# Peter's Story

Garner Ted Armstrong

D1221954

i

Peter shifted his position slightly, adjusting the horsehide scabbard that protected the razor-sharp edge of his Roman short sword he always carried.

Peter's father had purchased the sword from an Arabian trader who claimed he had bought it from a man of Alexandria who had taken it from a Roman mercenary in the battle at Actium. No matter the sword's history, Peter was happy for it. The sword had become a part of him. He used it for everything from scraping on the family boat when it needed repairs to helping in the mending and weaving of nets, from helping with the butchering of a sheep or goats they bought to slicing the fish he smoked for sale.

Maybe, Peter mused, the blade would yet serve him well, serve some greater purpose in this revolution of which Jesus spoke than the mundane chores of his business, or slapping some balky mule alongside the flank with the flat side of the heavy blade.

His eyes swept over the vast blue expanse of the Sea of Galilee, stretching away to the purple-hued distance. The water was dappled now with the blue-black shadows of this day's collection of cumulus that marched like so many white sheep toward the southeast, across the heights on the other side, where the steep slides of detritus showed grayish in the shimmering light that bespoke of the area of the Gadarenes, where people claimed a famous wild man lived among the tombs.

They had come here, panting with exertion, to follow Jesus' stocky figure as He climbed rapidly above them, and, taking comfortable seats about Him in this rocky amphitheaterlike flat with its breathtaking view, had settled down to listen to a major teaching session.

Jesus was known as a good builder and honest. His brothers gave you a fair share, hard work, and built true, and you could expect the work to come in at or below the estimates. Joseph had run the building trade from their home up in the tree-covered hills around Nazareth, and, after Joseph's death, Jesus had branched out a bit so that substantial homes, public buildings, sheds and warehouses in the whole Galilean region had been constructed by "Joseph and Sons, Contractors."

He looked plain enough, almost too plain the way Peter saw it; it might be better for the position of leadership He occupied and was soon to take if Jesus had some of the swashbuckling black handsomeness of, say, Judas Iscariot, or the sharper features and deep brown eyes of Luke, the physician. But, in spite of the fact He appeared so commonplace, so ordinary, with even, plain features, there was nothing ordinary about His voice, or the authority with which He spoke.

Peter heard the faint whisper of Luke's scratching now and then on the small slate he held on his knees and watched Matthew with his own note material. It was natural for Luke and Matthew to be taking such careful notes, Peter thought, what with Luke being a trained physician and in the habit of writing out his orders, receipts, prescriptions and the like, and Matt a publican, accustomed to making careful records of all kinds of personal business and property transactions for people. Luke and Matt were both skilled at a new short form of writing that had become popular, and no doubt were adding little shortcuts of their own. Peter wondered momentarily whether he ought to be taking his own notes until he thought ruefully how clumsily and slowly he wrote; he remembered how Andrew was the one who always kept the family business records or even wrote letters for Jona now that his hands shook so; he was widowed and had no one else to write for him.

Peter was glad they were keeping careful records. Someday soon it would be necessary to refer to them. No doubt open fighting would break out eventually, and in the aftermath of any revolution there would have to be a day of reckoning in some official form; maybe it would be like a new type of Sanhedrin or some other body of judges.

Peter's eyes swept the vast distances to the east again, and he mused of the ancient times he had heard described so vividly from the old ones, the elders and sages of the town, about how the kingdom of Solomon had stretched from Egypt to Persia and how his ships had circumnavigated all of Africa. They had brought ivory, peacocks, apes and all manner of strange creatures from the far, far lands of Put, leagues and leagues farther eastward from the glittering desert lands of the gentiles who lived with their camel and goat herds along the edges of the Red Sea. Solomon's mines, it was said, had been producing diamonds and fabulous jewels as big as a man's fist. From the terrifying country of eastern Africa, Solomon had even made himself a fabulous throne of the tusks of the gigantic thick-skinned, long-nosed animals the Greeks called "elephants." How many had it taken? Dozens, he supposed.

And Jesus was talking of a kingdom even greater than that—greater than Solomon's!

Imagine! A kingdom even greater than the greatness of Rome! Peter knew of the growing economy of the world's greatest empire in history; he knew at least something of the fabulous extravaganzas said to be held in Rome; of the growing traffic in exotic animals from Africa until it was said a lady of the court was virtually undressed without her own pet cheetah or leopard. Probably while he sat here Julius Caesar's own personal envoy was leading a centurion's force in search of the fabled unicorn of the African plains! While he sat here the ships of Rome plied the seas beyond the Gates of Hercules. Around Africa and to the far lands of the East, Caravans plodded through the soaring mountain passes beyond the lands of the Persians and brought silks, tapestries, spices, exquisite works of ivory and porcelain, paintings and delicately curved, razor sharp swords and knives. There were coins and tiny spice boxes made with cleverly inlaid pieces of rare woods and mother-of-pearl to be seen passing through. Precious little of these goods ever remained in Galilee, Idumea, Judea or the tetrarchies of Philip or Herod, though. They kept right on going; a golden, glittering, fabulous outpouring of the wealth of the world, right into the bulging treasure houses of the Caesar himself.

Peter had heard from dockyard laborers from the Syro-Phoenician ports talking of the new rumors that Roman sailors had heard about the fierce Northmen above the Islands of the Angaels and Kelts, that they had already colonized another whole new continent, another whole *world,* countless leagues to the west, far, far beyond Hercules' gates and over the unknown oceans.

He sighed. There was so much to be done. It was a big world, a fearsome one with the powerful forces at work within and without the empire. How could a tiny revolutionary force like this fight the might of Rome itself?

Peter knew it had been tried. His history teacher, Ben-yehuda, a wizened, stooped old man who had been to Carthage, to Rhodes and even to Rome, had lectured him often enough about the past 60 years of turbulence.

Why, only a little more than 27 years before Peter's own birth, Octavian had met Antony's ponderous battle-ships with a fleet of 200 lighter, handier vessels—and, when Antony found Cleopatra had sneaked off in the midst of the smoke and confusion, he ordered his own warship out of the battle, leaving his leaderless men to fight it out for themselves. Peter thought his own sword might have come from that battle.

Peter knew Herod—the skunk—had gone straight to Rhodes (Ben-yehuda claimed to have been there and knew all about it) to meet Octavian right after the battle to have his kingship over Palestine confirmed. His own mother-in-law, Miriam's mother, was friendly with Cleopatra, whom Herod had openly snubbed, wanting to flaunt his own power. The woman hoped Cleopatra could aid her in overthrowing her son-in-law. Though Antony had been a virtual mentor of Herod's and was Cleopatra's lover, the power of both was broken, and Octavian was in clear command of the field. Herod took the opportunity and slunk over to Rhodes to get himself a slice of the pie.

Peter's head would swim with these lessons as he heard the elderly Levite counting off the names, dates and places. The acid in his voice when he spoke of the chicanery of the family of Herods that was like a curse on the land was plain. Peter remembered how Ben-yehuda had talked of Herod's murder of many leaders in the Sanhedrin, and how he had seized their properties on some pretext or other. Herod had killed the high priest, a mutilated character who, it was alleged, had been a Babylonian.

Zacharias had been murdered. Herod had caused two of his own sons to be strangled and then killed another on his own deathbed. He died five days later, a murderer to the last, a killer of his own seed. Peter involuntarily shuddered at the thought of being embroiled in such filthy corruption, such intrigue, suspicion and hatred. His son, and successor to the throne, was little improvement.

It was no wonder Jesus' eyes fairly blazed when He spoke of the filthy hypocrisy of some of the political and spiritual leaders. He was familiar with the history of the times, much more so than Peter, for He was studious and possessed a keen memory.

Maybe Jesus would finally grow angry enough to use His vast powers in a *military* action—no matter their pitiful few in number, no matter the trained, brutal gentiles of Pilate's mercenaries. Remember Elijah and the prophets of Baal? Remember how the captains of fifty had turned into burnt, smelling cinders of broiled human flesh when they tried to take him? Remember Moses and the Red Sea and all of Pharaoh's armies? Remember Jehosaphat and so many others? Why, nothing could hold Him back if He ever decided to use His fabulous power!

For the present, though, it seemed Jesus was content just to build His popularity with the little folk and teach His own personal disciples the finest points of His entire philosophy and theology.

Peter knew when the time was truly ripe Jesus would

rally the throngs of tens of thousands and take His rightful place on the throne, overthrowing that pompous bag of lust, Herod, and then . . . then it would be on to Rome!

This was a well-remembered place to Simon who was called Peter—carrying the nostalgia of boyhood days when he had pretended to storm Roman citadels among these scattered boulders high on this mountain overlooking the sweeping expanse of Galilee off in the distance. He remembered how he would wield his wooden sword with piercing boyish yells, hacking away at the tall weeds and small trees, imagining himself at the head of a large armed force striking down the hated Romans before his wrath, dreaming boyish dreams as he acted out the hopes of the elders, such as his father, Jona, and his partner, Zebedee, who would sit on the jetty after a hard day on the nets and speak of "next year, in Jerusalem," when their country would be free at last.

It was this same high vista to which Peter's grandfather had come when he wanted to be alone with his thoughts. It was also the scene of one of their rare family outings when Simon had first seen little Elizabeth, a distant cousin, and then only a stripling of thirteen years—remembering how they exchanged shy glances, knowing the elders sat about and talked about their children, about future arrangements for dowries and marriages and such.

Now here he sat, powerful shoulders covered lightly against the breeze that had begun to sweep down the hills and ripple the surface of the lake below—brawny forearms, tanned, weathered face that had seen countless sunrises paint the lake below while he hurled his nets in the early morning light, working at his trade, fishing for his family's living—the frank brown eyes were deep-set beneath craggy brows, and the wide, generous mouth was mostly hidden by a brownish beard now bleached almost white around the edges from the hundreds of hours spent in the blazing sun with its reflected glare.

Just beyond him, and closer to Jesus, Luke wrote busily on his note slate, the sound of his scratchings not quite carrying to Peter above the sound of Jesus' voice, who had begun what sounded like a major, lengthy discourse.

Matthew, whom some called Levi, was also taking notes, and the others — ten more whom Jesus had chosen by name, plus many more who tagged along like Luke — were sitting or reclining here and there in a sprawling semicircle about Jesus.

Judas, who carried their common purse, sat closely together with Simon (who was a Canaanite), and Bartholomew could always be depended upon to be somewhere close. The three tended to spend much time together, just as both of Zebedee's sons, James and John, stuck close to Peter and Andrew, for they were from the same city and their fathers plied their trade together.

Simon, the big fisherman, couldn't help but feel the inevitable nostalgia of this moment; it had been many years since he had bothered to scale this height above the lake. It caused his mind to whirl with thoughts of the past.

His family had been fishermen for generations: simple, hard-working folk, roughened and weathered from the work. While much of the populace was illiterate, and dependent on the publicans for letters and figuring, Jona had earned enough to insist Peter and the others, especially Andrew (who was the scholar of the family), avail themselves of the tutelage of a couple of gifted Levites who held class, and who would teach in the home now and again — so Peter could read and write and could even speak a passable amount of Aramaic, as well as a bit of Greek.

Peter left the book work to Andrew when it came to their trading but was up to the task if the occasion demanded. He had never expected his life to be any different from that of his father and his clan, content to ply his trade at home with the wind and the waves, away from the crowds and the constant strife and talk in the markets and caravan yards, alone with his fishing chores and the weather.

But, with the turbulent politics of a troubled world, his own country under the heel of the Roman despot, and with that pompous bag of fatuous greed, Herod, sitting on his puppet's throne as if in pretense of great office (the while smarting, no doubt, over how his father had to trot

over there to Cyprus following his mentor's defeat at
Actium and practically beg Octavian for the crown), Peter
could only wonder about these rapidly changing times
—wonder whether the elders in the cities and towns were
correct in their calculations, and wonder whether this
Jesus of Nazareth was, in fact, the Messiah of whom they
all spoke.

There had been particularly emphatic gossip about
the Messiah during these past years because of odd occurrences about thirty years before when some strange priests
from Persia—some said they were students of the mysterious Zoroaster—had showed up in Bethlehem talking about
a star they had followed and claiming the Messiah had
been born there.

Peter had heard the stories often, as Jona and Zebedee
retold the tale, much embellished, no doubt.

Peter had heard much of the talk in the evenings about
the coming of this Messiah: a Deliverer, like Judas
Maccabaeus, or even a Joshua, or King David, who would
overthrow Herod and perhaps even Rome, who would
reestablish a kingdom even greater than that of Solomon.

The elders had continually speculated about who this
man should be and from whence he would come. Many
had taken to quizzically hanging onto every word of each
would-be rabble-rouser, who could be guaranteed an instant audience merely by raising his voice in the public
squares. A man named Theudas claimed to have strange
powers, raised up a group of rabble, it was said, who
followed him here and there as he would stand up in the
synagogues and preach to the people. A man named
Barabbas had collected a band that raided the villages from
down in the Arabah, the burning desert, and who was said
to give to the poor, even if he did loot the shops of the
merchants and steal from the caravans.

But for all their speculations about a coming Messiah, the people remained hopelessly passive and helpless.
Their feelings of futility proved contagious; seldom dared
any person say what he felt too openly. Oh, you could get
angry and make boasts when it was talking time after the
day's catch was smoked or salted, and the elders gathered

to exchange their philosophies and rumors. But, Peter observed, talk was all they did.

How well he knew that talk dwindled to awkward silence when the measured tramp of a squad of Roman soldiers came quick-stepping through the streets, their leathern skirts slapping against dusty, swarthy thighs, their short spears held at a trail, helmets jouncing as they trotted off on some errand or other at the orders of their centurion. Then the elders would become suddenly interested in the asses, or in the coals of the fire, or checking on the smoke fires in the huts where the fish were hanging.

Now, Peter thought, the time for all that talk and speculation was over.

The Messiah was actually *here*, right here in this mountain, beginning a powerful discourse to His followers, speaking things no man had ever heard before, startling his listeners into silence and wonderment. They had actually found the *Messiah*—this Jesus, a builder from Nazareth who had a business there and a home down below them in Capernaum; Jesus, the son of old Joseph who had died years ago, and who some claimed was the illegitimate son of the old man, who had died in disgrace and shame. Jesus had four brothers named James, Judas, Joses and Simon—and sisters at home. Though Peter only vaguely remembered the occasions he had met this same Jesus a time or two, when the Man from Nazareth would stop by their boats to purchase a little of the catch, or to spend time talking to Zebedee or Jona. Peter had paid little attention to Him during these times; there was nothing outstanding about Him, nothing particularly attractive in His appearance or His clothing.

But now Peter found Him totally fascinating!

This stirring, powerful leader had surprised him again when, only about an hour ago, He had terminated the growing argument with the large crowd down below in Capernaum and, looking at Peter over the heads of those surrounding Him on the bales of trade goods that had formed a pedestal of sorts, had nodded to Peter, strode through the crowd, signaling the others to follow, and, striding quickly through the streets of the city, had gained

the countryside and continued His walk around the shore
until He began to scale these heights.

He forced his thoughts back to the here and now.

The small flat was ringed by pink-hued, quartz-laden
rocks, and the others, Thaddeus, Bartholomew, Matthew
and Luke, Judas, John, James the son of Alphaeus, James,
John's brother, and all the rest were gathered around,
some sitting cross-legged on the ground and others on
nearby boulders or convenient fallen tree trunks.

As Jesus was speaking a few of the hardier of the
crowd had come panting up to the last rise, stopping as
they saw the host of disciples gathered close about Jesus,
and, brushing at their garments and wrapping their cloaks
more tightly around them against the brisk wind, stepped
quietly closer until they too could hear. What was it He had
been saying?

"Blessed are those who have opportunity to show
mercy; they are the ones who will be given mercy."

At this Peter could recall the absolute mercilessness
of most of the brutish, illiterate mercenaries in the Roman
army. It was commonplace to see strong, husky Roman
soldiers loading down the elderly of Peter's town with
their own knapsacks, mail sacks or other burdens; it was
commonplace to see them pushing older people out of their
simple dwellings and sleeping on the beds while forcing
the tenants of the house to sleep outside; it was commonplace to see people lashed in the public square for some
small infraction.

Peter remembered how sickened he had been when
on the occasion of a visit to the Syro-Phoenician seacoast
he had paused to watch the bales of cordage, hemp, cotton,
papyrus, fabrics, amphorae and trade goods of every sort
being swayed into the holds of some of the Roman ships.
He had seen the long rows of wealed, scarred backs of the
hapless wretches conscripted into the Roman ships as
galley slaves. Peter could only shudder at such a sight,
wondering how long even he, with his well-muscled
shoulders, arms and back, could stand up to the incredibly
cruel rigors of a slave galley.

Certainly no one in the Roman army that he had ever

met, with the possible exception of Alexios, a famous and kindly centurion who had actually put up the money to help build a synagogue, had ever shown anyone any mercy that he could recall!

Gathering his cloak even closer about his neck against the breeze and looking again at the dappled surface of the lake below, Peter's thoughts once more drifted back to his wife, Beth, and how she had been desolate when she learned he was picking up a small traveling kit and possibles bag and simply leaving to go tramping up and down the country following some tradesman from Nazareth who had some great ideas about revolution!

"Simon," she had said in that familiar, half-chiding tone, hands on ample hips, a wisp of her graying hair falling over one eye, the brow lightly smudged with flour that was being transferred to her dress from her hands, "now you listen to me! You've no business picking up and leaving your family—and your business! Why, you don't know anything about politics, religion and such. You've always been a simple, hardworking fisherman, and honest. You leave the politics and talk of new kingdoms to the elders in the village, the leaders of the synagogue, or those rabble out in the desert who go galloping off here and there to irritate the Roman garrisons! There are enough would-be revolutionaries to populate every city of refuge. You're a homebody, a father, and a partner with your father and brothers. You've got responsibilities!"

How they had argued! Finally, when she saw his mind was implacably set, she shrugged, bit her lower lip, blinked back the moisture that suddenly sprang to her eyes, and said, "You'll need your best walking boots and your warmest heavy cloak and, and . . ." Then she had turned, brushing angrily at the wisp of hair that fell over her eye, and fled into the sleeping quarters to help her husband get ready to leave.

But it hadn't been so bad. He had found Jesus intended spending a good deal of time within a reasonable radius of Capernaum, which wasn't very far from Bethsaida up here in Galilee, so he had opportunity to stop in and see the family fairly often and even to spend a night now and again. It was during these brief family reunions, or when Jesus Himself was a guest in their home, that Peter had held his family entranced with his glowing tales of the birth, childhood and early life of Jesus, with amazing tales of His great feats of power, His miracles and signs, His retorts to the persecutors, and His tenderness toward the sick, afflicted and the poor.

Peter's thoughts turned to the present again.

Here he was, a member of Jesus' own select group, sitting here on this mountain listening to a powerful discourse.

He became aware of Jesus' glance in his direction and brought his thoughts quickly back to the scene before him.

Luke was still taking rapid notes; Matt had paused and was looking thoughtfully at Judas. Jesus was saying, "*Blessed* are those who are persecuted for righteousness' sake . . ." Was He paying closer attention to Peter now, knowing his quickness of temper, his bold, blustering manner when threatened? Peter colored a little, looked at Jesus and nodded slightly, indicating he got the point. ". . . For *theirs* is the Kingdom of God."

There He goes again, Peter mused, saying the only way to help Him bring about His glorious new latter-day resurrection of Solomon's great kingdom under God was the exact opposite of what Peter would have supposed. Peter shifted the weight of his Roman short sword in his scabbard at his side, pulled the blade scarcely free of the scabbard and fingered its carefully honed edge tentatively.

What would he do, he thought, if someone tried to injure or murder Jesus? I'd slice his head in two like a ripe melon, he thought, with a mixture of bravado and doubt as he wondered what Jesus would think.

Looking at the other upturned faces and the rapt attention of the crowd, Peter thought, Ah, well, let the idealism and philosophy motivate these men. Jesus certainly knew how to cut right into the heart of the matter, into the innermost conscience of people, but, when fighting time came, Peter knew he would be ready. He liked and admired Jesus so much he couldn't bear the thought of anyone harming Him; Peter almost imagined himself as an older brother, protector and self-styled bodyguard to this Jesus, an anachronism of strong build, well-muscled arms and body, calloused hands and confident, sure manner, but who on the other hand spoke so much of gentleness, goodness, faith, peace, mercy, love and forgiveness.

The contrast was almost overwhelming. Jesus had gained this height many long steps ahead of the rest; even Peter had been laboring a little, his brow covered with sweat. There was power in Jesus' frame. Peter had seen Him force open huge doors when they balked on rusty hinges that two other slighter men couldn't budge; He had lifted big beams, heavy tables, large stones, and could leap up outer stairways three at a time as well as climb lofty slopes like this one with only a minimum of effort. Still, for all this obvious good physical condition, He remained a meek mannered, polite, unthreatening person.

That is, until His eyes blazed with anger and His voice rose in controlled intensity. Peter had seen that occur a time or two when a particularly incautious Pharisee's simpering complaints ignited some deep-seated indignation within the Lord. He had seen men shrink back before Him, briefly frightened by the sheer force of His person, His voice and His authority that seemed to radiate from Him.

Jesus was looking from one to the other of the crowd who were coming closer. He said, *"Blessed* are you when men shall revile you and persecute you and say every conceivable kind of evil against you falsely on account of Me. When that happens, then rejoice and be really glad and happy, because your ultimate reward carefully stored up for you in heaven above will be great beyond your wildest hopes and dreams. You are no different, because they persecuted God's prophets long before you in the same way.

"You are the salt of the earth . . ."

Exactly, mused Peter. But the proud Jewish race was being systematically exploited by the combined force of the Roman emperor and those hated symbols of his far-flung dominions: Pontius Pilate, governor of Judea; Herod, the tetrarch of Galilee; Herod's own brother, Philip, who sat on the tetrarchy of Ituraea; and Trachonitis and Lysanias, who was tetrarch of Abilene, north and east of the reach of Peter's gaze. "Salt," indeed. The combined produce of the whole region trickled into the holds of the Phoenician traders and Roman ships to flow into the emperor's coffers in Rome. Judea was being systematically plundered, not only of salt but of everything else.

Jesus continued His strong, authoritative message, His voice rising now with ringing clarity, shocking, angering, stunning His audience with statements such as had never been heard before.

*"Love* your enemies!" He cried. "Do *good* to them that hate you!" Murmurs would ripple through the crowd now and then. Peter heard, "This is *astonishing* teaching. He sounds so sure, so positive, not like our scribes!"

Jesus' voice rose above the growing breeze, His hair stirring and His clothing rustling as He gestured, saying, "Not everyone who says to Me 'Lord, Lord' shall enter the kingdom, but he who does the *will* of My Father who is in heaven!" His eyes snapping, He mimicked those who would come to Him in protest: "On that day many will say to Me, 'Lord, Lord, did we not prophesy in Your name, and cast out demons in Your name, and do many mighty works in Your name?' "

Matthew's hand fairly flew over his note slate now, and Luke was busy, hunched over, head bowed, writing. Peter saw Judas winking at Simon, the swarthy disciple from Canaan, and noticed Thomas sitting by with a puzzled frown creasing his not unpleasant, homely face.

Dropping the simpering tone, Jesus flashed, "And then will I declare to them, 'I never knew you. Depart from Me, you evildoers!' "

Jesus was nearing the end of this powerful discourse now, for the words were spaced, somber, and conveyed a strong warning.

Jesus said, "Everyone who hears these words of Mine and does them will be like a wise man who built his house on a rock. The rain came, and the floods came, and the winds blew, and buffeted that house, but it didn't fall because it was founded on a rock. But every man who hears these words of Mine and does not do them will be like a foolish man who built his house on the sand. The rains fell, and the floods came, and the winds blew and buffeted that house, and it fell and great was the fall of it."

A hush fell over the crowd of about three hundred. Then a growing crescendo of voices rose, with small groups gathering here and there and a number rushing to surround Jesus to ask questions.

Peter worked his way closer to Jesus, knowing many in the crowd were skeptical and hostile. Peter didn't understand the inner compulsion that made him assume the role of self-appointed protector and bodyguard, but somehow he couldn't resist the impulse.

Sometimes Jesus seemed so vulnerable. Not soft, just vulnerable and exposed.

Would some cowardly fanatic walk up to Jesus and call Him out on this statement about "turning the other cheek"? Peter supposed it likely.

Jesus might just do it, Peter thought to himself. If someone walked up and delivered a ringing blow to the side of the Lord's head, He would probably just stand there and turn the other cheek! But, by the time He did it, Peter reasoned, the man who dared lift a finger against Jesus of Nazareth would be prostrate on the ground with a lump the size of pomegranate decorating his ear!

But nothing happened except a few tiresome ones who seemed contentious and wanted to argue kept trying to interrupt Jesus and demand answers for their questions.

In due time Jesus beckoned to the disciples and, followed by the growing crowd, began descending the mountain along the trail toward Capernaum, visible in the distance.

As always, Peter tried to keep the crowds orderly, sometimes shouldering closely to Jesus, his big fisherman's hands placed firmly on an arm here and a shoulder there, guiding, steering people when they seemed about ready to mob one another in their eagerness to hear.

That night, when the crowds had finally been sent away and it was time to rest, Peter had time to spend a quiet hour with James and John.

"That was an astounding message Jesus gave us today," Simon Peter began.

James and John both nodded agreement.

"But what do you think about turning the other cheek, and loving your enemies, and doing good to people who hate you?" he continued. "Do you think it will work?"

"I doubt that the Lord meant for it to 'work,' " John said quietly.

"Well, then . . . ."

"If by 'work' you mean turning the other cheek

makes the other fellow quit hitting you, that is,'' John amended.

"But if he doesn't back off and quit hitting," Peter reasoned, hands held open as if in appeal, "are you supposed to stand there and let him half kill you and do nothing?"

"That's what the Messiah said," James put in.

"I know what He said, and I'm not arguing with it or disagreeing," Peter protested. "But what if some Roman soldier were raping your wife, James? Would you be required to just stand and watch?"

"I doubt very much that such could ever happen to one of His disciples," James replied. "In the first place, I believe God would protect us, that the Lord Himself could perform some sign or miracle and prevent such a thing from happening."

"Yes, but what if nothing like that happened?" Peter insisted.

"Maybe you'd better take it up with Jesus tomorrow," John replied, yawning and stretching. "Besides, He wasn't talking so much about the here and now as He was laying out rules for His coming kingdom. Didn't you hear how He said the meek would inherit the whole earth, that the way into the Kingdom of God was a narrow, rocky, difficult trail, and only the *few* would find it?"

Still puzzling, Peter sat by himself, lounging against the traveling packs before the still glowing embers in the hearth, and thought.

Jesus talked of His coming kingdom—spoke of putting an end to crime and violence, of the kind of government that would bring peace and establish principles of personal dignity, human rights and fairness for all men.

The *authority* in His voice was unmistakable, Peter thought.

The way He could hold a crowd spellbound, hanging on every word . . . Though plain of visage and commonplace in dress and appearance, He was anything but common when He spoke.

Peter marveled at Him.

Folding his calloused hands over his belly, now com-

fortably filled with this night's fare of kid stew and a sip of
Judean wine, Simon mused over the events of these past
incredible weeks.

He remembered how Andrew had come running up to
him in Bethsaida hard at work on the nets and said,
"Simon! Simon! We've found the Messiah! Come and
see!"

"You've found who?" Simon had laughed. "Andrew, have you been at the wineskins so early?" Chuckling, he had turned again to his work only to find Andrew
fairly hopping up and down with anxiety and saying again
and again he had found the Messiah, begging Simon to
come and see.

"Hold it! Hold it! Slow down a bit and tell me what
you're talking about," Simon had said, bemused by the
excitement his older brother was displaying.

"Why, Jesus. You know, Jesus of Nazareth, the
carpenter, the builder from up in Nazareth . . ."

"Couldn't be," Peter said with some doubt. "The
readers and scribes claim the Messiah will have to come
from Bethel or some place around Jerusalem or those
parts. There's no way a local man from up here could be
the Messiah!"

Andrew hurried along a winding trail that took them
toward the hills to the west and after a few miles' laborious
climbing came to a shakemaker's hut among the thickly
wooded cedar slopes.

As they walked the glistening waters of Galilee were
visible now and then through the trees, and the shade
helped, for it was hot and humid and Simon perspired
freely from his exertions.

Andrew stooped under the low eaves of a sheltered
gatepost, traversed a littered yard redolent with the smell
of freshly split cedar lengths, where adzes, mauls, wedges
and hammers could be seen lying about amid finished
shakes and trimmed boards.

Andrew entered a small bunkhouse and Simon followed.

Simon's eyes adjusted to the dim light as Andrew
said, "Greetings again, Master. This is my brother."

Simon turned to see a rather ordinary man rise. He was broad of shoulder, not very tall, perhaps an inch or so shorter than Peter's five foot ten (which was slightly above average for the time), with neat beard, wide-set, open eyes of the most striking blue, generous mouth and work roughened hands. He wore a plain, homespun garment of the finest wool with the broad stripe that said He was of the tribe of Judah. He had apparently just finished His morning meal and had been gathering up His traveling implements, preparing to tuck them into His leathern girdlelike belt that lay on the bench beside Him.

The friendly, assured eyes looked directly into Peter's as He grasped Peter's hand and said, ''I know who you are. You're Simon, Jona's son. But you're going to be called Peter [He used the Aramaic name *Cephas*, meaning a *stone* or *rock*] from now on!''

Peter mused back on that striking occurrence. What a talk they had had!

Surely this was the Messiah! Peter remembered how following that lengthy meeting Jesus had gone back with them to Bethsaida, and when He saw Philip Jesus had said, ''You're Philip, aren't you? Philip, I want you to come and follow Me!''

Peter knew Jesus had prayed *all night* one night over who His top twelve men ought to be. He had known some of the men rather well, certainly knew their families, their background, their basic character. Judas, now . . . well, some wondered about him. He was darkly handsome with close set, obsidian eyes, a little too quick to laugh and talk, too garrulous, and in Peter's view, a little too given to private haggling when it came to striking deals here and there in the marketplaces.

But Jesus had chosen him so he must be all right. Of course, there was a rumor out that Judas had had some sort of a mental problem when he was younger. It was said that he had a ''biting demon'' as a boy and had been involved in some dishonest scrapes, but that a well-to-do family and a leading Jewish lawyer, his mentor and teacher, had intervened in his behalf and had gotten him off. That was his business, of course, and Peter couldn't set much stock

in the tale that Judas had run across Jesus down in southern
Judea when Jesus was much younger, probably only about
fourteen, at one of the family Passover trips, and had bitten
Jesus on the cheek. Weird and likely untrue.

The twelve were certainly representative of every
conceivable talent, background, point of view, personality
and character. A doctor, a fisherman, a traveling-salesman
type, a publican, men of the land, of the mountains and of
the sea. There was not a dishonest, four-flusher among
them except maybe Judas.

That had been quite a time when Jesus had looked
straight at him and said, "I know you . . ." Peter remembered. He said it *twice,* actually. First up there where He
had lodged following His baptism, and later right down
there in the lake not too far from shore. He and Andrew
had gone out to try their luck one early morning with their
cast nets. They hadn't done so well, either. The autumn
winds made the water rough. Jesus had walked out on a
little jetty, cupped His hands and, hailing them in a strong,
clear voice, had said, "Come on along after Me, you two,
and I'll make you fishers of *men!*"

They had been expecting it. Then had followed the
scene with Beth, and they had picked up their meager
traveling packs and left. Now they were right back here in
home territory after having been all over the whole
Galilean region, with huge crowds gathering everywhere.
Why, some had come from clear down in Jerusalem and
further south and from over in the ten towns called "Decapolis" and from beyond the Jordan river.

It had been hard on Jona, left with the business and
only a few hired servants. It was also hard on old Zebedee,
James' and John's father, to continue their fisheries' part-
nership with only the hired help. James and John, Peter
remembered, had been sitting there, their nets stretched
from mast to bow spit and cascading down the rocky
breakwater working cross-legged on the mending. Jesus
had spoken to them previously, of course, but now it was
time to go, and, dropping their work where they were, they
kissed old Zebedee on his leathery cheek and acknowl-
edged his admonition to remember what he'd always

taught them. He showed mixed grief and joy knowing they were off to follow the great Messiah and that perhaps triumph or tragedy awaited.Then, resolutely, he had called the two servants, taken up the mending right where James and John had left it, and continued working the rest of the afternoon, brushing angrily at his eyes now and then and blinking fiercely as though he had trouble seeing.

Three days later there had been a large marriage feast at Cana in Galilee, and, because she was a close personal friend of the family, Mary was helping serve. Jesus and His disciples had also been invited. Peter hadn't wanted to go, but Jesus said there was a time for everything and many important people would be there. So Peter reluctantly but obediently went along.

After the feasting and drinking had been going on for some time, the wine proved to be inadequate for the very large crowd present.

Knowing that the wine was now exhausted and feeling some responsibility, Mary had come to Jesus and informed Him of the dilemma. "They are totally out of wine," Peter heard her say.

Jesus knew His mother expected Him to perform some special miracle to make up the short supply and so in a mildly chiding tone said, "Woman, whatever am I going to do with you? Don't you know that the time for Me to reveal who I am is not yet here?" Obviously Mary thought the occasion important and there were sufficient family considerations that she prevailed upon Jesus in spite of His gentle reminder, and He found her impossible to refuse.

Turning to some one of the nearby servants, she had said, "No matter what He tells you to do, see that you do it."

Peter well remembered that day! Mary had been so positive, so *sure*. Now Peter wouldn't be surprised at anything the Lord did.

He had long since come to understand why Mary was so sure of herself. Her long talks with John and a few chats with Peter had shown she had never forgotten the vividly remembered events of Jesus' birth.

Though Peter doubted that Jesus had used His amazing powers very much, he knew there must have been at least a few times when close members of the family had been spared severe personal injury or perhaps even healed of some sickness or wound that had occurred through work or play.

Anyway, Mary knew. She wasn't hoping or guessing. She just *knew* Jesus had the power to do something miraculous about the wine, and she had told those servants in a positive way.

Even though Jesus warned Mary the event might bring undue notoriety, He was nevertheless willing to perform the miracle knowing the wagging tongues of the servants and others attending the marriage feast might well carry the tale far and wide, bringing exclamations of doubt and disbelief wherever it was told.

It had been quite a party, a traditional wedding feast with hundreds of people milling about and Jesus' family there. After they had taken their leave, the whole crowd—all the disciples along with Mary, James, Joses, Simon, Jude and the girls—had gathered their animals, cinched up their packs and traveled back down the switch-back trails to Capernaum.

They weren't to stay long, however, because spring was becoming more obvious every day, the hills riotous with wild flowers and the days becoming noticeably longer and warmer. Passover wasn't very far away, and Jesus talked about their coming trip to Jerusalem.

Peter thought something really important was likely to happen down there. It would be only too logical for Jesus to use the most important spiritual occasion of the year, when tens of thousands of Jews from all over the whole Mediterranean world would be present. Why, some of the pilgrims came from clear up in Cappadocia, far above the city of Antioch in Syria, or even from Bithynia and Pontus on the shores of the sea they were calling "Pontus Euxinus" south of Dacia and bordered by Thracia and Bithynia. They came from all over the world, it seemed, and, if there was ever opportunity for Jesus to spread His doctrines of reform and this great new kingdom, it would be during the Passover. No wonder the

Romans always added special strength to their garrisons and insisted on stringent regulations concerning search of caravans for caches of arms or propaganda materials.

Pity. The Passover should be a deeply religious occasion. It was blasphemous, Peter thought, that the devout among the Jews couldn't even purify themselves, offer their sacrifices and proclaim their vows without having to see surly Libyans, Thracians, Gaelics or Hispanic mercenaries of the Roman legions, usually degenerate, unwashed, heavily armed and illiterate, looking on, making obviously bawdy and contemptuous comments about the Jews in their strange tongues.

But no matter. They were certainly used to it by now. Peter thought it might be possible for the high priest to perform his required rituals before ranks of thousands of threatening Romans with leveled spears! And to think some of those Pharisees could still boast they had never been anything but "free" and were never in "slavery to any man"!

Well, it was time for the trip and Peter was looking forward to it.

Probably He, James and John would have some special assignments to fulfill, maybe recruiting among some of the pilgrims from far-flung parts of the empire.

At long last Peter went to sleep, his dreams tumbled and chaotic, with Jesus' powerful voice stabbing his conscience again and again, "Love your enemies!" making him toss and turn.

The next morning they saddled up their pack animals, repacked their meager personal belongings and after a hurried breakfast took a little-used trail to the south.

The trip to Jerusalem consumed only four days. They pushed themselves and their animals fairly hard, keeping their pauses for food and rest to a minimum, for they deliberately avoided the crowded trails with the long camel trains of the more wealthy and kept to the rougher country, using the back trails.

Simon Peter stayed close to Jesus on this bright, fresh morning, listening to Him talk and nodding in agreement when He said they would go to the temple first thing after an early breakfast.

They camped among the old olive trees on the Mount of Olives, about a Sabbath day's journey from the temple, across the bubbling little brook they called "Kidron." It was a dry camp and they had filled their water jugs in Kidron and spread out their extra garments to dry after washing them in the stream.

Breakfast over and the chores done, they strode down the pathway to the brook, stepped across the stones placed there for the purpose and labored up the steep hill to the city gate.

A growing mutter of noise could be heard from the teeming streets. The cries of merchants, blatting of sheep and goats, the guttural, belching sound of the camels and the excited chatter of pilgrims meeting old friends all contrived to paint a confused, multicolored, teeming tapestry of life swirling among the ancient streets and walls.

A few people here and there called out to one or other of the disciples who recognized a friend now and then from Galilee or one of the other provinces. Judas smiled and winked at some of the merchants and shopkeepers sitting or standing over their wares. Luke was checking his writing materials carried in the skin bag slung over his left shoulder, and Matt paused briefly to purchase some parchment and then ran, panting, to catch up with Jesus's swift, sure stride.

Gaining the broad Court of the Gentiles, Jesus kept maneuvering through the throngs until He entered the temple itself.

They found themselves in the midst of a riotous cacophony of blatting sheep, lowing bullocks, bleating goats, and the high-pitched, professional whine of the money changers. Jesus stopped, grasped Peter's forearm in His powerful grip, and, fairly trembling with anger, beckoned to Peter to hand Him some halter cordage Peter had brought.

With growing pride and apprehension, Peter watched as Jesus swiftly tied lengths together, forming tight, compact little knots at the end of each one, until He had a fairly lethal-looking scourge of tough hemp in His powerful hands.

Jesus then strode up to the first table and unceremoniously dumped it over on the floor! A florid-faced, balding, barrel-chested little ogre, sitting there like some gloating spider with his carefully arranged trays of the coins of at least a dozen nations, gawked, sputtered, and then screeched in fright as the heavy table, striking his knees, propelled him over backward to sprawl in an awkward tangle of filthy robes, cascading coins, scrolls and ledgers onto the dusty floor!

Except for the sounds some of the animals made and the soft cooing of the doves in their cages, the great room fell silent as dozens of worshipers, change makers and the sellers of sacrificial creatures turned to stare in disbelief.

Jesus hadn't even paused.

He had already dumped three more tables over and was driving a growing herd of young bullocks, lambs and kids before Him, the hand-made cat-o'-nine-tails whistling down on a slow-moving rump here and there.

The next two tables he overturned had been hastily swept of their coin trays and ledgers, and their owners stood clutching their belongings to their middles, watching with mixed outrage and fear at this shocking violence—and right in the temple of God!

Peter helped, as did several of the others, to clear the last of the animals from the big room, sending them bawling and protesting into the early chill of the morning along with a number of their owners and a few perplexed purchasers who saw their money disappear into a chaotic pile on the dirty floor, and then saw their recently acquired sacrifices disappear into a herd of tossing rumps and heads.

Meanwhile, Jesus loudly shouted in a voice that fairly rang with anger, "Take these things out of here! Don't make my Father's house a house of merchandise!" He was outraged that the temple should be filled with animals, money-changing tables, offal, and the assorted accoutrements of the merchants.

It was a chaotic, turbid scene.

The officials gathered then, and Peter wondered if Jesus would strike one of them. He doubted it, yet he half-expectantly hoped the Lord meant this to be the magic moment of revolution.

"Now, see here!" demanded their leader. "Just by what *authority* do You think to do all this? What kind of credentials or signs will You show us to prove You have any authority?" several chimed in and a few muttered threats were heard.

Peter knew Jesus never played the petty little games of pretense by skirting around the main issues with useless words. Jesus read their desire to kill Him so He said, "Destroy this temple and in three days I will raise it up."

What did He mean?

The spokesman for the crowd snickered in derisive amusement. "The temple was a full forty-six years building and *You* claim *You* could raise it up in only *three days?*" His sardonic, patronizing tone indicated to the crowd he wanted to believe he was dealing with some madman.

He couldn't quite bring it off.

Jesus repeated His statement twice and, turning, left the temple with the disciples.

The act of throwing the money changers and their wares out of the temple caused a major stir among the pilgrims in the city. The people were gossiping about it in the shops and markets for days and not a single disciple of Jesus failed to hear His name constantly repeated.

During one quick trip for a simple purchase of food, Peter and John were hurrying along the crowded shops toward the dung gate and overheard a pompous Pharisee attended by his little scribe and two other admirers saying He ". . . said He would actually destroy the temple. That is a treasonous, anti-Jewish statement!" The little scribe nodded agreement and an exclamation of outrage came from three others standing by.

John grabbed Peter's arm, and the two paused as if to look at some footwear displayed in the next booth.

"But it would take a veritable army of men with all the machinery of demolition to even begin such a task . . ." protested a huge, wheezing merchant, spreading his sweating, fat palms upward and peering at the Pharisee from behind partially hooded eyes.

"It doesn't matter whether he would actually *try* it,"
protested the Pharisee. "The fact that He boasted He
would destroy the temple makes Him a dangerous revolutionary, a man who would sell out to the Romans, who
betrays the traditions of our fathers and the Scriptures
themselves!"

"But, but," stammered a swarthy proselyte standing
near, "they claim He also said He would build it up again
in only three days!"

"A ridiculous claim!" trumpeted the Pharisee. Why,
the temple was many, many years a-building, and this
imposter claims such powers?"

John joggled Peter's arm again and they moved on.

"They're deliberately making a case against Him,"
John said, looking worriedly about.

"Yes, they are," Peter admitted. "But He said nothing of the kind. I don't know exactly what He meant yet,
and I hope to ask Him soon, but it was something about
them, the Pharisees, plotting to destroy the temple and the
Lord raising it up again."

"And He said in only three days!"

"I know," Peter agreed. But, with the very miracle
power of God to back Him up, He could do it!"

"Do you think He was predicting the destruction of
the temple in a war?"

"I don't know," Peter admitted. "Perhaps."

"Well, if that were to happen, and Jesus and all of us
pitched in to restore it again, it would win the favor of the
whole nation!"

"That's true enough," Peter cast over his shoulder,
hurrying along the steep pathway toward Kidron. "If we
become the protectors and builders of the temple, well, it
would legitimize Christ's claim to the throne of David as
nothing else could—would mark the whole beginning
of a new age, a new empire!"

"Maybe that's what He plans," John wondered.

"I hope to find out soon," Peter affirmed again and
turned his attention to their climb, now that Kidron's
gurgling waters were behind them.

That night, when they finished supper and were sharing several songs together, Jesus' strong voice blending with those of James, Andrew, and John, and Peter's gruff monotone bravely keeping pace, one of the disciples who was watching the trail below came running up and said a wealthy official wanted to see Jesus.

"Who is he?" Jesus wondered.

"He is called Nicodemus and he is an important man, a ruler among the people," said the disciple, panting from running ahead.

Jesus indicated he should return and bring the man, and Peter hastily pitched in to clear away a place for the man to be seated among their packs and bedding.

More torches were lit, and Andrew fetched a wineskin to offer their guest.

After the introductions were over, Nicodemus gratefully sat down and, after looking nervously about him, began talking.

He went on for some little time saying, "Rabbi, we know You must be a teacher from God for no man could do the signs and miracles You do except God be with Him . . ." and then began asking about Jesus' strange messages about His kingdom. He wanted to know about His daily teaching sessions in the temple, about the overthrowing of the money changers' tables and the claims that Jesus said He would destroy the temple.

Jesus answered all his questions one by one and Nicodemus nodded, eyes widening in puzzlement and wonder.

Finally, he asked a question about the kingdom of which Jesus spoke so often.

Then Peter picked up his ears.

He heard Jesus say something so strange it puzzled all of them. Jesus said, "Truly, truly I am telling you, except a man be *born anew from above,* he cannot see the Kingdom of God!"

Wondering if He was joking, Nicodemus shook his head, looked puzzled and said, "But, Teacher, how can this be? How can any *man* enter his mother's womb and be born?"

Jesus went on, "Truly, truly I am telling you, except a man be *born* [there was that same word again!] of *water and the Spirit,* he cannot enter into the Kingdom of God!

"That which is born of flesh *is* flesh, and that which is born of the Spirit *is* spirit!"

A *spirit,* Peter thought, why, He seems to be saying a man can actually become a *spirit* instead of a man . . .

"Don't marvel that I said to you, 'You must be born anew,'" Jesus said, perceiving the puzzlement on the faces of those present and Nicodemus' bewildered look. "The wind blows wherever it will and you can hear the voice of the wind, but you don't know where it comes from or where it goes. *So* is everyone that is *born of the Spirit,"* He said earnestly.

Shaking his head slowly as if to clear his thoughts, Nicodemus asked, "How can such things be?"

"Are you a teacher, a rabbi, in Israel and yet you don't understand these things? Truly, truly I am telling you, we speak that we do know, and bear witness of that we have seen, and you receive not our witness. If I told you about earthly things and you don't believe those, then how shall you believe if I tell you heavenly things?

"And no man has ascended into heaven but He that descended out of heaven, even the Son of Man which is in heaven.

"And as Moses lifted up the serpent in the wilderness even so must the Son of Man be lifted up, that *whosoever believes in Him may have eternal* life!"

Think of *that!* Peter was both inspired and puzzled. He knew Jesus spoke in awe-inspiring tones of His coming kingdom, its grandeur, its greatness, and his reeling brain could only conceive of this "eternal life" in the vaguest possible way. Of course, Peter knew a little of the religious teachings of his people, knew some passages from the scrolls, and Jona had seen that his children memorized some of the important prophecies and psalms. But Peter had never thought of himself as "religious," and the promise of "eternal life" seemed very, very far away.

Likely, Jesus meant whoever believed in Him would have a part in a great kingdom that would last forever and forever. He knew Mary had said the angel claimed Jesus would inherit the very kingdom of David, and of "his throne there shall be no end . . ."

But Jesus continued, "For God so loved the world that He gave His only begotten Son, that whosoever believes on Him should not perish but have *eternal life!*"

Peter noted the amazed, puzzled and hopeful look on Nicodemus' face. He had believed, had wanted to believe, but was almost afraid to believe that this was, indeed, Messiah! He was hanging on every word.

"For God sent not the Son into the world to condemn the world, but that the world should be *saved* through Him. He that believes on Him is not condemned, but he that does not believe has been judged already because he has not believed on the name of the only begotten Son of God . . . and this is the judgment, that the light is come into the world, and men loved the darkness rather than the light, for their works were evil!

"For everyone that does evil hates the light and won't come to the light lest his works should be exposed. But he that accomplishes the truth comes to the light that his works can be made manifest, that they have been wrought in God."

After Nicodemus left, Peter and John lay awake for a long time, puzzling over Jesus' strange words.

This Passover and Days of Unleavened Bread in the environs of Jerusalem proved heady wine indeed. Jesus had the whole area on its ear with rumors, gossip and speculation.

He would spend hours answering questions and teaching in the temple, continually emphasizing to those in custodial chores to keep it clean and polished. Miracles were performed, many were healed of diseases, even leprosy, and the streets were abuzz with talk.

Following John the Baptist's example, Jesus instructed His disciples in how to baptize people unto repentance, how to talk to them about the forgiveness of sins, the symbolic burial of the old self and washing away of the past in Jordan's waters, to rise as if in resurrected newness of life and to live a clean and different life.

Those who humbly came to Jesus and asked for baptism were gathered in groups, and hardly a day passed but that several of the disciples would start the trek to one of the pools with a new group wanting to be baptized.

The rumor mills were alive and it was inevitable that the disciples should hear of the evil plotting of the Pharisees.

Hearing of it over dinner one night, Jesus gave instructions to return to Galilee. Their time in Jerusalem was over.

The next morning they packed up and left, wanting to be well on their way before first light.

Though arduous and forcing them to go without sleep, the trip was largely uneventful, save for Peter's consternation on the second morning to discover Jesus' bedroll empty and thinking He had been kidnapped. It was with great relief Peter discovered Jesus had arisen well before the others (it was remarkable how little sleep He seemed to require) and had gone away to pray.

Samaria divided the Tetrarchy of Herod Antipas at the waist, occupying the lands embracing the mountains to the south of Galilee and north of Jerusalem. Mount Ebal was near its center and the trail forked toward the Decapolis, the Sea of Galilee, and westerly toward the Mediterranean, Caesarea and Strato's famous tower.

Most of the Jewish pilgrims studiously avoided Samaria, holding the Samaritans in contempt as a filthy, ignorant, superstitious race of pariahs, not fit for common society.

In Jewish parlance, calling someone a "Samaritan" was tantamount to calling him demon-possessed, a wildly insane person.

Jesus ignored such racist feelings and took the direct routes, journeying freely through Samaria with His disciples as if He hadn't a care in the world. On their return trip to Jerusalem, having hurried for three days, they finally came to the fork in the main road through Samaria, at Sychar, where it was said the parcel of ground Jacob had given to his son Joseph so long ago remained, and where Joseph's famous well was located. Mount Ebal loomed faintly majestic in the distance.

It had been a long, hard trek that day. They were quite tired, and Jesus and the whole group lounged around the bordering stones of the well for a time when someone suggested that they let the Lord rest and go on into town and drum up something to eat.

After they had left to go into town, a woman from the village sauntered up to the well and at the sixth hour began to draw water to fill the two pots she had fetched on her yoke.

Jesus asked, "Will you draw Me some water too, please?"

The Samaritan woman was astonished. Jews were known to treat Samaritans like animals and beneath contempt. She asked, "How is it that You, a Jew, would ask a drink of a Samaritan woman? The Jews have no dealings whatsoever with Samaritans."

"If you knew the gift of God and who is asking you for a drink of water, you would have asked Me and I would have given you *living water*," Jesus said.

The woman placed the water jars on the ledge and began to lower one into the well. She laughed, "Sir, You have nothing with which to draw the water out and this is a very deep well, then where will You draw such 'living water'? Are You greater than our father Jacob, who gave us the well and drank from it himself together with his sons and cattle?"

"Everyone who drinks of *this* water will only grow thirsty again after a time," Jesus replied, "but whoever drinks of the water that I shall give him will never thirst, but the water that I shall give him will become in him a well of water springing up unto eternal life!"

She said sarcastically, "Sir, then please give me this water You're talking about so I'll never thirst again, and then I won't have to come all the way out of town to draw water from this well."

"Go call your husband and come back here," Jesus said.

"But I have no husband," she said, wondering why Jesus would interject talk of a husband when the two of them were out here alone.

"You're telling the truth there," said Jesus, "because you've already had *five* husbands, and the one with whom you're presently living is not your husband—you're certainly speaking truly enough."

The woman was astonished.

"Sir, I perceive that You are a prophet, a Jew, probably from Jerusalem.

"Our fathers worshiped in this mountain," she changed the subject, "and you Jews say that Jerusalem is the place where men ought to worship."

"Woman, believe me," Jesus retorted, "the hour is coming when neither in this mountain nor in Jerusalem shall you worship the Father. You worship that which you know nothing about, but we worship that which we *know,* for salvation is from the Jews. But the hour is coming, and even now is, when the true worshipers will worship the Father in spirit and in truth, for such does the Father seek to be His worshipers. *God is a Spirit,* and they that worship Him must worship in spirit and in truth!"

The woman said, "I know that Messiah is to come, who is called the Christ, and when He is come He will declare unto us all things." This she said tentatively, peering intently at this strong young stranger. Jesus looked at her and said, "I that am talking with you am He."

Peter and the disciples came back and saw that He was speaking with the woman, yet none of them bothered her by saying, "What are you doing?" or "Who are you looking for?" or asking Jesus, "Why are You speaking to her?"

The woman left her water pots and went quickly back into the city and told some of the men there, "Come and see a Man who told me everything that I ever did. Do you think this would be the Christ, the Messiah?"

Some of the citizens came out of the town and came toward Jesus. In the meanwhile Peter and the disciples had been begging Him to eat, knowing that He was very tired from the lengthy trip and had taken nothing for some time.

This scene at the well turned into another of these impromptu sermons. The townsfolk clustered about and the leaders asked many questions of Jesus. Peter hung back, a look of pain on his face. He didn't like having to journey through Samaria anyway, but why was Jesus wasting time on talking to them?

Wouldn't this kind of thing hurt His cause if it got out? Wouldn't loyal Jews be antagonized when they learned the Messiah had been freely socializing with a motley crowd of Samaritans from Sychar, and that the whole thing had begun by a lengthy conversation with a class A prostitute? Besides, Peter knew you couldn't trust any Samaritan. Why, they were as slippery as water on a moss rock, they'd as soon cut your throat as look at you, they'd slay their own grandmother for her purse — the way Peter had heard it. He couldn't see the logic behind staying here any further, but what was this?

Jesus had gotten up and beckoned to the others! He was turning toward the town! The leaders had been so absorbed in His teachings, it seemed many of them began to believe Jesus really *was* the Messiah and had been begging Him to remain longer. Peter knew Jesus could never turn down such earnestness, such hungry sincerity; He never had yet. So off up the path they went, and they remained there for two days.

Jesus seemed to really enjoy these two days; He was able to teach freely and directly. Peter knew He had avoided making any direct statements to the Jewish leaders in the temple that He was the true Messiah. He hadn't wanted to precipitate the revolution too soon, apparently, and had continually warned Peter and the others to "tell no man who I, the Son of Man, am." But here, in the midst of this childlike crowd of swarthy Samaritans, Jesus seemed to relax and enjoy speaking openly, telling them plainly, "I am the Messiah who is to come!"

Following the two days at Sychar, Jesus and the disciples went on to Galilee.

# III

It was wonderful to be in his own environment again, thought Peter as he heard Beth instructing the children in their morning chores. He stretched mightily and reached for his clothing, got out of bed and stamped into his short-topped fisherman's boots.

Stepping to the stone water pot, he dipped a gourd full of water, and, crossing to the stoop, went out and poured it over his head. He briskly rubbed the water off his face and beard, ran a brass curry through his hair, and strode to the family backhouse.

Afterward, he went to the jetty to inspect the two boats' early morning catch. Jona and Zebedee had been forced to return to the nets, together with two hired servants, and it was a poor harvest today. Simon Peter stooped to look into the fish well, the first light sparkling on the moisture still imprisoned in his beard.

"Not very many today," he said, as if to himself.

"But better than yesterday," said his father, who was beginning to carry their nets ashore for spreading and drying.

"Here, let me help," Peter said, taking the heavy burden and heading for the drying pegs. Privately, he felt shame for remaining so long in the bedclothes this morning—but Jona understood, probably, that he had been gone on a long journey, and time with Beth and the children was a chancy thing, what with Jesus seemingly keeping to a schedule only He knew. Peter scolded himself for not arising well before first light and going fishing himself.

Zebedee and the two others were setting themselves cross-legged on the fish cleaning slate, where they wielded sharp knives in deftly gutting the morning's catch.

"I see you finally got the tiles for piping you wanted," Peter said.

"Yes," Zebedee nodded, indicating the water sluicing across the lower edge of the slab of stone. "We could have taken time to bake them ourselves, perhaps, but it would have taken days, so we purchased these for a load of fish and a few of Beth's baskets." The piping had been set in a trough, dug in the soil and covered over with stones to protect their comparative fragility, and a steady flow of water from the spring above the house came gushing out of the tiles, to flow over their slate, providing a place for cleaning their catch.

"Did you try my suggestion about the fish guts?"

Jona looked up, and gestured to the fantail of the larger boat, saying, "We did, we did, and it works pretty good. We've been blessed with fairly good fishing until the storm about three days ago."

Earlier, Simon Peter had suggested they fashion a basket from netting material and equip it with stones for weights, placing all their entrails and heads in it, and lowering it onto the shallower parts of the lake bottom as chum.

"Just like you said, Simon," chimed in old Zebedee, without looking up. "The combination of the water pipes and taking all our leavings out as chum makes a far better operation. Hardly any flies any more, and the fishing has been better."

"Good for you," Peter said. "Jesus constantly talks about being clean. He always manages to bathe at least once a day unless it's impossible, and tells the rest of us it's healthier."

Tossing the last fish into a basket, Jona arose, tied a line to the handle, and lowered it briskly into the lake several times, rinsing the fish.

One of the servants was scooping up the fish entrails

and heads, carrying them to the boat, and placing them in their chumming basket. This done, he lowered it over the side, snubbing the line to a cleat. In moments, the area was as if no fish had been cleaned there, with only the sight of smaller, curious fish darting here and there in the shadow of the boats, among the rocks, as they fed on the smaller parts that had been sluiced into the lake.

A distant call from the house said breakfast was ready, and Peter turned back, with Jona keeping pace. Zebedee went toward his own home, and the two servants slung the catch across a burro's back and started toward the town market. Those fish they failed to sell within only a couple of hours would be returned to the smoke house or dried in the sun.

At breakfast, talk turned toward Peter's recent trip again, and for the fourth or fifth time he told everyone of Jesus' great show of chasing the money changers out of the temple.

Soon he knew it was time to go. The others were probably wondering when he would arrive—Jesus had said they were going to Nazareth soon; He wanted to visit His hometown for some reason—and perhaps they would set out today.

By the time Peter gained the street in front of Jesus' home in Capernaum, it was to find a sizable crowd already gathered and Jesus already deep in speech, teaching them.

Peter waited on the fringes of the crowd, and, after nearly an hour, decided to go the long way around, to the rear. Once inside (for the others were already there, and Bartholomew had seen Peter's intent), he asked the day's plans.

"He said we're going to Cana today," Bartholomew answered, "but the crowd gathered, and He doesn't seem to want to send them away."

But, about an hour later, Jesus dismissed the crowd, and they gathered their belongings and set out along the road to Cana.

Cana lay higher up, across some of the steep mountains from the city of Capernaum to the west and south.

They arrived just before dark, after an arduous trip,

and Jesus and His disciples stayed with a wealthy man Peter supposed to be a distant cousin, for he had seemed to know Mary well. Both Jesus' mother and Mary Magdalene had come along this time, and they moved at a far slower pace along the trails than they had on their trip back to Galilee from Jerusalem.

The next day, Jesus seemed inclined to teach in Cana, for when word went out among the people, a large crowd of several hundred gathered in the court of the house, and Jesus began teaching them.

He spoke powerfully about His new kingdom, speaking many parables and examples and warning the people to repent of their sins and ready their lives for the coming Kingdom of God.

"Not everyone who calls Me 'Lord, Lord' will enter the kingdom of My Father, but he that *does His will!*" Jesus said.

"But what *is* His will?" asked an elderly Pharisee.

"You have Moses and the prophets," Jesus answered. "And if you knew His will you would know Me. Whoever knows Me knows the Father, for I and the Father are One, and He is in Me, and I am in the Father!"

Peter could only shake his head in puzzlement at this, wondering exactly what Jesus meant. He could see it puzzled the crowd, too, for many began to whisper back and forth.

During His teaching, He was interrupted by a nobleman who, John whispered to Peter, was a land owner and well to do. Apparently the man had followed Jesus clear to Cana, learning Him gone from Capernaum, for he was begging Jesus to reverse His steps and come clear back to Capernaum to heal his son, who was near death.

Jesus said to the nobleman and to all the crowd, "Except you see signs and wonders, you will in no way believe!"

"But, Sir, Sir, I beg of You, please come down to Capernaum and heal my boy. Please, before he dies!"

"Go on back home—your son lives," Jesus said calmly with a friendly smile. One of the disciples accompanied the man as he left, and they encountered two of the nobleman's servants who had been dispatched from Capernaum to Cana to find him.

"Sir!" they called out loudly, piling off the camels they were riding, "your son has been healed! He's alive!"

"When did it happen?" he asked them.

"Why, it was yesterday, about the seventh hour, and his fever broke!" one said.

"But that is the exact moment when the Man called Jesus of Nazareth told me, 'Your son lives.' " he said aloud to himself. Peter heard later how the two disciples had continued back to Capernaum with him at his request and how the whole household—family and servants too—had been baptized!

A few days after leaving Cana, they arrived in Nazareth, the city set high in the mountains overlooking sweeping distances, redolent with the smell of pine, fir and cedar, and the place of Jesus' early life.

Perhaps Jesus intended making His official start here?

It would be likely, Peter thought.

That night he discussed his thoughts with James, Andrew and John.

Jesus' statements about His marvelous new kingdom never ceased to fire Peter's imagination—renew his determination and zeal.

Revolution was in the air; Simon could smell it. A deeply patriotic man, religiously so, Simon's entire life had been profoundly influenced by the constant references to the thundering orations of the prophet Isaiah; the grandeur and sweeping promises of Ezekiel and Zephaniah, and all the great seers of Judah and Israel.

Simon was innately contemptuous of lesser breeds of men who had not the tumultuous history and tradition of the Jewish people and of Israel: the gentiles and interlopers who were like a curse upon his nation as a punishment for the sins of his ancient forebears.

He was acutely conscious of his nationality, made more poignantly alive and bitter by the accommodations between the ruling Herods and tetrarchs and Rome. Though the Romans preferred not to intervene in the

domestic difficulties and intrigues (Simon knew the priestly castes' penchant for endless argument and labyrinthian
reasoning over every possible disagreement) of this turbulent land, and allowed the Sanhedrin to carry out its own
justice, the specter of occupation was always there, and
with it the possibility of sudden violence.

Simon would not have characterized himself as either
racist or religious, yet he was possessed of a profound
belief in God and a religiocultural concept of a racial
destiny.

"Messiah shall come soon" had been drummed into
his boyish ears until it was like a chant, the words coming
to him at odd moments, assailing his mind whenever
doubts about his nation's future came.

For years, the people had chattered on and on about
this supposed Messiah—who He was and from whence He
would come.

The sages and keepers of the scrolls were busy
searching out the most indirect references to this Messiah,
this prophet who would come, reading Daniel's promises
and reciting by memory the lilting poetry and song of King
David.

Abraham was his father, and Isaac, and Jacob. In
Simon's veins ran the blood of prophets, seers and poets,
the blood of the nation of Israel; born in slavery, exiled to
Babylon, risen to glittering heights, dashed to the ground
in subjugation; persecuted; afflicted, murdered, plundered—but not beaten.

"They can control your body, take your property and
force you to work for them," Jona had said, his old hands
shaking with fervor, ". . . but they can never control your
mind. Your mind is free, my son, free. You are a child of
Abraham, to whom God promised the whole world!
Someday soon, Messiah shall come—you'll see!" he
would say.

Did a family meal ever pass without Simon's young
ears hearing reference to the Israelitish nation's plight;
their yearning for a mighty Savior to lead them once again
to Solomon's glories? Did Simon ever hear a lesson from
Ben-yehuda without seeing the old eyes grow misty with

dreams of past greatness, and hear the Levite's voice grow impassioned with prophesied promises for the future?

And now Messiah had come! He was *here*.

It was unthinkable — impossible.

Simon had always imagined great things happening far off in some storybook land, like the fables and stories he had learned as a boy that had unreal and shadowy meaning. Always, the news would come from afar of great events.

But nothing ever happened to disturb the years-long monotony of their simple fishing trade, save the usual local happenings such as marriage feasts, burials of noblemen, arrivals of eastern caravans, or the ceremonies of changing a Roman centurion's billet with a new arrival from some part of the empire or other.

To think that Simon, whom Jesus had dubbed "Peter," could have been selected to stand at Messiah's side! Sometimes the unreality of it made Simon go back over the past again and again, if only to reassure himself.

Sometimes he had to seek quiet moments with John, who seemed closer to Jesus than the others, and rehearse some of the shocking things they had seen and heard, wondering about Jesus' incredible powers and bolstering their nagging doubts with each other's company.

"Why *me?*" Simon had asked himself a hundred times.

But it was happening. Messiah was here. This was reality. Simon Peter had rarely ever grasped the broader concept of empires and nations beyond Hercules, of affairs of state and international commerce. But now he found himself for the first time acutely conscious of this moment in history, feeling part of something which would soon shake the earth.

Was Nazareth to be the scene of a major, formal announcement?

"What do you think, John?" Peter asked, watching Luke carefully packing away his writing materials.

"About what?"

"About Jesus coming here, to Nazareth?" Peter insisted. "You know, about whether this is the time and place to begin establishing His kingdom!''

''It's possible, all right, for it is the place where He is well known and where His own family has lived for so long.''

''That's what I was thinking,'' Peter added. ''Probably, He intends making some formal announcement before the leaders of the synagogue and the town council tomorrow.''

''If he does, I'm certainly ready for whatever comes,'' Andrew chimed in.

''Do you think He'll show some great sign or wonder when He announces He is setting up the new kingdom?''

''I'm positive that's the way He will do it!'' John admitted. ''It never fails to amaze and dumbfound the leaders. There is nothing to hold Him back if He ever decides to use the mighty power of God to establish His kingdom!''

They discussed just what kind of miracle would be the most effective, and what Jesus might say and their part in it, until well past midnight, when it was time to turn in.

They were staying in the large home that had been Jesus' permanent home for more than twenty years. It featured the large sheds in the rear, where the building materials and tools were stored, and there were sheds for their animals and a large courtyard. Even if it was crowded, the entire group of more than one hundred men found places to sleep, some even rolling up in their bedrolls on the roof, while Mary invited Mary Magdalene, Joanna, who was the wife of Chuza, one of Herod's stewards, and several other women to share the women's quarters with her.

The next morning Jesus informed the others He was going to the synagogue.

Peter's scalp prickled.

This is it! he thought, fingering the horsehide scabbard of his blade. Today is the day. He glanced at James and John, and, rising, they followed.

The synagogue in Nazareth was, like most of the stone buildings that housed the worship services, quite small. As always, it was dim inside, the oil lamps casting a feverish, yellow glow in their wall niches, and only shafts of light penetrating the room from the slits along the topmost portions of the room, shutting out most of this glowing, fresh mountain morning.

Peter and the others stayed in the rear, for the place was full and there were not enough benches to go around. Peter, James and John and some of the others lounged against the pillars or the wall.

Sure enough, when it came time for the Scripture reading the wizened old man who carefully guarded the priceless treasures of handwritten scrolls came shuffling toward Jesus in his spiderlike, crippled gait (for he had been injured in early life and was stooped terribly) and handed to Jesus the scroll of the prophet Isaiah.

The oil lamps in their niches along the walls had blackened the stone with the smoke of years; the air was close and stifling and the place smelled of burnt oil, sweat and dust.

Jesus stood up and, moving to the reading place flanked by two lamps in their holders, solemnly unrolled the scroll, with the help of the old man, until He came to the place He wanted.

Now He began to read.

"The Spirit of the Lord is upon me, because he anointed me to preach good news to the poor; He has sent me to proclaim release to the captives and recovering of sight to the blind; to set at liberty them that are bruised and to proclaim the acceptable year of the Lord."

Finished, He rolled up the scroll and the old attendant scuttled back to the scroll room with it. A dead hush was on the crowd.

Peter wondered whether Jesus meant announcing that *this was the moment. Now* He would proclaim their en-slaved nation would be *released;* that the people would be *set at liberty* and that *this* was the intended year when God would establish Christ on His great throne!

Sure enough, Jesus said, *"Today has this scripture been fulfilled in your ears!"*

The whole audience was listening with shock and wonder. A few were looking worriedly at the authorities on their dais in front who were plucking at their garments, crossing and uncrossing their legs, blowing in their hands, readjusting their necks and reddening around the ears.

The services were at an end, and immediately a din of confused conversation filled the synagogue as the people broke into knots of discussion. Some had marveled at the ringing impact of His words and asked, "Do you suppose *He* could really be the Messiah?"

"Nonsense!" said the ruler of the synagogue. "Why, isn't that Joseph's boy there? And isn't he just a local boy? Why, his brothers and sisters are right *here!*"

Jesus said, "Doubtless you will quote to Me the oft-repeated parable, 'Physician, heal yourself.' You will tell Me, 'Whatever we have heard done at Capernaum, let's see You do it right here in Your own country.' " He went on, "Truly I say unto you, no prophet is acceptable in his own country, but I truly say unto you that there were many widows in Israel in the days of of Elijah. And, when heaven was shut up for three years and six months and a great famine came over the entire land, Elijah was sent to *none* of his own people, but was sent only to Zarephath, in the land of *Sidon,* unto a widow woman who lived there!

"Further, there were *many lepers* who lived in Israel in the time of Elisha the prophet, and *none* of those Israelitish lepers were cleansed, but only Naaman, who was a *Syrian!"*

"That's *blasphemy!"* screamed one. "Lies, lies, lies!" chorused others. "Just who does this upstart think He is to insult the traditions of the elders?" shouted another. "Kill Him! Kill Him! He's not fit to live!" they shouted.

The foremost men fell over themselves, several falling to the floor in a heap as they struggled to wrestle Jesus' arms behind Him, and began shoving, jostling Him ahead of them out of the synagogue. The disciples were scuffling with many of them, and some of the mob fell down in a heap of tangled clothing, waving arms and legs as the roar of a riot rose to echo from the stone walls.

Peter was alarmed! Why didn't the Lord *do* something? Why didn't He stand up and use His great power?

All He had to do was *quiet* this shouting rabble and *take command!*

With shock and disappointment, Peter and several of the others struggled to reach Jesus' side, Peter shoving a number aside.

It was absolute riot. A group seized Jesus and several others fell over themselves trying to help imprison His arms at His side so they could propel Him out of the synagogue.

Peter, Andrew and John finally struggled their way to the front ranks and began roughly shoving some of the leaders aside, as if in anger to seize Jesus and aid in having Him killed. Shouting out orders and adding to the confusion, they tripped two of the men in the front ranks, shoved a few others, and in the hysteria that ensued Peter stood up and shouted, "He's getting away! *Stop Him! Stop Him!* pointing to the side. Several shrieked and surged in that direction. Meanwhile, some of the other disciples had shoved their way to Jesus' side and, helping Him to His feet, had pulled their cloaks around their heads and His and mingled with the mob. It was crazy, and it was a tragic shame, Peter thought! Here they were, suddenly propelled from the heights of expectancy thinking Jesus was making the first public proclamation of a unilateral declaration of independence from Herod and from Rome, and, impossibly, it had degenerated into a riotous mob scene that could cost Him His life!

"I'm here, Lord!" Peter said with quiet intensity into the hooded face, at the same time roughly shouldering away a short, stocky man who was still clutching fiercely to Jesus' arm.

Jesus looked straight into Peter's eyes, smiled with an expression of great sadness and pulled His cloak about His face, stooping over and turning toward Simon Peter.

Thaddeus and Judas emerged from the pile of struggling bodies that was just now disentangling itself from the overturned benches in the front rows, and Peter's face crinkled into a grim mask as he watched two Pharisees stamping at the robes of one of their fellows who had fallen over one of the reading lamps, and whose robes were now flickering yellow with flames and sending up heavy, sooty smoke.

With his brow heavily perspiring, and feeling his body soaked with sweat, Peter shoved this and that one, constantly looking over the heads of the nearest rioters, pointing and shouting, ''There He goes! Don't let Him escape!''

They were outside, then, and the crowd that couldn't enter had swelled considerably, Peter saw.

Turning and pointing, Peter's frantic bellow succeeded in causing further confusion so that the newcomers struggled to enter as the outraged men from within were fighting to exit the door.

It was like a big wave splashing against the breakwater, Peter thought as he saw the wildly waving arms and flailing fists.

Already a number were stooping to dislodge the stones of the roadway, handing two or three to eager fellows who then turned to run after a struggling knot of men surging along the narrow alleyway toward a steep cliff only about two blocks distant.

Each time one would attempt to peer into Jesus' face, Peter would roughly shove him aside and bellow out, ''You're letting Him get away!'' and point over his head toward part of the crowd.

Quickening their stride, the disciples began working their way toward the fringes of the mob and headed toward the lower street that led back to the caravan yard.

Several Roman soldiers came trotting up the hill, their lances at trail, their short swords slapping against their leather-reinforced skirts.

Jesus and the disciples sauntered down the hill past the curious still flocking to the riot, past the soldiers and their officer who paid them no attention whatever, and continued out of the city, taking the hilly caravan trail back toward the main road.

It was a near thing.

Peter was more than mortified! He felt as if he himself had been cast over the cliff.

The shame of it was like gall. It nearly choked Peter

with bilious hurt when he thought of it! To have to hide their faces and run! Everything in him cried out against this humiliating defeat — and he wondered whether Jesus was *really* who He said He was after all.

Were the people in Nazareth right? Were His own brothers right when they scorned the idea He could be anyone beyond a simple builder? The conflicting thoughts were tormenting; there was a miracle in Cana, Peter remembered, but was it a trick of some sort? After all, *he* hadn't gotten up to supervise the pouring of water back there. Had some of the servants conspired?

Why, they had come from the triumphal occasion when Jesus had cleared the temple, from His powerful speeches against the religious leaders, from baptizing hundreds in Jordan, from the people of Sychem and their great interest, from Cana and another miracle. And then . . . Then Jesus had made what seemed like the first great step toward public declaration of what He intended doing and had been treated like a common criminal, like a man caught in the very act of murder, and had been summarily dragged, like some baggage, out of the synagogue!

They crossed the open caravan yards, gained the public square, deserted on this Sabbath day, and continued past Jesus' former home, where several disciples were instructed to tell the women and others all that had happened.

Jesus' breathing was steady again, and Peter walked beside Him, his big chest still heaving with his exertions, a dark scowl on his face.

No one else was saying anything.

Jesus just kept walking.

Peter began wondering whether He intended going further than the allotted "Sabbath day's journey" when He departed the main road and indicated they were to climb to a vantage point above the trail.

This done, they backed well away from the view of those passing below and made a temporary camp.

It was later that evening before Peter's tormented spirits permitted him to even speak. Was it all for nothing, then?

He asked Jesus where He intended going, and the Lord told him He was going to return to Capernaum.

*Capernaum.*

But they had only left the place a few days earlier —Peter supposing Cana was but a temporary stop on a triumphal journey that would conclude in Jerusalem!

That night Luke reminded Peter of an obscure prophecy concerning the Messiah, but Peter was disconsolate and paid little attention. Luke said, "But, Simon—Peter, I mean—the prophet Isaiah said, "The land of Zebulun and the land of Naphtali toward the sea, beyond Jordan, Galilee of the gentiles, the people which sat in darkness have seen a great light, and to them which sat in the region and shadow of death, to them did light spring up."

"So what does *that* mean?" Peter asked sardonically.

"Seems to me it means the Messiah would live and work for a time right in Capernaum, for it is 'by the sea, in the borders of Zebulun and Naphtali.' "

"Well, at least it's close to Bethsaida!" Peter said resignedly.

The next morning Peter asked Jesus, during their long walk on the first day of the week, about a visit home.

Peter tried to phrase it just right, speaking of old Jona and Zebedee and the condition of their two fishing boats, the hardships of their life, meager catches, many chores and short help. His tone implied to Jesus he felt they were skulking backward along their own back trail in defeat.

Peter hoped Jesus would understand how he felt.

Jesus understood all right. Too well.

So Peter went back to fishing.

# IV

It was a sad and disappointed Simon who returned to his family at Bethsaida. Sensing his mood, Elizabeth spoke little and avoided questions about their recent trip, preferring to give Simon time to marshal his thoughts.

He would inform them in time, she felt. Meanwhile, he was her husband for all this life, and, as a daughter of Abraham and obedient to the traditions of the fathers and Scriptures, her place was to be his helper and his wife.

Simon was grateful for the absence of curiosity and questions — grateful, too, for Beth's skillful way of insuring the children didn't come around with their irritating questions.

As the days passed, Simon found himself becoming more at peace with the decision he had made. Strange how recent memories would fade so quickly, once one was back in one's own environment.

With each black predawn rising to his boat and nets, Simon's spirits were healed. Every blistering, sun-drenched day that he helped spread their catch on the racks, the familiar sights and sounds carved away more of his keen disappointment.

The keening cry of a flock of gulls, diving, swooping down to light on the water, would send Simon scurrying to hoist his sail, or bark at the servant to help him with the sculls, to approach the birds as fast as they could, knowing they were feeding on a school of minnows, and that the larger fish would be just beneath, savagely tearing into their numbers.

It was therapeutic work.

The days stretched into more than two weeks and Simon could now begin to think back over the events of these past few months with greater clarity.

Was Jesus really the Messiah?

Simon had begun to wonder. Where he had believed it, now there were doubts.

Still, he had seen healings with his own eyes; he had known long hours of spellbound listening to the incredible teachings of this plain looking, nondescript, but intense young Man who could speak of the heavens, the whole universe, the world and all the kingdoms of it, and prophesy of His soon-coming Kingdom of God. He had thrilled to Jesus' overthrowing the money changers' tables; sipped good wine he knew had been only water.

No, yes, no, maybe. His head swam with conflicting thoughts. One day reassured, he believed again. The same afternoon he wondered. That night he doubted. In the morning he was sure again.

Meanwhile, he fished.

There came a day when he and Andrew were sitting cross-legged on the jetty, having placed the servant to shoo away the gulls that were trying to steal strips of drying fish from the racks, representing yesterday's catch.

They had arisen early and had cast their nets until their backs ached, and succeeded only in collecting some weeds and grass from the shallow bottom near shore.

The sun was hiding behind a lowering, slowly moving overcast. It was cool and still, so that a man's voice could be heard a good distance away.

Andrew paused, cocked his head and listened.

Simon heard it too—the sound of a large number of people talking, growing louder as they neared the fishing sheds and boats on the shore.

Sure enough, it was a group strung out along the broad cart path for several stone's throws, clamoring out their questions to Jesus! And here He came, swinging along the road, calling out over His shoulder—and then He saw Peter!

"Lord! It's *You!*" Peter said.

"Yes, Peter, it's Me," He answered. "Can I come into the boat?"

"Certainly, Teacher!" Peter said gladly and with a little shame. "Come ahead . . ."

"Wait a minute—stand back there! Make room. Make room!" Peter said, and then thought: It seems like I'm forever protecting this Man from the crowds.

Jesus stepped into the boat, and Peter and Andrew cast off, poling out into deeper water so the crowd couldn't follow. Jesus asked Peter to anchor here, and, taking a position atop the little cabin, began to teach.

His ringing words echoed clearly over the glassy water as He spoke powerfully of His coming Kingdom, and told the people they must *repent* and turn away from their carnal vanities to the truth of God. His words assailed Peter's painful conscience like biting blows of a whip!

Now He was concluding an inspiring, vivid sermon right from Peter's boat. And here Peter was, with the stench of fruitless fishing on him, back at his trade instead of following along in Jesus' steps.

The discourse finished, Jesus leapt lightly down and, smiling at Peter, said cheerfully, "Why don't you push on out deeper into the lake and let down your nets, Peter?"

"Master, we've been throwing the nets till our backs ache all morning long and haven't caught a thing except enough weeds to foul our nets. But, because You have said, I will do it!"

So they did.

When Peter and Andrew had begun to slowly circle, then close the net, they couldn't believe their eyes! The water was shimmering with blue-black, glistening fish, the whites of their bellies and sides flashing as they darted this way and that, hurling themselves against the closing nets. Several leapt free of the water—a swirling, packed mass! A *huge* catch! The largest catch they had ever seen, ever even *heard* about, in this inland sea. And *look at the size* of some of them!

Excitedly, they began attempting to draw the net into the waist of the boat. Andrew, Peter and two of the hired hands all crowded to the port, hauling on the nets, and began to spill the first part of the large fish into the boat, their thrashing bodies slithering against the scuppers, tails beating frantic tattoos, splattering the men with water. The side of the boat was dipping lower into the water until the waist was taking water faster than the scuppers could shed it overboard.

It began to appear as if they were perilously in danger of swamping!

Peter's head swam. "Oh, no! Another of these fantastic miracles!" And now, because he had deserted Jesus and gone back to fishing, the Lord was going to "bless" him with a catch so big with such big fish . . . wait a minute! What was he doing? Here he was, getting more excited about the size of the fish and their number than he had about Jesus' message, his selfishness and greed fairly oozing out of his pores, and he was trying to gather so many into the boat he was about to capsize them! What was Jesus thinking of him?

Here he was, like a pig in a slop trough, trying to drag so many huge fish into his boat, eyes glittering with thoughts of profit, that he was about to drown them all.

Turning to Jesus, Peter said, his voice catching, "Go ahead and leave me, Lord, because I'm not fit, and a sinful man!"

"Don't be afraid, Peter," Jesus said, "because you're going to be a fisher of men. From now on you'll only be catching *men!*"

So he still wants me to follow Him? Peter thought, shamefacedly. After thinking He had failed in Nazareth?

Grimly, he and Andrew began throwing much of the catch away, pitching the thrashing bodies out into the blue-green waters of the lake and keeping only a small number—much to the wide-eyed dismay of the servants, who were mumbling to themselves.

Andrew and Peter exchanged rueful glances.

Peter nodded at him, their decisions made. There was no need to talk.

They were standing in the midst of a fabulous miracle—feeling it with their hands. This Man could only be the very Son of God, the Messiah! *No* normal human being could do what He could do; this was the finger of God.

Peter shuddered as he pulled in the last of the net, casting anxious eyes at Jesus now and then, who had once again seated Himself atop the cabin, His back to the mast.

But Jesus was merely looking across the distances as if to see beyond the faintly visible shores on the eastern side; to see beyond Judea, and beyond their nation.

Peter knew now that he would stick it out through whatever failures or setbacks—he would follow Jesus wherever He went, no matter what came.

Then followed a time of intense activity. It seemed Jesus was ready now to work day and night, not sparing Himself any discomfort to accomplish His mission.

The following Sabbath, Jesus went to the synagogue. After reading the Scriptures in His inimitable manner, a person stood up and, with saucy, sarcastic voice, said, "Oh, why should we have anything to do with You, You 'Jesus of Nazareth.' *We* know who You are, the 'Holy One of God'; are You come here to destroy us?"

Strangely, Peter was to learn, demons always recognized Christ.

Jesus knew the minute the man stood up that he was possessed of an evil spirit and so said in a loud, authoritative voice, "You *be quiet* and come out of him!"

Aghast, the people witnessed the man thrown violently to the floor, writhing about, chewing on his tongue and foaming at the mouth, screeching in a frantic voice! Gradually, the spasmodic jerking of limbs subsided and the man lay breathing quietly.

His eyes fluttered open and he sat up and looked dazedly about.

He then stood and began talking in a rational mind.

Even the disciples were amazed. And some of the crowd commented, "What *is* this, this strange power He has? Why, even unclean spirits come out when He commands them!" Many people were present, so the rumor of the event in that little synagogue in Capernaum preceded them into the entire region of Galilee, and people spoke of it everywhere months later.

Immediately following this miracle, Jesus told the disciples He wanted to go back down to Bethsaida, and Peter suggested they all stay at his home. It would be crowded, of course, but they could manage, and with the nearby home of Zebedee and their small loft above the manger, plus their fisheries' sheds, they would have adequate room.

When they turned in at the gate, it was to hear from one of the servants that Peter's mother-in-law was lying in bed sick with a bad fever.

Peter thought that next early morning restive thoughts of recent events. It had been good to lie in Beth's arms again, in their own bed after a time away. Peter's dreams had been tormented with the violence of Nazareth as if seeing Jesus' body tumbling into space. Faces came and went: the leering officials in the temple demanding Jesus produce credentials. Peter tossed and turned with the feelings of shame over the meeting on the quay when Jesus had come striding along and asked Peter if He could use the boat as a floating platform to address the people before He was trampled underfoot.

He disengaged his left arm gently from beneath Beth's head (his arm was completely asleep), massaged it slowly, easing its unfeeling weight down on the top of the woolen coverlet so as not to awaken her.

What a woman she was. The miracle yesterday had done much to fill even Beth with wonder and awe, for all her earlier distress that her traditional, centuries-old way of life had been shattered by the lugubriousness of her fisherman husband picking up and trucking off after another of these would-be "deliverers" of the people. (Beth had been genuinely *afraid* for him, Peter knew, expecting his head had been addled by some cleverly spoken political slogans or such, and was terribly afraid he would be arrested and killed. Peter knew the fear was more than just concern over the children and what the neighbors would say; she was sincerely afraid for *him*.)

It was a day and age of arranged marriages.

Peter could remember the shy way she had smiled when he saw her face for the first time after her uncle (for

her father had been drowned in an accident while fishing—and they, too, had been fishing folk) had arranged
the dowry, and when the family was having the usual party
after the promises were made, the bargains struck, and the
local ruler of the synagogue asked to formalize the be-
trothal period. Peter had even resented—with a quick start
of guilt—all that folderol about "tokens of virginity." The
priest had to go through the ancient ritual, along with her
legal guardian; it was terribly embarrassing. Still, Peter
couldn't question the accepted rites of marriage; it was just
that something had begun to develop between him and
Beth that was, well, *special!*

Peter could remember the shy, wide-eyed way she
had looked at him. Why, it had set the blood to pulsing in
his temples and caused his hands to tremble, so he had
quickly clasped them behind him and struck a most dignified pose, attempting to mimic the looks he had seen in a
number of similar parties, when he had seen family marriages, and the six-month waiting period began.

Usually the men hardly deigned to look at the frightened little creatures that had been sold to them because of
financial, tribal and family considerations—unless the
word had gotten out that the girl was a spirited little filly
and someone special.

Beth's simple good looks, the spattering of freckles
across her nose, the generous lips and deep-set, brown
eyes showing flecks of amber—her deep auburn hair—had
taken his breath. Of course, there was nothing about the
shapeless bridal attire, with its layers of undergarments
and embroidered robes, that could reveal the slim, almost
athletic body that lay beneath, and Peter tried valiantly to
follow the urgent teachings of his father and the readings
he had heard in the synagogue to fight down the speculations that flooded maddeningly through his head.

Maybe some would have said she was too "skinny,"
if the clothing required at the time could have revealed it,
but Peter had found Beth was all woman and with hidden
fires that almost made him wonder if her passion, when
she allowed herself to express it, wasn't almost sinful. Not
that Peter felt it so; he felt himself a very fortunate man—a

man blessed.

After the children came along, Beth had gradually assumed a more matronly appearance; there were a few more fine lines around the corners of her friendly mouth, another couple of furrows in the brow, and a touch of gray here and there to bear testimony to the rigors of her work. Even if they were relatively successful and could afford at least one household servant and two men to help with the boat and the nets, Beth had always carried her share.

Peter thought, as he heard the cock crow distantly, how loving and almost cloying Beth had been last night, and how she had tried to show him she knew and understood now why he felt he *had* to follow the Master. She had quietly gone about her work during the few days after he had come back home, defeated, shamed and downcast.

They had never spoken of it, and yet when Beth had come to the quay thinking to refresh the water jugs and had seen Jesus and the crowd, and Peter sitting there looking both contrite and enraptured at the same time, she had placed the jug on the ground and had taken a seat on the rocks of the quay and listened intently to what Jesus had said.

And now her own mother had been spared; Beth had been truly frightened for her, Peter knew. He had seen the symptoms; Jesus had been so compassionate, so *understanding,* somehow! He *knew* Beth's heart and mind, it seemed—knew what these other men, unannounced, would mean to the household. He had walked over there, looked down at Beth's mother, who was flushed with high fever, with rapid, quick breathing and brightly burning, fever-charged eyes, and had reached out with His strong, broad hand and taken her hand in His, looked briefly up, spoken only a few words, almost as if in a sigh under the breath, and then, nodding His meaning to Beth's mother, had lifted her right up off that sickbed!

Well, that did it! Beth had been almost fawning in her thanks. And, though the women turned immediately to their work, to prepare a fine meal (it *had* been unusually good, of fresh fish, with a thick gruel of lamb and barley, and even fresh greens and home-baked loaves), Beth had turned to steal admiring glances at the Lord now and again, and Peter knew now that Beth would never again chide him for what he was doing.

Peter stirred and, carefully easing his feet to the floor, parted their hastily rigged privacy curtain of goat-hair tenting material and squinted at the bleak, brittle light of a new day. Time to get up, he thought, dreading having to leave the warmth of his wife, and even wondering whether . . . but, no, Jesus would be wanting to lay out the day, and he'd better be moving.

Going out to the loft where Jesus had insisted on sleeping (He had politely but firmly refused Peter's offer of their own bed and had insisted on sleeping out there, saying He really preferred it), Peter found it empty!

He stopped at the well, drew up a bucket, and, rinsing off his sleep-swollen face and running his comb through his mane of hair, began looking around for Jesus. He stopped by the kitchen door, which opened directly on the lake to the rear, and saw only a sleepy servant slowly gathering wood to start the morning fires. Puzzled, he began meandering out through the streets.

As the sun's rays began painting the mountains above him, he became mildly alarmed. He knew the Lord had many enemies, and had worried about Him sleeping out there by Himself. Could anything have happened to Him? Peter was past the last house on the higher ground, and, looking up as the pinkish hues of the sun began to swathe the mountainside, he thought he saw a man, or maybe a goat or a sheep, up there. No, it *was* a man, and coming down the trail now, briefly hidden by larger rocks or trees. And then, with a sigh of relief, Peter saw it was Jesus!

"Is everything all right, Lord?" He called.

"Fine, Peter," Jesus answered, and then commented on the beautiful morning God had given.

It was then Peter saw the reddish imprint of His forehead and recognized it for what it was: the imprint of Jesus' own clenched hand where He had cushioned His head as He had been praying . . .

Peter was to learn (and feel twinges of guilt at his own inattention or lethargy) that Jesus often did this: disappeared to a private place alone to pray.

They walked together back to the house to find everyone astir and their breakfast ready.

In the weeks that followed Jesus kept them moving at an almost breathless pace, as if an urgency was on Him to reach every town, village, hamlet or city in the whole Galilean region and in Decapolis and beyond.

Not only was Jesus seemingly concentrating on reaching as many of His own countrymen as possible, but one outstanding miracle in Capernaum showed He was willing to show mercy upon gentiles.

Years earlier, Peter had heard of the exploits of the favorite centurion around the northern part of the Sea of Galilee, Alexios. He was a well educated, intelligent man, married to a half-Jewish woman. Through her, he learned much of the Jews' religion, and, though he was not a convert, or a proselyte, he came to admire and respect their rich history.

Wealthy in his own right, and possessing substantial sums as a result of his exploits (officers were given shares of captured booty, depending on rank), he had been moved to contribute most of the money toward the construction of a new synagogue. The devout Jews all through the region talked of Alexios and his famous heroism. Was part of it exaggeration?

Peter didn't know, but old Ben-yehuda had told the story as if true in every detail.

Alexios had been involved in a lengthy seige against some embattled Halmanni, a fierce tribe of savage warriors who had taken refuge in a walled city of huge tree trunks far up in the Dacian foothills.

Alexios was under the command of General Aristubulos, a graduate of the Academy of Rome and fellow student of Titus.

Aristubulos was laboring along the trails, dragging a vast siege train. There were hundreds of horses and mules and eight thousand mercenaries dragging the ponderous stone launchers, battering rams and pitch kettles. The wagons and chariots were laden with all their cordage and hemp, tackle, springs, pulleys and blocks, trenching tools and sacks of square nails and spikes, all the equipment they would need for building trenches and protective battlements as they advanced to within hurling distance of the walls.

The Halmanni had refortified their captured city with thousands of huge tree trunks set deeply in the ground, sharpened at the top, with log runways around the perimeter. They were skilled bowmen and expert with the sling. Though they possessed no chariots, they mounted sturdy little horses and wore shields and helmets of iron.

They were a fierce, blond-bearded race, blue-eyed and standing two to three hands taller than the average Roman. They had come boiling out of Samatia above Pontus Euxinus, and the distant borders of the empire above Pannonia were seriously threatened by their increasing numbers.

They must be taught a lesson. A Roman lesson.

Should Rome allow even this one incursion to prove successful, the news would surely travel, and the whole northern flank of the empire from Germania to the plains of Dacia and the Oloia river drainage could be turned, and it might require several legions to contain.

The Halmanni needed to be dug out, and quickly.

The story said that Alexios, growing impatient with the long wait required for the ponderous siege train of Aristubulos to arrive, had developed an ingenious surprise. Perhaps it was a combination of the coup of the Persians under Darius the Mede and the Trojan Horse! Darius' men had diverted the course of the river and assaulted Babylon from within, walking under the river gates dry-shod while Belshazzar and his citizens were asleep following a drunken orgy. Everyone knew about the famous horse of Troy!

Alexios had been studying the site from a distant hill, pacing up and down, arms clasped behind his back. His juniors kept their distance when their commander was like this, knowing he was puzzling out some plan.

Water. The Halmanni had an inexhaustible supply, while his own men had to carry it in leathern buckets to their dry camp, in peril of scattered Halmanni scouts who would slip out of the town at night and attempt to waylay wood or water details.

The city sat squarely astride the small river, which surged against the logs of the river gate, disappearing within and flowing out the other side to fan out over a long, fertile valley whose small villages had been put to the torch and the fields left untended.

That river barrier intrigued Alexios. The current was strong, and few of his men could swim. Any man weighted down with shield, sword, helmet and bronze greaves would surely drown.

Alexios had been puzzling over the problem for over two hours, pacing until he paused, seeing a wood detail unloading its supply of dried sticks, branches and reeds.

Reeds!

To the startled soldier he said, "You, come here!"

"Sir!" he soldier said, more loudly than necessary, stamping his feet as he jerked to attention.

"Where did you get these?" Alexios asked, seizing one of the large reeds.

"Along the marsh yonder, sir!" the man said, turning to gesture beyond their camp, where a circling flight of ducks could be seen dropping toward the distant flags of green stalks that bordered a shallow slough.

Orders were barked to the men, and within minutes another load of the largest and strongest reeds were hacked down and brought to camp.

Alexios chose thirty of his men, some of whom could swim, and explained his plan.

They were to leave everything except sword and dagger; those would be strapped around their waists with only one belt, and their greaves, helmets, shields and leggings, even their clothing, would be left behind.

They extinguished one of their fires and built up several more, instructing the men to move back and forth before the flames to allow the Halmanni in the city to see their movements. From the muck of the ashes, they smeared themselves with black until they looked like hideous savages, their pale skins all but invisible in the growing darkness.

Alexios led them to the river bank, taking more than two miles to reach the forest beyond the slough, and then followed the river bank below the cut it made in the plain, so their shadowy progress would not be seen unless scouts were in the river bed itself.

He spent several minutes explaining what they would do.

It would take steel nerves, and no mistakes.

They would quietly advance to within a few hundred feet of the walls and slip into the river two or three at a time. They would seize a large, rounded stone, of which there were countless thousands along the banks and in the river, and, clenching the reed in their mouths, walk along the river bed with only the last two or three inches of reed projecting above. If water came into the reed, they would hold their breath, turn sharply right and move toward shallower water, lightly blowing the reed free.

If any man panicked and began thrashing about like a stranded whale, he could be picked off by bowmen from the parapets; one weak link in the chain and they were dead.

Alexios' speech had the desired effect. That, and a firm Roman grasp of the forearm and a ''good luck'' to each man personally.

If the plan worked, they were to continue past the river gate for a count of one hundred steps, which should carry them well beyond the guards on the walls. They would wait until just before false dawn for their attack, waiting until all their camp fires had long since been allowed to smolder out and the Halmanni had been convinced the Romans were asleep, except for their outposts.

Meanwhile, their remaining force would likewise blacken their bodies and leave all heavy armor behind, armed only with swords and bows — no helmets, no shields and no shin greaves — and steal as close as they dared to the two gates on the south and the dung and animal gate, much smaller, to the east. They would use the cover of the tree stumps that remained and move very slowly.

The faint murmuring of the river the only sound, Alexios and his men had slipped slowly into the icy river,

their faint gasps of breath coming as the shock of the water
hit them, and, lowering their bodies slowly, stooped to
pick up a large rock, weighing at least a quarter of their
body weight or more.

Their frozen progress was made terrifyingly difficult
by the slippery river rocks, and not a few of the men found
themselves losing their footing, filling their reeds with
water, and having to struggle toward shallower water to
pause, gasping furiously for air from their large reeds,
eyes wide with fright.

Another terrifying moment was holding their breath
when they were swept, their feet leaving the bottom for
several strides at a time, under the boiling wave caused by
the river gate.

But the noisy gurgling of the river gate current prevented their being heard, and the sleepy guards on the
parapet, lulled by the somnolent whisper of the river, and
believing the Romans asleep, did not notice.

It was to their peril.

Sleepy guards at the gates had awakened moments
later to see the unbelievable sight of naked, dripping men
falling upon them on silent feet, swords and daggers
plunging and hacking. The screams of the wounded and
dying alerted the men in their bull-skin huts, and those
along the walls, but all three gates were opened and hundreds of Romans came pouring in.

Soon the carnage was over.

With a loss of only thirty-seven men, most of those
from bowmen on the walls, Alexios' small force of a few
hundred had carried the city, overpowering a large garrison more than three times its size!

Aristubulos and his ponderous siege train had arrived
three days later to see the imperial flag flying from the
battlement and to be greeted at the gate by Alexios, resplendent in silver helmet and breastplate, sitting astride a
captured Halmanni horse.

Peter knew Alexios was much beloved by his men,
that he was, for all his fierce exploits in war, a well
educated and cultured man, and that he wore the honor of a
decoration from Caesar himself.

Though he was uncircumcised and a gentile, he was said to place much weight on the Scriptures, and he especially liked hearing the story of David and his heroism.

They were strolling along the colonnaded porches and arches of the finer part of Capernaum one day when they happened near the house where Alexios the centurion lived.

Peter remembered the vivid stories he had been told about Alexios when it occurred that Jesus met him personally.

Alexios had come striding out to see Jesus, and, when Peter identified Him, the officer said his household servant was very sick and asked Jesus to heal him!

"Imagine!" Peter thought. "One of the most famous of the Roman officers in the land, and, though he is not circumcised, he asks the Lord a heal a *servant,* a Jewish *servant.*"

"I will come and heal him," Jesus said, smiling.

"Don't bother Yourself, Lord," Alexios protested. "I am not worthy that You should come into my home, under my roof. I am not even worthy to appear here before You. Just say the word and I know my servant will be healed.

"For I am a man who is under authority," he continued, humbly. "And I have many soldiers under me. I tell this one 'go,' and he goes; another 'come here,' and he comes. I tell my servants 'do this' or 'do that,' and it is done."

Jesus' eyes widened at this, and He remarked to Peter and the others about the man's faith.

"I tell you," He said in a booming voice, "I have not found faith as great as this even among My own people in Israel. I tell you, many will come from the east and the west and sit down with Abraham, Isaac and Jacob in the Kingdom of God, but the sons of the kingdom . . ." turning to the Pharisees and scribes standing near, listening, ". . . shall be cast out into outer darkness, and there shall be weeping and gnashing of teeth!"

Peter beamed at Jesus and stood studying the glittering splendor of the silver breastplate Alexios wore.

"Go your way," Jesus said to the officer, "and as you have believed so it will be done!" Word came back before they had covered two blocks further that the centurion's servant had been completely healed!

That made quite a stir. Peter was happy now. It seemed as if the Master was really stepping up His campaign. He preached the most powerful, inspiring, encouraging messages, painting vivid word pictures of God's love and compassion to the people, and sometimes talking in puzzling, mystifying terms about His soon coming kingdom.

# V

Peter liked the urgency of Jesus' tone.

He would say, "The time is fulfilled. *Repent*, all of you, and believe this wonderful good news I'm telling you," or, "The Kingdom is at *hand*," and other such statements that continually buoyed Peter's faith and determination in spite of the nagging impatience for the revolution that kept plucking at the edge of his mind.

Wherever they went, the crowds gathered. They couldn't remain in any one place more than three days or people would show up from every part of the country. Why, some had even come from up in *Syria* and from Jerusalem and further south beyond Jordan.

One day a leper came to Jesus, beseeching Him loudly, prostrating himself on the earth and saying, "Lord, if You will You can make me clean from this filthy disease!" Jesus then performed an astonishing miracle.

Lepers were absolutely untouchable. People feared the dread disease, believing it to be highly contagious, and lepers were commanded to shout, "Leper! Leper!" when they came along the way so that others could give them wide berth. But Jesus, looking directly at the wretched man, being moved with deep compassion, walked up to him, put out His hand and actually *touched* him.

An audible gasp was heard from the crowd. Why, Jesus was risking *leprosy*, and everyone knew it was extremely contagious! He said, *"I will, be thou clean!"* Immediately, the leper's whitish, scarred face and hands changed to a healthy, ruddy glow, and he rose, completely healed!

Jesus began to strictly instruct him, saying, "See that you say nothing about this to anyone, but go your way privately and alone. Show yourself to the priest, and offer for your cleansing the things which Moses commanded which will be a witness to them!"

Instead, he went out and began to talk to everyone about his miraculous healing.

Because of the leper's tale, it became difficult for Jesus to enter openly into a city, so that He had to stay outside some of the towns (and thus outside of the jurisdiction of the local authorities), and the people, learning of His presence, would gather around Him in various wilderness areas where He and the disciples were encamped.

After a period of time, Jesus decided to go back to His home in Capernaum. After they had been there for some few days, word went out that He was once more in His house, so a large crowd gathered.

Some of the Pharisees and the doctors of the law were there, and, as Jesus was teaching a large group inside the covered public courtyard of His home, a group of people brought one of their buddies who was terribly sick with palsy and who could neither stand nor walk but had to be borne on a stretcher. They kept attempting to get closer to Jesus but couldn't because of the crowd. Gaining the roof by the outside stairway, they began to take up some of the tiles on the roof until a hole appeared.

Peter marveled that Jesus stood there, almost as if He *knew;* almost as if He had already seen *through* that rooftop and knew what was happening. Most men would have cried out an alarm, summoned help and rushed up to stop the vandalizing of their property! Not Jesus.

The men began to take up some of the roofing tiles, and those below, sitting about the large, inner court listening intently to Jesus, noticed some dust sifting down, and then a bright sliver of light appeared in the ceiling. Some rose and stepped back, brushing at the flecks of plaster that speckled their hair and clothing, and suddenly the teaching came to a halt.

Jesus stopped talking, for all eyes were on the growing hole in the roof.

The hole grew larger and larger until it was well over
five feet long and several feet wide. Peter wondered
whether the pranksters up there intended taking the whole
roof apart, and he began to have fears of an attempted
assassination. He tried to warn Jesus to duck or get behind
a protected place, and had assayed to gather several others
and run up there and put a stop to this, but Jesus just
smiled, put out His hand and indicated that Peter should
not interfere but stay where he was and watch.

A brilliant column of light now pierced the interior
court, giving life to innumerable, tiny dust particles like
thousands of little fireflies, and bathed a swath of the
curious seated around Jesus with harsh sunlight.

Peering upward, the crowd now saw several faces
appear in the large aperture that had been made, and then a
pallet was slowly lowered into the room, the lines bringing
with them additional small showers of dust.

On the pallet was an inert figure of a man.

"Of all the presumptuous . . ." began Thomas.

Jesus raised His hand and Thomas cut off his remark.

Others were commenting about the rude interruption,
and no small number had leapt to their feet to avoid the bits
of debris that had come tumbling into their midst.

Some were smiling, and many were looking from the
lowering pallet to Jesus, wondering what He would say
and do.

Finally, the pallet gently lowered to the floor, those
on the roof called out their wish, and two of the disciples
quickly untied the ends of rope affixed to the four handles.
The ropes swayed jerkily upward and disappeared to the
sight of more minor debris and dust cascading into the
room.

It was completely quiet now. No one moved.

Finally, Jesus rose, walked to the pallet and looked
down.

The crippled man lying there could only raise his
eyes, his face contorted with desire and hope.

With a smile, Jesus looked back at him and said,

"Son, your sins are forgiven!"

"What is this?" cried one of the officials of the publicans. "What is He claiming?"

"You mean to say you claim to have the power to *forgive sins?*" squawked another, sardonically.

Suddenly, what had been a fairly tranquil teaching session was taking on the overtones of another riot. A growing babble of voices began fiercely arguing what Jesus had said, the majority hooting their outrage that a mere man could claim such powers. "Blasphemy! That's what it is!" "Never heard such preposterous claims!" "What vanity!" "He can't be serious," laughed the mob.

Gesturing for silence, Jesus said in a ringing voice, "So you can understand that the Son of Man *has the authority*" — He raised His voice even louder — "on this earth to forgive sins, turning to the paralytic, who was still lying inert, "I am telling you, *get up from there, roll up your pallet* and go to your home!"

The man raised both arms instantly, and, placing his palms on the wooden brackets, sat up, gathered his feet under him, and stood.

A gasp of shock rippled through the crowd, and a ragged cheer came from above, where the faces of his friends had reappeared.

The man stooped, pulled the two rods out of the pallet and began rolling it up, with tears streaking his dusty face, his hands shaking with emotion, and looked up at Jesus, babbling out his thanks.

"It's some trick!" shouted one.

"He was planted!" added another. "That man wasn't really sick. He was just feigning sickness!" The Pharisees began nodding agreement, and an angry buzz of talk erupted again, with many claiming Jesus had blasphemed by claiming powers that belonged only to God.

The men above had disappeared, and the gaping hole remained.

Peter saw that several of the others, including Simon, from Canaan, and little James, Alphaeus' son, were flanking Jesus. Thinking Him safe from any attack here in His own home, Peter gestured to Andrew and pointed upward.

Would Jesus never weary of this continual controversy, wondered Peter, as he signaled Andrew to follow
him.

"What is it?" Andrew said, as they gained the corridor to the servants' quarters.

"The roof," Peter said, without comment.

Andrew trailed along with his brother, hearing the
fading sounds of angry talk echoing from the stone walls of
the covered courtyard they had left.

Gaining the rear, they crossed behind the walled rear
yards and came to the open stairway that led to the "road
of the roofs," as some rabbi had taken to calling them.

Several men were just rapidly descending, and Peter
called out to them, but they hurried past without pausing.

Now Andrew knew Peter's mission. He was going to
replace the stones and try to insure there was no damage.

Kneeling to help, Andrew asked, "What do you
think, Simon? Can He really forgive *sins?*"

"If He is Messiah, He can," Peter grunted, lifting
another stone into its metal bracket, and reaching for
another.

"But what kind of sins was He talking about?"

"Whatever it was that caused the man's injury, I
guess," Peter answered. "He apparently applies the intent
of God's laws even to the physical, bodily actions. You
know how fastidious He is about keeping clean and about
avoiding injury."

"But," Andrew protested, "since the Pharisees are
very strict about their belief that only God can forgive sins,
and since the Lord just said what He did, don't you think
there might be as much trouble here as we had in Nazareth?"

"I doubt it," Peter said, finished with his work,
standing to survey the stones and then kneeling to see if
they were straight. "In the first place, this is His own
house and not the synagogue. In the second place, these
Pharisees are not local people and have no standing here.
They were sent up from Jerusalem to report on Him."

"I suppose you're right," admitted Andrew, as they
descended the outer stairway again.

"I know I'm right, or I would have never left His side just now," Peter growled.

That was true enough, thought Andrew, for Peter had imagined himself a lieutenant of sorts, a bodyguard for Jesus. Andrew sometimes worried about the way Peter (it was becoming easier for Andrew to think of him as "Cephas," or "Petros," now, and it never failed to remind him of the revolutionary nature of their activities) kept allowing his hand to stray to his sword. He wondered what Jesus would say if Peter ever attacked anyone.

"By the way," Andrew said, grasping Peter's arm just before they reentered the rear of the house, "I heard today that John the Baptist is becoming very upset."

"Oh?" Peter stopped, tugged at his beard and waited.

"About Jesus' ignoring him," Andrew began.

"What do you mean 'ignoring'?" Peter asked, craning his neck to listen to the loud sounds still coming from within, his brow furrowing with concern.

Though Andrew realized he was only half listening, he decided to go on.

"Because John is in *prison*," he said, "and I have heard that several of his disciples are really concerned that Jesus has sent him no message, that He has shown no concern, almost as if Jesus doesn't even know about John's plight. And yet I told Him myself!"

"Don't worry!" Peter said, still cocking his ear toward the sounds coming from the corridor. "John will be released any day now. Herod will not dare touch him, not with so many thousands of converts, not with Jesus backing him so strongly."

"Even so," Andrew continued inexorably, "the disciples of John are beginning to remark about the contrast of John's poverty, his sacrifices. He's a Nazarite by vow, you know, and drinks no wine. And stories are told about Jesus attending wedding feasts and banquets, drinking, living in a fine home like this, wearing a fine robe and visiting in the homes of the wealthy."

Peter turned from the door, his full attention now on his brother.

"Do *you* believe all that garbage?" he demanded.

"Well, no," Andrew began. "But . . ."

"But nothing!" Peter interrupted. "Just think about it, brother, just think about it."

"I *am* thinking about it. That's why I'm asking you," Andrew protested.

"Look," Peter said wearily, "I know you were a devout disciple of John, and I know what you think of him, but there's nothing to really worry about. Jesus could just speak the word and John would be released from jail in minutes!"

"I know that!" Andrew protested. "That's not what I am getting at. I mean there is growing talk that Jesus has not even mentioned John lately; they claim He has forgotten him. Several are claiming Jesus is really only a disciple of John, like I was, that John baptized Him, as you'll recall."

"Well, the people look to John as a prophet, and I doubt that Jesus wants to ignore him," Peter rejoined. Then as an afterthought he added, "Let's talk to John about it tonight."

After the crowd had gone and supper was finished, Peter and Andrew sought John, and the three went back up to the roof, where several were preparing their bedrolls for sleeping.

Going to a far corner, they settled down to talk, for Peter had asked John if they could discuss something in private.

"What is it?" John asked, seating himself on his bedroll.

"Andrew is worried about John the Baptist being in prison—about talk he says is coming from John's disciples."

"What talk?"

"That Jesus' life-style is sumptuous, that He has been seen in the company of wealthy people, dined at banquets, and mostly that He has apparently intended doing nothing about John being in prison."

John sat cross-legged, scratched under his beard and stared across the roofs to the fading line of purple that etched the rugged line of hills against the distant sky.

"I'll tell you what I think," he began. "Remember, John said plainly, 'I must decrease, but He must increase,' meaning the Messiah. Remember, too, the political overtones.

"If Jesus went back to Jerusalem now and tried to effect some surprising sign to get John out of jail, what would happen?"

"Perhaps the beginning of the revolution—probably the beginning of His new kingdom!" said Peter.

"No," John said quietly. "We have talked much about it, Peter. Jesus is on some definite timetable of His own. You know very well He has said time and again, 'The time is not now,' or, 'The Father only knows the time,' and similar words."

"But surely that doesn't mean He'll let John die?" Andrew protested.

"I hope not. But I doubt very much that Jesus means to get Himself arrested and in the middle of a tangled legal mess involving Herod and Philip and the lusts of the Herodian household over the divorce issue. I would tend to believe Jesus is leaving the whole thing alone, that He knows what will happen in advance. He seems quite untroubled by the news."

They talked on for another hour or so, Andrew particularly troubled, for he had great love and respect for John.

It was the very next day that the reported gossip proved true in the form of a delegation from John in Jerusalem. Several of his disciples, including two of Andrew's friends, came to Jesus in Capernaum.

After they had been fed it was time for the meeting. Peter listened in mild dismay at the tone of their voices when they braced Jesus on the issue.

"Are you the One who was prophesied to come, or should we go look for another?" began their leader. Without even allowing an answer, another demanded of Jesus, "Why do John's disciples fast, but your own are eating and drinking?"

The tone of self-pity and irritation was obvious.

Peter could understand. He knew John's disciples were hard working, loyal to John with a fierceness that matched that of the most zealous Pharisees; he also knew that John's own life-style of abstinence, rigorous outdoor living, meager diet and frequent fastings had become like a religion unto itself, a virtual way of life.

To them John represented the epitome of righteous life. They couldn't understand why Jesus, having heard (for it was a nationally known event and had caused a great stir among tens of thousands of people) that John had been thrown in jail for resisting Herod's desire to marry illegally, had not come down there and effected his release. They felt that He ought to be showing grave concern, should be mourning, fasting and speaking of John to the people! Instead here He was conducting a great public ministry, sitting down at feasts, wedding suppers, or dining in the leaders' homes. And, it was said, gaining a reputation as a *winebibber*, a wino!

Peter knew their hurt, their inability to equate the contrast in Jesus' own mission with that of John.

Jesus answered, "Can the sons of the bridechamber fast while the bridegroom is with them? As long as they have the bridegroom with them they cannot fast! But the days will come when the bridegroom shall be taken away from them, and then they will fast!"

Then He said, "No one would patch up an old garment with a piece of new cloth; it would be glaringly obvious, and a new patch on old cloth would appear worse than the rend they were trying to conceal!

"Neither would anyone put new wine into old wineskins, else the wine would burst the old skins, and both the skins and the wine would be lost. But men put the new wine into fresh, unused wineskins so they can both grow old together. And, when anyone has drunk of the aged wine, he will never desire the new because he says, 'The old wine is good!' "

Peter tried to understand. Jesus was speaking about incongruity—contrasting situations that didn't go together.

His analogy about the bridegroom and fasting was

probably veiled reference to the wedding feast in Cana, and the rumors. But it made sense, Peter could see. If only John's disciples, and John the Baptist himself, could understand.

Peter knew no one would ever put newly fermented wine, wine that was still "working," into an old wineskin. Not only would the flavor be affected, but it would probably cause the skin to break in time. As Peter mused on all that Jesus meant, Jesus turned to the crowd and said, "And blessed is he who shall find no occasion of becoming offended at Me!"

He said many other things to John's disciples. As the men collected their packs and left, Jesus turned to the crowd and said, "Well, what did you expect? What did you go out there in the desert to see? Some reed shaking in the wind? What did you go out there to see? A man clothed in soft, expensive clothing? Look, those who wear such are in kings' palaces . . . but what did you go out there to see? A prophet? Yes! And I'll tell you this: You saw much more than just a prophet because this is the one of whom it is written, 'Behold, I send My messenger before thy face who shall prepare your way before you.'

"Truly, I am telling you, among those born of women there has not arisen a greater man than John the Baptist. Yet he that is but little in the Kingdom of Heaven is greater than he." Jesus continued, "And from the days of John the Baptist until now the Kingdom of Heaven suffers violence from violent men who try to treat that kingdom violently! All the law and the prophets were *until John*, and if you are willing to receive it, *this is* that 'Elijah,' which is to come. Whoever has ears to hear, let him hear!" Jesus finished.

Peter knew John, too, was like an emissary of this great new kingdom; as such, Jesus was according him diplomatic status, the stature of an ambassador or advance representative of that kingdom. Jesus was making it clear, then, that those who had violently seized John were guilty of doing violence to the platform and principle that represented the political, moral, social, economic and spiritual underpinnings of the kingdom itself. Further, He must have been referring to the violence in Nazareth when He had very nearly lost His life. But, more, He was showing publicly that John's ministry must be over!

Why, He had said, ''From the days of John the Baptist until now . . .'' almost like He had meant to imply the days of John the Baptist were *over*. Did Jesus know John was beyond saving? Did He know that any attempt to rescue John from prison might mean the premature finish of His own cause?

Surely Jesus had always spoken highly of John and had told the disciples of his place in Scripture, that he was the one who had come in the ''power and spirit of Elijah'' to ''prepare the *way*'' before Christ Himself! Now it seemed Jesus was saying John's great preparatory work was done, that ''the days of John the Baptist'' were over, and the ''days of the Son of Man'' were here.

Jesus continued, ''But unto what shall I liken this generation? It's like little children sitting about in the public marketplace and calling to their friends, 'We piped the tune, and you didn't dance to it! We wailed, and you didn't mourn!'

''For John came neither eating nor drinking, and they claim, 'He must be demon possessed!' But the Son of Man is come both eating and drinking, and they say, 'Look at that! A gluttonous man and a wino! A friend of publicans and sinners!' And wisdom is justified of her children!''

Peter could appreciate the lesson in incongruity. Jesus just didn't fit anyone's mold, even Peter's! John, albeit at the opposite spectrum of the two life-styles, didn't fit anyone's mold, either. Seemed people were never satisfied. No matter how much abstinence, hardship, self-sacrifice and the rigors of a wilderness, John just didn't fit the mold people had for him in their minds; he was ''different,'' somehow, and, since most always fear what is different, they branded him ''demon possessed.''

In contrast, since Jesus was known to attend wedding feasts, known to enjoy good food and wine and would talk in friendly tones to known sinners in the local towns, the people weren't satisfied with His example, either.

Just like little kids, Peter supposed. ''We call the

tune, but you don't dance the step! We name the game, and you don't play by the rules. You just don't *fit*, somehow!'' It was good Jesus was upholding John the way He was, for John was beloved and greatly admired by many, and Peter knew Jesus was totally sincere; He had great love and respect for John.

Who knows? Maybe by the time John's disciples return a miracle will have occurred and John would be sprung from jail anyhow. Peter wondered.

That same day, about midday, one of the leading Pharisees, a tall, haughty looking fellow in the full regalia of his office, asked Jesus to dine with him in his home. Peter knew it would be a setup; the patronizing, raspy voice grated on him like rusty fishhooks when the Pharisee asked Jesus to dine and Peter noticed the smirks exchanged when he sent a servant scurrying ahead to make preparation.

No doubt the man would attempt to trap Jesus in some insignificant breaking of tradition and defame Him later. It wouldn't be unthinkable that the man had arranged for an armed guard who would be there to arrest Jesus and hold Him for trial before the Sanhedrin if He fell into a trap.

Peter urged Him not to go, but the Lord was determined, so, reluctantly, Peter and a few of the others followed Jesus and entered the Pharisee's ample home. Nearing the front entry, Peter noticed the Pharisee, whose name was Simon, was kissing the cheeks of other well-known leaders of the community as they arrived. It was obvious Jesus and His men were to fend for themselves. Peter felt the blood rushing to his head. The Lord acted as if He hadn't noticed, but Peter knew better.

After the greetings and acknowledgments, they were seated, and, following a lengthy and formal prayer of thanks by Simon, they began to eat.

The hum of conversation filled the room as the servants passed among the guests, seeing to their water vases, bringing steaming plates of lamb, kid, vegetables, cheeses, herbs, greens and loaves of round, flat bread.

Peter paused, a succulent bite of lamb stew halfway to his mouth, and suddenly noticed a huddled figure down the table washing Jesus' feet! Several servants were whispering to one another, and two more across the room were pointing.

Those seated next to Simon, the host, followed the extended arms of the servants and saw the woman at Jesus' feet. With a look of pure disdain, one of them nudged Simon's elbow and gestured toward the scene.

A woman had somehow mingled with the servants and, gaining Jesus' side, knelt at His feet and was pouring an ointment from an alabaster cruse over His feet and weeping. She was using the very hair of her head, which tumbled gracefully over her shoulders, to wipe his feet!

"Oh, no!" Peter thought. "Not *here!*" He was quite accustomed to displays of emotion and acts of worship toward Jesus, but, knowing the woman by reputation (she was the best known town harlot), Peter was stunned. This could be disaster.

But Jesus merely looked down and smiled at her.

Simon was thinking, "No man who is a so-called prophet would ever have allowed such a slut to touch him!" so Jesus said, "Simon, I've got something to say to you!"

A hush had fallen over the tables, and all eyes turned toward Jesus. Simon, sitting across from Him, stroked his beard and smiled patronizingly.

"Say on, Teacher, say on!" Simon the Pharisee said with a short chuckle, acknowledging the smile and knowing glances of his compatriots.

"There was a lender," said Jesus, "who had two debtors. One of them owed five hundred pence and the other fifty. Now, neither of them had any money, both were broke and couldn't pay, so the lender forgave them both. Which of them, do you believe, will love his lender the most?"

"Why, I suppose it would be the one to whom he forgave the most."

"Well said, Simon!" Jesus retorted.

"Simon, you see this woman?" He said, turning to the woman who had not ceased her laving of His feet and her soft crying. "You know, it was obvious when I entered into your house that you gave me no water for my feet, but here is this woman, wetting my feet with her tears and wiping them with her own hair. You greeted me with no kiss (though you did all the others, and the slight was obvious), but she since the time I have come in and sat down has not ceased to kiss even my feet. You didn't offer me any oil to anoint and comb my hair, but she has been anointing my feet with ointment.

"Wherefore," He said, turning again to the woman, "her sins, which are many" (she nodded and more tears spilled out of her eyes as she looked straight into His face) "are forgiven!" With that the woman lowered her eyes and grasped His feet again, "for she loved much," Jesus continued, turning again to the gaping crowd of dinner guests and to Simon, "but to whom little is forgiven the same loves little!"

Gently He turned to the woman and said, "Your sins are forgiven!" A murmur of conversation rippled through the room, and several servants made as if to remove the woman, but Jesus warned them with a glance, and, taking the woman by the hand, lifted her up and said again, "Your faith has saved you [using the familiar]; go in peace!"

Peter heard the arguments raging as they made to leave later. Almost every Pharisee or obsequious Pharisee pleaser in the place was reasoning to himself, "Just who does He think He is . . . ? The very idea! To claim *He* has the very power to forgive sins!"

But others said Jesus *did* have that power, and Peter figured that Jesus' statement certainly proved He could forgive sins! If the woman didn't feel any more *guilt,* and if she was *free* now from her own mental anguish, and could face the future with confidence and a whole new beginning in life, why, wasn't that forgiveness?

Yes, Peter knew Jesus *did* have that power; He *believed* it! He knew the Master would chide one of His disciples now and again, and when they would sincerely say, "I'm sorry, Lord . . . I made a mistake!" He would look at them and with tiny crow's feet crinkling at the corners of his eyes would say, "I know you are. Forget it—you're forgiven!''

It could mean everything, Peter found. The possession of a clean, clear conscience could mean more than the wealth of the richest man. Money couldn't buy it—that zest and expectancy that awaited you in each new day, life with no guilt-ridden past hanging around your neck—life like a wellspring of fresh, gurgling branch water, and no apologies to anyone so long as you kept yourself right with God and with man.

*Sure,* He had the power to forgive sins! And the woman, no matter her past, Peter knew, was forgiven! And may the fleas of a whole herd of goats infest the beard of Simon the Pharisee for being so unforgiving . . . Oops! He shouldn't think like that. He had to chuckle at the thought, nevertheless. Simon the Pharisee. The man's whole life consisted of a religious pose—like walking down the proverbial hall of burnished bronze mirrors, striking this and that self-righteous posture, wondering how well he was impressing other lesser men of inferior spirituality.

# VI

One day Jesus was in the house and the crowd gathered quickly; so many were striving to find a place where they could hear Him that it was impossible to find room to eat their noon meal, and Peter and the others were worried. "Why, He must be *beside* Himself!" some were saying. He could be trampled in a crush like that, and Peter, with help from the others, had to effect a hasty rescue, shouldering their way through the crowd and saying, "Give way, give way, there!" in loud voices. Peter could be an imposing figure, with his fisherman's roughness, strong build and a voice that was used to calling across the wind and the waves. And he carried that sword . . .

Finally they had dispersed the crowd into more orderly ranks. Jesus was seated, teaching, when a distraught family managed to bring to Him a son possessed of a demon. Jesus cast out the demon with His command, and some of the Pharisees who were there from Jerusalem to spy on Him and attempt to compile witness against Him began saying, "He must be possessed of Beelzebub himself!" and, "It's by the prince of the devils He casts out devils!"

Jesus, knowing their thoughts, lifted up His voice and said to them all before the crowd, "How can Satan cast out Satan? And, if a house be divided against itself, that house will not stand. And, if Satan has risen up against himself and is divided, he cannot stand."

Letting the whiplash of His anger crackle through His

words, Jesus said, "And, if I by Beelzebub cast out demons, then by whom do *you* cast them out? Therefore, they shall be your judges! But, if I by the *Spirit of God* cast out demons, then is the *Kingdom of God* come upon you!"

Peter was excited at His anger and words! Now He was showing the kind of miracle-working *power* He would use when He came into His kingdom!

"How can a person enter into the home of a strong man," Jesus continued in a more reasoning tone, "and spoil his goods, except he first bind the strong man, *then* he will rob his home?" Puzzled, Peter wondered if the Lord meant that He had to bind up Satan and his demons *first* before He could assume complete spiritual control of His new kingdom.

Jesus' voice was rising in power again, and He was looking straight at the Pharisaical delegation from Jerusalem. "And truly I'm telling you, whoever is not with Me is against Me, and he that does not gather with Me is scattering. And I'm telling you that every sin and blasphemy shall be forgiven unto men, but the *blasphemy against the Holy Spirit* shall not be forgiven; it is an eternal sin. And whosoever shall speak a word against the Holy Spirit shall not be forgiven in this age or the age which is to come! Either make the tree good and the fruit of it good, or make the tree corrupt and its fruit corrupt, for the tree is known by its fruit!" He said with ringing power, "You generation of snakes! How can you, being evil, speak good things? For out of the abundance of the heart the mouth speaks. A good man out of his own good treasure brings forth good things, but an evil man out of his evil treasure brings forth evil things! And I'm telling you that every idle word that men shall speak they shall give account thereof in the day of judgment. For *by your words* you shall be justified, and *by your words* you shall be condemned!"

What a session! Peter watched as mixed anger, hatred, puzzlement, fear, contempt and feigned amusement washed across the faces of the religious leaders; saw their minds trying to cope with the razor sharp strokes of Jesus' words as He dared to call them a "generation of snakes.'' It was beautiful, Peter thought.

To show Jesus His support, Peter stood to one side, fixing first one and then another of the religious fanatics in the front ranks with an icy stare, hand on the hilt of his sword. Peter reveled in the role he was playing of self-appointed bodyguard to Jesus, and the one upon whom Jesus would depend for His personal protection and safety (with God's help, of course). Peter had helped to convey Him out of dangerous situations before, but this was different! Here in Galilee Jesus was clearly *in charge*. He was the leader, and the people by the thousands looked to Him as ''that prophet'' who is to come, or as Elijah, risen from the dead.

Meanwhile, in Jerusalem, Herod Antipas, one of the three sons of Herod the Great and the ruler on the puppet throne, was becoming extremely uneasy.

Daily, impossible tales reached his ears of this ''Jesus of Nazareth'' who was said to be massing thousands of loyal followers from among the common folk; travelers from Syria and Babylon who had stopped along the caravan routes in Galilee were spreading the most impossible rumors.

They claimed this Jesus had power to heal the deaf and maimed, to cast out the demons from demoniacs with a word, and even had power to raise the dead.

Herod's tormented mind put another twist to the stories, for the events of the past couple of weeks had caused him to toss sleeplessly on his mat, groaning aloud as he strove to drive from his mind the ghastly act he had been forced to commit because of his own foolishness.

Curse that fiendish woman in there, his wife! She must have the eyes of ten cats and the cunning of a snake! It was all her fault!

And now these wild tales about this ''Messiah'' up in Galilee had Herod convinced John the Baptist was *back from the grave* and would come to torment him.

He shuddered, remembering.

John the Baptist had said to him, ''It is not lawful for you to marry your own brother's wife.''

Herod desperately wanted to consolidate his own

position, and marrying Philip's wife, Herodias, was one of the most important political moves he could make. Little could he know the scheming woman had vast political desires of her own. Herod was striving to bring other tetrarchies into his own orbit, and Herodias was hoping to gain the throne and probably poison Herod and become reigning queen.

He had gone ahead with the marriage and, as talk mounted behind his back, decided to teach John the Baptist a lesson. Herodias herself leaked her plots to have John killed, so Herod thought to outwit her by having John cool his heels in prison.

He would be taught a lesson that way, and watch his mouth. Further, while he was under the royal guard, he would be out of harm's way. Do him good to think about his sayings, and contemplate what the consequences were to speak against the crown, Herod thought.

What were his *real* reasons for marrying Herodias?

She had dark, exciting beauty, flashing eyes and black hair, a kind of knowing, experienced, direct look that could set the blood coursing through his temples and give him an excited quickening of the heart.

But she also had a teenaged daughter.

The daughter, Salome, was absolutely breathtaking. Herod found himself daydreaming as much about the daughter as the mother now and again. And when the wedding was over, and the girl had risen on tiptoe to kiss his sagging cheeks and press his shoulders with her little, exciting hands, the faint smell of her perfume and the touch of her hair on his cheek had set him fairly snorting like a Roman chariot horse in a race. He hoped Herodias didn't see the way he patted her in more than fatherly familiarity now and then as she came near him during their endless series of dinners and parties.

What tragedy! He didn't want to think about it, but the thoughts assailed his mind like vinegar and he couldn't shake them.

It had been on his birthday, just a little over a week ago, when Herodias had outwitted him.

Had she actually seen his growing desires for her

daughter? Had she skillfully planted the girl in such a way that Herod would fall into her hands? He wondered.

They had been lounging before the low tables, nearing the end of a nearly four-hour Roman-style banquet. There had been endless courses of foods, and some, following the newly popular Roman custom, had turned to empty their stomachs in the vomiting troughs, rinse their mouths with wine and then continue to fill their stomachs with the endless array of delicacies the busy servants placed before them.

The third group of musicians had been playing, and a clanging of tambourines and cymbals announced a special bit of entertainment. Herod had belched his way through the kid and barley cakes, sipped more Idumean wine and peered through heavy-lidded eyes at the draped entry as a lithesome, scarcely clothed, beautiful young dancer began her slow, graceful, tantalizing dance.

As she came closer, Herod had sat bolt upright. It was Salome!

The child was a full-blown woman, he saw, for this was the first time he had ever seen her without her proper clothing in place.

She dipped and swayed, stepped lightly through an intricate dance of the Syrians, undulating her young hips and causing her slim waist and flat, brown little stomach to do the most fantastic things.

Herod thought he would go mad with desire.

With wine dribbling over his beard and staining his loosely fitting toga, he sat forward, completely entranced, as an idea began forming at the back of his wine-soaked brain.

When the dance was over, he gestured with his silver goblet and a servant leaned immediately to fill it with more wine.

"The girl! Bring her here at once!" he whispered.

Dracimus and Pargas seemed not to notice, and Herodias was not here this night, claiming a headache. But Herod's wine-clouded mind supposed his whisper was much softer than it was.

The girl came before him, bowed deeply and smiled.

"Come here, child, come here," he said, handing to her a bunch of grapes that had been chilled in the bottom of the water pots. "Sit by me."

She sat, and Herod congratulated her on the dance, expressing his amazement that she knew it so well and covertly eyeing her swelling bosom and strong young thighs. It was heady stuff indeed, having this young, beautiful creature sitting there with only the skimpy veils and decorated dancing costume that revealed a bare midriff and showed a good deal of supple skin.

Herod drunkenly made his proposition.

"Name the gift you desire, child," he said, expansively, and then added in an undertone, his eyes desperately striving to convey his whole meaning, "and it is yours, even up to half the kingdom!" he finished, spacing the words and emphasizing the word "kingdom."

"Oh, thank you, my lord," she said, sweetly, bowing lower and allowing his reddened eyes to peer lustfully down her bosom.

"May I have only a few minutes to think about my request and to change from my dancing costume?"

"Of course, child, of course," he breathed heavily, leaning over to pat her arm, not noticing the way she pulled back a little at the smell of his wine-laden breath.

Privately, Herod hoped the girl got his implied meaning. She had her own ambitions, no doubt. Her mother could be taken care of in one way or another, and, though Herod knew she could never be his if he poisoned the woman, there could be a convenient accident arranged.

He hoped the girl knew his promise of "half the kingdom" was genuine.

But the whole thing had gone sour as green wine. The dumb young thing had sailed straight to her mother, and Herodias, seeing Herod's plans and turning the situation to her own advantage, told the girl to go back into the banquet and demand John's head, all neatly laid out like some suckling pig on a charger, as a bizarre jest for the banquet.

Herod was dumbfounded. He had wanted to spare him, but he knew Herodias was wild with rage against John—wanted him dead. The woman must have a thousand eyes, he told himself. She sensed somehow that he could have gotten rid of her, married the daughter and gotten around all of John's objections; Salome is not "my brother Philip's wife," he said to himself, imitating John's tone when he had warned him of his infraction of Jewish law. Curses! The whole sordid mess was hanging around his neck like a decaying, uncured camel's skin.

He sighed, remembering.

He had to open his big mouth and make a wild promise right in front of his most trusted aides. And, to keep their respect and retain any semblance of true kingly office, he knew that once a promise had passed his lips it was as if it had the force of law.

The stupid girl!

Instead of seeing what he plainly implied—marriage (eventually)—she had gone prancing in to her mother, exactly as she had been instructed, probably, and spilled the beans. No telling what Herodias had thought; they had never discussed it. But she had proved more clever than Herod could ever have imagined.

Trapped, he had given in, calling the captain of the palace guard and instructing him to send orders to the prison. When he had struggled out of the aching hangover the next day, he could scarcely believe what he had done! He had remembered Salome coming back, walking in that sensuous, promising way of hers, and had been aghast when she had said, "You said I could have anything, even up to half the kingdom. Did you really mean it?"

"Of course, child!" he had exclaimed with a significant look and loaded tone of voice.

"Then I'll have the head of John the Baptist on a charger as a present for my mother!" she had demanded.

*How could he have done it?* he asked himself.

Yet he had.

The guardsmen had come back within less than an hour, and, like a grisly jest, as if to parody some special course at the banquet, they had borne John's head on a silver charger, garlanded with leaves and sprigs of grapevines. Sickened, Herod had told them to take the thing out of his sight, and, following Salome's gestures, they had carried it straight to Herodias.

Herod had been outwitted at every turn. Now, instead of being able to seek John's eventual blessing, he had become his murderer—no matter how hard he tried to claim charges of "treason, revolution, sedition" and say John was plotting the overthrow of Herod's government. Further, with John dead, Herodias had pointedly explained that none of the other religious leaders dared question his marriage to her, Philip or no Philip, and through subtle means had let him know she understood his secret hopes toward her beautiful daughter.

So now the streets of Jerusalem were alive with wild rumors about this "Jesus of Nazareth." Miracles had been performed, it was said. They claimed he had turned water into wine, could heal the sick, the blind and the dumb, could even raise the dead. Many claimed he must be "Elijah that is to come"; others said he was one of the great prophets, reincarnated, resurrected from the dead!

As for Herod, *he* was convinced in his heart that this must be John the Baptist come back from the dead!

He remembered how he had allowed John's servants to claim the headless body, and how they had apparently managed to arrange a special tomb.

Herod's scalp prickled. Was this the beginning of the end? He had been acutely aware of the incredible period of intrigue, betrayals, murder, corruption and exploitation that had marked the reign of his father who had at first seemed so skillful at retaining his throne. He was lucky to be alive, when he really thought about it.

He remembered how many times he had heard the story—and the warnings that had been given him by his mother as well as their household sages and teachers. His father, Herod the Great, had allied himself with the Arabian nobility and had become a ruler of Palestine under Hyrcanus II. But, when Rome decided to use armed might in Palestine, sending Pompey there personally, Antipater had been discerning enough to know Rome would finally prevail and so skillfully managed an alliance with Pompey's representative.

Herod's grandfather had managed to commend himself both to Caesar and Mark Antony and, after the famous battle of Pharsalia, was made both a procurator and a citizen of Rome as a result.

His father had begun ruling from early youth when Herod's grandfather had died at age seventy-five.

He had set the whole East on fire with his swift actions, brutal subjection of potential rivals; he had the dangerous archbrigand Hezekiah, who had made serious incursions into the Syrian border, murdered. The assassination of Hezekiah gave some of the nobility among the Jews in Jerusalem a pretext to get rid of him, since they all hated his Idumaean ancestry. And Hyrcanus had possessed the audacity to command him to appear before the Sanhedrin.

He had promptly appeared with a large armed force, and the members of the Sanhedrin who had been openly bragging about how they would take care of this youthful upstart who had exceeded their own authority in executing Hezekiah were meekly overawed and said not a word.

A trial of sorts had ensued, but Herod had sent off an envoy to persuade the governor of Syria to demand his acquittal, and the resultant deal found him in Galilee, absconding with considerable wealth.

Years later he had returned to Palestine, but the intervening period had found him in Rome after the Arabians, who were his people on his mother's side, had repudiated him and Antony made him a tetrarch. Later Antony used his influence to persuade the Senate (with the full agreement of Octavian) to name him king of Judea.

When he came back to Jerusalem, it was in the company of Antony and plenty of Roman troops, who were entirely at his disposal, and he laid siege to the city and took it by storm.

He had been smart enough then to marry Mariamne, a Hasmonaean princess, and put out the word to the Pharisees to accept his rule as a direct judgment from God.

A short while later, he had forty-five members of the Sanhedrin murdered and confiscated their possessions.

Little had he realized that his marriage to Mariamne had brought enemies right into his own household, and that his mother-in-law was plotting to have him overthrown, finding Cleopatra of Egypt a handy ally—for Herod had openly spurned her, and Cleopatra was blistering mad, no matter that her lover, Antony, was Herod's mentor.

It had been a turbulent, wild, impossible period of time. With the huge battle at Actium over, Herod the Great had executed Hyrcanus and then went to Rhodes to meet the victorious Octavian, whose ships had so recently burned the fleet of Herod's own protector and mentor, Antony. Octavian had confirmed Herod's position, and he had returned in triumph to govern Palestine.

Then had followed the ugly period when the monster (Herod thought of him as that now, father or no father) had listened to family intrigue and had two of Mariamne's own sons (who he suspected were plotting against him) assassinated—they were strangled at Sebaste.

Then, even on his own deathbed, he had listened to stories that his own son had been plotting against him, so he sent to Caesar Augustus and obtained permission to put him to death.

One of the most colossal blunders of all had been his decree to kill all the infants following the visit of the Magi, and then he had ordered his own son killed so that the father followed the presently ruling Herod's brother in death by only five days.

No wonder a traditional epigram began to be circulated by Emperor Augustus which read, "It was better to be Herod's *swine* than a *son* of Herod."

Somehow he, Herod, the present ruler, had to avert the abominable disasters that had plagued the lineage. Hadn't he begun to build a beautiful new city that he named "Tiberius" on the Sea of Galilee? Wasn't he already finishing fortifying the towns of Sepphoris and Betharamptha in Peraea?

He was wily and clever (it made him furious that rumors had reached his ears that this upstart "Jesus of Nazareth" had referred to him as a "fox"), and somehow it must be possible to prevent this mindless mistake from costing him his power and wealth.

As Herod was battling his tortured thoughts in his palace, Jesus and His disciples were stepping up their pace. Peter was continually amazed at the Lord's tireless physical strength, His seeming disregard for sleep and the way He would fast and arise early to spend much time in prayer.

The news of John's death had come as a terrible blow, especially to Andrew, and it required many a long talk from Peter to calm his brother and remind him of all that Jesus said.

"He said there was no greater man!" Peter said for the tenth time, at least.

"I know. But I still believe we could have *done* something," Andrew argued.

They covered the same ground monotonously, Peter explaining, with John's help, that an armed attempt against the dungeon, guarded by Herod's own palace guard, was impossible; that the Sanhedrin needed only a small pretext and Jesus would suffer the same fate; that breaking religious traditions was one thing and open defiance of the law (even if it was corrupt) was another.

Andrew had been disconsolate, and Jesus had tried to help him understand.

The late summer blazed hot and dry, with only infrequent thundershowers to give the land the moisture it needed, and the trails were dusty and long.

All through the long months that followed, Jesus traveled ceaselessly throughout Galilee and Decapolis, continually returning to Capernaum as a kind of home base. He taught, preached, answered endless questions, healed hundreds of sick people and skillfully tangled up the Pharisees, who dogged His steps, with His direct words.

He preached in Chorazin, Nain, Cana, Bethsaida, Capernaum and Tiberius and in dozens of towns and villages on this and the other side of the sea until Peter lost all track of time.

On those occasions when Peter, Andrew, John and James were able to spend a day or so with their families in Bethsaida, Peter would rise early to help with the fishing chores. But it was always only a matter of one or two days at the most and they would be off again, following along as Jesus continually told the crowds, *"Repent,* all of you! And believe the gospel!''

They would create no small stir upon entering the smaller towns, for it was unusual to see a group of strong young men, accompanied by their servant women and animals, traveling about away from the main caravan trails.

Mary, Mary Magdalene and Joanna, who was wife to Chuza, a servant of Herod himself, traveled with them much of the time, seeing to their packs, washing their clothing in the streams and preparing their meals.

Always there were those who came following along from one town to the next to spread stories in the public squares about Jesus' powerful words and His mysterious talk of the "Kingdom of God" that was just ahead, or to tell how He had healed them or their children.

It would never require more than an hour, barely time for them to arrange lodging or to set up a camp near a stream or a well, when the local townsfolk began clamoring for Jesus and bringing their sick.

As winter neared, Jesus began spending even more time near Capernaum, teaching in His own home from time to time, or entering the synagogue and reading and answering questions.

Things had been going fairly smoothly for some time now, for they had avoided any direct confrontations with any officials from Jerusalem as long as they kept to the smaller towns. But, as sure as they spent more than one day at a time in a larger city, like Capernaum, the officials would show up, usually with a spy from Jerusalem with them, trying to trap Jesus in His words.

This was the second day of the week and they had only been back in Capernaum for a night and a morning when Peter was particularly puzzled by something Jesus said.

They were in the house again and a small group of officials arrived to request a special visit. Apparently, they hoped it would be a showdown, of sorts—hoped to put an end to Jesus' continual teaching.

They stood in the court and their leader said, pompously, "Master, we want to see some sign, some definite proof of Your authority from You!"

"An evil and adulterous generation seeks after a *'sign,'* " Jesus said, "but there shall be no sign given to it except the sign of the prophet Jonah. For, just as Jonah was three days and three nights in the belly of the great fish, *so* shall the Son of Man be three days and three nights in the heart of the earth!"

What did He mean by *that?* Peter wondered. Though Peter was familiar with the story of Jonah, he had found himself seeing possible flaws in it and had experienced doubts, especially since he was a fisherman. Peter didn't know that much about saltwater fish, but he had exchanged tales with the fishermen of the Syro-Phoenician coasts and from Joppa on the few occasions when he had been there.

He marveled at their tales of huge fish, caught right off the bottom, and which had to be dragged aboard by large lines when they would try to swallow a huge glob of pigs' entrails that some of the gentiles were wont to use as bait! Peter had a difficult time understanding their stories, separating the fact from fiction, their belief in strange gods of the seas, in a boy who rode on a dolphin, and of monsters, dragons, serpents and the place far beyond the Gates of Hercules where some said there were vast and far lands peopled by giants with one eye, and of the songs of nude maids who would lure hapless sailors onto their rock-studded shoals, and of mermaids. But Peter could believe there were huge fish, maybe big enough to swallow a man; he just had trouble believing any man could survive it, let alone three days and three nights! But what did Jesus *mean* "in the heart of the earth"? Did He mean He would go in hiding somewhere? Did He mean out in the Arabah, that bleak, windblown tinderbox of heat, scorpions and centipedes that was the land of the wandering goat keepers of the gentiles? Would he descend into a cellar somewhere and remain there as a "sign" of some kind?

Jesus was continuing, "The men of Nineveh shall stand up in the judgment with this generation and shall condemn it, for they repented at the preaching of Jonah. And, behold, a greater than Jonah is here. The queen of the south shall rise up in the judgment with this generation and shall condemn it, for she came from the ends of the earth to hear the wisdom of Solomon. And a greater than Solomon is here!"

Then Jesus delivered another scorching warning to the scribes and Pharisees who were spreading the accusation that Jesus' miracles were done in cooperation with "Beelzebub," the prince of demons!

"But the unclean spirit, when it is gone out of the man, passes through dry, waterless places seeking rest and doesn't find it. Then he says, 'I will return to my house where I came from,' and when he is come he finds it empty, swept and garnished. Then he goes and takes with himself seven other spirits more evil than himself, and they all enter in and dwell there! And the last state of that man becomes worse than the first! Even so shall it be also unto this evil generation!"

As usual, the word had been spread, and a large and growing crowd was here, many coming inside unbidden and many more jamming the door and foyer.

While Jesus was speaking, Peter noticed someone attempting to attract his attention outside. Squeezing past those who blocked the door, he looked for the man who had gestured and discovered another of the disciples, who said, "Listen! Jesus' own mother and His brothers and sisters are outside and want to speak with Him!"

Peter relayed the message to Jesus that Mary and the others (James, Joses, Simon, Jude and the girls) were standing around outside and couldn't come in because of the crowd. Hearing this, Jesus stretched out His hands, gesturing with a sweeping motion to indicate to the entire crowd, and said, "Behold, My mother and My brethren, for whoever it is who will *do* the will of God, My Father, who is in heaven, that person is My brother or My sister or My mother.

"My mother and My brethren are those who not only

hear the Word of God but *do* it!''

Finally, Peter and the others had begun urging the people to leave, saying Jesus' family was waiting and that He was growing tired and that He would no doubt be speaking to them again later or tomorrow.

Jesus spent a little time with His family in private while Peter and Zebedee's two sons ran to the docks to obtain a boat at Jesus' instructions.

The minute Jesus exited from the house, the crowds began to swarm along after Him, and they soon came to the rock jetty where Peter, James and John were standing ready with the boats. After Jesus stepped aboard, they poled away from shore. The other disciples urged the people to be seated wherever they could to wait for Jesus to speak to them.

Peter urged Jesus to eat a quick snack and drink from the cooled water jug he had lowered overside into the cooler depths of the lake. And, thus refreshed, Jesus seated Himself atop the little cabin and began to speak to them in strange-sounding stories (''parables,'' He told Peter they were).

Hours later, after Jesus finished His lengthy teaching session, Jesus wanted to cross to the other side of the lake and avail Himself of darkness so the crowds wouldn't have time to discover immediately where He went, so they pushed away from the landing and set the sail to catch the nighttime breeze that would carry them across.

# VII

They decided to sleep in shifts. The boat began pitching gently, and Peter saw how the lights of the one following were winking faintly as the freshening breeze threatened to blow out the lamp at the masthead. The big lugsail was drawing full, and the boat began to plunge more heavily, spray breaking over the bowsprit as they ran before the wind. Peter was sailing, and Jesus, exhausted from the long, rigorous day, was below in the stern sound asleep and oblivious to the increased tossing of the deck.

The wind was fairly howling around their ears now, and Peter's words were whipped away as he hailed James and the others, who were fully awake and beginning to show concern, to reef the sail. This finished, they soon double-reefed it, and, as the wind increased, John shouted, "This wind will snap the mast if we don't heave to. If it goes, the sail will drag us broadside to these waves and we could turn turtle!"

Peter nodded, and, shouting orders to James and Matthew to signal the others to heave to, they manhandled the sail down, nearly losing their grip on the flapping sail. It seemed determined to shake them off into the waves.

Throwing out the sea anchor, they brought the bow around until their direction was reversed, and now they faced the shrieking gale, the bows dipping into the waves, shipping green water that foamed and hissed along the deck to fill the scuppers and pour overside. Water flung by the wind hit their faces in stinging spindrift. Now that their direction was reversed, they could dimly see the pitching, dancing light of the other boat ahead of them making strange, corkscrewing motions as it pitched and heeled over when a fresh gust struck.

The waves were monstrous now, the largest Peter had ever experienced! Many a time Peter had seen these land breezes rushing back toward the Arabah as if in retaliation for the constant east winds blowing across the lake from the heights. But now it was clear their very lives were in danger, and it was likely they could swamp!

How could He do it? Peter wondered, looking down at Jesus below the weather deck in the stern cabin, protected from the howling blast of the wind. The deck moved so violently Peter could not keep his feet without hanging on. The wind was rattling lines against the mast, setting up discordant howls as it tore at the rigging and flung spray at them from the crashing whitecaps that were taking on the size of ocean breakers. Yet Jesus seemed totally oblivious, completely asleep. Peter wondered if He should be awakened and warned to find something floatable to cling to if they were overturned or swamped, the way the others had, but he hesitated. Jesus had put in one of the longest days so far, and Peter hated to awaken Him.

Straining to see the others, his clothing rippling against his skin and his hair streaming straight across his face, Peter found he could no longer see the lights on the mast of the boat following them! Either the wind had blown them out . . . . He looked up. Yes, their own lamp was out, so perhaps the others were still afloat.

The timbers of the aging craft were straining audibly as the water came crashing over the bow to be dashed into spray against the splash rail and cabin, and hissed along the deck over Peter's feet. Most of the others were huddling in the lee of the meager shelter of the tiny cabin, shielding their eyes from the stinging spindrift, casting anxious glances toward Peter's bulky figure where he held firmly to the tiller, checking their sea anchor line. The sea anchor, nothing more than discarded sections of net with large leathern buckets affixed, provided a dragging weight, thus keeping the bow to the waves and for the time being, at least, insured they would not be rolling wildly in the troughs.

Somewhat irked by the somnolently indifferent figure of Jesus, sound asleep out of the wind and the spray, Peter lashed the tiller down and flung himself full length on the deck so as to let head and shoulders hang partially through the space of the hatch, with its ladder leading below.

He shouted, "Master, *save us!*" The fear caused his voice to rise into an unnatural pitch. "Save us or we're all going to drown! *Don't You care?*"

Rising at the first shout, Jesus had sat up, glanced upward at Peter's anxious face and clambered up the ladder.

Gaining the deck, Jesus steadied Himself by clinging to the handlines running from cabin to stern and, seeing the frightened faces and looking at the huge waves hissing and frothing, their tops raggedly whitecapped, said to them all, "Why are you so filled with *fear,* you of *little faith?*"

Then, bracing Himself against the wind, He stood straight up, and, holding out His hands as if to physically catch the force of the wind in His own hands, He said, addressing the waves and the wind, "Shalom! Peace! *Be still!*"

Almost instantly the shrieking of the boat ceased, the waves began to subside, and the boat's pitching, corkscrewing motion slowed. Some were sick, and others clung to the boat in a listless manner from the soporific motion and constant din.

A great calm came over the whole sea, and they could see distant figures moving about on the boat ahead of them.

Their fear of drowning was replaced with total awe! What kind of Man is this? Peter thought. Why, *even the wind and the waves obey Him!*

"Why are you so fearful?" Jesus was saying to them all, though addressing Peter first. "Haven't you yet learned to *have faith? Where is your faith?*" Peter could only hesitantly stammer out his apologies and thank Jesus for what He had done, shaking his head in bewilderment at what he had seen.

Later they hauled in the sea anchor, set the sail again, and, aided by the big sweeps (for there was almost no wind now), they continued on their journey. Jesus had again lain down astern, and the others talked of their experience through the rest of the trip. Both Mark and Matthew began immediately jotting down notes, now that they could find a steady enough platform on which to write, for they wanted to remember well this incident later.

They made a landing in the early morning hours, and some went ashore to find a place to sleep in the deserted area near their boats, while others elected to stay where they were and catch a couple of hours' rest.

Finally, after breakfast, repacking their clothing after gathering it from the rigging where it had been drying following the drenching of the night before, they began to climb along the rocky hillsides that rose steeply a short distance from the shore, toward the country of the Gadarenes.

There were rumors about two crazy men who lived in the graveyard that served several nearby villages.

It was said they were possessed of evil spirits, and that one of them was so insane with demons that he would frequently tear his clothes to shreds and appear to be flung violently to the ground, that he was continually wearing bruises and lacerations from these violent rages and spells.

Though his relatives tried to clothe him or talk to him in moments when he seemed lucid, most of the townsfolk were terribly afraid of him, it was said. Armed groups had tried to capture him to hold him in a safe place so he wouldn't come raging out of the tombs to frighten wayfarers and scare the daylights out of children who had become too adventuresome and who, out of curiosity, would try to get near enough to watch his antics.

They were afraid he might seriously hurt someone.

However, even though they had succeeded a time or two in binding him—not without considerable damage to some of their own number—they had no sooner strapped his hands together with horsehair ropes, leathern straps or even chains than some violent rage would seize him and he would burst the bonds, even *chains,* and, screaming out at his antagonists, send them scurrying away as fast as they could go.

He became a legend in the area. Day and night in the graveyard up on the mountainside he would be screaming, wailing, sobbing and cutting himself with sharp rocks.

When this man saw Jesus from a long distance away, he ran forward and, worshiping Him, screamed with a loud voice, "What am I going to do with You, Jesus, You Son of the most high God? I adjure You by God, do not torment me! Are You come to torment me before the time?"

Jesus, looking at the man, spoke directly to the demon who had used the man's voice and said, "What is your name?"

It answered, "My name is *Legion,* for we are many," and then began to beseech Jesus not to command them to go completely out of the country.

On the nearby mountain slope a huge herd of pigs was feeding. The demons besought Jesus, saying, "Send us into those swine so we can enter into them."

Jesus said, "Go!"

Immediately the unclean spirits left the man and entered into the swine.

The disciples looked on in amazement as the pigs began to squeal with terror, the entire herd rushing down the steep talus slope, tumbling down like a multicolored avalanche, with a cacophony of loud grunts, clattering rocks and squeals. The entire herd of about two thousand pigs lunged into the lake in a muddy froth. The whole big herd was drowned!

The swineherds ran as fast as their legs would take them to the nearest town, excitedly telling everything they had seen.

When a delegation from the town came out, they found that the man who had been such a notorious plague to them and their children was sitting quietly beside Jesus, fully clothed in garments the disciples had provided, and in his right mind. They were terribly afraid when they saw this, and some of the swineherds related how Jesus had cast the demons out and how the big herd of pigs had stampeded into the lake.

Immediately the delegation from the town began to beseech Jesus to leave the area, for they feared Him. Jesus walked back down to the shore and began to climb into the boat again. The man, now in his normal mind, begged Jesus to take him along.

Jesus said He would not permit it, but said instead, "Go to your own family and friends and tell them what great things the Lord has done for you, and how He has had mercy on you!" From that time on, the man went on his way and began to tell everyone who would listen in the towns of Decapolis the great things Jesus had done for him so that all who heard him were amazed.

Jesus and the disciples returned back to the other side of the Sea to Capernaum. Their return trip was memorable to Peter. After the big blow that threatened their lives in the previous crossing, it was pleasant to catch the fresh breeze that spread rippling patterns on the sea as it pushed its cooling air back toward the heights, even if it meant tacking often, lying as close to the wind as possible, and taking much longer than usual.

Several of the men caught up on lost sleep, and Jesus had joined Peter at the tiller after arising from a nap Himself.

Andrew was sitting atop the little cabin splicing some lines that had parted in the big storm, while James, who was equally experienced in the handling of the boats, stood at the tiller of their smaller companion tossing along behind them, its rounded bows bursting through the larger waves in a sparkling shower of spray.

Peter was continually amazed at the fund of knowledge Jesus possessed.

Their conversation wandered from the weather to the subject of the hide and tallow shops and leathern-making. Jesus asked a question about their sea anchors.

Tossing along in the freshening breeze like this, with Jesus' sole attention on their own conversation, Peter couldn't help thinking about the vastness of what they were trying to do.

Hermon loomed vast in the purple distance, and the evenly scattered cumulus clouds marched over their heads like fluffy sheep headed eastward toward Persia. Beyond them a whole world lay in prostrate subjection to the emperor at Rome. Tales reached their ears of some minor fracas here or there, usually months later than the fact and probably much embellished by the time it reached their ears.

The products of the whole world were flowing like a never-ending stream from fabled Cornucopia right into the palaces of the rich in Rome while Peter and his people (strange that he had begun to take a more paternal view of the masses of suffering peoples of his homeland now that Jesus' teachings had begun to inspire him) labored for pittances, either bordering on or living in actual squalid poverty. Not that the tradesmen couldn't carve out a comfortable living if they applied themselves and knew the right people.

Peter knew of bronze and iron workers who managed to pile up sizable fortunes by contracting to supply the Romans with various weapons while keeping up a lively business with their local clients and the Eastern caravans. Usually they kept their sword and spearhead molds and worked as weapons smelters, casting the shields, breastplates, helmets and shin guards that had become fashionable in a back lot out of sight from prying eyes.

Peter supposed the natural human instinct to survive led to many a loyal Jew compromising his conscience by cooperation with the Romans.

While displaying a full line of plows, hoes, adzes, awls, knives, rakes, scrapers, rings, buckles and pulleys for the fishing trades or harness makers, many an enterprising metalworker was carrying on a brisk business out of his back lot, saddling up the camels and mules with their packs after dark when their clandestine contacts called upon them.

Even Samaritans, those untouchables of society, were known to be go-betweens for some of the Eastern traders, who usually had direct contacts with the shippers in Tyre and Sidon, or at Joppa, where the ships were loaded for their trips to Asia, Greece and Italy or the islands in between.

Peter knew of at least two major clay quarries that were prospering in the manufacture of amphorae, those huge jugs that served so many purposes and which, almost completely encased in hemp slings, carried the water and wine supplies for the ships at sea. They came in every conceivable size and shape, from the tiny pots and lamps for household niches and walls to the ponderous jugs carried aboard ships or set in concrete, side by side, in the front of the wine shops.

Jesus' conversation with Peter ranged from all these things to the stories of exotic animals being trapped in Africa and taken to Rome for the games. Always, though, He would interject some observations about the rottenness of human nature, the thievery, dishonesty and especially the hypocrisy of people.

They fetched the jetty on their final tack, and Peter was acutely sorry to see their return trip end. He knew that, as sure as people found out Jesus was back inside His home in Capernaum, the crowds would gather. They tied up the boats, and Peter instructed Judas to give a small offering to Jona and Zebedee, who had been absent from their boats for two days, before accompanying Jesus and the others up the side roads to Capernaum.

Sure enough, it was less than two hours later that a sizable crowd had gathered outside, and many were noisily calling for Jesus to appear. One of the main leaders of the local synagogue, Jairus by name, managed to approach closely to Jesus through the crowd, and, overcome with grief and apprehension, threw himself down at Jesus' feet, begging Him, "Please come and heal my little daughter! She is at the point of death, perhaps has died already. I beg of You, come and lay Your hands on her that she can be made whole and live!"

The little girl was about twelve years of age.

Jesus told Jairus He would come and heal the girl, and as they headed toward Jairus' home another great miracle occurred.

# VIII

As usual, Peter was beside Jesus, fulfilling his role as bodyguard and protector, trying to keep some semblance of order in what was usually a disorderly, sometimes loud and shouting crowd.

It was as if many thought Jesus was the most fascinating sight they had ever seen, yet many of them went away thinking they had seen Jesus when in fact their friends had pointed out another of the disciples or merely one of the Pharisees in some confrontation or another with Jesus.

Often people would come to John or walk up to Peter and ask, "Are *you* Jesus of Nazareth?" and they would shake their heads and say no. Jesus was so common looking and dressed so similarly to the others that He was difficult for people to find in a crowd.

As they were turning to go, Peter thought he saw a hand reach out and take hold of Jesus' outer cloak. It was only a flicker of motion, and there were others there jostling one another in an attempt to see Jesus or talk to Him, so Peter didn't worry.

Suddenly Jesus stopped.

He said, "Who is it that has touched me?"

Peter said, "Lord, the whole crowd is gathered all around You with everyone pressing against everyone else and jostling and shoving us, and You are asking, 'Who touched Me?' "

He said, "Well, *somebody* touched Me, for I felt virtue go out of Me!"

A woman came forward and tremblingly told Jesus she had been sick for many years, had spent her meager savings and all she could earn on physicians in a vain attempt to stanch a continual issue of blood that seriously weakened her and threatened her life. She said she knew that if she could *touch* Jesus she would be healed! She explained that she had been healed instantly! She babbled her apologies and her thanks, telling Jesus she had meant no harm and that she didn't wish to bother Him, but she had been so desperate to be healed.

Jesus looked at her and tenderly said, "Be of good cheer, daughter of Israel. Your faith has made you whole! Go in peace!"

Shortly following this incident Jesus saw one of Jairus' servants running breathlessly to Jairus, telling him sorrowfully that it was too late. Jarius' daughter had died only moments earlier.

Jairus was overcome with grief. He stood with head down, hands tightly clenched, and, struggling to control his voice, told Jesus to forget his request; it was too late.

Jesus quietly told him He would continue, that the little girl was "only sleeping."

A crowd of hangers-on, consisting of a sprinkling of religious antagonists, skeptics, local wags and the merely curious, was tagging along with some of Jesus' disciples.

Arriving at Jairus' prominent home, He entered the vestibule, slipped off His street shoes, allowed a softly crying servant to wash His feet, set aside His outer cloak and turned toward the family's sleeping quarters, led by a stricken Jairus.

At the door Jairus' wife and several close relatives looked up.

Seeing the heartbroken look Jairus and his wife exchanged, Jesus said, "Don't worry about it. I am sure she is only sleeping."

One or two laughed bitterly, the tears coursing down their faces, expressing their dismay that some outsider would come into the sleeping quarters of a private home to the deathbed where a tragedy had occurred and play such a cruel joke as to allege that the child had not in fact died but was only sleeping!

Who was this interloper? What business was it of His that Jairus suffered family grief through the death of a daughter? Wasn't His sounding off in the synagogue —confusing and embarrassing people, always stirring up trouble by defying established customs and tradition— enough?

And now here He was as if He could do anything about death itself. Several sneered, and one friend of the family who had knowledge of the physicians and had offered cures, told Jesus, "She's *dead.* Of that I'm certain. I checked the pulse myself . . ."

"She's dead, *dead,* do You hear?"

Jesus indicated to Jairus that he should clear the room of everyone, including the professional wailers, flute players, keeners and mourners (it was the custom to so lament the dead) who were making a din with their moribund dirge. Jairus stopped the musicians and with the help of his servants cleared the room.

As he was ushering them out, Jesus said to the crowd, "Make way there, and don't carry on crying like that. The girl is not dead—she's only sleeping!"

Some laughed at Him scornfully, wondering aloud why Jairus didn't throw this pretender and His followers out. Jesus had allowed only His closest three disciples, Peter, James and John, to enter the house with Him. And, when the crowd had been ushered outside, the door closed and the noise ceased, Jesus, together with Jairus, his wife and the three disciples, went directly to the girl's bedside.

Looking up to heaven, Jesus prayed silently, calling upon His Father in heaven to hear and to answer.

Stooping over, Jesus took the girl by the hand and said to her, *"Talitha, cumi!"* (which meant "Miss, arise!"). The twelve-year-old girl opened her eyes, blinked, yawned and sat up. Standing, she held out her arms to her parents, who tearfully embraced her, babbling their thanks to Jesus. The girl looked about in amazement at all these strangers and at her parents' actions. She had been terribly ill, growing weaker and weaker, and had only wanted to be left alone and be allowed to sleep for a while.

The servants had kept going and coming, and everyone was crying so much it exhausted her. She had felt herself drifting into a deep, deep, black sleep, and then . . . nothing.

Now here were both her father and mother tearfully lavishing thanks on this stranger and His three companions.

"Did you see *that?*" Peter asked James and John.

"Yes, and she had to be really dead," answered James. "A physician has been right here all along, and she had been dead long enough for them to summon the mourners and begin the death rituals."

"No question about it!" John said. *"Another impossible miracle, just like Elijah!"*

But Jesus was solemnly telling Jairus and his wife, "Don't tell anyone about this; keep all your opinions to yourself. Just be thankful to God in private, but don't tell the story abroad. And, by the way, I would suppose your daughter needs good, solid food now. She'll be hungry!"

It was while Jesus was on His way back to Capernaum from Jairus' home that two blind men heard the crowd passing and, hearing the voice of Jesus, began following after the crowd, tapping their canes on the stones and crying out in loud voices, "Please have mercy on us, O son of David!"

Finally they managed to get close enough with the help of their friends and Jesus noticed them.

Jesus turned to them and said, "Do you believe that I am *able* to do this?"

They both answered, "Yes, Lord!" Reaching out, He touched them on their eyes, saying, "It will be done to you exactly according to your faith!"

Both of them immediately began to see! Jesus encouraged the men not to tell any other person about the miraculous healing. Peter couldn't believe his ears.

This custom of Jesus—admonishing those who were so ecstatic over their healing—puzzled and irritated Peter. Who could be a better witness to Jesus' great miracle working power than those on whom such mind-boggling miracles had fallen? Why, a *blind* man, no, a virtual *army* of the blind by now, Peter supposed, with friends and relatives to support their stories, could give powerful testimony to Jesus' wondrous gifts. There were dozens who had been deaf, a host of former lepers and other disease-ridden folk, and even those who had been *raised from the dead*, who could testify! Of course, it was doubtful anyone would believe a person claiming, "I was *dead*," Peter supposed, but deafness, blindness, demon possession, leprosy and venereal disease, distorted limbs, child deformities—people could present powerful witness to *those* healings!

But Jesus seemed determined to keep Himself as low-key as possible. He was especially concerned that too much pressure might be brought to bear on Him "too soon"; He was forever talking to the disciples privately about the "time when the Son of Man will be offered up" or "delivered into the hands of sinners," or about the "time of the Son of Man" that was to come, which Jesus said the "Father knew."

He seemed very conscious of the *timing* of everything; He was cautious not to precipitate some terrible confrontation before He was fully ready. Peter could only suppose the Lord had some even greater dazzling miracle in store for the leaders in Jerusalem, some great sign that would make them faint dead away in fright and surprise, and that He intended waiting until the stage was set for the final act in this years-long drama ushering in a new government for Israel, the soon-coming *kingdom* Jesus described!

Still Peter wished Jesus would enthusiastically encourage those He healed to "tell as many people as you can" about it.

The Pharisees tried to counter the growing fame of Jesus by continually planting the rumor that Jesus was managing to perform these miracles by "trickery," saying, "He is doing it by the prince of the demons, feigning to cast out demons!"

Now that the crowds were so large, and Jesus was surrounded by enough of His own disciples, He did not fear to go back into His own country, and they journeyed back to Nazareth again.

Peter was not a little apprehensive over this appearance again in Nazareth, especially since Jesus had been in the center of a riot and had nearly gotten Himself killed there earlier. But Jesus' following was immense and growing, and rumors had no doubt reached Nazareth just like the other cities, though the local people no doubt scoffed that this was that same "local man, the carpenter's son," who had made that outrageous statement to the leaders in the synagogue that time many months ago.

And yet here He was, teaching the people in the *same synagogue.*

This time, though, Peter was ready! Never again would he doubt Jesus, he knew, not after seeing the dead raised up and seeing the Man put out His hands and calm a raging storm; seeing Him heal deaf, dumb, blind and maimed; seeing Him cast out a veritable army of demons from a strong man. No, Peter would stick tight to His side now no matter what came.

Jesus was finished with His brief lesson now, and the people who listened to Him were absolutely astonished!

Some were saying to one another, "Where in the world could these men be given these things? What is this special wisdom that this Man claims to have, and what are these rumors about the mighty works we hear being wrought by His hand?

"Isn't it that carpenter, Mary's son, and the brother of James, Joses, Judas and Simon?

"And aren't His own sisters right here in the local community?"

They were all totally offended by Him. So Jesus, knowing their thoughts and minds, said, "A prophet is not without honor except in *his own country,* and among his *own relatives,* and *in his own home!"*

Jesus told Peter and the others that He could "do no mighty work" here, except that from time to time, in private, He would lay His hands on a few sick people who came humbly and wanted to be healed.

Peter was learning another lesson he would remember later. It seemed *faith* was sometimes a two-way street. It seemed Jesus Himself was affected by it. When He had calmed the storm, it was His *own* faith and His own belief in God and His power. But when it came to healing people Peter noticed there was faith present, either in the form of a parent on behalf of a child, or the living for the dead, or the sick for themselves! It seemed it took "faith mixed with faith" for great healings to occur. Not that Jesus didn't have the power to heal no matter what, Peter supposed, but, since healing was an act of love, of compassion and concern, and not some flamboyant extravaganza calculated to mesmerize a crowd, Peter knew Jesus always did it quietly, and then told those healed to be quiet about it. No wonder, then, that He could do no mighty work in Nazareth, because the extreme distaste toward Him (yes, even from those brothers of His, in His *own family*) was such that it blunted the keen edge of faith, made it null and void.

Not long after this Peter was in deep conversation with John and asked about the progress of his notes. In Peter's mind he hoped John or else Luke or Matthew would be sure to include some of the important points of family history.

He was disappointed when John explained to him that Jesus had been extremely close-mouthed about His early years, only giving the men the sketchiest items concerning His birth and early years (and most of the details, even then, had come from Mary and Elizabeth, who loved telling the story).

"John," Peter complained, "anyone reading this story of yours later is going to think the Lord never stopped to eat, sleep, exercise, bathe or even relax and talk about common, day-to-day things with us. You make it look like all He does is walk about from one confrontation with the Pharisees to another, from one speech to another, and never put in any of the interesting details!"

"I know, Peter," John answered with a sigh, "but we are all very, very busy. Even the women work very hard keeping our clothing and baggage in good repair. And the Lord has told me time and time again not to waste time writing about the things He says are 'unessential.' ''

''We both know,'' he continued with a shrug of his shoulders, ''that if I were to try to write it *all* — you know, *everything* we share together — no one would even believe it!''

''You're probably right.''

''I know I'm right!'' John said. ''Our society is not ready for the kind of knowledge and experience Jesus is giving to us, Peter. Much of what He does with us privately, even the little, personal things, like His singing, or how handy He is with the chores and the animals, how strong He is when it comes to packing up and how He never fails to turn everything that happens into some observation about life . . .''

''I know,'' Peter responded. ''He has even been known to comment about the 'spiritual meaning' of inward cleanliness when He makes some observation about a man doing his daily duty.''

John chuckled. ''That's what I mean.'' No one would every believe it. The life we share with Him is so, well, so *human!*''

''Do you think sharing even some of those 'human' moments, as you call them, will take away from His dignity somehow?''

''Probably.''

''You see, Peter,'' he continued, ''people don't like to think about their leaders being just like *they* are. They don't like to dwell on the fact that they grow just as tired or dirty, that they have their minor annoyances and frustrations — though I have never seen Jesus react the way most of us do to any frustration whatsoever — or even their personal appetites.''

''For example,'' he continued, ''you and I both know Jesus has never overindulged in wine once, right?''

''Right.''

''And yet, just because He changed water into wine and has been seen sipping wine out of the finest goblets with some of the leaders, either Jew or Roman, the enemies call Him a 'wine bibber,' a 'wino,' and claim He is a man of great physical appetite!''

"I know," Peter said. "But unless you at least describe *some* of His personal habits, the way He likes to enjoy wine but never overdoes it, the way He holds check on His eating — why, He scarcely eats as much as a stripling, and I know He fasts sometimes for several days, even if He keeps His strength up pretty well — unless you describe enough of Him to let people know how completely *human* He is . . ."

"Don't worry about it, Peter," John said. "I intend showing at the very beginning of the book I'm writing that He is not only *human*, but that He is the very Son of God!"

"Do you really believe that?" Peter had asked.

"Of course! Don't you?"

"I guess so," Peter had said. "I don't see how it is possible — I mean for Him to be the very Offspring of God. And yet I know He has the very supernatural *powers* of heaven! I have seen Him stop the winds and waves, and raise the dead, and . . ."

They talked often like this, as did all the others. And as they did their puzzlement, admiration and awe of their Leader increased.

Their conversation was interrupted by the arrival of Andrew, who told them something new was afoot and that Jesus wanted them.

Peter was excited! The Lord had sent out word that He wanted a special meeting of the entire twelve!

# IX

Something was definitely in the wind. Peter knew Jesus had been especially intense with His lessons to them, remarking on this or that healing and discussing at length some of the more difficult cases of demon possession, as well as repeating over and over again the basics of the good news He wanted preached about His soon-coming reign. He had been particularly keen on instructing them to avoid the gentile areas, that the message should go first and foremost to the "lost sheep," as He called them, of the *House of Israel!* Peter had heard all his life of the "dispersion," those Israelites who had been enslaved in successive waves of invasion under ancient Assyria, and of the troubles during the reign of King Pekah of the Northern Kingdom. Tiglath-Pileser, the king of Assyria, had swept through this whole land, including Galilee, and taken tens of thousands captive and dispersed them in Assyrian encampments.

Peter had been taught his history well, for the tutors of this land of Galilee were especially interested in the wars of the past that had raged back and forth across this crossroads of trade, commerce, culture and religion.

Capernaum, at the northern edge of the sea, while a splendid example of Grecian and Herodian architecture, was a place of large trading bazaars, storage sheds and horse and camel stables for the caravans. A natural meeting place of north, south, east and west, it was a place of many languages, many cultures.

Peter's education had necessarily been cosmopolitan from rubbing shoulders with strangers from far places and listening to the elders speak of faraway lands and customs.

Peter remembered how graphically his teacher had described when Ahaz was king of Judah and Hoshea was reigning up in Samaria, Israel's capital city. King Shalmaneser of Assyria had besieged Samaria for three whole years and had finally captured it, taking vast numbers of unfortunate Israelites into captivity up into the Assyrian lands of Halah and Habor by the river they called "Gozan." They had sent large bands of them into many cities of the Medes to be servants working for the gentiles in their homes, on their farms or with their animals and at their trades.

These invasions had happened not once but many times following Jeroboam's succession and the creation of the two separate kingdoms of Israel with a capital at Samaria, up here in the north, and Judah with its capital in Jerusalem.

There were uncounted tens of thousands of the modern descendants of those ancient Israelites, Peter knew, scattered all over the lands across the snowy mountains beyond Thrace and Dacia and on the islands from which the Phoenician traders and Roman ships brought metals for the tools of war.

It would be some task, Peter thought, if they were to go preach to *all* the "dispersion" of the "lost sheep of the House of Israel," for it was said many of them were established in colonies beyond the seas, in vast new lands only vaguely rumored of in the talk of seafarers from Gaul.

He had heard some of the older ones along the dockyards in Joppa talking of the fearsome, hairy giants that lived in the bleak, rain-drenched islands far to the north beyond the Gates of Hercules and who called themselves the *Tuatha de Danaan,* the Tribe of Dan. Their land was called "Dan's Mark," Peter thought he remembered, and there had been Jewish people who had settled nearby, for the seamen said a part of the mainland to the east in a vast, almost landlocked sea was called "Jute Land."

It would be fabulous, Peter imagined, once Jesus'

new kingdom was established, if He delegated some of them to captain expeditions to many of these exotic, far-off places and take news of the vast, empire-shaking revolution that had begun and encourage these peoples to recognize Jesus' rule and to cooperate with Him in trade.

At length, when they were all seated, Jesus began speaking to them about an exciting new adventure. He was sending them out at last *on their own,* and each man was going along with one other so there would be six pairs of them (Peter hoped the Lord didn't send him with Judas, for he had difficulty liking the man because of his shifty eyes and his swarthy, secretive look), and they were to begin traveling far and wide, taking the message of Jesus' coming kingdom to the people!

Matthew was busily taking notes again, looking around and listing the names of all those present. Peter glanced at what he was writing, "Names: 12 — Simon (called 'Petros'), A'drew, bro., Phip, Bart,'' and the abbreviated names of all the others.

Jesus said, "Don't go into any of the gentile countries, and do not even enter into any Samaritan city. You are to go, rather, to the 'lost sheep' of the House of Israel! As you travel you are to preach, saying as your main theme, 'The Kingdom of God is right at hand!'

"I want *you* to heal the sick, raise the dead . . .'' Wow! Peter thought! He want *us, me,* to try to perform some of the same miraculous, fabulous, shocking, surprising, impossible miracles *He* has been able to perform! Peter's scalp prickled with expectancy. *Raise the dead.* Would God perform such miracles through a man such as me? Peter wondered.

". . . Cleanse lepers, cast out demons,'' Jesus was saying, "and, remember, you have received these great gifts and this commission *freely,* so *give* of your gifts and your knowledge *freely.*

"Don't worry about taking an undue amount of gold or silver in your purse or even brass; you won't require any special traveling money in your wallets nor even an extra coat or walking stick. The laborer is perfectly worthy of his hire! So, whatever town or village into which you enter, search out there who is worthy and of reputation before God and you will be able to stay there until you need to leave for another town.

"When you come upon such a house, greet the home owner with respect and use My name, and if the house is worthy let your peace come upon it. If it be not worthy, then let your peace return to you. But, whoever will not receive you or listen to your message, when you depart from that city, then shake off the very dust from your feet!

"For I am telling you, it will be far more tolerable for the land of Sodom and Gomorrah in the day of judgment than for that city."

Peter passionately hoped that "day of judgment" for these impudent cities was not far away!

It invariably thrilled Peter when Jesus' voice would ring out with power like this, speaking of the future day of reckoning of judgment and government, of the revolution. It seemed that just when Peter would find himself growing overly anxious because the Lord tended to delay, just when he found himself sinking into gloomy moods of impatience and doubt, Jesus would shore up his sagging courage with such statements.

Peter's spirits soared. He would remember these ringing words, and if necessary he would repeat them —loudly!

This must be one of the last really major moves Jesus would make prior to marching on Jerusalem. Apparently He wanted the entire group to go far and wide, simultaneously covering as many major towns and villages as they could, because He planned an immediate move following their return.

Peter perked up his ears and listened more intently.

"Now, look!" Jesus continued. "I am sending you out like gentle sheep in the midst of a pack of wolves! I want you to be as wise as serpents but harmless as doves. Be very careful, beware of them.

"These are the ones who will deliver you up to their courts, and in their churches and synagogues they will have you whipped. Yes, and you will be brought even before governors and kings for My name's sake, as a testimony against them and the gentiles.

"If and when this happens, and you are delivered up, don't take any undue, anxious thought about how or what you shall speak. It will be given to you at the appropriate time what you shall say! It is not you who will do the speaking, but the *Spirit of your Father* that will speak in you.

"I am telling you the time will come when brother will deliver up brother to death, and the father his own child. And children will rise up against their parents and cause them to be put to death!

"You shall be hated of all men for My name's sake, but he that endures to the end, the same shall be saved!

"If they shall persecute you in one city, then flee from that one to the next one because I am telling you the truth. You will not have accomplished fulfilling this great commission among all the cities of Israel until the Son of Man be come!

"Remember that a disciple is not above his master, nor a servant above his lord. It is sufficient for the disciple that he be *like* his master, and the servant as is his lord. If they have called the Master of the house 'prince of demons, Beelzebub,' how much more will they disparage His household, meaning you!

"Do not fear them, therefore, because there is nothing covered that will not ultimately be revealed, nor hid that will not become known!

"What I tell you in private meetings or in darkness, you speak in the light; what you hear privately in the ear, shout from the rooftops!

"And do not be afraid of them who are able to kill your physical body but are not able to kill the life itself, but rather fear him who is able to destroy both life and body in Gehenna fire!"

So some of them might even be killed; some might not be coming back! Peter looked speculatively about and wondered. There was Simon the Canaanite over there, and, while Peter was a bit uncomfortable that Jesus had chosen such a dark-skinned man as one of the twelve, he knew the Lord wanted a representative group and that

Jesus had a great deal of pity and affection for the black peoples of nearby lands, and even for the Samaritans. Would Simon fall victim to racial prejudices, trying to preach this powerful message to the "lost sheep of the House of Israel"? What about Peter's own brother, Andrew? What would that do to the family? Somehow Peter never remotely allowed the shadow of a thought into his mind that *he* could die in some riotous melee. He could vaguely see himself in this or that confrontation; the scene would invariably end with Peter in full command of the field, silencing the detractors with his words and performing some great sign to shock them into submission. But he couldn't imagine any bodily harm coming to him.

Peter's hand strayed to the hilt of his Roman short sword at his side. He had never used it in anger except to strike a balky mule with the flat of the blade now and then. But he had no doubts about being found equal to the task if and when Jesus called upon him to put the sword to its designed purpose: splitting heads!

Peter could identify with Jesus' statement about a man's foes being those of his own household; it seemed Jesus' own brothers, James, Joses, Simon and Jude, publicly disclaimed Him, didn't believe He was who He said He was, didn't believe He was able to produce such great signs and miracles. Ah, well, familiarity breeds contempt . . . and Peter knew by now that Jesus could only produce those great miracles when the simple, believing, hoping people were looking to Him out of great sorrow of heart. He'd have to remember that! If a pack of doubters was present, he had better not try to use Jesus' name in casting out any demons or healing any sick; he'd better follow Jesus's example exactly . . .

So they left. Peter took Bartholomew, Judas went with Simon, James teamed up with Andrew, and John went with James, the son of Alphaeus, while Thomas and Philip paired off. Matthew left with Lebbaeus, whom they called Thaddeus.

They fanned out in all directions, Peter and Bart following the steep foot hills and stopping in towns and villages throughout the region. They would always inquire as to the village elders and first determine if they had heard of Jesus, if they knew of the ministry of John and if they believed Jesus was the Messiah.

Where they found interest, belief or even curiosity, they remained a day or two, gaining the approval and permission of the elders to speak to the people. Where they were greeted with hostility, they solemnly took off their traveling shoes, wiped the dust from them, turned around and left.

Peter's first few attempts at speaking were poor, he thought. But one day, as an irate heckler seemed determined to interrupt his message with hoots of scorn and ridicule, saying, "And just who do you think yourself to be, you of rough Galilean speech and fisherman's garb? Are you some prophet?" Peter found himself developing a theme that helped him throughout the remainder of their journey.

"Who am I? I am Simon who is called Peter, a fisherman by trade and a Galilean, right enough. As for my being a prophet, I tell you, no! Look, all of you. I didn't want to believe any of this either! I was tending my family business, working my boat and nets, when Jesus of Nazareth told me to come and follow Him. I did, until He was almost killed at Nazareth by His own countrymen. I returned to my nets, believing the whole thing a misadventure.

"But Jesus came to my boat again and I saw with my own eyes a great miracle." Peter glowingly described the day he nearly swamped their boat trying to drag so many great fish into it, and continued to tell of the little deaf girl, the blind men, the water turning into wine and Jesus fearlessly calming the storm. His voice rose in intensity, and he began quoting the prophets, especially Isaiah and Daniel, saying, "This *is* Messiah who was to come; He is the Son of Man, the Son of God!

"Repent, all of you, and clean up your lives, for the time of salvation is come to this village! *Repent!* Repent, and *believe the gospel!*"

Peter was amazed at how the words came. He could suddenly remember Jesus' parables and analogies. He would say, "The Kingdom of God is like finding a pearl of great price. A man would sell his whole house and all his belongings to buy that one pearl!"

Peter found the crowds listened more favorably when he showed them how he, too, had disbelieved. As he showed them how he had been convinced of Jesus' great calling and commission in spite of himself; how he could not deny the things he had seen with his own eyes and heard with his own ears, it seemed to win them over, make them listen with less skepticism.

In some villages, he and Bartholomew would baptize a dozen or more, sometimes a whole family. In others, the leaders rejected him, and he and Bartholomew would copy Jesus' speech against Bethsaida and Chorazin, saying, "Woe unto this town. It will be better for Sodom and Gomorrah in the day of judgment than for you!"

As they traveled, Peter and Bartholomew became more confident.

Thrice they had been assailed by demoniacs.

Each time, with the hair rising along the back of his neck, Peter found himself afraid. But each time, with a prayer to God in His mind, He had commanded, "In the name of Jesus Christ of Nazareth, I command you to *go!*" And each time the demoniac had been thrown to the ground in a violent, frothing fit, and then had been helped, dazed and only semiconscious, to his feet and had looked about him in amazement and in his right mind.

He would begin explaining that he had been as if in a dream, as if one part of him *knew* what he was doing and saying, but that there was an uncontrollable urge to act crazy, to fly into mindless rages and resort to violence.

Bartholomew was becoming a powerful speaker too. He would speak in his clipped, precise way of the miracles he had witnessed, and, when the afflicted came to him and Peter with their sick, they would pray, lay their hands on the sick and look with gratitude and amazement when they were healed instantly!

Their trip lasted for several weeks.

Making a circuitous journey through Kadesh Naphtali, and reaching the coast south of Tyre, they continued along the coast until coming to Accho Ptolemais, turned eastward and ascended the River Ramah to its headwaters, crossed the ridge and followed another drainage down to Magdala and thence back to Tiberius, on the Sea of Galilee.

"We must have preached to at least fifteen thousand people!" Peter said as they strode into Tiberius.

"At least!" said Bart, breathing heavily and planting his walking staff with a thump on the stones of the thoroughfare.

They came to an inn, off-shouldered their small packs and laid their staffs across them against the stable wall.

Beating at the dust on his short skirts, Peter walked to the water cistern, pushed aside a burro and dipped cupped handfuls of water onto his dusty hair and beard.

Bart followed, and they laughed with relief as the rank smelling water bit into the dust and grime of their last twelve miles. Wiping their heads and faces with cloth toweling from Bart's pack, they entered the low stoop, rising beyond the lintel to adjust their eyes to the semi-gloom.

The place was small, only two other customers at this late afternoon time, and they asked for barley and lentil soup of the youngster who piped to them the meager fare.

"And water—do you have a well?" Bart asked.

"Yes, sir, deep and cold," the lad responded.

When he had left to fetch their soup and water, Peter said, "Well, Bart, what do you think? Were we successful?" Peter couldn't quite rid himself of the feeling of failure because of the villages that had proved hostile.

"We'll know when we ask the Lord," Bart said. "I'm anxious to know how Judas and Simon got along, where they went and how they did."

"Why just Judas and Simon?" Peter asked with rising interest.

"Oh, nothing special. I just wonder whether Judas spent as much time preaching as he did haggling over a deal."

"But Jesus said to take no extra money or scrip. We had barely a day's supply with us when we left, and here we are, able to give money for this soup because of those who gave us of their tithes and gifts.''

''I know,'' Bart admitted. ''But I'll wager Judas arrives back with a lot more than he started with.''

''You believe him dishonest, then?''

''I don't really know. And perhaps I should not be talking about it, for it is only a feeling I have. I have seen him haggling endlessly over only a few pennies' worth of bread when the price was obviously low, and he never makes any reports to Jesus or anyone else about money matters.''

''True. He keeps the common purse, though, and Jesus seems to say nothing.''

''I just can't believe Judas would use the cover of Jesus' name and the preaching of the kingdom for personal gain. But there is something about his sharp features, the way he whines and argues, the way he moves his hands . . .''

''I have thought the same thoughts, Peter said, moving back to allow the lad to place a wooden bowl of steaming soup before him. ''But I have nothing substantial with which to back it up.''

''Maybe,'' he said as an afterthought, ''we should follow Jesus' example and believe the best, believe him completely honest unless Jesus Himself shows us otherwise.''

''You're probably right,'' admitted Bartholomew, digging into the thick soup of savory barley and lentils. ''It's just that we have had an exhausting, yet exciting, interesting trip. We have both lost much weight; we have preached to thousands, been spat on, nearly stoned, chased out of towns, and yet have been used to heal the sick and preach the gospel. And I know you and I had opportunities for accepting larger gifts than we should!''

''I know,'' Peter said. ''Can you imagine? Why, if we had been interested in self-gain, we could have returned riding horses or camels, driving a herd of firstlings before us and with purses full!'' Peter thought back to the many times grateful people had wanted to give them a bullock or a foal because a son or daughter had been healed. One town elder had wanted to give them a small sack of Roman silver, which they had refused.

"But we couldn't have lived with ourselves," Bart said, reaching for the clay water urn.

"I'm glad we stuck to Jesus' instructions—to the letter," Peter affirmed.

"I wonder if Judas did . . ." Bart said.

"Well, we'll know tomorrow, or the next day. For it is the fifth day, and by Sabbath I believe all will have returned to Capernaum," said Peter, stretching hugely and stifling a yawn.

"We'll have to travel fast tomorrow and get to Capernaum as soon as we can," said Bartholomew ruefully, "for our purse is nearly empty now. Maybe good for two more meals."

"Forget it," Peter reassured him. "I know many good people along the shores of the sea. We'll not lack for food or a shelter even if our preaching part of the journey is over."

They had traveled on through Tiberius, gained the open shores to the north and remained overnight in the loft of a fisherman's stable before resuming their trek to Capernaum, which they reached late the following afternoon, on preparation day.

When they arrived back in Capernaum, their bodies caked with the dust of the trails, Joanna and Mary Magdalene took their packs, laid out fresh clothing for them and told them that four other teams had come in only yesterday, that most of them were finishing up last-minute chores before Sabbath.

Judas and Simon the Canaanite had arrived this morning.

Inquiring about their condition as if in casual interest, Bart found to his relief they had arrived with no cattle, no horses. Unless Judas had secretly filled his purse, then, there was apparently no evidence of any wrongdoing.

They didn't see Jesus until the morning, for He was by Himself, they said, on the mountain to the west.

That Sabbath morning, with all the disciples and Jesus gathered in the court following a late breakfast of smoked fish, bread, leeks and olives, followed by generous slices of goat cheese and milk, the disciples began excitedly relating their experiences to Jesus.

He would smile and nod, sometimes laugh with them at a humorous story and comment on their experiences.

It was amazing how similar were the experiences of each. With no extra outer garments, no extra shoes, it had proved to be exactly as Jesus had predicted: Whenever the nights turned chilly and they lacked an extra cloak, it seemed there was a willing person to offer them the loan of one; when they needed food it was freely set before them; when their shoes wore thin it was noted by generous persons from place to place and they were given a new pair.

Some of them related excitedly how they had been a little frightened to have been arrested at the behest of religious leaders, hauled into a local tribunal and had to spend anxious hours wondering about their fate.

True to Jesus' predictions, they had found the exact words with which to confound and confuse their enemies so that the only result of such isolated occasions was a further witness, not only to the general public but the local officialdom as well.

Peter exclaimed how remarkable it was that just the right words seemed to come at the right time, and all the disciples commented about the marked similarity of the experiences they had undergone.

It seemed one unit of two had no sooner begun to explain about a particular event than others were nodding and exclaiming they had experienced the same thing exactly!

Peter was tremendously encouraged. Surely the time was growing near when the Lord would announce the beginning of His new kingdom, when they would march on Jerusalem, picking up tens of thousands on the way, and proclaim Him King! Peter knew they could rally uncounted thousands around this Man. And how unselfish He had been; He didn't try to monopolize the glory; He always told people *not* to go out and sing His praises when a miracle occurred and had even allowed the disciples to earn a little glory of their own by permitting them (no, *ordering* them) to go out and perform such tremendous feats in units of two.

It was further proof He intended they have leading roles in the new government to be formed; He would make good His word.

# X

Peter was mildly irritated.

They had come to Bethsaida for a couple of days, and now Zebedee's wife had come over. James' and John's mother was too forward to Peter's way of thinking, and always concerned about her sons. It was normal the woman would want her two sons to succeed, but she was continually asking questions about how Jesus accepted them, and trying to promote their cause.

Now she was at it again.

"James and John—they are well?" she asked.

"Quite well, yes," Peter said.

"And they'll be here tomorrow?"

"I suppose so," Peter said, looking up to check the skies. "Even if it rains, it shouldn't slow them by much. The Lord wants to take a few days off and go over into the wilderness beyond the Gergesenes where no one will know us." Peter was immediately sorry he volunteered such information. The woman had a rather free tongue, and the last thing he wanted was to see a group of people following them across the Sea of Galilee and pestering Jesus.

"We heard rumors that Messiah sent you out on your own," she said matter-of-factly.

"They're true," Peter responded, glad for the change of subject. "I heard their stories. Doubtless they'll be anxious to tell you all about it tomorrow," Peter finished, turning back to the lines he was rigging.

Beth came out then and chatted with the woman for a few minutes while Peter contrived to appear sufficiently occupied that he was asked no more questions.

He went into their house then and gladly listened to his young son and daughter telling him about their lessons. It seemed a new Levite had joined the teaching staff that worked under the keeper of the scrolls at the synagogue, and this man, a fairly young man of not much more than Peter's own 34 years, had been to Rome and to Alexandria and Memphis. He knew much about world conditions, and both of the children were enthusiastic about what they had learned. Peter was amazed at their outbursts; it had been all but impossible to encourage them in their lessons when old Zach, their local linguist, croaked at them with his trembling voice and tried to force them to do their vocabulary lessons in Greek. It was a wonderful family reunion. Aging Jona presided over the meal — fish, inevitably — but spiced this time with some special herbs that had come all the way from Persia that Beth had saved for a special occasion. Beth had wrapped the fish in succulent leaves, placing the herbs and goat's butter inside the fish, and then covered the fish in clay and put them in the oven. When the clay was baked, she broke it open with sharp raps from a hammer, and, when the leaves fell away, there was the fish with all the juices sealed in, the savory steam rising from it making Peter's mouth water. It was marvelous, the way you could lift every bone in the fish completely free by a little effort, leaving two boneless fillets lying in the juices.

Together with the greens Beth had cooked, and bread she had baked with bits of leek mixed into the dough, it had been a family meal to remember.

The next morning Peter knew Jesus and the others would be arriving within a few hours, probably before noon, so he and Andrew hurried to ready the boats. He knew Jesus would want to leave immediately, and knew the reason for it.

The moment His presence was known here in Bethsaida, Jesus would draw huge crowds like a magnet. But only a few of the professional fishermen could afford boats, and none of the hangers-on could follow them.

Besides, with the distant shore shimmering on the far horizon, it would be virtually impossible for questing eyes to see exactly where they landed. And, by the time any enterprising ones had traveled completely around by land, they would be long gone.

Peter felt some small amount of mixed shame and gratitude about Jesus' thoughtfulness in sending him on ahead to be with the family overnight. Peter positively blushed when he wondered if Jesus had thought of Peter spending the night with Beth . . . Probably not, Peter thought. It had only been the Lord's consideration for the family.

Still, though, Jesus was openly frank about family matters and family responsibilities. They even discussed sex from time to time and the ridiculous rumors about Jesus' own origins that the Pharisees kept alive.

Peter knew Jesus was not prudish. Yet He kept Himself rigidly apart from the females as much as He could.

Perhaps that was the very reason so many of them were so enthralled by Him. "Forbidden fruit," Peter almost said aloud, shaking his head.

Jesus' very unobtainability seemed to carry a surprising attraction to many of the women. Mary Magdalene was so obvious it was positively embarrassing. Anyone could see she was completely in love with Him, and yet, aside from the gestures of friendliness He would show anyone else, Jesus hardly seemed to notice the poor woman.

Gratitude first . . . and then . . .

Peter knew Jesus was not handsome, not even attractive in any physical way like Judas was and a few of the others. But, for all His plainness, His flawless character endeared many to Him.

Peter's thoughts were interrupted by the arrival of Simon the Canaanite, who said the Lord and the others weren't far from the town and would want to board directly.

Peter supervised the packing of the last of their foodstuffs, and, together with Andrew, insured the two boats were ready to cast off. His good-byes already said, he looked eagerly for Jesus and the others to arrive.

Two hours later they were well across the sea—the big lugsail drawing as they ran right before the wind on their way to the wilderness for a few days' rest.

They beached the boats, leaving them in the care of a young man they hired for the purpose, and the next four hours found them well beyond the towns, winding their way into the tree-covered slopes of the undulating hills beyond.

One wonderful night camping out, relaxing and listening to Jesus' sayings, before singing some songs around the fire, was all they had.

By the next morning here came seven men with two women and some sick children, and before noon the crowd had swollen to hundreds, and still they came. They shared their meager rations with the first arrivals, and were soon exhausted. Peter listened to Andrew telling him they were out of food, but he doubted if the Lord knew it, as surrounded by the people as He was.

Several began wondering if Jesus would send the people away soon and move on.

Finally Peter thought he would intervene, so he walked through the crowds sitting around Jesus and said, "Lord, couldn't you send them away now? They have been here for hours, and this is a desolate area, nothing to forage for food. And perhaps they should be thinking about lodging and something to eat."

"Well," He said, looking up at Peter, "then give them something to eat." Peter answered, "What shall we do? We don't have anywhere near enough to feed a crowd of thousands of people like this. Furthermore, all the money we have is two hundred pennies. And, even if we went to a nearby town and bought two hundred pennies' worth of bread, it wouldn't be anywhere near enough to go around! There wouldn't even be a scrap of bread for each one of them with such a crowd."

Jesus said, "All right, how many loaves of bread do you have? Go and look!" Andrew, Peter's brother said, "One of the young lads who has been following us has five loaves of barley bread and two fish, but what good is this among such a crowd?''

Jesus then told His disciples, ''Tell the crowd to find a place to sit. I will leave it up to you to organize their numbers in groups of about a hundred or fifty or so.''

Then, receiving the basket of loaves and the two wrapped fish from the young lad, Jesus looked up to heaven and asked God's blessing in prayer and, reaching into the basket, began to break the loaves of bread, giving the bread as He did so to the disciples as they stood in line to receive the food from His hands.

The disciples, looking past one another, craning to see what He was doing, noticed that He would reach into the basket, break a loaf of bread, then reach into the basket and break another loaf of bread, handing each several fish as He did so, and it seemed the basket was filled with an inexhaustible supply!

After about an hour, when the disciples had finished the task of feeding the great crowd (there were at least five thousand men and enough women and children to make a crowd of over ten thousand people), they passed among them, gathering up that which was left until they collected *twelve baskets* full of scraps of bread and leftover fish!

Hundreds of people were absolutely astounded! A rumor was rippling all through the crowd about the ''cornucopia basket,'' the incredible miracle Jesus was performing of feeding such a massive group from only a handful of loaves and two fishes! They were commenting about the tremendous quality of the food and praising God and glorifying Jesus and giving Him thanks. The disciples were looking at one another in dismay, shaking their heads in amazement as they gathered up the remaining fragments. Constantly Peter thought, ''Now I've seen everything!''

Judas, Peter thought, was probably wondering why in the world Jesus did not charge at least some small sum for the meal! Many of the people began to talk in loud, animated voices about the fabulous miracle.

Peter knew the crowd was on fire with zeal. They were chattering happily. Peter had overheard many a comment, ''Just like Moses in the wilderness and the manna from heaven!'' and ''He can do *anything!* No miracle is beyond Him!''

It was not surprising that some of those who had been in the audiences of the disciples' recent trip were here, and their relatives. Not surprising, either, that a few had managed to arrive from Peter's own hometown (that resulting from Zebedee's wife's loose tongue, no doubt).

The miraculous meal was catalytic.

They had been sitting here, spread out by their groups, just as Peter and the others had placed them, and patiently waiting as the disciples came bearing baskets *full* of fish and bread! What fish it was too! Smoked lightly, it seemed, and the bread was marvelous!

The stories of healings of some of the sick children had spread like wildfire through the crowd, and many a young teenager could be seen seeking friends and relatives, bearing messages for them among the crowds from their families.

The enthusiasm was infectious.

''Let's go right now and begin the march!'' One older man urged.

''Nonsense!'' said another sitting nearby. ''How will the whole mass of us make it to Jerusalem without being set upon by the Romans, and, besides, how can we eat?'' He had scarcely finished when the laughter of the one who had spoken first interrupted him.

''Eat?'' He had said derisively. ''Your belly is even now happily growling with miraculous food that He gave you and you wonder about food?'' That silenced the man, and their leader continued, ''And so what if some crazy Romans show up? Jesus of Nazareth can take care of them. Didn't He stop even the waves and the wind?'' Turning, he saw Peter.

''Peter!'' he said, ''You were there. You *saw* it. Tell them!''

''It's true,'' Peter admitted. ''I was there, and I saw it. He put out His hands and said ''shalom'' to the storm, and it became calm within minutes!'' The group marveled; the hum of conversation grew into a cacophony of sound.

At this the group got to their feet, and the elder who

had been the spokesman beckoned to Peter and began striding toward Jesus.

Peter went along, wondering how the Lord would respond to this excited enthusiasm. For once, Peter saw, there was not a single dissenting voice, not a single Pharisee, publican or Sadducee in the crowd. No one had challenged Him. Had Jesus actually planned this?

As the word spread, hundreds more rose and marched toward Jesus where He was seated with a few of the disciples, eating.

They drew up before Him, and the elder said, ''Lord, we know You are from God, we know You are the very *Messiah* sent to redeem our nation. *Now* is Your time. *Now* is the time for the delivery of God's people Israel!''

''Amen!'' and ''Hallelujah!'' shouted hundreds.

''Men,'' said the elder who had appointed himself spokesman for the group, ''are you with me?''

''Yes! Yes!'' they shouted. ''Let's go. Let's march now!'' shouted another from back in the crowd. ''We're through waiting!'' said someone else.

The shouting became a tumult, and the forward ranks made as if to hoist Jesus to their shoulders and begin marching toward Jerusalem.

But Jesus stopped them with His word.

''Wait!'' He commanded in a loud voice.

They stopped, and Jesus asked for all to be seated again.

Then, in a powerful dissertation, He thanked them for their enthusiasm and began explaining, as He had to His own disciples so often, that this was ''not His time,'' but that only the Father ''knew the times that He had before ordained,'' and that Jesus must not go to Jerusalem now.

It was only by sheer force of His personality that He prevented them from bodily seizing Him and placing Him on their shoulders, beginning a march, Peter saw.

Peter found himself caught up in the infectious enthusiasm of the crowd. He, too, had wished the Lord would seize this magic moment and begin a march of triumph. What could be better timing? They could gather tens of thousands en route.

Peter was scarcely able to contain his disappointment when Jesus began firmly telling the crowd He had no intention of going to Jerusalem just yet, that it was not for them to know the times and seasons the Father kept secret unto Himself; that there was much yet to be accomplished.

# XI

Peter was surprised and a little mystified when Jesus instructed them to return back across the Sea of Galilee and leave Him here. The crowd took almost a full hour to disperse. Hundreds pressed forward for a last word, to see Jesus or to grasp His forearm and reconfirm their willingness to start the march then and there.

Finally Jesus turned to Peter and instructed him to take the others and return across to Bethsaida without Him.

"But, Lord!" Peter began to protest. "Surely we can't all go and leave You here alone . . ."

Jesus stopped him with a raised hand and reminded him that He would not be alone, glancing upward. Involuntarily, Peter's eyes followed Jesus' glance, but he didn't see anything except the dying purplish hues of the sun's last rays tinging some of the highest clouds. But he knew what Jesus meant. He meant angels. Peter knew that Jesus relished spending time alone in wilderness or mountain areas praying. Peter had become accustomed to Jesus' early morning disappearances by now, but he was genuinely concerned about leaving Him over here in these rugged lands of crude villages.

He knew the people were not all as civilized and friendly as those who were even now trudging toward their homes, supposing Jesus would be leaving with the boats. What if a few of them returned to make sure?

But Jesus insisted, so Peter and the others returned to

the shore, and, after giving a small tip to their youthful boat watcher, they poled away from the shore to catch the night breeze that would force them to lie closely to the wind, tacking their way across. Peter's lifelong experience with the sea had conditioned him to this daily phenomenon. And, though he couldn't explain how the cooling air descending over the lake would be drawn toward the ovenlike heat and dryness of the Arabah to the east in a daily cycle of thermals, he was wary enough to know that sometimes those late afternoon and early evening breezes could whip up dangerous whitecaps.

With Peter at one tiller and Andrew at the other, the journey began.

Only a few minutes from shore Peter lit their shielded light and hoisted it on the mainmast, where Andrew, tacking along behind, could catch sight of it.

Some of the others immediately lay down to sleep, and Peter was content to man the tiller, bracing his elbow against it to steady himself as the boat began rearing to meet the oncoming waves like a spirited horse. Before long it appeared another full gale would soon be blowing.

Everyone had left the bow and foredeck and was either in the tiny cabin or below right before Peter's feet, where the hatchway shone dully with flickering orange light as someone moved in front of the oil lamp he had lit.

Peter always worried about some lubber casting about with a lamp below decks lest a fire occur.

The growing shriek of the wind made Peter reluctantly decide to heave to. His mind went back to that other time when he had been severely frightened and he flushed with embarrassment at the recollection. But Jesus was not aboard to calm the winds this time, and, with the quartering waves already beginning to come aboard as green water smashing against the coamings and hissing along the scuppers, it was time to heave to.

The sail was like a living thing. It obstinately tried to throw them into the sea or smash them against the mast as they struggled to quiet its wild flappings. But in due time they had it furled and lashed in place, and there was nothing left but to keep anxious eyes on the wind and check their leeway to make sure they weren't pushed aground against rocks that would pound holes in the bottom. The big sea anchor was out, and Peter guessed they weren't making more than two knots to leeward, if that.

Andrew had followed his example when he saw the dull whiteness of Peter's lugsail disappear, and Peter could see the faint outlines of the other boat about a hundred yards to port, the bows coming almost clear of the water as it rose up each crest, the wave passing amidship to pitch the boat sickeningly into the trough. The wave, passing under the stern, caused the boat to pitch steeply forward, and then another would burst against the bow, forcing it up steeply again like a bucking horse.

Peter felt cold water splattering across his ankles. Looking down, he was just in time to see water coming out of the hatchway. John, or someone down there, had opened the lower hatch to the bilges then and had organized a three man bucket brigade.

The working of the seams in these rough waters would have added several inches to the bilge.

Peter thought of growling at someone to send another man to the top of the hatch, handing the bucket free of the hatchway before slopping it along the deck like that, but his feet were thoroughly soaked anyway, so he said nothing.

Instead, he lashed the tiller, knowing it was practically useless with their heavy sea anchor out, and climbed atop the cabin to lean back against the mainmast. He listened to the creaking sounds, felt the hum of the lines transmitted to the mast, gently throbbing at his back. When the rising bows met each larger wave, the boat was suddenly snubbed short by the drag of the sea anchor. Much of the wave top crashed over the bow, flinging spray against Peter's back even at this height.

His thoughts turned back to the scene on the heights, and he felt stirrings of doubt and discouragement again. It would have been a marvelous thing, he thought, if the Lord had acquiesced to the suggestions of the leaders over there; they could have made six or eight miles before dark, and in the days ahead they could have grown larger in each town or village they passed. They could have been twenty thousand strong by the time they reached Jerusalem!

Peter's mind whirled with conflicting thoughts.

Sometimes, guiltily, he found himself wondering if he were a part of some mad dream. The familiar sights, sounds and smells of his own fishing boat probably did that to him, and spending some time with Beth and the children at home. In a way, his anticipation dulled by reality, his hungers satisfied and a new experience under way, Peter could vaguely berate himself for enjoying these brief visits home, for he found himself with the same mental conflicts that had torn him before.

He would say the most outrageous things to himself. "Is He who He really says He is?" "What am I doing here?" and, "Why *me,* of all people? Why does everything always have to happen to *me?*" Then, perversely, his mind would say, "Shut up, you fool. Haven't you *seen* the miracles with your own eyes" (it was positively puzzling how a fabulous miracle could lose its luster with the passing of weeks or months, but it happened), "and haven't you seen a consistency in the Lord's behavior, a determination and dedication that would shame any lesser man?"

Peter found himself going back over his entire life now and then, nostalgically reaching back to his youth.

He had not been a particularly happy youngster, though there were the moments of excitement or triumph which came along to counter the times of sickness, grinding poverty and disappointment.

He fancied this wind blowing his hair, rattling the lines, creaking the mast and causing the boat to plunge like this was blowing unimpeded clear across the great sea, all the way from Italy.

Out there, on that great sea back about the time Peter's father had been a small boy, the greatest naval battle of all history had occurred.

Peter had seen relics in the homes of coast dwellers who claimed this or that piece of wood or portion of sweep or oar had come floating ashore months after the galleys of Antony's and Cleopatra's fleets had suffered defeat at

Actium.

His father had told him of the great battle, how it was said there were at least two hundred ships on each side and how the ships of Octavian, lighter and far handier than the ponderous battleships of Antony, had made use of quick skirmishing tactics, avoiding closing with the huge ships whose heavy artillery could have crushed them, and had won a great victory.

It had been on the second day of the Roman ninth month, Peter remembered—it was a date his history teacher insisted he remember—when the great naval battle had been fought and Cleopatra suddenly withdrew her squadron of vessels when she saw how the battle was going. The historians claimed Antony was shocked and outraged and slipped off behind her, leaving his fleet, which was subsequently set on fire and mainly destroyed. Thousands of men had died with the ponderous hulks. Many, laden with the huge throwing stones, had sunk to the bottom, taking their hapless galley slaves with them still chained to their seats.

Would there ever be a time of peace?

Wars were being fought here and there even now, Peter knew. Scarcely a ship arrived from Rome or Africa that did not bring news of some new conflagration somewhere.

Out there at the very source of this wind that whipped up these waves, Peter imagined, there might even now be some great naval battle occurring, or perhaps the ships of Roman trade were plunging along, carrying cargo or fighting men to some distant shore.

Peter felt movement below him and heard John grunting with exertion as he climbed up to seat himself beside Peter, leaning partly against Peter's shoulder and partly against the mast.

"Another windy night," John said.

"It'll die down in another hour or so. It always does," Peter said, and then wondered why he had added the thought.

"How do you think Jesus will come back to Bethsaida?" John asked.

"Do you worry about Him?"

"Yes, I do, although I guess I shouldn't," John admitted.

"John," began Peter, "do you believe the Lord is really going to carry through with His plans to set up His kingdom?"

"Of course. Don't you?"

"Yes, I guess so, but it seems He is always hesitant just when the time is ripe. Like only hours ago that crowd was ready to take Him on their shoulders and begin marching to the streets of Jerusalem," Peter said, not without chagrin.

"You heard what He said," John chided. "He has some greater plans that He gets from His Father in heaven. He is on some time schedule He says we can't understand yet.

"I know, but I wish I could understand it, then perhaps I wouldn't be so anxious."

"Well, you know what He says about patience."

"Are you patient, John?"

"Oh, I find myself growing impatient for something dramatic to happen just like everyone else, I suppose, but I have seen so many astounding miracles by now I guess I have learned to wait on Him to decide. Besides, He keeps saying it is not for us to know the times and seasons, and even hints that *He* might not know exactly. It's like He is waiting for some sign from above."

"But it seems such a waste," Peter countered, "to allow that enthusiastic crowd to disperse when there wasn't a single Pharisee among them. We could have grown into four or five times that number by the time we reached Jerusalem."

"Peter," John said with a touch of irony, "remember David's sin? He numbered Israel." And then, to avoid seeming overly critical, "Don't you believe that a man who has the power of raising the dead, of changing water into wine and even calming the winds and waves, could do anything He wants to do without the support of a screaming mob?"

"You're right, John," Peter answered, shifting position so as to ease his back against the mast.

The two fell quiet, for it was an effort to speak above the howl of the wind through the rigging and the splashing of the waves against the bows.

What was that? Peter thought he heard a thin, piercing sound, almost like a scream from a vast distance. Looking toward the other boat, he thought he saw a pair of wildly gesticulating men. They were yelling thinly, the wind distorting the sounds, and pointing. Just then a loud yell sent the hair along his neck rising when someone right aft by the tiller screamed out, "It is a *spirit! A spirit! A spirit walking on the water!*" said John, right in his ear.

Peter's eyes followed the pointing arm and there, ghostlike in the dim light, was a human form gliding slowly across the waves toward them.

Peter felt his sharp intake of breath, the quickening of his pulse, as he grasped the mast and rose to his feet for a better look.

What would Jesus do if He were here? What would He expect them to do?

Rebuke this creature? Drive it away? He found himself passionately wishing Jesus were here, or hoping James or John, or someone, would stand by him and help.

It was coming closer and closer, and Peter found his palms sweating (even though the breeze was cold) and his scalp prickling. What would Jesus expect him to do? Well, He's expecting you to handle the situation like He would, Peter answered himself.

Some of the others were babbling excitedly and pointing, and, as if hearing their voices, the figure turned toward them and said loudly, "Cheer up! Don't be afraid! It's *Me!*"

They all recognized the voice instantly. "It's Jesus!" someone said.

Peter wondered. What if they had made a mistake? Was it *really* Him? He thought he knew a way to make sure if it were really Jesus. He called out, "Lord, if it is really You, then bid me to walk out there to You on the waters, just like You are!"

"Come ahead!" Jesus called.

Peter lowered himself over the thwart, stepped on the water, and, seeing Jesus' robe faintly shining in the darkness, actually began to *walk on the water* toward Jesus. But, as the wind blew harder and Peter began to look around him in amazement at the waves that were splashing over his feet, dumbfounded that he was able to actually walk on liquid, he began to sink!

Frightened, for though he was a strong swimmer he was fully clothed and he knew he might drown in this heavy chop, he began to shout at the top of his lungs, *"Lord! Save me! Save me!"*

Immediately Jesus walked to Peter and, stretching forth His hand, grasped him and said, "Oh, you of little faith, *why did you doubt?"*

Holding Peter by the arm, He strode directly to the boat and, climbing up over the thwart, went into the boat. Immediately the wind ceased.

Peter and the disciples, seeing this utterly fantastic occurrence, all knelt, bowed their heads and said, "Truly You are the very Son of God!"

Excited babble broke out among them as Jesus descended into the ship and seated Himself.

John looked at Peter, strode aft to unlash the tiller while Peter struggled to get the sea anchor in.

Peter got the message in the look.

It was as if John were saying, "See, didn't I tell you not to worry?"

With the sea anchor gotten in, sails hoisted and both boats slowly under way again, Peter had time to ponder this remarkable experience. He looked overboard there at the waves and water he had known all his life and thought, "Did I really *do* that? It was *incredible*."

He tried to recapture what had gone through his mind when he had first taken that foolish, daring, frightened, courageous step (for it had been all those things, he guessed) and actually *stood,* right back there about a hundred yards or so, and walked. And it had had felt just like walking on some solid yet gently fluid or moving substance, a strange sensation indeed!

Strange that as long as his mind kept saying, "He's

doing it—we're *both* doing it,'' he was getting along fine, taking step after step. But the moment his mind told him to look down into the water itself, see the slosh of waves over his feet and wonder how this could be possible, he felt himself being engulfed, like the water was slowly admitting his body as if he had stepped into a pool of quicksand. With his mind on Christ, he admitted, he had accomplished (or God had, rather, he corrected himself) an absolute *miracle,* and with his mind on himself he had canceled out the miraculous power.

Peter was embarrassed. He had let Jesus down again.

When the Lord had said, *"Why did you doubt?"* He had said it with a *smile,* almost as if He had been disappointed too, and like He might have enjoyed a walk out there with Peter on the waves. The weirdest thoughts that suddenly came made Peter involuntarily chuckle out loud. He could almost see, in his mind's eye, what might have happened if he hadn't gotten frightened and had to cry out to be rescued. Why, the whole two shiploads of them would have probably followed suit, and he could imagine how incredible it might have looked to some poor fisherman in a passing boat to see about thirteen grown men cavorting about on the water. Thaddeus would have probably tried handsprings, Peter thought, and the unfortunate fisherman would have probably never touched another drop of the grape for the rest of his life.

It could have been quite a story, but now Peter hoped they wouldn't bother telling it.

Jesus had said He wanted to go to Capernaum this time instead of Bethsaida, so Peter changed course. Some of the others could return the boats so Jona and Zebedee wouldn't have to send servants after them or come themselves.

It was graying in the east, the marbled columns of the public buildings near the bay in Capernaum faintly gleaming in the half light. Peter and Andrew warped their boats alongside as John and Simon leaped ashore with the hawsers to tie up.

They unloaded their packs and sent two men ahead to inform the servants in the Lord's house He would arrive within a few minutes.

Peter hoped they didn't have to face some large crowds this morning, for his legs had long ago reminded him how many hours it had been since he had last lain abed. Strange that it seemed like a week or more since he had wakened out of warm, deep sleep alongside Beth and then began the journey across the sea, but it had been only yesterday.

They trudged through the lightening streets, their footfalls echoing faintly from the walls as a curious face peered out of an upper window now and then.

Twice they passed small groups of people leading their donkeys laden with foods from the countryside, farmers heading to the marketplace, intent on arranging for a choice stall to sell their food.

Little could Peter know that the next few hours would bring another of these emotion-charged, heated confrontations—and, of all unbelievable things, with some of the very people who had only yesterday been ready to hoist Jesus upon their shoulders and march on Jerusalem!

The women were busily preparing food as the men arrived, stowing their dunnage in various rooms, washing up and expecting a good breakfast and perhaps a nap before noon.

Peter ate with Jesus, James and John, while some of the others dispersed on errands of their own or retired to the sleeping quarters to snooze.

Peter's mind seemed to hear, from a vast distance, a dim voice in his ear. He thought for a moment he was back on the boat with the rocking motion he felt. But then he came fully awake and here was Mary gently pushing on his shoulders and saying, ''Peter! Wake up! There is a large crowd gathering outside. Some of them are saying they came all the way around the north shore from a meeting the Lord had yesterday. They have asked around the docks and in the streets, and they say they know He is here.''

Peter sat up, ruefully regarded the sun's shadows that told him it was barely midday, scratched his hair, ran his hands over his beard to smooth it and stood, hating the smell of his own clothes after several soakings, for he hadn't bothered to change.

"Where's Jesus?" He asked.

"He's sleeping upstairs," she answered.

"Well, you'd better wake Him while I go see what's happening," he instructed, and then turned toward the door at the end of the main court. Halfway there he thought he had better answer another even more urgent business first, so turned aside, went out through the kitchen, and stood against the back wall of the old building adjacent to the house.

Peter returned to the door, hearing the noisy crowd outside, and was opening the door when here came Jesus behind him, and the people who were noisily calling to each other and talking loudly, catching sight of Him, let up a cheer.

Oh! Peter thought, Mary was right. Some of these men are the same people who were over there yesterday.

About that time one of their number stepped forward and said he had rowed clear across the lake in the early morning stillness. He said, "Master" (calling Jesus "Rabbi," or "Teacher"), *"when did You come over here?"*

At this, Jesus said a positively astonishing thing, making Peter's eyes involuntarily blink in total surprise.

He said, "You're not looking for Me but because you are hungry again. Don't seek for the bread that fails! You're not here because you saw signs and wonders, but because you think I'll feed you! Don't labor so hard for the bread that will perish, but labor for the meat that will never perish, unto eternal life, which the Son of Man will give unto you, because Him has the Father sealed."

Peter was shocked.

Why was He insulting these people who had worked so hard to catch up with Him? Many of them had puzzled, almost hurt expressions, and the man who had been admonished about being more interested in getting a free meal than the spiritual things was positively furious.

Why did Jesus insist on making people suddenly come face to face with themselves? Peter knew the feeling; it hurt like a whip. And he guessed the man who had been brought up short was miserable just now, having been soundly rebuked in front of his peers.

". . . Bread from heaven," Jesus was saying, as Peter noticed Luke scribbling away at his ever present slate, and there was Matthew, and even John, all doing the same thing, as if all of them expected this would develop into something they would want to record.

Peter listened attentively. Some kind of argument was developing over "bread," probably because the man had been stung by Jesus' words about the "bread that perishes" and the admonition to seek for "eternal bread." Jesus was speaking in similes again, using analogous representations, knowing full well that most of the people wouldn't understand what He was saying.

"Well, Moses gave our fathers bread from heaven, and yet they are all dead . . ." countered one.

"No, it wasn't *Moses* who gave your fathers that bread, but My Father, who gives you the true bread out of heaven. The bread of God is that which comes down out of heaven and gives life unto the world."

Puzzled, the spokesman for the crowd said, "Then, please, Lord, give us of that kind of bread. We would like to eat only *that* bread from now on!"

Was there sarcasm in that statement?

Jesus said, *"I am* the bread of life. He that comes to Me will not hunger, and he that believes on Me shall never thirst. But I said unto you that you have seen Me and yet believed not. All which the Father has given Me shall come unto Me, and him that comes to Me I will in no wise cast out. For I am come down from heaven, not to accomplish My own will, but to do the will of Him that sent Me. And this *is* the will of Him that sent Me, that of all which He has given Me I should lose nothing, but should raise it up at the last day!

"For this is the will of My Father, that everyone that beholds the Son, and believes on Him, should have eternal life; I will raise him up at the last day."

Peter heard how the leaders of the religious sects grabbed this opportunity and began to murmur and gossip among the crowd concerning Jesus because He claimed,

"I am the bread which came down out of heaven." One of their leaders said, "Isn't this that Jesus, the one who came from Nazareth, Joseph's boy, whose own father and mother we know?

"Since we know of His boyhood and background, and the town in which He lives, how in the world can He now claim, 'I am come down out of heaven'?"

Jesus said, "Don't bother wondering and spreading doubt among yourselves. No man can come to Me except the Father which has sent Me draw him, and I will raise him up at the last day!

"Sure, your fathers ate manna in the wilderness, and nevertheless they all died! *This* is the bread which comes down out of heaven that a man can eat of and never die! *I am* the *living bread* which came down out of heaven; if any man eat of this bread he will live forever. Yes, and the bread which I will give is My *very own flesh* which I will give for the life of the world!"

Immediately following this powerful discourse, a hubbub of shouting arguments broke out among the spiritual leaders' caucus. Some in outrage and amazement said, "How can this Man give us the very flesh of His own body to eat?" Others were saying, "Now He is advocating cannibalism! Well, I never heard of such a thing! Did you hear that?" Other such complaints were rumbling through the crowd.

Jesus said, "Truly, truly, I am telling you this: Except you eat the flesh of the Son of Man and drink His blood, you do not have life in yourselves!

"He that eats My flesh and drinks My blood has eternal life, and I will raise him up at the last day. For My flesh is meat indeed, and My blood is drink indeed. He that eats My flesh and drinks My blood abides in Me, and I in him. As the Father sent Me, and I live because of the Father, so he that eats of Me, he also shall live through Me, because of Me.

"This, meaning Me, My life, My body, is the bread which came down out of heaven, not as the fathers did eat manna in the wilderness and still died, but he that eats this bread will live for all eternity!"

At this Peter and many of the disciples were dumb-founded. They did not understand the saying any more than did the religious leaders. Judas seized the opportunity to attempt to disaffect others of the disciples, and one of them was heard to say, "This is a really tough thing to say. Who in the world can listen to such words and understand them?"

But Jesus, knowing that His disciples were murmuring, answered, "Does this cause you to stumble? What then if you should see the Son of Man ascending up to where He came from? It is the Spirit that quickens, that makes alive; the flesh profits absolutely nothing! The words that I have spoken unto you are spirit and are life! But there are some of you" (casting His eyes over Judas and some of the others) "that believe not!"

Jesus knew from the very beginning who they were who would not believe, and which one of the disciples would betray Him. He said, "For this cause have I said unto you that no man can come unto Me except it be given him of the Father!"

Peter was shaken to his boot soles. What was Jesus doing? Why, with only a few words it seemed the Messiah would wipe out all these months of hard labor!

The rumble of male voices rose to a cacophony of sound as dozens broke up into argument and vehement protest.

"What *is* this, anyway?" Peter heard one say. "Who ever heard of someone eating the very flesh and drinking the blood of another man?"

"Yeah! What a violation of the law itself!" chimed in another. "How can He be saying such things?"

"No surer way to turn the people away," said a small swarthy fellow from the Negev beyond Jordan, identified by his dress. "The people won't support foolish talk like 'drinking blood' and 'eating flesh' from a leader." His voice was drowned by dozens of other similarly outraged as snatches of protest reached Peter's smarting ears.

Peter tried to stop some who were disgustedly making as if to leave. Shaking off his grasp, one hawk-faced fellow, an obvious leader of a sizable group, said, "Go away, Simon. Maybe you don't care about your wife and children, but the rest of us are sick and tired of waiting for the revolution! We came out here for *action,* and at no small cost to ourselves, not to be harangued with strange-sounded words about drinking human blood!''

Peter's frantic gaze saw how James, John and even Bartholomew and Simon, the dark Canaanite, had surrounded Jesus, thinking He might be in danger.

He worked his way closer to the Teacher, wanting to speak to Him about all this, when Jesus, looking straight through him, it seemed, said, ''Well, Peter are you going to leave Me too?''

The shame of Nazareth came back to Peter. The racing thoughts tumbled through his mind in quick succession as he remembered the incomprehensible miracles, the magic basket of fish and bread, walking on water, the changing of water into wine and even the raising of the dead!

It was as if his whole life flashed in front of his eyes in only moments.

He was torn with indecision for what seemed like an interminable period of time. Here was the very cream of their future officer corps; the trained, experienced, loyal, hard-working, dedicated cadre of their future government disintegrating right before their eyes! Why, it was *mutiny!* Yet Jesus stood there like a captain on the quarterdeck with his crew jumping aboard his cutter, bailing out, leaving the ship and yet doing nothing!

Why didn't He raise His voice and rebuke them? Why didn't He somehow *correct* the misunderstandings? Surely there must be some way to modify the hard words He had used; surely He didn't literally mean there would be some bizarre ceremony in which they would have to partake of His own blood?

The steady eyes were unnerving and calming at the same time. Peter thought about returning to the tedious boredom of his nets. He thought longingly of whiling away the time when the lake was too rough for fishing in front of his own fire with Beth and the children, or sitting in the door of one of his favorite shops in Bethsaida, exchanging the latest news from the Persian caravans or travelers from Greece or Rome. He thought of that moment when his brother Andrew had found Peter working on his nets and had said breathlessly, ''We have found the Messiah!'' The scene at Nain flashed through his mind when Jesus had stopped the men carrying a wrapped body on a bier and the young man had been raised from the dead! The resolve Peter had made after Jesus found him in his boat and used it as a speaking platform came back suddenly.

He had made a commitment. He had decided he would follow this Man to the death. This was disaster. It was a major setback, but it wasn't as if all was lost. There were, Peter had learned on many an occasion when half a catch had been lost through the ripping of a net, ''other fish in the sea.'' He would stay. No matter what. Besides, Jesus was more than just an ordinary human being, Peter knew that! Somehow Peter knew, he *wanted* to know, that Jesus was really who He said He was! He could regather those men in an instant, probably! He could raise up another group! Why, perhaps He intended letting them go back to where they came from knowing they would be replaced by another force their same size with the rest of the disciples, and the ones who were even now noisily leaving their company would become unwitting recruiters for yet additional hundreds. After all, they couldn't forget, nor could they deny, the experiences they had shared!

No, he would not leave!

He met the level eyes. The question had been put squarely to him, and a number of others were waiting for his answer.

He said, ''Lord, where shall we go? *You* have the words of truth about living forever, and we have believed, and we *know* that You are the Holy One of God!'' Peter hadn't intended to say it just exactly like that, but somehow the words had come tumbling out. He had felt like he was being guided by an unseen force, like he had been intended to say those words. Besides, the ones on the fence needed to hear some encouragement!

''Wasn't I the One who *chose* all of you, all twelve of

you, and yet one of you is a demon?'' said Jesus. John was
writing hastily, recording the whole scene, Peter knew.

Well, not all of them had left, but too many, Peter
thought. Still, he got the point. Jesus reminded them that
''many were called, but few were *chosen*'' The twelve had
been *chosen,* hand-picked, specially selected.

If Jesus had chosen the twelve with such deliberate
care, and even after an all-night prayer (which Peter knew
about), and yet had intentionally allowed Himself to include a thief like Judas among the twelve and even allowed
Judas to handle the money when He *knew* Judas was a
thief, then Jesus *must have foreknown* His strong words
about His body and blood would drive many away.

He never did anything without a *purpose* in mind,
Peter supposed. So maybe He even knew which ones
would leave and why and which would stay and why.

Probably.

The days that followed were sober times.

Peter's doubts came up like bile in his throat time and
time again when he thought back to the scene. The group
had been like a tightly knit cadre of brothers commonly
bound together by the deepest commitments.

Their fireside talks had been punctuated by the rough
good humor of co-conspirators, men of the land and of the
sea who would seek to right the wrongs, overthrow the
profligate, pot-gutted pompous asses of the Romish puppet governments, and restore the Jewish state to its rightful
greatness.

Hadn't each one of them heard the prayers of their
elders?

Hadn't they listened by the timeless hours to the
reading of Isaiah or another of the prophets, and the
cantors of the synagogues or the scribes in the marketplace
talking of the promises to ''the daughter of Zion'' or the
great promises of the prophets directed to the ''cities of
Judah''? Surely it was time. Surely Jesus, the very Messiah, the miracle worker from Galilee, was the One! Or
was He?

Peter found himself retracing his thoughts back to the
beginnings of his acquaintance with Jesus. He had com-

pletely mystified Peter on more than one occasion when He didn't measure up to Peter's idea of what the Messiah should be like.

Peter's memories sawed at his conscience when he thought of his many mistakes in harshly speaking to Jesus because he misunderstood. Like that time when he had said without thinking, "Lord, *save us*—we're about to *drown*. Don't You *care?*"

But each time Peter went through this exercise he progressed quickly through all the experiences with Jesus, all the incredible miracles, and came up with the same answer.

"He *really is* the *very Son of God*—I mean, the *real* One—the very divine One who came from a miracle from God, the Redeemer, the Savior, the Messiah!" Peter knew it, and still the lingering doubts assailed his mind.

Days passed without any major events.

Soon some of the leading Pharisees from Jerusalem were said to be finding lodgings in Capernaum, and Peter heard rumors in the shops that they were preparing questions about the disciples' eating habits. Judas had bought some supplies, and several of the others had heard loose talk about the casual manner of the disciples, that of simply wiping off the outer dirt from fruits, or scraping a choice vegetable with a knife, or brushing a succulent grape against their garments before popping it into their mouths.

No doubt they were here because of the rumors of dissidents having left Jesus and they hoped to find His popularity on the wane. Well, they were due to bitter disappointment, Peter thought.

The disciples carried the tales to the Lord, and He seemed willing enough to meet these Jerusalem Pharisees and their scribes over the issue of "defiled bread," or ceremonially unclean food.

Peter was told that the Pharisees were gathering outside His house and that they had been talking up His alleged infraction of law—the encouragement of His followers to ignore the ceremonial washings—and that a large crowd had collected, waiting to see what Jesus would say.

The disciples told Jesus about it, and Jesus went out to listen to their complaints. The Pharisees and scribes asked Him, ''How come Your disciples do not live according to the tradition of their elders, but eat their food with ceremonially defiled hands?''

Jesus retorted, ''Well did Isaiah prophesy of you hypocrites. As it is written, 'This people honors Me with their lips, but their heart is far from Me. But in vain do they worship Me, teaching as their doctrines the precepts of men.'

''You wholly reject the commandment of God and cling to your traditions.

''Listen to Me, everybody, and understand this! There is nothing from without the man that going into his body can 'defile' him! But the things which proceed from within the man, those are the things that defile the man!''

Jesus went back into the house and Peter and His disciples gathered around Him, asking Him what He meant by the parable and telling Him that ''of course you know the Pharisees were terribly offended when they heard this saying!''

Jesus said, ''Every plant which my heavenly Father has not planted will be rooted up. Don't bother with them, let them alone! They are blind guides, and if the blind guide the blind both will stumble into a pit!''

Peter spoke up and said, ''Explain to us the parable, will You, Lord?''

Jesus, looking at Peter in gentle rebuke, said, ''Are you also without any understanding?

''Don't you understand that whatever it is from the outside environment that goes into a man cannot defile him, because it doesn't enter into his heart—that is, his spirit, his mind or his character—but it enters into his belly and eventually passes out of the body through the elimination tract?

''But the things which proceed out of the *mouth* of the man stem from the innermost thoughts of his heart, his mind, his conscience and his character.

''For from within, from the heart of man, proceed

evil thoughts: fornication, thefts, murders, adulteries, covetings, wickedness, deceit, lasciviousness and evil interpretation of things, rantings and railings, pride, foolishness, false witnessing and every assorted form of evil!

"All these things come from deeply *within* the man, and these *defile* the man. But to eat with hands which have not been ceremonially scrubbed time and again can never defile a man!"

Peter's ears burned, and he felt his neck warming, supposing it was flushing and giving away his embarrassment before all the others. Of course. He should have seen the analogy before he opened his big mouth again, but somehow his impetuous nature seemed determined to make him plunge on like a madly galloping horse stumbling straight into the midst of a snarling pack of she-lions.

He felt like a fool.

But he understood.

With his usual incisive logic, Jesus had made it clear that no amount of ceremonial washings, scrubbings, pourings, launderings or soapings could make a man truly clean. The freshly washed Pharisee was still a murderplotting, conniving, lusting, greedy, backbiting, self-righteous, thieving son of a . . .—no, he shouldn't say that—who was black dirty inside.

Peter supposed it was a good thing God hadn't made evil thoughts as obvious as dirt or disease. Lounging around the kitchen long after the others had gone to bed that night, Peter sipped meditatively at a skin of Galilean wine and tried to sooth his injured pride.

Jesus was asleep upstairs, and the others were in various rooms; some had decided to remain out in the courtyard since the night was balmy.

Thinking over what the Lord had said, Peter allowed his thoughts to stray to Judas again. Judas seemed very careful when it came to washings and ablutions, and he was always making some comment that seemed to Peter critical of the Lord, complaining when Jesus would instruct him to go into the shambles and buy a choice leg of lamb, that perhaps they could have gone without meat on this day (since the Pharisees fasted twice in the week, and the disciples almost never did) and saved the money, or, better yet, give some small offering to the poor.

Peter wondered at that. Of all their number, Judas was the one most like a Pharisee. He spoke continually of generosity toward the poor and harped on paying strict attention to religious custom as if he were afraid to offend the religious leaders. Why?

Peter had never known a person any more sensitive to his personal reputation than Judas was. Yet Peter knew John suspected Judas had been possessed of sticky fingers now and again. Did Jesus know? Of course He did. Hadn't He said one of them had a demon? The Lord seemed to have some sixth sense; He could virtually read their minds, so Peter suspected that Jesus knew whatever it was Judas was doing.

Tilting his head back, he raised the wineskin to his lips and allowed another small sip to trickle down his throat. The Pharisees had tried to be "astonished" at Jesus' doctrine again, and an angry muttering had ensued when some of them tried to take special exception to Jesus' calling their myriad laws and regulations the "commandments of men" and their own "traditions."

Peter was learning. The ultimate in hypocrisy, he guessed, was a simpering, holier-than-thou, posturing, pretending, busily scrubbing Pharisee half-drowning himself in ceremonial ablutions. Thinking back to Jesus' rebuke and His strong words about the thoughts of the heart, Peter guessed those Pharisees' hearts were about as slimy and black as Peter's own hands after cleaning a whole catch of fish. He knew it was inevitable that a man ingested some "honest dirt" in his lifetime, and had wondered about it. But Jesus had made it plain that honest dirt that might find its way down an unsuspecting gullet as a part of a meal, or from unwashed hands, didn't "defile" that man spiritually. It might make him sick, Peter guessed, if he ate enough dirt, but it didn't defile him in God's sight.

And here were the Pharisees (and Judas, some of the time) scrubbing away, washing, dipping, pouring and trying to remain spotlessly clean, all the while thinking thoughts of avarice, greed, hatred, lust, vanity, plotting how to trap Jesus. Well, Peter thought, closing up the wineskin and returning it to its peg on the wall, he wasn't the only one whose ears had burned today; a whole flock of Pharisees had gotten it worse than he had.

He'd better get to sleep, he supposed, for, judging by the sonorous sounds coming from the common court through the door, the others were oblivious by now.

He had heard the others saying Jesus was thinking about a trip to the northern seacoast soon. Peter could relish that possibility; they would be in the Syro-Phoenician seacoast and completely away from the Pharisees who trailed along after them, probably. Maybe it would be a vacation of sorts.

Peter's mind grew sluggishly tired with thoughts of miles of white beach, bright sun dancing on a crashing green and white surf, and some interesting talks with some of the saltwater fishermen in the area.

# XII

Early dawn found them on their way, having arisen well before daylight, packed fresh clothing, loaded the animals and said their good-byes to Mary, Mary Magdalene and the other women.

Several of the women had worked many hours to make sure their clothing was in order, and Peter knew Mary Magdalene had stoked a fire in their largest cooking oven, hanging Jesus' soft inner cloak of the finest wool in the room to dry. The good woman knew enough to keep the garment well away from the fire, hanging it up over wooden pegs so as to spread it out, but not let the fabric dry too quickly.

They had wanted to escape notice as much as they could, and so, at the expense of several hours' sleep, they had packed up and left before most of the city was awake.

Their route took them almost straight north for some hours, following the course of the creek that drained into the Sea of Galilee, and then they turned upstream toward the northwest and followed the narrow valley of a tributary to its source, crested a rugged ridge of lower mountains with the snowcapped peak of Hermon visible off to their right, and saw the blue Mediterranean through the haze in the distance.

They used a little-traveled trail away from the main roads, Jesus preferring the solitude.

Whenever they traveled like this, Peter could relax and devote his mind solely to the efforts of their progress.

Their animals were nondescript, their clothing plain, and their appearance like that of any other group of travelers. Peter knew it was only rarely that Jesus was recognized, and then only if someone had been in direct conversation with Him (or confrontation, more likely) in the past.

Up here, descending a narrow defile along a creek that led to the sea, they were departing Galilee and entering the Syro-Phoenician coast. Peter passionately hoped the Lord wouldn't mind spending a few days along the beaches, with fishing villages nearby, or even in Tyre (which the Arabs pronounced "Tsur"), where Peter would be able to chat with the tradesmen, hear of the latest gossip from passing coasters who carried trade goods from the Grecian islands to Syria, and down the Palestinian coast to Egypt and Africa. There would always be a few of the strange-looking Dhows from the Nile anchored in Tyre, and some galleys from Rome, too, likely. Here, among these gentile people, they would be completely anonymous.

Peter didn't like the gentiles much; he had a natural aversion to them that was probably built into him from the dozens of sessions in the synagogues when he was a boy. Ancient Israel had mixed itself among the gentiles, Peter was taught, and God's judgments followed. Had they utterly exterminated the pagan tribes like the Hivites, Jebusites, Perizzites, Philistines (they were entering ancient Philistia even now) and others, they would have been spared the centuries-long conflicts that came.

That night they camped along a vineyard wall, paying the owner for use of his stable and for fodder. Tomorrow they would reach the sea.

The next two or three days were marvelous for Peter. They traveled little, and Jesus seemed content to allow them plenty of leisure time. Several times they waded out into the surf, and the few that knew how to swim enjoyed diving through the breakers and racing one another back and forth.

Peter was glad Jesus had allowed them this time for relaxation. Jesus came swimming alongside, the clear water, blue sky and foaming breakers dazzlingly brilliant in the bright sun, and suggested a race to Peter. It had been all Peter could do to stay even with Him, but it had been neck and neck until they tired and then Jesus, laughing with the joy of flailing away at the waves, turned toward shore and He and Peter ran splashing through the shallower surf to lie in the sun and let the beads of moisture slowly dry on their skin, feeling the stickiness that came with the tiny rings of whitish salt that remained where each droplet dried. Peter saw that Jesus had fallen asleep, and wondered if his own beard were crusted with sand and salty brine like Jesus' was.

Later they all washed themselves free of the saltwater in a creek that came tumbling along through the rocks to form brackish pools in the dunes. It was a memorable night, for two of them had tried their luck with hand lines while wading in the surf, and they had caught five large fish, bluish-gray in color, that could be seen chasing small fish through the shallows. Peter had seen the type before at a fishmonger's shed down in Joppa, and they proved delicious eating. They scooped out a hollow in the sand near the creek, lined it with rocks, and then, after cleaning the fish, lined their bodies with herbs, wrapped them in large grape leaves wet from the creek, and covered them over with a layer of clean sand. They started a fire over the top of the fish, and, after it had burnt down to glowing coals, scraped the ashes away, took out the fish from their thick wrappings to find them thoroughly baked. The flesh fell easily away from the bones and had a succulent moist and tender flavor. The fish, together with dried fruit, fresh berries and a dessert of grapes followed by a sip of wine from the wineskins, made a memorable meal.

Peter had enjoyed that day and evening meal immensely. It was fun to lean back and enjoy some songs together that evening, listening to the occasional stamping of their animals' feet, the distant sound of the surf, and talking into the late hours over a dwindling camp fire.

Peter wondered if Jesus' shoulders and back were as warm as his own. Peter knew he had been accustomed to the sun, but it had been many months now since he had labored on his boat for days on end, stripped to the waist, or even entirely naked, and he noted how Jesus' back and shoulders didn't appear even as accustomed to the sun's rays as Peter's own.

They packed up and moved further north along the coast the next day and found lodgings in a small village. It was here their delightful vacation came to an abrupt end.

A woman, one of the dark Canaanitish people who lived in the Phoenician shore, sidled up to Simon the Canaanite and began questioning him when she grew curious about the group of men with their packs and animals, and without any women or children along. She knew where they came from just by looking at the striping on their robes.

It turned out she had heard many of the stories about this "Jesus of Nazareth" and His miracles from some Syrian traders who had been present in some of the large Galilean cities who had seen some of Jesus' miracles.

She had been there yesterday, and now here she was again! Pestering Simon and the others, she asked, "Which one is Jesus? Who is He? Where is this 'Jesus of Nazareth?' I've got a daughter terribly afflicted by a demon. Could He come and heal her?"

On this occasion Peter saw what was happening: The woman had approached Simon, Judas, Matthew and two of the others as they were inspecting some fruits in a shop, and Peter urged Jesus, James and John to move on ahead in the hopes the woman wouldn't spot Jesus and cause some public disturbance.

The last thing Peter wanted right now was another riotous crowd scene. He was still shaken from their loss of so many disciples; still concerned about the attitudes of disappointment in some, and hoped they could extend their stay along this pleasant coast for at least a few more days.

Repeatedly some of them had tried to send the woman away.

Peter thought he'd better inform the Lord about it, and so brought up the statement Jesus had made about not going into gentile areas, and that He was sent only to the "lost sheep of the House of Israel."

Peter said, "Let's send her away, Lord, because she is whining along after us continually, and is beginning to cause a good deal of public notice!"

Jesus agreed, "That's right, I wasn't sent but to the lost sheep of the House of Israel," He said.

But the woman had apparently caught some of the men's glances too many times, for here she came straight toward them. She looked at Jesus, fell down on her knees and grabbed Him by the ankles, sobbing out, "Lord, help me! Help me!"

Jesus looked down at her but decided not to respond, and said nothing.

The woman continued pleading, persisting in hanging on to Jesus' feet even though He made as if to leave. Peter was about to seize her by the shoulders and lift her up when Jesus warned him with a glance and said to the woman, "It is not fit to take the children's meat and cast it to the dogs; the children must first be filled!"

She answered, "Yes, Lord, that's true, but still the dogs eat of the crumbs that fall from the children's table!"

Surprised by this humble attitude, Jesus quickly answered the woman, "Lady, you have *great faith*. It will be done unto you exactly as you wish!"

He told the woman to go away to her home, that her daughter would be healed.

Sure enough, the woman went back to her house and found her daughter stretched out upon the bed, just as normal as ever, with the demon gone!

Peter had pled with Jesus to leave at once, to head back to their camp of the other night and avoid any noisy mobs, but Jesus said no and seemed content to wait for the woman's return.

Surely nothing could be gained by remaining here any further. Of what use could these gentiles be, Peter wondered? Even if Jesus managed to impress them by the thousands with His signs and wonders, would they be of any real use when the revolution occurred?

They would never be accepted in Jerusalem—the Jews would reject them outright—and if Jesus wanted to impress the Syrians, then the place to do it was Damascus, or some of the larger cities, not here in the villages of the seacoast.

But Peter's arguments fell on deaf ears and, sure enough, here came an excited crowd, with the woman in the van, excitedly rolling her eyes, gesticulating, crying out aloud and pointing to Jesus and the others, saying, ''There they are—there He is—didn't I tell you? That's the famous Healer, the Jesus from Nazareth, the One they say is the Messiah!''

Peter knew the vacation was over.

Though it took a time to disengage themselves from the curious townsfolk, they finally managed to gain the main road again and so headed back down toward Tyre, passing through its narrow streets and crowded warehouse area, stopped briefly in Sidon and continued back toward Galilee.

Surely they hadn't come this arduous distance just for the sake of this single event? Peter wondered. They discussed it among themselves on the trip back to Galilee, which was accomplished much more rapidly than their journey here.

They went further south, along the coast, before turning eastward to cross the hills, so arriving in the mountains near Galilee not far from the place where Jesus had delivered His Sermon on the Mount.

Though he was still mystified by many of Jesus' seeming moods, or some of the things He said, he was learning how Jesus never went out of His way to fit the mold of other people, acting as they expected Him to act, saying things the way they wanted them said, satisfying their vanity and pride by being exactly the kind of ''Messiah'' they expected!

Peter knew there were those who would have been outraged when Jesus first ignored, and then turned down, the Canaanitish woman's tearful requests; they would have surely stumbled at His strong statement about it not being fitting that the children's meat should be ''cast to the dogs.'' Some wanted Jesus to go about emptying grave- yards, exhausting Himself by running about the country- side on a fast horse, healing every single sick person within hundreds of miles.

Some were positive Jesus wanted nothing so badly as to spend time with them in their own homes, and to listen to their problems and their personal ideas and philosophies. Peter was learning more and more about human nature, and about vanity, and ego.

He was even learning a little about his own, hopefully.

No, Jesus just didn't fit the mold.

He never yet tried to make a show of a miracle, Peter knew, unless it was a completely private show to the disciples themselves, like that dumbfounding time of walking on water, or privately raising Jairus' daughter from the dead!

If it hadn't been for those powerful miracles, Peter knew several of the twelve would have gone away when the whole group of others left, just because they were angry when Jesus wouldn't start the revolution then, and had said what He did about His body being "bread from heaven" and that they had to eat of His flesh, and (Peter winced a little) "drink His blood."

Whatever He meant by this, Peter knew He would make it clear in time.

Meanwhile, Peter could ponder whether this seeming aloofness of Jesus wasn't hurting the cause.

Even though He might have not gone out of His way here and there to rush off and perform some special miracle for someone, Peter knew Jesus could always be depended upon to show great compassion when families were especially grieved with terrible personal problems, sickness, deformities, or the like.

The next morning a family brought to Him their son, who was both deaf and dumb.

They besought Jesus to lay His hands upon him. But, seeing the bewildered look in the boy's face, that he did not understand the excitement of his parents and the crowd, Jesus decided to take him aside privately. When they reached a place where the two of them could be alone, Jesus, knowing He needed to signal to the deaf lad what He was about to do, looked meaningfully into his eyes, put

His fingers deeply into the boy's ears, signaling that He was going to open them. Then, nodding to the boy he should do likewise, Jesus turned to one side and spat, touching the tip of his tongue.

The boy nodded he understood, and so, looking up to heaven, Jesus sighed deeply, and, placing His fingers once more in the boy's ears, said, *"Ephphatha!* Be opened!"

Instantly the boy's ears were opened, and the boy, turning to the side, spat out an object which had become dislodged in his mouth (tissue that had prevented his tongue from moving as freely as it should), and the boy was able to speak!

Peter knew Jesus had instructed the boy and his parents, as He returned him to them, that they should tell no one about it.

The young lad was eagerly and vociferously thanking Jesus, shaking His hand, babbling out his deepest gratitude with his startled ears hearing the sound of his own voice, forming the words with difficulty, but tearfully thanking Jesus over and over again! The sounds he made were like strange monotones, poorly formed, and loud, remarkably loud.

Peter was moved to hear Jesus help the boy by teaching him his first few words, and how to form the sounds.

Jesus spoke to the boy, slowly forming the words by exaggerating the motions of lip and tongue, and helping the boy understand how to form the same sounds. He pointed upward, and spoke God's name and said, "Your Father which is in heaven has made you hear."

The parents were overwhelmed with tearful gratitude, and they showed it effusively. Again Peter heard Jesus tell them to be thankful toward God, and as a family, but not to noise this event abroad. He told them to rejoice quietly, and to enjoy teaching their son to use his new powers of hearing and speech, offering any gifts they were of a mind to, but to avoid spreading word of the miracle, and keeping Jesus' identity private.

Peter wondered if they were even listening very carefully, what with repeatedly hugging and embracing their son, pointing to themselves, and having him say "father" and "mother," and learning to pronounce his own name. At each successful sound they would all laugh and cry anew, and the hugging and embracing would start all over again.

Nevertheless, the more He would tell people not to spread word of His compassionate miracles abroad, the more they published it.

As a result, great crowds once again began following after Jesus in this area of the Decapolis to which they had arrived, bringing their lame, blind, dumb, maimed and deformed, as well as many others of various diseases and afflictions.

Jesus, having great compassion on them, healed them all. The crowd that had assembled out here in the countryside were amazed when they saw people who were well known in their own communities as dumb, and who could not talk, now speaking sensibly; when they saw those who had been maimed in terrible accidents made whole; when they saw the formerly crippled actually walking; when they saw the town blind people seeing and praising God because of their newfound eyesight, they lifted up their voices in prayer and thanksgiving and glorified the God of Israel!

After three days of this, Jesus said, "I have compassion on this huge crowd because they have been here now for three long days and most of them have not had a bite to eat in that time. I can't send them away fasting, for many of them simply will not make it all the way back to their homes; they have come from so far."

Peter was to wish he had bitten his tongue, later, for having said, "How can we possibly be able to feed all of these people here in this place out in the country?"

He asked, "How many loaves have you?" And someone answered, "Seven." Then, ascertaining they also had a few small fish with them, He commanded the multitude to sit down on the ground and took the seven loaves and the fish, gave thanks and began to break as He had once before in an area not too distant from this place. He handed the food to His disciples, who passed it out among the thousands of people.

Was He going crazy? Peter wondered. He couldn't believe his own eyes! They would no sooner reach into the basket and bring out a smoked fish and hand it to an eager pair of hands than it appeared there were more fish in the basket than when they began!

With the memory of that other time not so very long ago, and not far from here, Peter wondered whether a similar event would be repeated. Would this vast crowd of several thousand try to hoist the Lord on their shoulders and forcibly carry Him away to Jerusalem and make Him king?

The hands were reaching, grasping, eagerly seizing each morsel of smoked fish the disciples would dig out of that basket. Peter wondered whether some in the crowd, seeing the size of the basket and the throngs of hundreds reaching out for food, wouldn't begin to wonder when the basket was not empty long before it reached them.

Strange how one could never become accustomed to miracles! Each marvelous wonder Jesus accomplished left Peter as amazed and incredulous as before. He could never quite grow nonchalant about some strange phenomenon like this, and, since the miraculous appearance of seemingly limitless food in the bottom of a basket had happened once before, Peter was particularly curious.

He wanted to see somehow with his own eyes the fish materializing out of thin air. But the faster he would try to empty the basket the more fish seemed to remain. Once he decided to try to turn the basket over and empty it completely. All he succeeded in doing was spilling about two dozen fish all over the laps of people seated in their group—to angry cries of dismay!

"Hold it—don't spill it all over the ground. You're wasting precious food!" they complained.

Peter turned the basket aright, and to his amazement it was as full as before!

His scalp prickled and gooseflesh arose along his spine. He was witnessing another of the fabulous miracles Jesus could work, right before his very startled eyes!

Peter found himself wondering whether Jesus was

creating new food right out of thin air or whether the existing food was dividing in some way. It almost hurt his head to think about it, but he couldn't deny what his own eyes told him.

He changes water into wine, Peter thought, raises the dead, heals leprosy, deafness and blindness; He walks on the water and calms even the winds and waves. And now, for the second time, He is producing food where there was none! Truly He is the *very Son of God!* Only the creative powers of the universe could do this. Only the same power that had brought the whole world and all that is upon it into being could do what Peter had witnessed Jesus doing!

Jesus was seated, teaching the crowd, which had quieted with the business of devouring their impromptu snack of smoked fish and bread. The food caused an almost unbearable thirst, and several were going back and forth to the stream that coursed its way over the rocks, forming several small pools as it dropped toward the lake.

This crowd proved far less excitable than the other, and Jesus was telling of some great sign He would give.

What was this?

Peter listened to Jesus speaking about the "Son of Man shall be in the heart of the earth" just like Jonah was exactly three days and three nights in the belly of the great fish. He seemed to be precisely specific about the time period. Peter heard Him say it very carefully, and watched Matthew copy it down.

But why?

Where was this place that He called "the heart of the earth"?

Would He go back into the wilderness, hiding out for several days, and then emerge as King?

Peter knew the time of Jonah's near torture in the belly of the great fish was viewed as a punishment from God of sorts, the final sign from the Creator that Jonah was expected to preach to Nineveh as God had commanded. Did Jesus need to undergo yet some further test?

Those who were arguing with Jesus were mumbling among themselves about this strange "sign" He said He would leave.

No doubt the fact that some of the Pharisees were present here contributed to the comparative solemnity of this group, as opposed to the other group a time back which had wanted to seize Jesus bodily and propel Him to Jerusalem.

But in due time the episode was over, and Jesus signaled to Peter that it was time to go back and retrieve the boat from the watcher and leave the area.

They gradually took their leave, with dozens crowding close to thank the disciples for the food, or to try to hear Jesus' words more carefully. Andrew went on ahead to prepare the boat for an immediate departure. They would be a little crowded this time, for they had brought only the one boat across with them.

The trail narrowed to a deep defile leading along the creek bed, making it necessary to either jump across or use the steppingstones that were here and there. They had to cross the creek several times on their descent to the narrow plain of the coast. The steepness of the trail and the narrowness of the path shook off all but the hardiest of those in the crowd who seemed determined to follow, and Peter could see several distant figures standing on the brink, waving, as Jesus and the others clambered over the coaming into the boat.

Peter took the tiller, and, as they poled free of the shore, Andrew and Simon the Canaanite, with help from James and Thaddeus, unfurled the sail.

Soon they were lying over to a mild breeze and clipping along at a good four knots or so, and Peter could begin to appreciate the strange events of these past hours in retrospect. He had been so busy passing out food he had taken none himself. Now he chided himself for it for he had intended to taste of the food to see if there was any difference in the new food Jesus had created and other fare they had carried with them.

The thought of food made his stomach rumble, and Peter called out to John about it. A quick survey discovered they had but one measly loaf of bread between them!

They were sadly talking about it and contemplating several more hours without food when Jesus said, ''Take heed, and beware of the leaven of the Pharisees and Sadducees!''

Peter and the disciples began to reason among themselves, saying, ''He must be commenting about the fact that we have no bread.'' But Jesus, perceiving their thoughts, said, ''Oh, you of little faith, why is it you reason among yourselves that we have no bread?'' (In Jesus' thoughts it was utterly incongruous for His disciples to worry about the fact that this tiny group of twelve had no bread when only hours before they had, for the second time, passed out *tons* of it to a crowd of many thousands, taking up sufficient baskets full of leftovers that would have adequately provided for their current journey!) He said, ''Don't you remember the seven loaves for the four thousand, and how many baskets you took up?

''How is it you don't understand that I wasn't talking to you about bread?'' I was saying, 'Beware of the leaven of the Pharisees and the Sadducees.' ''

He even asked the disciples, ''When I broke those five loaves among the five thousand, how many baskets did you take up?'' They answered, ''Twelve!''

''And when I broke the seven loaves among the four thousand, how many baskets full of broken pieces did you take up?''

And they answered, ''Seven.'' And He said, ''How is it you still do not understand?''

They finally got the point. He was urging them to beware of the *teachings* of the Pharisees and Sadducees!

Peter got it. His mother had explained to him as a boy why they left that lump of dough outside, covered with a fine cloth to keep the insects away, or left it on a fine spring morning on a shelf in the open window of the cooking area.

She said when the air got to it after a couple of days the bread would rise when cooked. But if she ground the meal and cooked it immediately it was always flat. Peter had listened to the rabbi explain about the ''bread of haste'' their forefathers had eaten on that ''night to be much remembered'' when they had been thrust out of Egypt. There hadn't been time, then, to let their dough sit so the leaven could work through it.

No one had ever seen leaven, but they knew how it worked. Something in the air caused the dough to swell gradually, and when it was baked it filled with tiny air bubbles, making the bread lighter, softer and easier to eat. The women would save out a portion of their leavened dough and mix it in with the fresh mixed batch, for they had learned centuries ago that this hastened the process, and the new batch didn't even have to sit outside or in the window all night.

Peter mused over Jesus' example. The leaven was insidious, secretive, hidden and invisible. Yet it completely changed the character of the dough. Further, it caused the baked bread to become ''puffed up,'' and the analogy to Pharisaical pomposity and self-righteousness was obvious.

The one thing Jesus seemed to detest more than any other was hypocrisy.

Pretense, deception, posturing and public poses of goodness to conceal a murderous spirit of hatred frequently caused Him to speak with indignation and anger—a biting edge to His words that cracked like a wagonmaster's whip and that made even the disciples sit up and take notice, and they were accustomed to His speech.

The ''leaven'' of the Pharisees must mean the self-righteous hypocrisy of the group—their personal pomposity and vanity and their careful attention to legalistic trivia without any genuine feelings of empathy, love and consideration for their fellows.

Finally they arrived at Bethsaida, and they had no sooner come back to Peter's hometown when a group of friends brought a blind man before Jesus, beseeching Him to touch him and heal him. Jesus looked at the man, seeing the deformed eyes, the dull, whitish orbs, covered with a film of dust—hopelessly opaque—and blind.

Jesus was filled with compassion for the man. But, because He knew very few would understand what He was about to do, He decided to lead the blind man by the hand, out of the village of Bethsaida, and attempted to find a private place alone, telling the others not to follow. He took the man by the elbow and began to guide him over steps and other obstacles and up a steep path until they found a place away from the crowds. Finally Jesus indicated the man was to stop by pressure on the man's arm, and, turning to him, Jesus deliberately told him what He was about to do. Since there was no water or other fluid around, Jesus took saliva from His mouth, gently applied it to the man's sightless, dust-filled eyes, and asked the man, "Do you see anything yet?"

The man looked, and, seeing some people walking at a distance, said, "Yes, I believe I see men, but it almost looks like they are trees walking!"

For the second time Jesus applied saliva, reached up and touched the man's eyes gently, and this time the man's eyesight was fully restored!

The man began to babble his profuse thanks, praising Jesus and thanking God. Jesus said, "Go on back now to your own home, and be careful not to return even through Bethsaida, which we have just left. I don't want anyone else to know about this just yet." The man, overcome with emotion, grasped Jesus' hand and arm, looking directly into His eyes with his newfound eyesight, and thanked Him emotionally, with tears, assuring Him he would do as He had said.

# XIII

It was a welcome respite to remain in Bethsaida for a few days, and Peter even found time to help aging Jona with his nets and to see to the stepping of a new mast. The other had been put to considerable strain in the storms of not so long ago, and Jona had pointed out a split in the base, in the bilge against the keel.

It was not an easy operation to rig block and tackle and pull the old mast out and then to lower the new one in and secure it, but Peter enjoyed the hard, sweaty labor and enjoyed being around the familiar sights of home.

In the evenings he fascinated Beth and the children with tales of their recent trips and Jesus' miracles. The children wanted to know over and over again about the time when Peter tried to walk on the water, and, eyes wide and mouths open, asked him how it felt when he first took a few steps.

The next morning Peter laughed so hard he had to sit down after he watched his son step down from the jetty, pause for a long time, stare out at the water and then step into the lake straight over his head! The boy had come up thrashing around, grasped the jetty, and, hauling himself out again, sat dejectedly contemplating the spreading pool of water around him and his sodden clothes.

But the brief respite was soon over, for Jesus told Peter that same day He wanted to go into some of the villages around Caesarea Philippi.

Beth was used to their comings and goings now, and

went about the business of helping the two Marys ready their clothing and pack with quiet efficiency.

They covered almost twenty miles in the first day and nearly as many the next. They took the river route north of Bethsaida along the Jordan, passing opposite Chorazin, and finally turned up the valley that led to the foothills of the Iturean Mountains. This was part of the Tetrarchy of Philip, and the countryside was spectacular with the snow-clad heights of Hermon in the distance.

A conversation had developed about some of the fantastic stories people were spreading about Jesus, about who they thought He was, and He no doubt overheard.

As they doubled back and forth along the steep hillside, gaining elevation, they paused for a time for a rest, and Jesus asked several of them, "And whom do they say I, the Son of Man, really am?"

"Well," said Simon the Canaanite, "some of them claim You're Jeremiah, Isaiah, Elijah or one of the other prophets."

Several others added names they had heard, and the men were chuckling over the absurdities of some of them when Jesus said, "And who do *you* say that I am?"

Several looked down, or at each other, and they all hesitated.

But not Peter. He looked right at Jesus and said, "You are the Christ, the Son of the Living God!"

Jesus, pleased with Peter's answer, said, "Blessed are you, Simon the son of Jona, for flesh and blood have not revealed this to you but my Father, who is in heaven. And I will tell you this. You are *Petros*" (using the Greek language, meaning a small stone, or a pebble) "but upon this *Petra*," He said, gesturing first to Himself, and then to all the others, I will build my *Ekklezia!*"

Peter knew why Jesus had used the different word, *Petra,* for a large *rock.* He had heard the readers in the synagogue in Bethsaida often enough referring to the Messiah that was to come as the ROCK and had heard tales of the Stone upon which Jacob had laid his head when he had visions of heaven. He had heard of references in David's Psalms too about a *rock* that would be like a craggy cliff, a secure bastion or hiding place for God's people.

It was thrilling to Peter to be included as a part of the foundation of the new government, and more than just a part—an important part, one of the original twelve who had been right at Jesus' side continually.

Peter liked the sound of the name Jesus had given him: *Petros,* or a stone. Now, hearing Jesus use for the first time a similar name for Himself, *Petra,* or a craggy *rock,* Peter was touched at the similarity.

Jesus was continuing, speaking to all, "And the gates of the grave will not prevail against it, and I will give to you the keys to the Kingdom of Heaven, and whatsoever you shall bind on earth will be bound in heaven, and whatever you loose on earth shall be loosed in heaven!"

Peter was exhilarated at His words.

The Master was pleased at Peter's answer and was making one of His most profound declarations about their coming government, about His rule which was to begin. Peter would obviously have a major part in it, right there beside Jesus in some large capacity. They all would!

Peter took the statement about "the gates of the grave" to be a near guarantee of immunity against death! Jesus had the very power over the grave. "The gates of the grave will never prevail against it . . ." Jesus had said.

Hadn't Peter witnessed Jesus raise Jairus' twelve-year-old daughter with his own eyes? Hadn't Peter seen dozens upon dozens of miraculous healings. And hadn't he himself been gratefully pleased and surprised when he had called upon Jesus' name in some sick persons' behalf and seen them immediately healed?

Jesus must mean that He and the disciples would be given supernatural protection; that their plans would succeed where so many others had failed, that this coming revolution would sweep throughout Trachonitis, Galilee, Judea, Decapolis, the Tetrarchy of Philip and far, far beyond!

Now He was warning them again, "It's good that *you* know who I am, that I am the very Christ, but keep it to yourselves. Most especially don't argue with others about Me; don't try to *convince* anyone I am the Christ; My time is not yet come . . .''

Peter shook his head in the affirmative. So it wouldn't be now; and that probably meant the time would not be ripe again until the coming spring when tens of thousands would be in Jerusalem for the Passover. It was obvious they would lack support if anything happened now.

But wait. What was this?

Jesus was saying, "I am going to have to suffer many terrible things: indignities and tortures . . . The ones behind it will be the chief priests and the Pharisees—I will be delivered into their hands to be killed. But, after the third day, I will rise from the dead . . .''

Peter's ears scarcely heard the statements about "rising from the dead" for his shock at hearing of an impending arrest, cruel tortures and death.

Leaping to his feet, Peter seized Jesus by both shoulders and, overcome with outrage and emotion, said, *"Never,* Lord! I won't let them take You! Don't *say* such things! I'll protect You. Nothing like that will ever happen to You!''

Jesus stood looking at Peter, and, seeing the rest of the disciples' startled looks, rebuked him, saying, "Get thee behind Me, Satan! You are a stumblingblock to Me, and you savor not the things of God, but the things of men.''

Peter was near tears with shock and shame.

Jesus said to the others, "Come over here and listen!'' When they had gathered around more closely, He said, "If any man will come after Me, then he must deny himself and take up his cross daily and follow Me!

"For whoever would seek to save his physical life will lose it. And whoever would lose his life for My sake and the sake of the gospel shall save it.

"What profit is it to a man even if he gain rulership over the whole world and yet forfeit his eternal life? What will a man give in exchange for his life, not only his life now but his life forever?''

Jesus said, looking at Peter again, "And I will tell you this! Whoever it is that is ashamed of Me and My words in this adulterous and sinful generation, the Son of

Man shall also be ashamed of him when He comes in the glory of the Father and with His holy angels!

"Truly I tell you," He continued. "There are some here of you who are standing by who will in no wise taste of death until they actually *see* the Kingdom of God with power, and the Son of Man coming in the full regalia of His kingdom!"

Some six to eight days later, Jesus took Peter, James and John and walked for two days until they came to the heights of Hermon. Here their eyes could see a limitless vista in all directions.

It was here that one of the most striking events of Peter's life took place. It was here he understood Jesus' words about seeing the kingdom in advance.

While Peter, James and John were dozing, they seemed to overhear voices and looked around to see a bright light shining and discovered men talking. As they listened, they heard a discussion of Jesus' impending death and events which would transpire in Jerusalem.

A bright cloud suddenly overshadowed them and a voice came out of the cloud which said, "This is My beloved Son in whom I am well pleased; My chosen; listen to Him!" After the booming voice came out of the cloud, the disciples got on their knees, with their hands and faces to the ground, shaking with fright.

They had to shield their eyes from Jesus for it appeared His garment was shining with an iridescent hue. He was speaking to two other persons whom He called by name!

He said *"Moses"* and *"Elijah"*! They too were wearing garments which appeared to be shimmering and dazzling white, and even the very skin of Jesus was altered so that it appeared translucent.

Jesus came to the three disciples and, touching them on the shoulder, said: "Come on, get up, and don't be afraid any more."

They reluctantly got up, looking around in fear, and saw only Jesus standing there alone.

Now Peter began to understand what Jesus had meant when He had said earlier that there "be some of you standing here who shall in no wise taste of death until you see the Son of Man coming in His kingdom!'' They had *seen a vision* of that kingdom, seen Jesus as if He were no longer just human, but divine!

It was while they were winding their way along the narrow mountain trails on their return that they stopped for a rest and Jesus told them, ''Be sure you don't tell anyone at all about this vision until after I have risen from the dead!''

They all nodded assent, but as they were talking during the remaining days they continually began to comment about just what Jesus could mean ''rising from the dead.''

Peter felt the trip and the vision were aimed especially at him; he still felt like he was in disfavor because of his emotional outburst a few days earlier when he had grabbed Jesus and sounded like he thought he was captain of the guard or something. Nevertheless, Peter was deeply affected by the scene.

When they rejoined the disciples, it was to find a large crowd gathered about with some of the scribes questioning them, attempting to trap them in their words.

When the multitude saw Jesus and His three disciples returning, they ran to meet Him. Jesus asked, ''What questions are you bringing to them?''

One of the crowd said, ''Master, I brought unto You my son who has a dumb spirit; he is a lunatic and suffers epilepsy, suffering grievously, because whenever the demon grabs him it dashes him to the ground, throws him often into the fire or the water, and he froths at the mouth and grinds his teeth, and he looks like he may be dying!

''I told all of this to Your disciples, begging them to cast it out, but they were not able!''

Jesus, looking increduously at the disciples, said, ''Oh, faithless generation, how long will I be with you? How long shall I bear with you and endure your faithlessness? Bring him here to Me!''

Then they brought the man, and when the demon saw Jesus he immediately threw the man to the ground, where he wallowed in an agony, grinding his teeth, chewing his tongue and foaming at the mouth.

Jesus asked the father, "How long has he been like this? When did this thing come upon him?"

And the father said, "From the time he was a little baby. And often the demon would cast him into the fire so he would be burned, or into the waters to destroy him by drowning! But if You can do anything please have compassion upon us and help us!"

Jesus said, *"If you can* — listen! *All things* are possible to him that *believes!"*

The father cried out in anguish and said, "Lord, I believe. *Help me with my unbelief!"* When Jesus saw that a large crowd was collecting, running to see what was happening with the man wallowing on the ground, He rebuked the unclean spirit in a firm voice, "You dumb and deaf spirit, I command you to come out of him and enter no more into him!"

With a loud shriek and a last spasm, the young man's muscles quieted and he became as if dead. The crowd began to murmur that perhaps the boy was in fact dead, but Jesus, stooping, took him by the hand and raised him up.

The boy gained his feet and looked around. His parents spoke to him and found he was in a normal mind!

Some of the crowd began to once again accuse that He "casts out demons by the prince of demons, Beelzebub," but Jesus and His disciples went back into His house at Capernaum.

When they were alone, the disciples asked Him privately, "Why could not we cast it out?" He said, "Because of your little faith!

"This kind does not come out but by prayer and fasting! If you would pray and fast, then everything will be possible to you!

"I tell you, if you have faith like a grain of mustard seed—one of the tiniest of seeds, which eventually becomes one of the largest of herbs—you will be able to say unto a mountain, 'Remove hence to yonder place,' and it will obey you, because *nothing* will be impossibe to you!"

Peter couldn't help being a little smug about the rebuke given to the others.

As they dispersed the crowd, and took their leave of the tearful, voluble family who embraced Jesus and stammered out their thanks, Peter turned to Andrew and said, "When the cat's away the mice will play."

"What do you mean?" Andrew whispered back.

"I mean, they must have been whiling away the time and not paying attention to their duty," Peter confided. "Did me good to see someone else get a public chewing out for a change," he said, a little unfairly.

"But they *tried* to cast out that demon . . ."

"Yes, *tried,* but failed!" Peter cut in. "If they had been really fired up the way they were on the evangelistic trip, they would have succeeded."

"Well . . . yes, I suppose so," Andrew agreed. "But, remember, Jesus said something about *'this kind'* of demon. Maybe it was a more tenacious spirit, one that had more power, or something."

"But they were powerless," Peter said, unwilling to miss savoring a moment of smugness. "It's only when they have Jesus' constant example before them — watching Him refuse meals, seeing how He is missing from the bedroll in the mornings and finding Him coming back with His forehead red from knuckling it during prayer — that they pay attention to their duty and do likewise. It's no wonder Jesus chose just me, James and John — oh, sorry, brother, I didn't mean . . ."

"It's all right, Peter," his brother said. "I think you're right. When Jesus isn't continually after us, teaching us, correcting us and setting His example before us, I know we let down."

To mollify him, Peter patronized, "Well, I probably couldn't have cast him out either," but privately he wondered. He liked to think the demon would have obeyed him, just as others had. But Peter hadn't really been fasting much, and hadn't prayed as much as he should. Hadn't he and the others fallen asleep back there on the mountain when Jesus was praying so long and hard, and then had been transfigured before them?

He decided to let the matter drop. He had probably hurt Andrew's feelings a little, and felt like a fool for acting superior.

They continued to the house in Capernaum without further talk, and the next morning Peter was just finishing his call of nature in the privy in the rear when he heard Joanna calling him from the kitchen.

A few moments later he intercepted her just before she climbed to the sleeping quarters, still calling his name.

"What is it?"

"Oh, Simon—I mean Peter," she said. "There are three officials at the door who claim they are tax collectors. I can't find Jesus, so I told them you were here . . ."

"I'll go see," he said, and turned toward the entry.

He stepped outside to confront an angular, tall official, a Sadducee, by his dress, who wore a leathern hat with its official emblem of the temple upon it.

"Does your Master pay the drachma?" the tall one demanded imperiously.

His two cohorts looked up at Peter, one with writing materials and a large collection bag at his side with its many pockets and bulges. They were smiling, faintly, as if they expected Peter to say Jesus would refuse to pay the temple tax that they heard would be collected throughout the provinces.

A small crowd was beginning to gather, for the collectors had stopped at other homes in the street and many knew Jesus' house would be visited. Just as Peter said, "Yes," he felt a presence behind him and, turning, saw it was Jesus and some of the others.

Jesus had apparently let Himself in the back, probably returning from another solitary trip to the mountain, and now He was here.

"What do you think, Simon?" Jesus asked, shouldering to the front and speaking loudly enough for the growing crowd to hear. " . . . The kings of the world—from whom do they exact their taxes and tribute? From their own family, their sons, or from strangers?"

Peter thought only a moment before answering, "Why, from strangers!"

"Therefore, the sons must be free!" Jesus said loudly. "But, lest we give them an occasion against us, go out into the lake, cast a hook and take up the first fish you catch . . .''

Peter thought he must be hearing things. What?

"Look in his mouth," Jesus continued, impossibly, "and there you will find a shekel. That you can take and give it to them for both you and Me, a half-shekel from each of us!"

"A *fish?* Go to the lake and *fish?*" Peter blurted out.

But Jesus insisted, and so, wondering what strange sign Jesus had in mind, Peter grabbed up his fisherman's boots and set out.

Was there some hidden meaning Jesus intended? Was this like a warning from Jonah, a veiled reference to how he was vomited up out of the great fish to carry God's warning to Nineveh? Was it a bizarre method of showing contempt for the heavy tax burdens imposed upon the people by likening it to something a fish would throw up?

"No, Jesus wouldn't do that," Peter mused. Probably, He's only showing them that as citizens of our own country we should be paying taxes to *no* one."

Peter poled away from shore, engrossed in his thoughts. Then, fixing cut bait to a weighted hand line, cast it past the bow and let it settle. Soon the line began moving away from the boat. Peter took up the slack until he could feel faint motion throbbing up the line and, with a powerful motion, set the hook. He pulled the struggling fish in. Excitedly he disengaged the hook from the two pound fish and, seizing it by the lower jaw, opened its mouth and looked in. Incredible! There, almost swallowed, but with its edge protruding from the fish's throat, was a shiny coin! Of course, Peter knew he had caught fish on shiny objects before, knew they would grab at such objects allowed to wobble through the water, so he reasoned some unfortunate soul had dropped the coin from a dock, or from a boat, and the fish had struck at it as it danced toward the bottom. That was logical enough, but *how could Jesus have known all that?* And *how could I have caught this exact fish?*"

Peter was amazed all over again. Surely Jesus had the very powers of God Himself; could see, and know, *every-*

*thing.*

Peter returned to the house in Capernaum, displayed the coin to Jesus and then paid it into the tax collectors' hands. It was a curious event and one that would be retold often.

Jesus said He wanted to travel again to reach even more of the towns and cities of this whole Galilee, and so they left Capernaum and began traversing the countryside.

They moved at a fairly steady clip, stopping here and there in small towns where Jesus would preach to the people and heal their sick. The coneys were scurrying about, Peter saw, carrying seeds they gathered in cheek pouches for winter storage. The mornings were growing crisp with the hint of autumn, and the late summer showers came more frequently, with several days of thick overcast moving slowly along, the mists obscuring the taller mountain peaks and drifting through the evergreens along the ridges.

It seemed Jesus was on a schedule only He knew, driven to go to the smallest hamlet and even to reach scattered farmers and shepherds who were moving their flocks down from the summer ranges and heading them toward the sheepfolds and lower grazing grounds.

Camping along a tiny rivulet one evening, Peter took John with Him, dug into his pack and obtained a small net he used for seining fish. The mesh was only about a half inch wide, and he carried yards of it.

Gleaning his purpose, John began savoring the evening's meal.

"Noticed a flight a while ago," Peter said, beginning to climb.

"I know what you mean," John agreed, following behind him.

They neared the top of a low ridge, and Peter surveyed the terrain. Satisfied, he began descending to a notch in the ridge above a small pool formed in the rocks, where he saw the flutter of white wings now and then.

They arrived at the tree-studded notch, and Peter unraveled the net, handing the other end to John, who climbed to the opposite side.

They strung it just below the brow of the ridge, between two short pinions, and anchored it at the bottom with stones tied with short lengths of string.

Then they moved back into the trees and sat down to wait.

The little doves of the country used flyways to water in the evenings, their darting, erratic wingbeats making them appear like little gray-white leaves fluttering in a wind. They would speed up the valley on the other side, rising to the ridge from the grain fields below, and, cutting the top of the ridge with only feet to spare, zoom down the notch to land at the pond for water. Peter had spotted some of the early arrivals and wanted a good catch for supper.

They hadn't long to wait. The first small flock tumbled like chaff before the wind into the net. Some flew over it, and not a few, flapping their wings madly, managed to extricate themselves. But many were stuck fast, plunging their necks into the small mesh, the feathers then fanning out and blocking their attempts to pull themselves free.

Several times John and Peter would run to the net, disengage each bird, quickly pull its head off, hold the wildly flapping body toward the ground for proper bleeding and stuff it into their sacks.

By full dusk they took down the net and returned to camp.

It was a delicious meal they enjoyed that night, with breast of turtle dove broiled over an open fire.

The next morning they hit the trail toward a smallish village which could be seen below them, sending two of the disciples ahead to find lodgings, for Jesus wanted to sleep indoors tonight and spend the day teaching in the village.

When they reached the main trail from the mountain pathways they had followed, it was to encounter the two runners coming back with the news that there was not a single room to be had in the town.

About that time a youngish fellow came along the main road and loudly called to Peter, "Where is this Jesus of Nazareth I've been hearing about?"

He was impeccably dressed in clean, rather expensive clothing, carrying writer's materials and a leather packet slung over his shoulders.

Peter paused and allowed the man to catch up.

He shook hands and looked him over. A scribe, by the look of him, with soft hands and precise speech.

Peter thought he ought to introduce him to Jesus; there was no way the scribe could find which one He was in this crowd with so many dressed exactly alike and Jesus' regular features so indistinguishable from so many others', and, besides, Peter was impressed that a scribe would be sincerely seeking Jesus out. Usually they were in cahoots with the simpering Pharisees, and were a haughty, disdainful lot, managing to falsify records, misread documents and even alter inheritances and wills. Most people didn't trust them; they had heard too many stories about how the illiterate folk would be ripped off by the scribes who would read various official-looking documents to them posted in the public squares and marketplaces that would invariably cost the poor more money.

But when Peter pointed out Jesus the scribe ran directly to Him and said, "Master! I'm here to follow you wherever You go!"

Jesus looked at him, seeing the immaculate dress, the writer's equipment and the soft hands. Obviously the man was not accustomed to leaving his comfortable quarters very often. He was a scribe who worked indoors out of the sun and who slept in a comfortable bed every night.

Jesus had heard the word. They would probably be camping out again tonight.

He said, "Foxes have dens, and the birds of the heaven have nests, but the Son of Man has nowhere to lay his head."

Several others had arrived and one said, "Lord, I'll follow you, but let me go back home first and see to the burying of my father and then I'll catch up later."

Jesus said, "Let the dead bury their dead, but you go and publish abroad the news about the Kingdom of God!"

Another piped up and said, "I'll follow you too, Lord, but let me first run back home and say good-bye to everybody in the house.''

Jesus looked steadily at him and said, ''No man, having once put his hand to the plow and looking back, is fit for the Kingdom of God!''

Autumn leaves were a maze of earthy colors by the time they wound their way along the main caravan trail from the north back down to Bethsaida and Capernaum. The Feast of Trumpets was past, and it was nearing Atonement and the Feast of Tabernacles.

Peter was disgusted with Jesus' brothers, for no matter how many times he would tell them over and over again of the marvelous miracles he had seen with his own eyes, they wouldn't believe him.

Joses was particularly vehement.

''Why, then,'' he would argue, ''doesn't He do these miracles right out in the open where everyone can see them, if He can really do miracles, like you claim?''

James, Simon and Juda agreed, as did their sisters.

They were in Capernaum again, and this time the family had come to visit. Mary was sad to see the young men becoming so abrasive with Jesus. The argument took place at a family dinner with Jesus, Joses, Juda, the girls and James and John, Zebedee's sons, and Peter and Andrew present.

James was saying, ''Why don't You leave Galilee, Jesus, and go down to Jerusalem when the city will be teeming with thousands so all Your followers and the crowds can see Your works You are doing? It doesn't make any sense to do these things Peter claims You do in secret. No one who is claiming to be a king would do anything in secret, but would seek to become as famous as he could, to do everything openly.

'So, if You really can do all these things Peter claims,'' he finished, ''why don't You really manifest Yourself to the world?''

Jesus just smiled kindly at His brothers and family and said, ''Because My time has not yet come.''

He decided to add a gentle rebuke to His words and said, ''Your time is now; you're always ready to leap in and do whatever comes to mind, and for you that would appear right, because you are of this world and the world will not hate you. It can't hate you because you are a part of it. But Me it hates because I say to the world that its works are evil! You go ahead,'' He continued with a smile to gentle His words, and a kindly look to His mother, who was listening intently. ''You all go ahead to the Feast in Jerusalem, but I'm not going up there yet'' (they always spoke of Jerusalem as ''up,'' even though it was to the south of them, because of its lofty place atop the mountains) ''because My time is not yet fulfilled.''

The dinner came to a peaceful enough end, and it was very clear to the family He intended doing just as He said.

The brothers muttered about it, and to them it was proof Jesus was not really who He said He was. Hadn't they practically called Him a fraud? Hadn't they offered Him the opportunity to go to Jerusalem as a family and begin producing these miracles in front of thousands?

To them Jesus' demurrer was proof enough that He was embarrassed, that He doubted if anything striking would happen.

The next morning the others packed up and left, taking several asses and two camels, for they intended being away from home more than two weeks.

Jesus and His disciples remained behind.

Two days later Jesus sent several of the men as messengers ahead to act as pathfinders for them, to arrange lodgings in some of the towns in Samaria (the other Jews would be giving Samaria wide berth for they had nothing to do with them, and Jesus, by going through the region, intended traveling incognito, thus arriving at the Feast of Tabernacles unannounced). The messengers were to explain to the innkeepers that it would only be for one night at each place, and perhaps not the entire night at that.

They left, and when they had crossed the border and were approaching the first Samaritan village, their messengers met them with bad news.

''Master, I'm sorry, but when they found out You intend going up to Jerusalem to the Feast they became angry, knowing we are Jews and resenting the religion, and refused us any place to stay!''

Peter saw red.

This was ridiculous! They had covered over forty miles in barely a day and a half, and everyone was dusty, thirsty, hungry and half done in. Peter was of the firm conviction that this trip to Jerusalem, after such a long absence, would be the final time for the coup. There would be thousands there from all over the empire, from Crete, Cappadocia, Corinth and Rome.

They had seen several caravans bearing Jews from Syria and Asia headed down the coast route, and Peter knew most of the people Jesus had healed—the two big groups of four and five thousand He had fed, and many others—why, there would be at least twenty thousand people they had reached *personally* who would be there.

Elijah, standing on the top of his hill with the emissaries of wicked King Ahab burnt to cinders, flashed to mind.

He blurted out, "Lord, do You want us to bid *fire* to come down from heaven and *consume* those miserable Samaritans?"

Jesus turned and said, "You don't know what spirit you are of! The Son of Man did not come to *destroy* men's lives, but to *save* men's lives!

"We'll simply keep going. There are more villages ahead, and we can find a place to stay later."

Peter was embarrassed. He had allowed himself to get carried away with the more military aspects of their campaign. He so fervently wanted Jesus to show *force* that he had forgotten Jesus' attitude toward human suffering.

To Peter the Samaritan area would probably be one of the very first to be cleaned up. Deportation would be necessary, probably, to chase those heathen people away from their sacred "mountain" and put some good solid Jewish colonies in their place. He got indignant to think a stinking little Samaritan town (which should rejoice to even think that any self-respecting Jew would deign to remain overnight) would have the gall to send a party of this size away when it would mean such a financial boon.

But he simply shut his mouth, got back on the bony back of the big, swaybacked ass he was riding, and kept plodding along with the others.

The creature peeled back its lips, exposing long, yellowed teeth, and proceeded to peal out a wheezing hee-haw that echoed back from the sides of the rocky defile they were traversing. Peter's hand strayed to the hilt of his short sword, thinking to lay the flat of the blade alongside the offending beast's head, when Jesus turned around, looked first at Peter and then at the ass, and put His head back and laughed out loud! Peter colored, and then removed his hand and began roaring with laughter.

He got the message—and Jesus knew it.

The remainder of the trip was completed without incident worthy of John's or Matthew's notes; they went through Samaria, and thence by little-traveled trails, avoiding the crowds pouring into Judea, and went toward the city of Jerusalem.

They found an elderly land owner within an hour's easy ride of Jerusalem and, arranging provender and rudimentary lodgings, remained with him out of sight of the crowds for a few days.

Finally, in the middle of the Feast, Jesus decided to go straight into Jerusalem and show Himself openly in the temple.

Peter had reconnoitered the Feast several times, taking different disciples with him now and then. Judas seemed particularly anxious to spend a good deal of time in the city, haranguing the merchants and talking to friends he had known in the shops.

They received all the latest gossip.

The crowds were abuzz with talk about Jesus of Nazareth. One could hear snatches of conversation in the public places and in the temple. The Pharisees were continually asking, "Where is He?", wanting to find Him so they could trap Him into some alleged infraction and put Him in prison, and the crowds were speaking guardedly. Most said, "He's a good man!" but afraid to express it too openly because they feared the Jewish leadership.

Peter told Jesus all the latest and warned Him that the Jews wanted to have Him arrested. Peter was growing impatient again, quizzical about Jesus' plans. Was He going to wait until the Last Great Day and display Himself openly, performing some great and fabulous miracle, rally the crowds and proclaim Himself king? Peter hoped so with a growing impatience!

They had missed many an opportunity, and there could be no better time, surely, than now. Visitors were here from as far away as Rome, Jews from every part of Asia, from Cappadocia, Bithynia, Crete, Arabia, Africa, Egypt, Syria, Babylon—everywhere.

The Feast was always an exciting time, lacking the somber character of the Passover. It was a time of rejoicing, camping out in little "booths" or tiny "tabernacles" made of makeshift materials. Why, many of the people in the city moved up to the rooftops—the kids especially excited—and made temporary shelters out of palm fronds, boards, cloth, hides and other materials, sleeping out and eating atop their houses.

Those wealthy enough to have large courtyards moved into the court, and the surrounding countryside was colorful with the thousands of temporary dwellings that seemed to fill every space. Sanitation was always a problem, as was obtaining adequate water. Many a servant or wife grew angrily impatient at having to wait two hours or more at the well nearest them for water, and every creek site was taken up long since, with those downstream always complaining when some thoughtless character let his camel or ass stomp around in the water, sending clouds of mud downstream, befouling it for everyone else.

Peter was glad they were on the outskirts away from most of the hubbub and staying with an old friend of one of the disciples (Peter thought it was Thaddeus' father-in-law), who was blessed with a good spring behind the house and made a pittance from selling water.

They were camped in the ravine back of the house near the well, away from the road, enjoying the leisure, when Jesus told Peter to follow Him; He was going into the temple.

James, John and several others followed along, and it wasn't long before they were elbowing their way through the throngs that had gathered in Solomon's porch in the main temple area.

Jesus was recognized by the keeper of the scrolls, and several of the more moderate of the Pharisees, and it was a fairly simple matter for Him to be asked to take the chair for a teaching session.

As He began to teach, the crowd in His area began to swell, many excitedly running to fetch their friends and relatives.

"How can this character know anything, how can He be a scholar or know letters when it's obvious He never attended one of the major accredited schools?" some asked.

"What is He doing there?" said one plaintively, and another said, "Yeah, just who does He think He is?"

But Jesus raised His voice, hearing the murmuring, and said, "My teaching is *not Mine;* it's not My own invention, but His that sent Me! If any man is willing to accomplish His will, he will know about this teaching — whether it is from God or not—or whether I am just saying it out of My own conjecture. Anyone who speaks from his own personal authority is only seeking to aggrandize himself. But he that seeks to glorify Him that sent Him, that person is true and no unrighteousness will be found in him. Didn't Moses give you the law, and yet none of you is really obeying the law? Why are you seeking to kill Me?"

A roar went up from the crowd, and a leading Pharisee shouted out, "You must be demon possessed! Who seeks to kill You?"

"I accomplished one work and you are amazed! Yet Moses gave you circumcision—not that Moses invented it, but it came from the fathers—and so you circumcise a man child even if it is on the Sabbath day. If a man receives circumcision on the Sabbath, so you are careful not to break the law of Moses, are you right to be angry with Me because I made a man completely whole on the Sabbath? You need to judge righteous judgment, and not judge according to appearance!"

"Isn't that the One they're trying to kill?" asked an anonymous voice from the crowd.

"It sure is, and yet here He is speaking openly in the temple and no one is laying a hand on Him," said another. "Yeah. Do you suppose it's because the rulers really know this One *is* the Christ and that's why they're afraid?"

"No. Remember, when Christ comes we're not supposed to know where He'll come from, but everybody knows where this Man comes from," said another.

"You both know Me," cried Jesus aloud, "and you know where I come from, that I am not come of Myself, but He that sent Me is true, and you don't know Him! I know Him because I came from Him, and He sent Me!"

At this a growling cadre of the officers, gathering around members of the Sanhedrin, began arguing about whether to take Him right then and there. Peter was growing concerned. The crowd was clearly on Jesus' side, and many were saying, "This must indeed be the Christ!" It seemed the enthusiasm of the crowd dampened the plans of the officers sufficiently so that they hesitated and did not arrest Him.

John was saying to Peter, "Don't worry about Him being arrested today, Peter. It's not His time for that." While Peter was still wondering about what John meant by "not His time," Jesus spoke aloud, quieting the crowd again. "I am only going to be with you for a little while, and then I will go to Him that sent Me. You will look for Me, and you will not find Me, and where I go you cannot come!"

The Jews began asking, "Where is it He plans going where we can't find Him? Will He go to the scattered ones among the Greeks or go teach Greeks? What is this saying, 'You will look for Me, but you can't find Me'?"

The teaching sessions were tumultuous during the final days of the Feast. Peter was increasingly anxious about Jesus' safety, and just as concerned over this seeming exercise in futility: spending time and effort and not accomplishing much (for He performed no special miracles whatsoever during these days) except creating additional controversy among the people and the leaders, and yet running daily risk of being arrested or assassinated by some fool zealot who might try to earn the reward Peter was told the Jews had privately offered.

Peter was glad when it was finally the Last Great Day of the Feast. Perhaps this was the moment; it was certainly the final opportunity for this year.

If Jesus intended doing anything in a large public gathering, there would be no opportunity until early spring, at the next Passover. All these thousands would be long since scattered over the whole empire and would have grown forgetful of events during the Feast by then.

But Jesus began speaking out in what Peter thought was a plain appeal to follow Him!

He was saying, "If any man thirst, let him come unto Me and drink. He that believes on Me, as the Scriptures have said, out of his belly shall flow rivers of living water!" John told Peter Jesus was speaking this "of the Spirit," however, and both John and Peter were puzzled about the exact meaning, thinking it had to do with some yet unaccomplished sign or miracle.

Again, Jesus' teachings in the temple caused great public debate and gossip, many believing He was the Messiah and others vehemently arguing that He couldn't be, for "how could the Messiah, the Christ, come out of Galilee?"

That night Thomas and Bartholomew had good news in camp.

They had overheard a spirited argument between Nicodemus, a very highly respected member of the Sanhedrin and a leading Pharisee (the same Nicodemus who had come to Jesus at night that time because he didn't want to be recognized, fearing retaliation from his fellows), who had quieted some of the mob.

They had been cursing the crowds, saying, "Who are these rabble, anyway? They are an illiterate mob of know-nothings; they don't know anything about the law. *We* are the ones in authority; *we* know the law!"

Nicodemus had said, "True, but does our law judge a man except it first hear from himself personally and know exactly what he does?"

"What are you, Nicodemus?" shrieked a pear-shaped little Pharisee, his bald pate glistening with sweat.

"Are you some illiterate Galilean too? You go back and search the written Word and see if there is any prophecy about a prophet arising in Galilee!"

The little man shook his heavy jowls, waving stubby fingers in the air, punctuating his anger with jerky gestures toward Nicodemus. Nicodemus sighed, looked over at Thomas and Bart, without remembering them, and, signaling to his household servants who accompanied him, reiterated his parting warning and left the temple.

It was good news.

Even though Jesus obviously had not intended to seize the opportunity of this Feast for a major move, His appearance in the middle of the temple on the Last Great Day and His daily confrontations with the Pharisees and publicans had gained further notoriety, and thousands of Jews and proselytes were gossiping their heads off in every camp, tent and house and along every creek and in every marketplace, and on the tops of every home for miles.

"Jesus of Nazareth," and "He's a godsend," and "He's a good man," and "He's a fake," and "He's another Theudas or Barabbas," and "He'll get His come-uppance," and "He healed my daughter" would be heard.

The officers of the temple charged with arresting Him could only complain to their leaders, "We have never in all our lives heard a Man speak so engagingly, so powerfully and convincingly. We could do nothing! The crowd would have turned on us and we could have been in danger!"

This was much to the disgust of their murder-plotting leaders.

There was one major political development Jesus' appearance in the temple and His blatant challenges to both the priestly caste (the Sadducees) in charge of the building and its rituals, and the Sanhedrin (the Pharisees) had caused. Finally He had succeeded, without intending it, in uniting the two quarreling groups. Willing to abandon their internecine squabbles in order to face a common enemy, they were willingly plotting together, planning His murder!

# XIV

The next day Peter found himself in the middle of one of the funniest and most embarrassing events of his three and a half years with Jesus!

On this morning they awakened to Jesus' cheerful voice, finding Him washed, dressed and having already spent more than an hour's time in the olive groves atop the mount, and, after a hasty breakfast, they followed curiously as He headed for the temple again.

They supposed that now the Feast of Tabernacles was over and the thousands of Jews and proselytes from all over the empire would be packing up and leaving (their early morning sleep had been interrupted by the echoes of hoofs on stone, guttural snorts of camels and muffled braying of asses as at least two caravans had wound their way along the brook below and had headed down the Jordan trails), and wondered why Jesus would bother going back now that the crowds were leaving.

But they went into the temple and Jesus sat down in the reader's chair—and the curious began to gather. Clearly He intended teaching again.

Peter and several others liked to flank Him, or even mingle with the crowd, to keep a sharp eye on them. They feared moments like that of yesterday and the day before when a man could be shoved here and there with the push of the crowd, tempers flaring. The leaders of the Jews were trembling with their helpless rage, obviously wanting to see Him dead.

Today it seemed the Pharisees were quiet.

It wasn't long before Peter saw why.

A noisy interruption began when a whole group of Pharisees pushed their way through the crowd, halting Jesus' words in midsentence, a sobbing woman struggling feebly against the grip of two of them.

The poor woman was striving to hide her face in her shoulders, her arms being pinned, and was looking down and weeping. She was being half dragged, half carried by the men.

The Pharisees halted squarely in front of Jesus, and their leader, gesturing to the woman, said, "This woman has been caught in the very act of adultery! Now, the law of Moses commands us to *stone* her to death, but what do *You* say we ought to do about her?"

Peter drew in his breath.

He knew the Lord would never condone stoning. He had spoken too much of mercy and forgiveness in their ears and had talked of the abuses of the law wherein false witnesses could condemn an innocent person to death just to get possession of their property or to remove a potential political competitor. Jesus would never say she ought to be stoned! Yet if He didn't it would make Him look like He was flying in the face of the sacred law, defying the written word that so plainly spelled out the exact punishments for specific sins! If He did that, they would have Him on a grave charge, one that could mean His actual death! Peter found a fine film of perspiration on his brow as he edged closer to Jesus, loosening his sword in its scabbard. He looked hard at Thomas, Simon and James, hoping they would stand with him for he may have to fight his way through this crowd. He would protect the Lord to the last!

What was Jesus doing?

No answer—just a dramatic gesture. Leaving the chair, He wrote with His finger in the dust of the floor. The Pharisees were completely baffled. The throng was pressing close, and several of the leading publicans were striving to see what Jesus was doing.

The Pharisees, true to their rigid pecking order, shuffled themselves about so that their eldest, and therefore the most respected, could maneuver into the best position behind Jesus to His right to see what He was doing.

By now Peter was at the Lord's side on the left. He peered over Jesus' shoulder and blinked.

The words were a *series of names*.

They read something like "Nabuis—Ronda; Nicolas—Rhoda; Judas—Lucia; Zebuliah—Priscilla" and seemed to be a series of men's and women's names linked together.

Peter was first puzzled. The elder Pharisee gasped, grasped his robe and flung it hastily over his shoulders and, struggling to regain his composure, his face settling into a rigid mask, pushed his way through the crowd and hastily left. Someone had whispered his name.

"Judas," wasn't it?

Peter glanced again at Jesus' writing.

By now the second of the Pharisees was taking the place of the first, and he, too, peered over Jesus' shoulder, casting a puzzled look at the hastily departing back of Judas-ben-Levi, who was leaving. He then stared down at the words.

Almost as if carefully rehearsed, he stiffened, gasped, flung his cape about him and stalked through the pathway Judas was making, quickly beating a retreat!

Then Peter understood.

But *how could Jesus know?* Obviously the linking of these names was so shocking, so stunning to these posturing, swaggering leaders of "righteousness," that there had been some hanky-panky in their *own* lives, and it was the *same sin* of which the woman was accused: adultery!

Peter began grinning broadly, and a low, rumbling chuckle came from his big chest. Jesus glanced up at him, answered him with a grin of His own (did it have just a hint of mischievousness around the edges?) and kept right on writing.

Here came the third, and the fourth, and the fifth.

And there they went, like a ridiculous, shamefaced parade, each one in his turn, from the eldest to the youngest, peering intently at the words Jesus was writing, wonderment growing into fright as each saw the other before him hurrying away, only to blush beet red and follow his elder as quickly as his feet would carry him.

Peter saw Jesus was determined to carry out the drama to its conclusion.

When the last Pharisee was heaving himself through the crowd, and while several of them could still hear His words, Jesus straightened up, and, looking at the woman who was by now staring at the letters, with tears still marking her face, He said, "Woman, whatever happened to your accusers? Isn't there anyone here to condemn you?"

"No, Lord, there isn't anybody here," she said.

"Well, then, neither do I accuse you," said Jesus. "Go along now, and from now on—don't sin any more!"

With a grateful sob and blushing face, the woman cloaked her face, turned away and fled.

At this Peter burst out laughing, and so did several others in the front ranks who had seen the writing. But Jesus was compassionate to the last. With the mission accomplished, He quickly erased the names, and as an excited babble broke out He signaled to the disciples that He would go into the temple treasury room and teach there.

For hours He taught!

Peter wondered if He would ever tire as He said, "You judge after the flesh, and I do not judge anyone," and "If a man keep My word, he shall never see death!"

What amazed Peter was that the very Jews who originally had said they "believed 'on' Him" began to argue with Him, and within a few hours were so angry they wanted to stone Him.

Again Peter worried.

*Why?* Why did Jesus seem intent on antagonizing them? It seemed just as the masses were inspired to give Him popular acclaim He would single out a rotten attitude here and there, or enter into a lengthy diatribe with some simpering, posturing, self-righteous Pharisee, and, before you knew what was happening, a violent confrontation had developed.

By the time the session was over, Peter and the others

had to once again protect Jesus from stoning!

A violent argument developed, swirling primarily around the Jews' extreme chauvinism and racial pride. It was triggered when Jesus said, "You shall know the truth, and the truth shall make you *free.*"

One of the Pharisees answered scornfully, "We are Abraham's seed and have never yet been in bondage to any man. How can You say, 'You shall be made free'?"

Peter barely suppressed an angry retort himself at that one.

Could that self-righteous nut be serious? Here they were, within only a stone's throw of a Roman garrison, kept nearby the temple because of the frequent religious altercations and the need for a show of Roman force; they were but a few minutes' walk of Pontius Pilate's sumptuous residence with its resplendent balconies and interior courtyard with fountains and pools. They were heavily taxed, and any citizen could be commandeered to carry Roman burdens or do taskwork at any time by some ugly Roman soldier. Yet this ridiculous Pharisee could claim "we have never been in bondage to any man"!

Jesus looked squarely at him and with rising voice said, "Truly I am telling you, everyone who *commits sin*" (with a finger pointing directly at the Pharisee) "is the bondservant of *sin,* and the bondservant will not abide in the house forever" (was He making oblique reference to the temple as well as the kingdom He would set up as "God's House"?), "but the Son abides forever!

"If the Son shall make you free, you will be *really* free! I know you are Abraham's seed, yet you seek to kill Me because my Word doesn't find any place to remain in you. I am telling you the things I have seen of *My* Father, and you can speak only of *your* father" (which Peter knew meant Jesus was contrasting *His* Father, God in heaven, with *their* "father," who was Satan the devil, and the father of liars).

"Our father is Abraham!" shrieked a balding, heavily jowled publican, plainly stung by Jesus' implication.

"If you were Abraham's children, then you would be doing the works of Abraham. But now you are trying to find a way to *kill* Me, a Man that has told you the truth, which I have heard from God. Abraham did nothing like this!

"You are doing the works of your father . . ." Jesus concluded with a ring of anger in His voice.

"We weren't born of *fornication,* shouted a tall, sallow-faced Pharisee near the back of the crowd. "Yeah, He's that illegitimate son of Joseph we heard about," said another. And "bastard" could be heard under the breath of several.

Peter was mad.

Leave it to some rotten Pharisee to stoop to the tactics of personal attack when argument failed! Every time the pseudointellectual ran out of fuel, he could only resort to personal attacks. To Peter, having heard Jesus comment on this peculiarity of blind, carnal human nature, it was one of the oldest dodges in the world. If you couldn't answer the other man's arguments, just attack him personally!

Peter made as if to move toward the man, but Jesus stayed him with a gesture and a look, and he stayed where he was.

Peter could see Jesus was growing very angry. His voice was ringing out, fairly shaking with indignation and echoing off the distant walls so that others were beginning to gather around. The crowd must number more than seven hundred, Peter thought, and more were calling to their friends outside.

"If God were your father," Jesus said in a loud voice, "you would *love Me,* for I came from God Himself. I do not speak of Myself, but *He that sent Me.* I'll tell you why you cannot understand My teachings, because it is impossible for you to hear and understand My word, since it comes from the Father above! No, you are of *your father the devil,* and the lusts of your father *you will do.* He was a killer from the very beginning and did not stand for the truth, because there is no truth in him. When he tells a lie, he speaks on his own, because he is a liar and the father of lies! But because I speak the *truth* you don't believe Me!

"Which one of you could convict Me of sinning? If I speak the truth — and it *is* the truth — then why don't you believe Me?''

"Isn't it true that you're only a Samaritan," said a little rotund man with dripping sarcasm, "and *have a demon?*"

"*I have no demon!*" Jesus answered in force. "But *I* honor *My Father,* and YOU DISHONOR ME! I seek not My own aggrandizement; there is another that seeks and that will judge! If you knew My words, you would never see death!''

"Now we *know* You are demon possessed," screamed one of the Jews as others were saying, "Yes, a *demon!* A demon!''

"Abraham is *dead!*" the tall Pharisee yelled, "and the prophets are *dead,* and yet You are saying if a man keeps *Your* word he will never see death? Well, then, are You claiming to be *greater than Abraham,* who is *dead,* and even the prophets, who are all *dead?* Just who is it You are trying to make Yourself into?''

"If I glorify *Myself,* then My glory is as nothing; it is My Father who glorifies Me, of whom you claim that He is your God! Yet you have never known Him, and *I know Him;* and if I should claim 'I don't know Him' just to satisfy you, then I would be a liar, just like you are. But I *do* know Him and I keep His word! Your father Abraham rejoiced to see My day, and he saw it and was glad!''

"What are you talking about. You can't be fifty years old yet and yet You claim to have actually *seen Abraham?*"

"Truly, truly, I am telling you, even before Abraham was *I AM!*"

That did it!

That reference to the very name God used when speaking to Moses out ot the burning bush — "I AM" — that did it! With a shriek of rage, the tall Pharisee lunged for Jesus. Several others surged forward, tripping over the rotund balding fellow, who squealed, "Don't step on me, don't step on me!''

Shoving, screaming, yelling — a wild melee ensued as Jesus ducked down between Peter and Andrew, and His other disciples formed a cordon of bodies around Him. If

Thaddeus over there let a loose elbow bring that gasping look of glazed-eyed pain to the sallow-faced Pharisee who was struggling for breath, was it Thaddeus' fault?

Peter dearly longed to ring that tall fellow's bell for him, laying his Roman short sword up alongside his pompous head, but his first duty was to Jesus, and they needed to get out of here now before this screaming crowd could seize Him.

Covering the Lord's head, they jostled their way among the remainder of the disciples. The people were packed so thickly that the sheer weight of the crowd made it impossible to move for most of them. They were trampling each other, pummeling each other, and now and then a rock sailed over the heads of the rear echelons to thump an exposed head, shoulder or forearm, bringing forth a sharp cry of pain and outrage from the recipient.

They struggled through the screaming crowd with Jesus saying, "Careful, Peter. Don't hurt anyone. They don't know what they're doing," with Peter giving a shove here and there that even he knew was unnecessarily rough.

The soaring columns of the temple seemed to sway dizzily above them, and the cries, shouts, screams and yelling of the crowd echoed hollowly from the walls and the distant ceiling like a rising crescendo of a mad orchestra in dissonant rebellion.

It was a subdued group that trudged through the volubly talking crowds along the steep trails down to the brook Kidron, forded the stream and then climbed among the olive groves to camp that night. They all knew how near a thing it had been, but Jesus was almost nonchalant, quietly confident, seemingly unaware that His very life had nearly been forfeit. Did Peter overhear Him saying to John, in answer to another of John's interminable questions, "Because, John, it was *not My time yet*"?

They were dead weary by the time a meager supper was over, and Peter didn't even feel like singing.

Peter stretched his arms over his head, rolled over on his side and looked at the huddled figure of Jesus only a few feet distant, head resting on a pack, the firelight faintly

playing over His wide shoulders, and wondered if the chill
of this mountain was beginning to creep through that one
robe He wore, and which He had gathered around Him
now in sleep.

On impulse, Peter stealthily got up, fumbled in his
pack that he was using for a pillow and, taking his big,
rough fisherman's cloak, stepped softly to the Lord's side
and gently covered Him with it. He turned, then, and was
about to step back to his own pallet by the gnarled trunk of
an olive tree when a quiet voice said, "Thank you, faithful
servant. Thank you, Peter."

"Thank *You,* Lord," Peter said, "And good night to
You."

"Good night, Peter," He said.

It was another hour before Peter went to sleep, the
distant keening of a wailer signaling the death of a loved
one in a family that occupied one of the hovels across the
valley coming to him faintly on the night breeze.

He kept starting at the slightest sound, wondering if a
spy had discovered who Jesus was, or whether the Pharisees were even now creeping up on them with an armed
guard. Peter had tucked his sword under his pack, and the
familiar haft gave him comfort when he reached for it to
make sure it was in its place.

If not now, if not during the Feast that was now past,
then *when?* he wondered.

But Jesus knew what He was doing, and so Peter
consoled himself, determined to remain by the Lord's side
and see this thing through, no matter what.

The next few days were to bring another profound
lesson in human nature.

Jesus noticed a beggar, well known about the gates of
Jerusalem, who had been born blind. Some of the disciples, curious about cause and effect and the punishments
for sin, asked Him, "Master, who sinned? Who caused
this blindness? Was it this man, or his parents, that he
should have been born blind?"

Peter was very puzzled over the answer.

"Neither this man nor his parents sinned; he was born
blind so that the works of God should be made manifest

through Him. We must work the works of Him that sent Me while it is day, for the night is coming when no man can work. While I am in the world I am the light of the world.''

After finishing this strong, short speech, He spat on the dust of the ground and, using His finger to stir it into a clay, took a little between thumb and forefinger and gently daubed it over the ugly, whitish, sightless orbs of the blind man.

Then He said, ''Go, now, and wash off your eyes in the Siloam pool.'' Miraculously, as the blind man washed off the drying clay the accumulated matter on his eyes came off too, and he could *see*. He was reaching out, touching familiar places—the street corners he was so accustomed to, here a tree and there an awning in front of a shop, looking up in delight when remembered voices identified a familiar friend, staring in amazement when he saw their faces!

The miracle began an excited public stirring, and many of his friends became so ecstatic and curious they wanted him to accompany them to the leaders of the Sanhedrin, the Pharisees.

Many asked, ''Isn't that the blind beggar?'' and other said, ''No, you must be mistaken. How could his eyes have been opened?''

''How did He open your eyes, if He really did?'' asked one of the leading Pharisees.

''Well, He anointed my eyes with clay, and . . .''

''Who—*who* anointed your eyes?''

''Jesus—you know, the Man they call Jesus of Nazareth. He anointed my eyes with clay, like I was saying, and told me, 'Go and wash in Siloam,' and so I went down there and I washed off my eyes. When I did, I received my sight!'' he finished, voice rising in joy, happily blinking about at his friends and grasping the forearm of one shopkeeper who had been a generous friend.

''Where *is* this Jesus of Nazareth?'' asked the Pharisee.

''I don't know where He went,'' came the answer.

''Surely this man cannot be from God, because He

does not keep the Sabbath!'' said one.

"But,'' protested another, reasonably, ''can a man who is not of God, who is a sinner, perform such miracles?'' A babble of voices rose then as the group broke into shouts and arguments. At length, when the noise died down somewhat, the leader turned to the formerly blind again and demanded, ''What do *you* claim about Him, since you say He opened your eyes?''

''I believe He is a prophet!''

''We'll see about that,'' said the leader and gave orders to call the parents of the man to the hearing.

The parents were brought before the leaders.

''Is this your son that you claim was born blind?'' they asked.

''Yes, that's our boy all right. But as to how he now sees, we don't know,'' came the impossible answer. What was this? A parent so frightened of being ''put out'' from their cherished synagogue that they could not experience even the normal human emotions (what was ''normal'' about a miracle like this?) of the unbounded *joy* one would think they would feel?

Peter could not abide fear religion! To him the hated memories of Romans tramping through Bethsaida, and the many tales aged Jona had put deeply in his mind, made him yearn passionately for the freedoms and blessings of complete independence for this verdant land and an end to the stifling control of the religious leaders that made people act like these poor parents were.

Was it possible these parents were so brainwashed by the remembered ceremonies of a local synagogue, so totally convinced of the near infallibility of the religious leaders, that they could not stand before God *alone?*

Peter thought how it should have gone!

Why, if it had been me, he thought, I would have demanded, ''Now, just wait a minute! Anyone knows a *miracle* can come only from God! You men claim to represent God! Therefore, you can only *rejoice* that this man has been healed by a great miracle!

''What's your problem? *You* passed by this man in the streets for *years* and none of *you* could heal him! Now here is the blind beggar before you — seeing — and you want to claim it is *evil,* merely because the *blind* was cured on the Sabbath day?'' Peter thought of another example Jesus had used. He would say, ''Doesn't your own law claim you can help a dumb beast out of a mud hole on the Sabbath so an animal doesn't suffer? How much more valuable is a precious human life, and *eyesight,* than the hind leg of old Judah-ben-Zith's off-ox?'' (Peter liked that line.)

''I demand to know where He is!'' Peter would have said.

''I want to know *why* you religious leaders do not recognize Him!''

Then, if they ''cast him out'' from their tightly knit little group of huddled sheep, so be it!

But the parents had *not* taken a stand for God. They had been so afraid of their eternal destiny, so fearful to be ostracized from beloved friends and associates, so terrified of being ''alone'' in the world, without the feeling of security, of 'belonging' that was afforded by the rituals of the synagogue, that they cowed in fear.

His parents answered, ''We know that this is our son, and that he was born blind. But how he now sees we do not know, or who opened his eyes, we know not. Ask him. He is of age; let him speak for himself!''

*Unbelievable!* Instead of tearfully grabbing their son, pounding him joyfully on the back and happily sharing the experience of *seeing* for the first time in his life, showing him flowers, trees, the countryside nearby and sharing his very first sunset, they cowed in fear before these posturing religious bigots.

Here were the leaders who ''sat in Moses' seat,'' according to the Lord Himself, deliberately *dividing a family* because of their own desire for power and money!

Tragically, the parents could only stand with downcast eyes, trembling in fear. How could they abandon it all? Why, *every day* they were required to think about and to serve the synagogue. They attended faithfully, paid their tithes, watched the sacrifices, bought turtle doves and once or twice a year a young bullock or a goat. They fasted often and said their prayers. They rejoiced in the feasts, visiting happily with dozens of remembered friends from faraway places. If they took a stand now and grabbed their son and rejoiced, throwing caution to the winds and showing belief in this miracle and acceptance of Jesus Christ as a prophet, it would mean they would be *put out*. And that meant no more social life, and worse it meant *being cut off from God!*

That the parents were staying with a crumbling, dying religion, one of hatred, chicanery, persecution, power politics, avarice, greed, cunning and every evil, utterly devoid of love, mercy and goodness, never occurred to them. It was "their" religion; they had been reared in it, and they felt they should "stay with it"!

The parents knew through warnings from friends that the Jews had agreed already that if anyone dared to confess that Jesus was the Christ he would be *put out* of the synagogue!

Again the leader turned to the son and demanded pompously, "Give glory to God; we know that this man is a sinner!"

The son answered honestly, "Whether He is a sinner or not, I do not know. But one thing I know, that whereas I was blind—I have been blind for all my life and have never seen—*now I see!"*

"All right, you say He healed you, but what did He do, what did He use, *how* did He do it?" queried a Pharisee, hoping desperately to find some minor technicality of lawbreaking to use against Jesus.

"I just finished telling you the whole story, and apparently you didn't listen to me. Why do you want to hear it again?" the formerly blind asked, and then, with a smile and a chuckle (for he really didn't care what they thought at this point; what had the synagogue ever done for *him?*), "Are you thinking of training to become one of His disciples?"

This was too much!

*"You* are His disciple and *we* are the disciples of Moses! As for this Man, we don't know where He came from!"

"Why, here is an unbelievable thing. You, the religious leaders, claim you don't know where He came from, and yet He *healed my eyes* and I have my sight! We know that God does not hear sinners, and if any man be a worshiper of God, and do His will, him He hears! No one has ever heard of a man having his eyes opened who was *born blind!* If this man were not of God, He couldn't accomplish anything."

"Just who do you think you are, trying to teach *us?*" the leader shrieked. "You who were born in sins!" In a rage, they grabbed the young man by the arms, and, in front of the startled eyes of his parents, they half dragged, half carried him and threw him out of the building onto the street.

The parents remained where they were. They would have lost fellowship with the synagogue.

After hearing the story Jesus sought out the young man and finally found him joyously meeting friends and quizzically matching remembered voices with the new faces he was seeing—enjoying the marvels of his new-found vision.

"Do you believe on the Son of God?" Jesus asked.

"Who is he, Lord, that I may believe on Him?"

"You have already seen Him, and it is He who now speaks with you!"

"Lord, I believe!" said the formerly blind and, kneeling and grasping Jesus' hand, pressed it to tear-stained cheeks and worshiped Him in the crowded market-place.

Knowing that several of the Pharisees were present, Jesus said loudly enough for them to hear, "For judgment I am come into this world, that they which see may not see, and they who see may become blind."

A Pharisee drew near and demanded, "Are we, then, blind?"

"If you were blind, you would have no sin, for you would not be responsible. But you claim 'We see!' and therefore your sin remains!"

The Pharisee nearly choked with rage and would have entered into another lengthy harangue, but Peter and the others urged Jesus to leave.

# XV

The Feast was now past, and winter would soon be here.

The first frost of the season had painted the leaves with bright hues; the harvest was over, the fields being gleaned of their last produce by the poor, the haze of cooking fires hanging in the higher valleys.

As they descended the forested slopes from Jerusalem, they saw fields riotous with golden, rust, brown and green.

Jesus and the others had gone on back to Galilee by the usual roads, but Peter, Andrew and Thomas had asked to stop by Simon the Tanner's shop down in Joppa. It was far out of the way, but Peter knew Simon was a loyal believer in Jesus, and he was up on most of the latest information, talking with ship owners, sailors and tradesmen from many nations.

As they passed the browning fields, they noticed many threshing operations in progress, the women using the ancient hand method of beating the sheaves against the stone floors and the oxen patiently plodding around and around as the grain was shoveled under the huge round stone they pulled, pulverizing the grain into flour.

Peter sneezed violently.

"Me too," said Andrew, rubbing his red nose. "Sometimes, if I get too close to a threshing floor, it makes my eyes water for days."

"A fairly good harvest this year," commented

Thomas.

"Yes, but you'd be surprised how much of it will be loaded aboard ships to be taken to Rome," said Peter bitterly.

"Yeah, or confiscated by the Romans for their garrisons," said Andrew.

"Or taxed by Herod," added Thomas, matching the futile tone.

"Well, not for much longer," Peter said, quickening his stride. Shifting the heavy sword further to the side to prevent it chafing his leg, he said, "If the Lord sets up His kingdom next spring, He'll see to it Isaiah's prophecy about every man having his own land, his own fig tree, fields and cattle, comes true!"

They continued talking about the tremendous reforms that would occur, how the outpouring of Judea's wealth to Rome would cease, heavy taxation stop and the oppression of the people be replaced with true freedom and opportunity.

A day later they came to Simon's shop in Joppa.

Here in Joppa it was almost as if there was no autumn or spring. The weather had a sameness to it, except for a chance storm that would turn the normally blue Mediterranean into a dull, leaden gray and send huge, muddied breakers crashing into the shores as the last of one of the "euroclydons," as the seafaring men called them, would blow themselves out on these shores.

Peter wanted to purchase another set of heavier boots. Simon was incredibly busy now. Huge bales of rare and exotic hides awaited his racks and smoke. He had hired more help, Peter noticed, and one bale of zebra hides was quickly snapped up by a Roman whose wife had rare tastes.

Simon made footwear by taking some of the wild animals' hides and turning them inside out so the hair or fur was inside and the coarsely finished hide on the outside. Several layers of tough skins, sometimes from a wild ox from Africa with black, stiff hair and incredibly thick, tough hide, was then stitched to the bottoms and laced with decorative sinew.

Andrew and Thomas had each come with a shopping list from others whose shoes had seen the wear of many dusty paths, muddy creek beds and city streets — and winter was near.

They enjoyed Simon's evening stories. After he had satisfied the last customer and given instructions to the last servant, they would talk by the big indoor ovens in the main cooking room.

The talk was of Persia and the islands beyond Hercules, and of monstrous animals in Africa that seamen swore had only one horn jutting out from the front of their head. Simon wanted fervently to see one, but no one had yet succeeded in capturing the beast, for it was said to be the fleetest of all the gazelles, and wary.

They talked about a strange, short, bandy-legged man wearing bundles of skins that flopped here and there with tails, ears and colorful leavings who had a sallow complexion with deep pockmarks and squinted, puffy eyes who had stopped in yesterday.

Simon wondered aloud if all those people from the far lands beyond Persia didn't get that way from living in the perpetual snows that made them squint so.

The little fellow was full of questions about a strange star that had appeared more than thirty years ago that a caste of priests in his country had made up prayers and chants about, Simon said.

Peter wished he had been there to see the man and to tell him what he knew about the Magi, the star and Herod. Priests of Zoroaster, some claimed. Peter didn't know, but he was impressed with the civilizations of the East of which so little was known. Punching holes in their money made sense, for it was custom to string it in circles, and when a man had the money around his leg, arm or neck it was far harder to misplace, lose or have someone steal.

Simon spoke of the latest shipwrecks and of naval battles and fracases here and there. He seemed to be a fountain source of everything that was going on, and Peter was hoping he could remember most of it in case Jesus wanted to receive any news of other areas.

Soon, Peter told Simon, a new government would be

in charge.

The heavy taxes Simon paid, and the surcharges on the things he imported, could be lifted and the country would be returned to the ancient tithing practice. It seemed the Romans wanted to tax even the air they breathed, and many a bawdy joke had been told about whether they would tax marriage!

The visit to Joppa was over too soon. Peter wanted to hurry back to Galilee now, after telling Simon that Jesus had intended sending out a full *seventy* men now, just the way he and the other eleven had been sent.

They made good time back to Capernaum, arriving three days after leaving Joppa with weary pack animals, and then handed out their purchases, much to the delight of all. Judas ruefully looked over the stuff, noting each purchase according to the record Andrew had kept, and turned up a lip when he was handed the meager change and counted it carefully.

Peter smirked at him and turned away. Judas bothered him, with his incredible concern for money and the way he was always fingering their coin sacks. Peter was glad Judas had been thwarted from taking this side trip with them. What if Judas had lifted something from them? Peter fervently hoped he could catch the swarthy little crook with his hand deep in the till, but Peter was no publican, and there was no way he could demand a weekly accounting when Jesus seemed unconcerned about it.

A few days later Jesus spent a long time in earnest speech with seventy of the one hundred twenty who were with them most of the time, sending them in teams of two and instructing them almost exactly as Peter and the others had been instructed earlier.

This time things were really heating up! With *seventy* men — thirty-five teams — out there stirring up the people and giving advance notice that Jesus and the others were coming, Peter expected that things were shaping up so that the coming Passover season would lead to the final revolution.

There followed weeks of wearying labor, weeks of hard travel, of confrontation, or miracles and wonders, and of the crowds, always attentive, happy, shouting, rejoicing crowds, with the Pharisees' and Sadducees' spies and agitators among them trying to stir up trouble, and following about after Jesus with their rumors of "bastard" and "winesot," "a glutton" and "He breaks the Sabbath."

All that winter they trudged up and down the country, experiencing one major event after another. Peter was particularly struck by Jesus' reference to the dividing of families in all that was happening. His ears really pricked up when Jesus said, "Do you suppose I came to send *peace* to this earth? I tell you no! But rather division. For there shall be from here on five in a house, and three will be against two, and two against three. They will even be divided between father and son; the son against the father and the father against the son, and a mother against her own daughter, and daughter against her mother, and mother-in-law against daughter-in-law, and daughter-in-law against mother-in-law. No, I didn't come to send peace, but a sword!"

Peter reveled in this message of a sword and the stern rebukes and warnings to the Pharisees. It must mean Jesus would soon reveal His "time" He always spoke about. Peter was both elated and apprehensive. Jesus often talked of being "delivered up," and that He would be given into the "hands of sinners," and similar statements.

Peter supposed He would allow Himself to be mistreated in some way. And then, when the Jews had shown what true hypocrites they were, He would shock the whole population with a great sign and accomplish His enthronement in Jerusalem.

They were in Peraea for several months, journeying beyond Jordan to Bethany, when some of the Parisees warned Jesus about Herod Antipas.

A messenger from the Pharisees said, "You had better get out of this region because Herod would love to kill You!"

It was here, in the villages of Peraea, that He was accused so vehemently of being "the friend of publicans, harlots and sinners!"

To Peter these were exhausting months. Yet, a shocking event occurred, one which seemed to pale into insignificance all Jesus' other miracles, if that were possible.

A messenger had been sent by the sisters, Mary and Martha. He arrived with hair plastered to head, having ridden miles through a cold, driving rain.

His tired animal was unsaddled, rubbed and fed by a servant, and when he had been given dry clothing and brought to Jesus he said, "Lord, Lazarus, whom You love, is terribly sick!"

"This sickness is not unto death," Jesus said quietly, "but for the glory of God that the Son of God may be glorified by it."

The man nodded, smiling, but later voiced his doubts. It seemed both sisters were beside themselves with worry. Lazarus had suddenly taken sick, with high fever and dramatic weight loss. He was delirious with fever.

Peter knew the messenger was hopeful Jesus would saddle up and hit the trail immediately, and the man was clearly resentful when he awakened to find Jesus and the others eating a breakfast in the kitchen with the innkeeper and his wife and making no attempt to leave.

The messenger promptly left, flogging his braying donkey down the road as fast as its short legs would carry it, no doubt primed to tell Mary and Martha that the Lord was in no special hurry.

As a matter of fact, Jesus stayed two days right where He was, and then they began their journey to Bethany.

Thomas, Thaddeus and Simon the Canaanite all carried the same warnings to Him, saying how the rumors were widespread that if He dared show Himself openly in Jerusalem or the nearby environs again it was as good as giving Himself into the hands of the Pharisees, that they were plotting to stone Him to death as soon as they found Him.

Jesus insisted on going, saying, "Our friend Lazarus has fallen asleep, but I am going down there to awaken him."

"Lord, if he's only sleeping, then certainly he'll recover," they said.

John knew that Jesus meant Lazarus was already dead, but when John voiced the idea to Peter they both wondered how He could have known.

Finally, Jesus confirmed it.

"Lazarus is *dead*," He said. "And I am happy for your sake that I wasn't there during his illness — to the purpose that *you may believe!*

"Come on, let's be going," He finished.

Thomas had been especially close to the family and counted Lazarus as one of his best friends. Thomas, who had been very fidgety and upset for the past two days, let out a sob of grief. "Let's go down there and die with him!"

Of course, Thomas had not been present in Jairus' home, as Peter had, nor had he been on the mount and seen the transfiguration, for that matter. Still, Peter had told the full account of Jairus' daughter, but perhaps Thomas still doubted. Several of the men had taken to calling Thomas "Didymus," or "The Doubter," because of his timid, negative nature.

When they finally arrived in Bethany, it was to be met on the road by Martha, who burst into tears when she saw Jesus and said, "Lord, if You had only been here my brother surely would have survived. You could have saved him. I'm sure he wouldn't have died!"

Peter grimaced to himself. The woman was so obvious in her little female ways. Sure, he knew she was sick with grief, but the irk she felt toward Mary's apparent inside track (which it wasn't) with Jesus and her small disapprovals of Jesus' conduct came to the surface rather plainly. This was not only a plaintive cry from heartbreak, it was also a little female rebuke.

But she mollified it when she finished, "But even now I know whatever you ask of God He will give You."

"Your brother will rise again," Jesus said confidently.

"I know he will Lord; I know he will rise in the resurrection in the last day," she said, thinking He meant countless years into the future.

"I am the resurrection and the life, and he that believes on Me, even if he dies, yet shall he live; and whoever lives and believes on Me shall never die! Do you believe this, Martha?''

''Oh, yes, Lord! Of course I do. You know I believe You are the Christ, the Messiah, the Son of God; that One who was to come into this world!''

They continued their walk to the house, leading their pack animals, and Martha hurried on ahead to arrive breathlessly in the house, calling, ''Mary, the Master is here, and He is calling for you!''

Some of the wailers saw her get up hastily and leave, and they followed, supposing she was going to go back to the tombs and weep there.

Jesus was still coming along the track with the disciples and a growing crowd of people when Mary finally found Him. She fell down at His feet and said, ''Lord, if You had only been here my brother would not have died!''

Peter patted Mary gently on the shoulder and tried to comfort her as Jesus stood with the emotions of the moment playing across His face.

Jesus looked about and saw the friends and relatives and professional mourners. He saw Mary, with stooped shoulders, head hung, hair in disarray, reddened eyes and runny nose, sobbing out loud.

To all these weeping relatives, death was the ultimate finality. It was the slam of that final door from which there was no reprieve. Lazarus had been a favorite of them all, a man of great good humor, sparkling wit and good personality.

Peter heard Jesus groan within Himself.

Seeing the terrible anguish of Mary, and having a deep personal affection toward them that He had, seeing the weeping and wailing of all the other people around, Jesus asked, ''Where have you buried him?'' They said, brokenheartedly, ''This way, Lord. Come and see the tomb!''

At this, Jesus wept!

The Jews said, ''Look how much He loved him!'' But some of them said, ''Couldn't this Man, who opened the eyes of him that was blind, have caused that this man should not die?'' Again, Peter heard Jesus groaning within Himself because of their lack of faith. Coming to the tomb, Jesus said, ''Take away the stone!''

Martha said, ''Lord, by this time there will be a terrible stench because he has been dead four days now!'' Jesus said to her, ''Didn't I tell you that if you believe you would see the glory of God?'' He gestured they should do as He said, and so Peter and some of the disciples assisted in rolling away the stone.

Jesus lifted His eyes to the skies and said, ''Father, I thank You that you heard me and I know that You hear Me always. But, because of the crowd that stands around, I said it that they may believe that You did send Me!'' When He had prayed briefly, He cried out in a loud voice, *''LAZARUS! COME FORTH!''*

With a gasp of amazement, the crowd fell back as if seeing an apparition. A figure stirred, emerged from the gloom of the cave and came out, bound both hand and foot with grave wrappings! Even his face was bound about with a napkin, and he had his hands extended before him, walking zombielike, because of the hindrance of all the grave clothes.

Jesus said, ''Loose him, and let him go!''

The women were hanging back, shocked and afraid, but Peter and Andrew stepped up to unwind the burial clothes. Lazarus was already talking the minute they had his face uncovered, and he shouted out his recognition of Jesus and asked, ''Whatever happened?'' and ''Where am I?'' and ''Who are all these people, Mary?''

Mary and Martha took turns grasping and kissing Jesus' hand, kneeling before Him (had there been fewer people about, Peter suspected, Mary would have grabbed Him in a bear hug for sheer delight).

The wailers and relatives were standing there open-mouthed, stunned.

Some of them began to recover and were heard saying, ''But how did he *breathe* in there?'' and ''Well, the rabbi that pronounced him dead just must have made a mistake!'' Another began to recount how he was about to butcher an ox once that he had struck in the head with a maul over two hours before and the animal had gotten up, lunged at him and run off.

Peter smiled.

Leave it to these people and in a few hours Lazarus wouldn't have been dead at all. Those who were not right here, standing here and witnessing what had occurred with their own eyes, would have no hopes of hearing a clear version of what had really taken place, not with the prejudices of religion a party to it.

But many of the Jews there believed.

Peter was happy to see several of the leaders humbly drop to their knees and thank God aloud, and then come up to Jesus and acknowledge Him as Lord and thank Him for what He had done! That was a breakthrough, Peter thought!

What a *fabulous miracle!*

Peter still found himself moving as if in a dream. Was this really happening? Had Lazarus really been dead? Of *course,* he had! And now he was *alive!* Peter had seen the dead raised before, but this was nothing a man became accustomed to! His skin was prickled into gooseflesh, and his hair fairly stood up.

That voice. Jesus had spoken with such a ring of confidence and such *surety* when He had commanded, "LAZARUS, COME FORTH!" Peter rarely heard that tone in the Master's voice. Jesus *knew* Lazarus would hear Him! There was no bravado here, no mere show of human ego or vanity! This was the very work of God!

Peter was reminded of how Pharaoh's magicians had finally come to their chief and had said in hushed and awed tones, "This is the finger of God!"

But there they went, Peter noticed, a group of the hardheads, murmuring among themselves. They began questioning Mary about what she had given Lazarus and what kind of food and drink he had for the last hours before his "death," and which rabbi had pronounced him dead, and how long she claimed he had been buried in the tomb.

They hurried off, then, for a meeting.

John went along and was in time to hear them conclude the meeting. Caiaphas was the high priest that year;

it was his course of office. They were worriedly saying, "Whatever will we do? If we let Him keep doing all these signs, the Romans will surely intervene and we'll lose our very nationality." Caiaphas said, "You don't know anything at all! Nor do you seem to understand that it is expedient for you that one man should die for the people that the whole nation perish not!"

He looked amazed at what he had said, and wondered why he had said it. But the Holy Spirit prompted the saying, being a prophecy that Jesus should die, not only for the nation but that He might die for everyone, and gather together into one nation all the children of God. That was what John told Peter that night.

But there was an evil aftermath, because John knew the final, formal decision was now made, and they were taking counsel about how to kill Jesus.

For Peter's part, he spent hours encouraging the others to do their part and protect the Lord. Peter felt the responsibility keenly.

The days passed with Jesus giving many more parables and healing ten men all at once, one of whom, to Peter's great distaste, was a Samaritan, and yet he proved to be the only one of the whole group who came back to Jesus to give thanks. What a bunch of ingrates, Peter thought.

Jesus seemed determined to drive home the new idea he had planted in their minds. For instance, when they came to Jericho in the foothills above the Dead Sea, they stayed with Zacchaeus after Jesus convinced him who He was by telling the little man to climb down from the tree he was in (he was so short he had to climb up there to see over the crowds).

While they were at Zacchaeus' home, the arguments had raged wildly back and forth as the disciples' expectancies were honed razor sharp, believing that Jesus would establish the kingdom almost any day now with a great, dramatic march on Jerusalem.

It had been a long, tough winter.

Peter had enjoyed only one brief visit home and had been unable to really unwind and relax with the family as he had wanted, for he was sorely disappointed in the entire affair down there in Jerusalem during the Feast and afterwards.

The boots he had purchased from his friend Simon the Tanner were in sad condition now, for they had carried him countless miles. They had covered the whole Peraean area, and Jesus became ever more intense, spending longer periods of time by Himself, rising very early in the mornings and not always getting enough sleep, Peter thought.

The trips down the Jordan valley had been respite from the colder nights of the hill country, and the greater warmth and humidity were more to Peter's liking, living close to the sea the way he had.

The first new growth came earliest down along the river with the fields here already green with their winter wheat and barley.

Soon it would be time for the priests to take out a sample sheaf, in the famous "wave sheaf" ceremony, holding it up to God in praise and waving it as if for God to see. Peter had been taught that wave sheaf symbolized a Messiah, in some way, as if the first of the first fruits of the whole world.

Soon the families would choose out their unblemished lamb or kid and set it aside in preparation for the ancient ceremony of the Passover. The disciples saw increasing traffic along the trails, sometimes large groups of a hundred or more traveling to Jerusalem for the Passover just ahead.

Jerusalem was already buzzing with rumors. The chief priests were sure Jesus would try something dramatic at this coming Passover. The whole countryside from Galilee to Judea was rife with talk about the Messiah. Thousands said He was that Prophet who should come, and others argued He was just another Theudas or would-be Maccabean revolutionary.

But a rumor that chilled and enraged Peter was that some of the priests had begun to plot how they could trap Lazarus in some alleged sin and stone him to death!

Imagine that!

The common people regarded Lazarus as a curiosity

(hundreds of them were continually journeying to Bethany, which was only a few furlongs from Jerusalem and less than half a day's easy walk), and they would pester the family until Lazarus would consent to talk to them and answer their questions.

As a living example of one of Jesus' greatest miracles, the leaders felt they could not allow him to stay alive!

Peter was amazed at the utter hatred of these religious fanatics! "Can you imagine trying to *put to death* a man God has *just raised from the dead?*" Peter would say to himself.

It was only another seven days to the Passover, and they were taking a full day to cover the final miles to Bethany when news came to them about the plots being hatched against Jesus and Lazarus.

They stopped along the road at a small hostel for a noonday meal of lentils and roasted ears of corn, washing it down with the cool water of a spring that welled out from the base of a huge upthrust of rock. Below them along the trail another large caravan plodded along, the carts jouncing over the rutted road, with at least sixty animals in the train. The jingling of the ox harnesses came faintly on the breeze. Peter was relaxing with Thomas, leaning back against a pack, when he heard a startled "What?" from James over by the spring.

Peter walked over and listened.

"He said they spread the word through the city that anyone who sees Jesus is commanded instantly to run to the chief priests."

"So what?" scoffed Bartholomew. "They'll never betray Him like that. He's too popular with the people, and they're afraid of the priests."

"That's the whole point! Their fear!" said the messenger. "They are so afraid they'll be put out of their synagogues that many of them are openly saying they'll cooperate with the priests and reveal His whereabouts if He shows Himself."

"I can't believe they would do that," said Peter.

"Then think back about that blind boy's family," the new arrival continued. "The parents were so frightened they couldn't even embrace their son. And, remember, they stayed right there in the synagogue while the priests put the son out, and they were not allowed to have anything further to do with him!''

''That's true enough,'' Peter admitted. ''But what was this you were saying about Lazarus?''

''Just that he has become a major source of irritation to the priests. So many people have been over to Bethany to see him and are talking about his being raised from the tomb that he is one of the most important attractions in the country! It's one thing to hear rumors about so-called 'big works,' but another to saddle your camel, ride over and talk to a living miracle!''

''I see,'' said Peter. ''Then you mean it is true; they are actually plotting to kill Lazarus too?''

''It's true, all right!'' he affirmed.

They talked on about the mood of the general populace. Strange, Peter though, how people could be controlled by fear of being ''put out'' from their familiar surroundings. But ''put out'' from *what?*

Put out from a fear-ridden religious organization that kept its followers in a state of apprehension and doubt? Peter supposed the common fold would doltishly follow along even if the leaders in the synagogue were caught in bloody-handed murder. Somehow they had absolved themselves of all personal responsibility.

That was where Jesus' teachings ran head on into those of the Pharisees and religious fanatics. He taught personal responsibility, personal choice; He continuously emphasized the fact that every man stood alone before God and that he couldn't get into the glittering kingdom of which Jesus spoke on someone else's shirttails.

So now they were plotting to kill Lazarus!

''Rumor has it a meeting took place between the chief priests themselves and they're trying to arrange Lazarus' death,'' the messenger said, looking at Peter.

''Well, we'll warn Lazarus and Mary. Maybe Jesus will feel they should leave town. Maybe they should go up into Galilee until Jesus sets up His kingdom and brings down the present priesthood.'' Turning to Bartholomew,

Peter said, "Bart, why don't you saddle up and get over there and then come on back tonight. I think Jesus may want to go into Jerusalem tomorrow."

"I'll go right away," Bart said and turned to saddle up one of their pack animals that was standing by the seep, its tail switching flies. Bart and the messenger jogged out of sight below while Peter and the others went back down to the hostel to tell Jesus and the disciples of this latest development.

The following morning Jesus told Peter, "Go into that village over there and as soon as you enter it you'll find a colt tied that has never been ridden. When you find him, untie the colt and bring him to Me. And if anyone says anything to you just answer, 'The Lord has need of him,' and they will tell you to take him."

Peter wondered if He had already sent a messenger into the town yesterday, or had seen a vision, or had somehow used His supernatural powers to communicate to the owner of the colt. But, no matter, after all the miracles he had seen he wasn't about to doubt Jesus' ability to produce a free ride on a new colt.

# XVI

In a small house on the edge of the village, old Ben Chusa was excited as he greeted his wife at breakfast that morning. He couldn't wait to tell her about the mysterious dream he had had the night before.

He had been carefully gentling a beautiful white colt from his favorite jenny, leading it about, stroking it and talking to it, feeding it by hand, until the animal had become like a pet, though never yet ridden. Tomorrow he intended saddling up and taking the young colt over the winding trail up into Jerusalem and showing her off to some friends.

But that night he had a vision. It seemed a voice had spoken to him that he should delay his journey, that the foal was not to be ridden but that "the Lord has need of him." In his mind's eye, he seemed to see a long, long caravan of people, thousands and thousands of people in a huge crowd thronging the streets and running beside a plain-looking man who smiled and waved here and there, who seemed to be the center of attention.

The dream had been filled with sound and excitement. And, wonder of all wonders, just as the crowd seemed to shout the loudest, with people clapping their hands and crying aloud with joy, old Ben's watery eyes noticed that the man who was moving along the way, surrounded by so many people, was riding his newly gentled foal!

It seemed a voice had spoken to him; he couldn't

remember. But somehow he felt that he should have the animal ready, that perhaps the person he had seen in the dream would come for him. Ben Chusa was happy.

He was a praying man, and he had heard this Jesus of Nazareth teach at least twice in the temple.

His wife laughed at his dream and said, ''Go on, now, Ben Chusa, and don't deprive yourself of riding to the market today to show the new foal. You know how hard you have worked to prepare him and how long you have waited for this day.''

But he was adamant. ''What's a few more hours?'' he asked. ''If the Prophet comes and asks for him, as I saw in the dream, then I will know. If not, then there's time to go into the city tomorrow.''

She clucked at him longer, chuckling about his dreams, thinking how he was growing older and more prone to believe in almost everything that happened or was said as having some special significance.

As for herself, she couldn't believe in such things as dreams and visions, not since the time when her own mother had seen a vivid dream that the Messiah would soon come, even in her lifetime, and He had not. She had died after a long and painful illness, still thinking a prophet could show up any day and heal her.

She finished their breakfast cleanup chores and began gathering old Chusa's clothes into a bag for washing. Today she would join the other women down along the flat rocks on Kidron, even though it meant a steep climb back up, for she didn't want to go all the way to the washing rocks by the wells in the city. Ben Chusa was muttering to the foal out by the shed and currying the animal again as she started to leave the door.

Just then two men rounded the final bend of the trail below them.

''Chusa!'' she called out nervously, for strangers were a rarity up this trail that led to their own house and three others of their closest neighbors.

Their shed, like several others, formed a wall along the street. There was a door opening onto the street. The neighbors' sheds adjoined, and the wall was like a solid, white structure broken only by the doors which opened into each neighbor's shed and the animal yards beyond.

Her husband looked up then and, seeing the men approaching, led the foal to the trail outside and tied him at the door.

Whatever was he doing? she pondered. Sometimes pilgrims coming to Jerusalem for the Passover would come this way, though it was further around than the main trail below, for they wished provender for their animals, or there was food to be purchased from the small village or a spare room to rent. But lately there had been reports of thieves. Some of them were brazen enough to move about the countryside in small gangs, keeping the Romans busy. It was said an entire force under a centurion was scouring the nearby hills for Barabbas and his gang right this minute, and that they might have him any time. She was nervous about Ben Chusa leaving the foal outside like that.

A couple of the neighbors were looking quizzically at the men too.

The first was a stocky, brown-bearded fellow who carried a Roman short sword around his waist. He was powerfully built, with brawny shoulders, huge hands and well-developed calves exposed to the sun beneath the outer skirt he wore that stopped just above the knees.

The two men, spying the foal, strode directly to him and began untying the knot.

"Hey! You men there!" said one of the neighbors, running over. "What do you think you're doing with that foal?"

Two others trotted over, and old Ben Chusa walked out the gate and up the trail to the door of his shed where they were gathered.

He got there just in time to hear the big brown-bearded man say, "The Lord has need of him."

Ben Chusa interrupted, saying, "You're—you're with . . ."

Peter smiled at him and, finishing untying the knot, repeated his statement. Ben Chusa lifted a hand to stay his neighbor, saying, "Of course, of course, take him, and welcome."

"Chusa!" his wife called out, you're—you're not going to just stand there and let those strangers steal your prize foal . . ."

"Hush, woman, remember the dream?" he said.

"Go ahead, go ahead," he told Peter and Luke, looking intently at them, eyes dropping to Peter's sword and Luke's writer's inkhorn and papers at his side. "I knew you'd come—I had a dream."

The old eyes were watery, and his hand trembled a little as he reached out to stroke the young foal and re-assure the animal as it shied from Peter's hand.

"Here, you'll want this. He's partial to it," said Ben Chusa, handing Peter some fresh roots he had brought to feed the foal. "I have gentled him with hand feeding and special care. Intended to ride him into the markets today and show him off to my friends, but now . . ."

The voice trailed away as Peter smiled, accepted the roots with a rumbling thank-you, and, signaling to his companion, began leading the young animal away back down the steeply winding path.

Ben Chusa watched them out of sight and, seeing his wife still shielding her eyes against the morning glare, looking from the departing men and the foal to her husband, he hurried to her and said, "Well, woman, go on, go on, lay out my best robe and let's get cleaned up and ready to go to the gate. Didn't I tell you this would happen? Didn't I tell you?"

You're only an old fool who has just watched two thieves walk away with your prize foal, that's all," she said sarcastically. "And furthermore . . ."

"Shut up, woman," he said, voice rising and a bright, happy look coming into his eyes, "and get in there and draw me a bath from the water cistern like I told you. I'm going to the gate because there's going to be a parade, just as sure as my dream, and you'll see the Lord Himself riding into Jerusalem today, riding into glory, and on the back of my very own foal! Go on, go on . . ."

Stunned by the force of his own voice and not a little moved by the intensity and almost youthful exuberance of his passion, his wife, flustered at his newfound energy, ducked into their little house and rushed to the fire now nearly dead on the hearth, quickly seizing the bellows to bring it back to life for the warming of the water.

Maybe—just maybe—there was something to old Ben Chusa's dream after all.

Peter and Luke talked animatedly about the exciting developments.

"This is it, Luke—I know it!" Peter said.

"Seems to be, all right. If He intends entering the city so publicly, I know it will draw huge crowds."

"And you know as well as I do that many of the disciples will be running to tell special friends already, for we have had the full group with us for some time now."

"That's true," Luke admitted.

"What do you think? Will He go first to the temple or directly to Herod's house? Or would He go first to Pontius Pilate's residence, or would He think to assemble the Sanhedrin and throw them down from office?"

"Somehow He would almost have to do all of that at once!" Luke said, chewing on his lip. "But my guess is the temple."

Peter fell silent, striding along, leading the beautiful white foal, thinking back along the thousands of hours, the days, months and years. At last.

How many times had he been bitterly disappointed? How many times had doubts about Jesus *ever* setting up His fabulous kingdom assailed his mind, made him wonder if Jesus was truly who He said He was, the very Son of God?

So many times he had angrily fought down his protests when it seemed the Lord had passed up golden opportunities, like that time up in the heights above the Sea of Galilee when five thousand people would have hoisted Him to their shoulders and begun a triumphal march on the capital.

Now that the two teams of thirty-five each had spread the word through dozens of towns and cities, and some of them had even gone into Jerusalem and its suburbs ahead of them, Peter expected the day had really arrived.

Jesus was talking to some of the traveling teams when

they brought the foal up to Him along the olive groves on the Mount of Olives.

There was no saddle that would fit the animal, and so they took their outer cloaks and garments and made a several-layered, comfortable, makeshift saddle for Him.

They began.

Peter positively danced with joy — skipping along and thinking the strangest thoughts, like the way David leapt and danced before the Ark of the Covenant when he had it brought back from Kirjathjearim from the Philistines. When people would ask, "What's happening? What's going on?" he would joyously say, "Jesus of Nazareth, our *King,* is going to Jerusalem today!"

People were sticking their heads out of the windows of the houses clustered along Kidron, and neighbors were calling to one another. Crowds began to gather.

Peter saw many running along the higher road by the corner of the wall of the city and calling out to those along the way.

A swelling sound began as the crowds thickened, and then Peter saw that one man had climbed a palm tree and thrown down some green fronds, hacking away at them with a sharp field hand's knife. The men below grabbed them up and, waving them in the air, ran to Jesus' foal and carefully placed them down before Him.

Others, inspired by this display, began taking off their outer garments and spreading them before the foal.

It became like an exciting, breathless game to see if they could prevent a single hoof of the animal from stepping on the stones of the road, grabbing up the fronds and clothing as it passed and passing them along to those in front and laying them down again.

Someone shouted, "Hosanna!" and Peter was startled to find it was his own voice! "Blessed be our *King!*" shouted another of the disciples. Soon all the disciples were roaring out a marching chant, saying, "Peace in heaven! Glory in the highest!" and "Blessed be the King that comes in the name of the Lord!"

The crowds took up the chant until it thundered and roared, echoed and re-echoed against the walls of the city and up and down Kidron. The crowd had grown to more than three or four thousand by now, and they weren't even to the gate yet!

And here came the first obstacle. Peter and Luke ran forward to help clear the path and found some of the leading Pharisees standing squarely in the middle of the road. Rather than bodily remove them, they stood by, wondering what Jesus' reaction would be.

As the foal plodded along, the people busily laying down their garments and the palm fronds, the leader stepped aside, and, as Jesus drew near, he challenged, "Rabbi, *rebuke* Your disciples!"

"Yes, rebuke them," said his cohort. "They are blaspheming and causing a tumult here that is not allowed!"

"I tell you," answered Jesus in a loud voice, "if these should hold their peace, the very stones here would cry out!"

"Hosanna!" the shouting continued, pealing across the valley of the Kidron and splitting the clear morning air with a growing thunder as Jesus continued along the curving roadway, climbing ever higher toward the main city gate.

The Pharisee, muttering dark threats and saying, "We'll see about this!" scurried along the roadway, struggling to break through the crowds and gain the city gate ahead of Jesus. He failed, however, for the people were too densely packed and too excited to pay any attention to him.

Ben Chusa and his wife had perched atop a stone wall along the way, bordering a small orchard of a neighbor who lived on the main road. As the noise and shouting began, he kept standing up, almost losing his footing, to see the better. Soon his faded vision saw men and women, children among them, running along, leaping, dancing, pirouetting in the pathways and waving palm fronds —hundreds of fronds, olive branches and other greenery—the people shouting and crowding the streets to see.

And here came the procession, orderly ranks of at least fifty men all joyously shouting "Hosanna!" and

"Praise God! Blessed be our KING!" The men just behind were busily laying down *garments,* and even palm fronds, making a soft pathway for—*for his own foal!*

"Look!" he exulted, pointing a crooked finger. "Look!" His wife stared in incredulity.

"My dream! My dream!" said Ben Chusa. "It was real, it was true!"

"Hosanna!" the crowd shouted. "Blessed be the King that comes in the name of the Lord!" "Shalom! Peace!" cried those crowded near the wall beneath Ben Chusa and his wife. And then even his wife took up the cries, wringing her hands in her apron, and tears running down her cheeks. "Praise God!" and "Blessed be our King!" she said.

As the procession drew loudly abreast of Ben Chusa's perch, he thought he looked straight into the face of the plain-looking Man who sat on his favorite foal, thought he saw the lips form a silent "thank you" and saw a meaningful nod before his view was again blotted out by hundreds of waving palm fronds and olive branches.

Ben Chusa was so happy he thought his heart would quit. To *think* of it, the promised Messiah was here, this Jesus of Nazareth *really was* that Prophet who would come. He had seen Him and this crowd in his dream, and there was his own foal that he had so carefully and lovingly gentled and trained, never yet daring to ride until the big day—today! But it was not for him to ride, but his very King! He was overawed.

"Hosanna!" the crowd was shouting as the sounds gradually diminished with the passing of thousands of shuffling feet. And beside the foal Ben Chusa saw the two men who had come for the animal, the stocky, brown-bearded one walking along with his Roman short sword slapping his large thighs, shouting aloud along with the others and skipping and leaping now and then, shaking hands, patting people on the shoulders and with a big grin splitting his weathered face.

Rounding the corner high up near the wall, Peter noticed Jesus pull up and stop. The shouting nearest Him died down, with the disciples wondering why He had

stopped. Gradually the front ranks kept saying ''Quiet!''
and ''Shush!'' to those behind until the crowds fell silent.

Jesus was looking at the city, and tears were now
coursing down His cheeks. Peter's heart leapt—what?

''If you had only known, even you, at least in *this,
your* day, the things that pertain to the *peace* that could be
yours! But now they are hidden from your eyes!'' Jesus
said, voice breaking now and then.

''For the days shall come upon you,'' He said, voice
pealing out so that thousands could hear, ''that your enemies shall cast a trench about you and surround you on
every side, and shall lay you even with the ground, and
your children with you, and they shall not leave in you one
stone atop another, because you did not know the time of
your visitation!''

Peter's mind recalled another time when Jesus had
wept over the city, and his racing mind thought that
perhaps the Lord was speaking of yet future wars. Surely
He wasn't talking of this next generation? Was He not even
now about to enter the city and take over the government to
prevent the very calamities He now predicted? Peter's
head was swimming.

The march began again and immediately the shouting
was taken up, and the tumult became even louder as the
thousands swelled to more thousands, and the whole city
stirred.

At length they reached the temple gates, and, entering the massive courtyard, Jesus stopped, handed the reins
of the nose halter He used to James and got down from the
foal, giving instructions to another disciple, who turned
and began leading the animal back into the street, no doubt
heading for old Ben Chusa's house.

Jesus then strode purposefully toward the massive
building with His disciples, all of them now, flanking Him
on every side. Peter cried, ''Make way there!'' and helped
to part a pathway through the chanting, shouting people.

Entering the temple, Jesus immediately fixed a stern,
angry look on the nearest of the money changers' tables.

Striding to the nearest table, He grasped the front of it
and turned it over, complete with coins, metal bars, turtle

dove cages and even some piles of clothing that had been traded. The wizened little money changer who had been hunched over his trays like a miserly little clerk let out a squawk of fright and fell over his stool trying to get out of the way, ending up sprawled headlong among rolling coins and fluttering doves that were shedding feathers in their frantic attempt to break free from their cages.

*"My* house is the house of *prayer,"* He said loudly, "and you have made it into a den of thieves!"

With a shout of accord, the other disciples joined in. Peter grabbed the next table and began making mayhem of the money changers' tables and driving the animals out. The crowd soon joyously followed suit until there was not an animal, nor a dove's cage, nor a single money changer's table remaining in the temple.

Peter wondered if all of them had successfully retrieved all their money, but he frankly didn't care. They were cheats and crooks anyway. The thought about what Judas had been doing while he was helping throw down the money changers' tables went fleetingly through his mind, but Jesus was now mounting a dais in the main room and was being seated for a teaching session, and so Peter sent for John, James and some of the others and strode swiftly to His side.

That teaching session was tumultuously successful. Jesus spoke with real power and authority, and the people nodded and said, "That's true!" The Pharisees, chief priests and elders continually sought to find some argument against Him, with Jesus silencing them every time.

Jesus was a growing puzzle to Peter for the next few days as the Passover grew nearer. Instead of following up on the massive demonstration when He entered the city and marching on Herod's palace or even deposing the Sanhedrin, He seemed content to engage in almost endless confrontations in the temple.

Peter struggled with himself to be patient, knowing Jesus' plan was right.

# XVII

Judas couldn't understand Jesus' complete aloofness from money, and yet he was thankful for it; it meant Jesus never checked up to see how their financial condition was—only asked Judas to buy this or that from time to time, and even if some person tried to press a tithe into the Lord's hand to help them in their travels He always told them to take it to Judas, and didn't seem to want to even touch the coins. Judas' conscience could still rankle now and then, but he had managed long ago to justify himself completely in his financial schemes. He imagined Jesus would finally put him in charge of the whole treasury of the great new kingdom of which He spoke.

Judas' imagination went wild at the spectacular sight of him, Judas, being the one in total charge of the whole economy. Talk about *rich!* He thought of some of the ancient brazen vessels in the temple treasury, and even some shields and swords said to belong to David's time that had been recovered from the rubble when Zerubbabel and Ezra had begun to reconstruct the temple following the captivity in Babylon. Why, there were treasures to be contemplated that made his palms grow clammy and his eyes glaze over with a fevered heat. He was interested in archaeology too. He wanted very badly to investigate the rumors he had heard as a boy in the south of Judah about King Solomon's mines down near the Red Sea and along the soaring heights of Africa that spiced the stories of traders who came from distant lands where strange and exotic birds and animals lived.

Of late, Judas had allowed himself to dream beyond the lesser position of overseer of the treasury; his rambling imagination had probed into the weirdest possible areas. He had come to actually hate Jesus, hate His procrastination, His habit of demurring to attacks, and His lack of perception of how to use the power of the mob.

Why, He could have taken over the government a long time ago, if He had just used the gift of speaking He had, His strange powers of miracle-working, and allowed the herd to catapult Him into the very room of Herod himself—and even beyond Herod—to proclaim Himself absolute monarch, sending representatives to Rome and arranging complete recognition of the new government by pointing out the obvious disadvantages of another long, tedious campaign against Palestine—the vast expenditures in money, material and manpower—when the wealth of Palestine could continue to flow to Rome, by treaties of mutual respect and mutual protection.

Judas imagined he would convince the emperor by a quick military coup and add to the emperor's conquered territories. Caesar could hardly be angered by news of a successful military adventure wherein his imperial coffers were suddenly the richer by millions.

He would weigh the alternatives between choosing to view the takeover of Palestine as a threat to his empire in the East or the alternative of recognizing her, under Judas, as a partner, bound together by trading agreements, mutual defense pacts and Judas' commitment to Rome's further expansion.

Why, he could promise the Roman garrisons an increase in pay, better quarters and great rewards if they would assist in training the masses of rabble he would forge into an army. What if news of the revolution were tempered by the arrival of ten thousand slaves? Caesar could use the men in his galleys (even Judas could shudder a little at the thought, but, then, what difference would it really make?), and the women as household slaves for thousands of his nobles and favorites.

His mind plunged on and on.

He would send an expert in copper and mining to Rome, would have him explain how successful expeditions into Africa, and into the fabled land of "Put" from which Solomon had brought apes, ivory and peacocks, could increase the flow of valuable metals for arms, metals for all purposes. There were the new experiments in making hollow tubes of metal for conducting water from place to place to who knew what.

"Aes cyprium" would be plentiful, if he could locate the fabled King Solomon's mines. Most people were calling the metal "cyprium" for short, or, in the language of the common folk, "cuprum." Little could Judas know that, centuries later, the greenish, reddish metal used in the cheapest coins and, when alloyed with tin for spears and swords, would be perverted to "copper."

Would Peter go along? Would Andrew, or James, or John? Judas wondered; he doubted it. The only way would be if Peter were sufficiently disgusted over the Lord's continual refusal to fight, His continual backing down in the face of threats. Judas knew Peter's moods, knew how Peter sulked when his natural impetuosity, combined with his considerable physique and muscular development, led him to take direct action. He had seen the dozens of times that Peter's horny hand had strayed to the hilt of his Roman short sword he carried, seen him work himself into a sweat, hacking a brush for starting a fire with unnecesary vigor, as if he wished the brush were Roman heads instead of firewood.

Judas had spoken often enough to Thaddeus, and to Simon, the swarthy disciple from Canaan, and to Alphaeus' son, James. Even Bartholomew had allowed himself to give voice to some apprehension over the future and had expressed fear that Jesus might give up just before the final step in the coup were complete.

Judas' emotions would run wild at times like this, when he would abandon himself to impossible dreams, and yet . . . was it so impossible? Jesus seemed reluctant to seize just the right opportunities. Certainly that huge mob of five thousand people in the Galilean heights had been at a fever pitch for action. Why, they were going to take Jesus *forcibly* and put Him on their shoulders for a triumphal march into the capital.

Judas knew Jesus wasn't making anywhere near enough mileage out of the fabulous miracle-working power He had. Time and again the Lord would tell the members of the mob (Judas never thought of the masses of people as anything other than a herd, a flock or a mob; his contempt for the common people was a part of him) not to mention the miracles to anyone when a more clever person would have contrived to perform the miracles right in front of the most influential people possible, right in the eyesight of the leaders, backed up by sufficient of the herd to ensure he wouldn't dare deny it.

In the beginning Judas had a love-hate relationship with Jesus. He loved, admired and even feared Him. He didn't recognize that he also envied Him and would have been profoundly shocked if someone had accused him of it. It was just that his scheming mind could quickly analyze possibilities for immense profits when it seemed Jesus was oblivious to such opportunities. They could easily have placed leaders in charge of a few here and a few there, Judas thought; could have designated captains of tens, fifties, hundreds and thousands. It was the ancient pattern, probably the pattern of David's army, and was certainly the governmental system Moses used. The herd would fall into it naturally, for it had been taught them since their youth. They could have had upwards of two hundred thousand men ready to march by now, and instead Jesus had managed to frighten away even a significant number of their original one hundred and twenty.

Judas would slip into dark and dangerous moods, even imagining what would happen if Jesus were killed in one of the many riots when the angry leaders incited the crowds. Who would seize power? Peter would try, probably. Certainly John and Andrew were incapable of it, forever hanging back and soft spoken. John's manner made Judas' flesh crawl. He seemed so fawning, so obsequious around Jesus, and the Lord actually appeared to enjoy his company. It made Judas' blood boil to see the continual snubs he had been handed. Almost every time some special thing was about to occur, Jesus called James, Peter and John over to Him, and the four of them would set out with never a by-your-leave.

Judas passionately wanted to know where they had gone and what had happened when they had disappeared in the direction of Hermon that time and stayed away for days on end. Peter's manner had been one of renewed awe, and even fear toward the Lord after they had returned, and Judas couldn't for the life of him find out why. He had tried to pump them, but their lips were firmly sealed, and even after Judas had plied Peter with a special wineskin he said he had purchased at a bargain (which he had, but not with Peter in mind) and watched him put away more than half of it, Peter's tongue stayed firmly fastened in his head.

Judas loved Jesus dearly, he told himself. He loved Him more than all the others put together; deserved to be far closer to the Lord because of that deep affection, was more fiercely loyal, more concerned, more dedicated to the great causes. Judas couldn't know that his love for Christ was a self-centered love of desire toward Jesus because of jealousy, that his own mind deluded himself into confusing his desperate desire for sharing (or hogging) the limelight, being at the center of power, the focus of attention, with love. To him it *was* love, the only kind of love he really had yet experienced, for the true love of outgoing concern for that person being loved was totally foreign to him; he had never felt it.

That love Judas felt drove him into the darkest moods of depression when he saw Jesus falling short of the kind of Jesus Judas wanted Him to be. Judas deeply loved the Jesus of his dreams, a Jesus nearer Judas' own heart's desire, made in the image of a great, powerful leader who mesmerized the masses with stentorian thunder, who was of the stuff of emperors, kings, generals, who inspired only loyalty and abject, servile love in His subjects. Judas' perceptions of Jesus—the perfect Jesus the way Judas imagined He should be—became clouded with self-image. Judas couldn't know he was listening to an inner voice from the most subtle, powerful, persuasive spirit being on earth, Satan himself. He only knew that everyone said you got angriest at the ones you loved the most and so convinced himself his frequent private rages over Jesus' conduct were only because he saw Jesus falling short of Judas' own image of Him—hurting Himself, as it were —and Judas believed his outrage was completely justified.

From the beginning of his travels with the Lord, Judas had been content to be the treasurer, adviser in money matters and the special person trusted with specific duties uniquely his own (because of his vast experience, personal training and expertise, of course). Judas frequently told Simon the Canaanite, who was one of his most willing listeners, how he had given up a lucrative exchange and banking business to live this life of sacrifice. He waxed eloquent with Simon about how he would surely have controlled half the publicans in Jerusalem by now, would have reorganized the entire foreign exchange system at the borders and would have been coming to the notice of Herod himself because of his financial and legal genius.

He despised John, that a simple fisherman should have Jesus' attention, be at His side so much of the time and be privy to special information, accompanying the Lord on mysterious side trips—when He, Judas, was obviously more intelligent, better educated and more qualified in ever way to be at Jesus' right hand—constantly galled him. Besides, John had made a slur once, following a purchase Judas had made. With that secret part of his mind that didn't let Judas look at himself plainly, his deepest consciousness, he hated himself. But with his other self he fought fiercely to maintain a pose of total integrity, honesty and financial expertise.

He wondered, with the dark side of his mind, whether John knew he had been covertly pilfering from their common funds. Yet, with fierce intensity, he continually struck the pose of honest innocence, and, in order to shut the mouths of those who would dare impugn his "integrity," he would fly into uncontrollable rages at any slight.

John had made some notes that time, and Judas had managed to sneak a look at them. John had written: "Judas; carries bag; thief?" There was more: rambling lines about a possible betrayal!

A thief?

He had stormed over those notes for days before confronting John during one of Jesus' absences for prayer. But first he had made various threats against John to Simon, and to Thaddeus, and Bartholomew. He would go to the Sanhedrin itself, he had ranted. To bear false witness was a crime punishable by stoning!

"I will sue him for everything he is worth, and his family too. I'll have him in and out of a court of law for the next five years!" he had screamed to Simon! He knew Simon would carry the story to John and hoped that would be sufficient to scare John off, make him change his mind. And, under the threat of being tied up in lawsuits, or charged with a major crime, perhaps he would back off and not mention Judas in his damnable notes.

He waited for days without noticing any thawing in John's attitude.

John and Simon the Canaanite were the only two around the camp when he had returned early from a nearby village; Jesus was up in the nearby mountains and the others were either with Him or scattered about attending to their own matters. Judas had opened the conversation by complaining about the cheating villagers in the market, muttering aloud that "you can't trust any of those thieving cheats" and defaming all publicans, customs-house men (with a deliberate slur on Matthew's reputation) and money changers. Then he launched into a long diatribe about his own background, reputation and honesty.

He said, "John, you gave up nothing, really! You can go back to your family fisheries business and everything will be there waiting for you just as it was. You lose nothing. Any inheritance will be secure for you and your family. But me? I left a lucrative business, gave up everything! I was at the absolute top of the class, sitting at the feet of Zacchaeus' top three Levites, who taught me all there is to know about financial matters, even minting, and mining, and foreign exchange! I am a man with a reputation among the entire financial community, and I know the law! I will not stand having my reputation questioned!"

John had merely continued cleaning their utensils, scrubbing them with the sand of the creekbed and packing them away in the packs, leaning against the trees.

Judas couldn't stand the thought of John coming out with any specifics right in front of Simon, the swarthy disciple from Canaan, so he decided not to demand John go and alter his notes right there and then. Probably the other tack, that of frightening him so badly he would never dare use those notes or show them to anyone else, was best.

"Thank God the Lord gave me the responsibility of treasurer, handling all our financial affairs, John!" Judas laughed, trying to change his approach. "With your simple fisherman's honesty you'd probably have been stolen blind by these filthy thieves in the markets these days. You'd probably be unable to hang onto what we have, let alone see it increase by skillful dealing and saving money for all of us the way I have done."

John had been noncommittal, and that had galled Judas all the more, but after he had waxed eloquent over several examples of the dishonesty of others, and given himself plaudits for his financial genius, and the savings he was making their group, he broke off the conversation. Besides, here came Peter and James and, not far behind them, the others. Judas hoped his warning had been plain; hoped it would do the job.

At least John was a mild mannered, closed-mouthed sort. Jesus couldn't stand gossipers, and one of the things that endeared Him to John was John's stolid qualities. Judas feverishly hoped John would not defame him to Jesus; he couldn't stand that!

Perhaps one of the things Judas coveted the most was simple *approval* from Jesus—being noticed, held in esteem and appreciated. But no matter how hard he strove to capture the Lord's favor, no matter the hints he dropped or the stories he related about how expertly he had handled some sly money changer who had tried to rob their common purse by clipping coins, it seemed Jesus continually had that quiet reserve, that steady look that burned right through Judas' heart and that made him fidget nervously, finding himself running out of words, blinking furiously and looking aside.

The more he strove for reputation, the more his mind became embittered toward the Lord. It wasn't fair! He, Judas, would make all of them put together ashamed. He would show them! He was the only *really* astute, well-educated, "professional" in the entire group! Why, even Matthew, whose name was Levi, seemed to be an unambitious clerk. Anyone who had worked for so long in the customs department handling all that money and yet was not wealthy, and who had immediately left what should have been a promising professional career and followed Jesus—the man had to be stupid! No—Peter and Andrew—simple fishermen! The same for James and John! Their very hands and clothing reminded Judas of the reek of the fishmongers' shops along the waterfronts.

Luke? A petty peddler of herbs and potions. Perhaps he knew a thing or two about the workings of the body, and was a physician of sorts, but to Judas' best information Luke was poor enough and had never made much money. Judas was contemptuous of anyone who didn't know the value of gold—money—and who couldn't prove his worth by seeing to it that a substantial amount of the stuff stayed in his own pockets.

Here they were, with all the ingredients necessary for one of the greatest revolutions in the world. It boggled Judas' mind.

First there were the restive masses, exploited from both the Romans and their own puppet leaders, the Herods and their kin, like the various tetrarchs. They were notorious for their sumptuous living and their appetites that lay clearly beyond the Torah. Further, the struggling herders, farmers, fishers, coopers, carpenters, traders and the dozens of other occupations were so stringently taxed, or cheated, by the publicans, threatened out of their money by the Pharisees or robbed by Romans soldiers—all this provided fertile breeding ground for promised reform in the person of a powerful leader who could promise redistribution of wealth, promise every family a piece of the land and the freedom to work it.

Second, there was the fervent hope of Israel, the coming of Messiah! Weekly in the temple, and daily in every home, the prayers and supplications spoke of the hope of revolution, the coming of Messiah to restore the grandeur of the kingdom. Didn't the prophets promise that the glory of the temple, and therefore the kingdom it represented, would be even greater than the splendor of Solomon's own? Of course, the elderly spoke behind their hands and softly in the marketplaces and the wineshops whenever a Roman chanced along who just might understand Hebrew, but they spoke of it nevertheless. Never was a family supper enjoyed without the elder of the house referring to delivery—a Messiah—restoration!

Rumors of Rome's military needs from beyond the Gates of Hercules to Africa, and from here in Palestine to India, kept many a mother casting anxious glances at a strong young son who could be conscripted to serve. The rigors of the legions were well known, and the brutality such rigors bred. Runaways and deserters ended up as galley slaves, likely, or, if they were fortunate, dead. But death through crucifixion, that most brutal of methods whereby a person was mortally wounded through scourging and then hoisted aloft to croak out his desperate pain, terrible thirst and prayers for death for hours in a blazing sun—even the galleys were to be chosen over such a fate. What chance was there? Judas suspected many a mother had gouged out the eye of a beloved baby boy just to make him unfit for duty in the legions and a better beggar on the streets. There were plenty of those.

If ever a people were ripe for revolution, it was the Jewish people of this Herodian period. Exploited, downtrodden, poverty stricken, diseased—lepers walked along the roads crying out "Leper! Leper!" so the others could hastily give them wide berth. The ghastly disfigurements of those hapless wretches who had survived the army, or even the galleys (very rare, indeed), were evident in the streets. Feeble beggars who could scarcely rise from their pallets lay, covered with flies, right at the city gates. One could scarcely go shopping or visiting in the markets without a dozen of the scarecrow figures clutching at the hem of his garment, begging.

And in the midst of all this suffering strode a strong, young, powerful Man, a Man of the trades, right out of their own miserable ranks, from Galilee—Jesus, Son of Joseph the contractor and carpenter; Jesus, who spoke for all the people and who called Himself ''Son of Man'' and even ''the Son of God.''

And the *people believed,* Judas mused. How they believed! He had produced food where there was none; walked on water, restored withered hands, changed water into the finest wine, strode authoritatively into the temple itself and thrown the cheating exchangers and cattle dealers out. He had even raised the dead! Jairus' daughter and the whole family willingly repeated the story to all who would listen, and the widow at Nain and her boy bore witness! So did Lazarus.

Yet Jesus hesitated!

But *now,* or even *last year,* was the time!

Why did He continue to wait?

Judas didn't know. He only knew that the fantastic opportunity might not ever again present itself, knew that rumors already said the Romans were thinking of asking for reinforcements to quell any future uprisings. He hoped, passionately, that either Jesus would act soon, or that somehow he, Judas, could be given a greater dimension in the direction of their growing cadre of leaders and bring about the coup himself!

And what better time than *now,* during this Passover season? Would there be some opportunity for Judas to replace Jesus, to take over the others? He had made significant headway with Simon the Canaanite and some others, but there was always the chance the Lord would change and quit playing favorites with John and James and Peter! The streets of the city were teeming with people from all over the eastern part of the empire, and Jesus seemed intent on exposing Himself to the crowds. Perhaps He did intend to do something truly dramatic this Passover.

There were a number of Greeks at the Passover. Greek traders dealt with some of the frontier cities, especally Bethsaida, and it happened that some of them had known Philip, who was another of the disciples from that city.

They found him and asked if it were possible for them to see Jesus. Philip said he would check to find out and told Andrew about it. Andrew, Peter's brother, took Philip to see Jesus. Jesus not only agreed to let the Greeks see Him, but seized the opportunity to give a mysterious but very powerful message about being "lifted up from the earth" and said, "And I, if I be lifted up from the earth, will draw all men unto Myself!"

It seemed some of the Greeks were from cities in Asia, like Ephesus (where the great temples of Diana and Asklepios were), and even from Corinth and Thessalonica. One of them was named Titus, like the great Roman general, and there were several other common Greek names.

Jesus was spending up to nine hours in the temple each day, and, as the Passover grew nearer, His messages grew more powerful and intense and caused continual controversy.

Each evening He would leave with His disciples and walk all the way back across the brook Kidron and climb the hills up to the Mount of Olives.

# XVIII

The day finally came when Jesus completely silenced the Pharisees and Sadducees.

Peter was standing a little behind the slightly raised teacher's dais and looking over the crowd, assuming his unconscious role as Jesus' protector and personal bodyguard. It was a thankless job in many ways, but he couldn't help himself. He was impatient for the tide of events to hurry on. Surely the approaching Passover was it! Jesus' whole manner, His growing seriousness, the time He spent in the night and early morning away from the others, the sparing way He ate and His weight loss showed that He was growing more deeply concerned about the near future.

Peter felt it would have to happen on the first day of Unleavened Bread, doubting if Jesus would do anything spectacular to interrupt the solemnity of the Passover sacrifice.

The crowd was restive but attentive. Here and there the groups parted to allow a Pharisee or scribe to exit, and Peter could see a small knot of men standing just inside the door talking quietly together. They were all Pharisees, judging by their robes, and they were angry.

"And whosoever shall exalt himself shall be humbled; and whosoever shall humble himself shall be exalted," Jesus was saying, and then, lifting up His voice and standing, He pointed directly to the crowd back in the distance by the door and said loudly, "And *woe unto you, you scribes and Pharisees, you hypocrites!* Because you shut the kingdom of heaven against men, you yourselves are making no attempt to enter God's kingdom, and you try not to permit anyone else to enter, either!

*"Woe unto you, you blind guides!"* Jesus shouted.

Peter's heart was beating faster. This was more like it! Now the Lord was standing there shouting, His voice fairly shaking with outrage, and He was gesturing, pointing to the men as He spoke. The crowd was so quiet you could hear Jesus' words echoing from the walls. Jesus kept on the pressure, saying loudly, *"Woe* unto you, scribes and Pharisees, *hypocrites!* You tithe mint and anise and cumin, and yet you leave undone the weightier matters of the law: judgment, mercy and faith! These things you ought to have done, but you ought not leave the other undone!

"You blind guides, that strain at a gnat and swallow a camel!

*"Woe* unto you, scribes and Pharisees, *you hypocrites!*

"You scrub and cleanse cups and platters to get them perfectly clean on the outside, but within they are full of extortion and excess. You *blind Pharisees,* first cleanse the inside of the cup and the platter so the outside can become clean also!

*"Woe* unto you, scribes and Pharisees, *you hypocrites!* For you are like whited sepulchers, which outwardly appear beautiful but within are filled with the bones of dead men and of every uncleanness. Even so, you like to outwardly appear 'righteous' to men, but inside you are full of hypocrisy and lawlessness!

*"Woe* to you, scribes and Pharisees, *you hypocrites!* You build the sepulchers of the prophets, and garnish the tombs of the righteous, and you say, 'If we had lived in the days of our fathers we would not have been partakers with them in the blood of the prophets!' You are a witness unto yourselves that you are the sons of those who slew the prophets, and you are *exactly like they were!* So fill up the full measure of your father, *you snakes,* you *generation of vipers!"*

*"Fantastic!"* Peter exulted.

This was a new Jesus to the people, in complete control, masterful, powerful, dominant! He was speaking with power. Gone now was any vestige of the willingness to be heckled, belittled or ridiculed. No, this moment Jesus spoke as if He owned the temple and was in complete authority! Peter found he had patches of gooseflesh on his arms, found his scalp prickling! This was a fantastic condemnation, after all these years, and the final *silencing* of these rotten, self-righteous, posturing religious leaders. Jesus was scathing them, His words lashing out like cutting whips, just as He had scourged the animals from this place, and He wasn't letting up!

"How *can* you escape the damnation of Gehenna fire?" He thundered.

"I send you prophets, men of wisdom, and scribes, and some of them you will murder and crucify! Some of them you will scourge in your churches, and you will persecute them from city to city so that upon you is come the blood of all the righteous that has been shed on earth, from the blood of Abel the righteous unto the blood of Zechariah the son of Barachiah, whom you killed between the very sanctuary and the altar of the temple itself!

"Truly, I am telling you" (He was speaking now to the whole crowd) "all these things shall come upon this very generation!

"O Jerusalem, Jerusalem," He said, voice breaking with emotion, gesturing widely, to encompass the whole city, "which kills the prophets and stones them that are sent unto her! How often would I have gathered your children together, even like a mother hen her chicks under her wings. But you wouldn't have it! So look now! Your house is left unto you *desolate!*

"Because I'm telling you, you shall not see Me from now on, until the time when you will say, 'Blessed is He that comes in the name of the Lord!' "

Finishing this powerful speech, Jesus stood a moment, glaring at the Pharisees and looking over the people. Not a person spoke. The temple seemed to continue ringing with His voice, as if His personality pervaded every corner of this huge room. The Pharisees were blazingly angry, their faces as fierce as some starving hawk about to swoop down on a helpless field mouse. But they did nothing, said nothing.

Jesus stepped down, and, and, beckoning to Peter and the others, headed toward the temple treasury. The crowd began breaking up, a low murmur beginning as the stunned people began discussing all they had just heard.

They left the temple then, and some of the disciples commented about the huge stones, the gigantic columns and the walls.

Jesus answered, "See all these great buildings here? I'm telling you the days are coming when there won't be one stone left atop another!"

Late that evening, when they were back on the Mount of Olives, Peter was overawed by the sketch of gigantic happenings Jesus outlined for the future!

Why, it seemed the very elements of nature would be involved in the monstrous upheavals Jesus predicted!

Matt, busily scribbling notes, was overawed too. Luke was pensive, writing as fast as he could, as Jesus said, "There will come deceivers, so you had better take heed that no man lead even *you* astray! There will come false prophets, and even false Christs, and they will lead many astray.

"And you will hear of wars and rumors of wars, but don't be upset over that, because all these things I'm telling you must come to pass. But the end is not yet!

"For nation shall rise against nation, and kingdom against kingdom . . ."

"Then He won't suddenly bring peace!" Peter mused. "Then, it must be like I thought back in the beginning. We'll probably form some alliances with close neighbors. Rome will probably declare war, and we'll have a time of wars for maybe many years yet." His mind raced ahead with the possibilities. Would Jesus ask him to be some great general? Would they always succeed? Surely, with His supernatural powers they would win their battles! It would be like David's time and the time of Solomon's expansion all over again.

First, they would have to take care of the Samaritans

and the gentiles up in the Decapolis, and those Syrians. Then there would be Egypt and Libya, all of northern Africa. Why, they might even take all of Asia before Rome could respond.

"And there shall be famines and earthquakes in divers places," Jesus continued. "But all these things are just the beginning of tribulation. And before all these," He said, looking directly at Peter and the others, "they shall deliver you up to their councils and shall beat you, and kill some of you!"

Peter could only nod philosophically. But Lazarus had been brought back. Couldn't Jesus do the same for me? He thought.

"And they will deliver you up into their synagogues, and you will be thrown into prisons and be brought before kings and governors for My name's sake.

"Many false prophets will arise and deceive many. And, because lawlessness will abound, the love of many will wax cold. But he that endures to the very end, that person shall be saved.

"This good news about My kingdom shall be preached in the whole world for a testimony to all nations, and then shall the end come.

"And when you see the abomination of desolation spoken of by Daniel the prophet standing in the Holy Place, then let those who are in Judea flee to the mountains. And him that is up atop the house should not come down to take anything with him that is in the house, and those in the fields had better not return to the house for a cloak, because those will be the days of vengeance! Woe to those who are expecting a child or nursing in those days, and you had better pray you do not have to flee in the winter, or on a Sabbath day, because then shall be great tribulation, a time such as never before from the beginning of the world until then. And except those days would be shortened there wouldn't be any human beings left alive on earth!

"But for the sake of the very elect those days shall be cut short!

"And if any man say to you then, 'Look, here is

Christ!' or 'Look, there is Christ!' believe him not. Because there will arise many a false prophet or false Christ, and they will lead many astray, even you very elect, if it were possible.

"You'd better take heed, because I have told you everything beforehand!"

It was a sober group who rolled into their blankets that night.

Peter lay awake what seemed like half the night, staring up at the winking stars, thinking of the vastness of the world out there, and even of the heavens.

Jesus' words spoke of massive upheavals, major nations warring against other kingdoms, the whole *world* at war! He said famines would come.

Peter thought of Beth and the children. His mind went back to their quiet days in Galilee, before this powerful, puzzling, magnetic, mysterious, lovable, frightening Man had told him, "I know you. You're Simon, the son of Jona. Come with Me and I'll make you a fisher of men!" Their lives had been difficult; it was not easy making a living off the fisheries industry, but it had been adequate, and they didn't want for food or a roof over their heads.

Now, for the past three and a half years, he had been traipsing all over the country and had experienced one emotional crisis after another. He had experienced triumph, joy, fear, disillusionment, worry, anger, hurt, bewilderment; every conceivable range of emotion had tugged at him.

He thought back to the feeding of the two large groups and their attempt to begin the march on Jerusalem. His mind went to the time when he had temporarily abandoned Jesus, only to have Him stride up to the jetty and ask if He could use Peter's boat as a speaking platform. He thought of his embarrassment when Jesus had called him "Satan" or something like that, and puzzled over that incredible scene atop Hermon when it seemed Jesus' skin glowed and he had actually seen a vision of men who had been dead for centuries! The storm, and how Jesus calmed it—and the time he walked out there and joined Jesus on the water!

The stars blinked at him as the cool night slowly passed, and Peter's mind whirled with thoughts of great naval battles, armies marching in faraway Europe and across Persia. He sighed and gathered his cloak closer around him. Would he himself be killed? Would Jesus send him to some far country to risk his life in raising up an army?

Just as he was finally about to drift off into uneasy sleep, he thought he heard Jesus stir, and, looking over that way, under the olive tree, was amazed to see Him rise, run His fingers through His hair, step into His shoes and walk away among the trees. According to the stars, and the faint hint of false dawn, Peter had been lying there for the whole night, and Jesus was up already, no doubt going off alone somewhere to pray.

Peter rolled over and tried to quiet his racing thoughts. Finally sheer exhaustion overcame him and he slept.

It seemed moments later that the clinking of pots and pans said someone was readying their breakfast, and Peter scratched his hand across his beard and tried to blink the grit out of reddened, tired eyes. The brightness of this clear but hazy dawn hurt his vision, and he stumbled out of his robes and went to the cistern for water.

Jesus had talked of vast signs in the heavens, stars actually falling and the sun blood-red or black as sackcloth and the moon not even shining. Peter had not slept much, his mind tormenting him with pictures of heavenly signs and miracles, the tumult of war, vast naval battles, the cry of helpless women and children, always with Beth's face or those of his children coming before his mind.

Somehow he had hoped there would be a time of almost instant peace; Jesus' teachings certainly spoke of such a time. And yet here was Jesus warning them again about a time of riotous turmoil, of danger, persecution, suffering, and even death.

How long would it take?

Years?

Surely such a global conflict would last for a long time, maybe even beyond Peter's lifetime. He sighed tiredly, combed his tangled hair, splashed icy water over his face and felt it coursing down his chin under his beard.

That morning was a bad one for Peter. He felt like his eyes were full of trail grit, and his head seemed to continually ring with Jesus' exclamations of "Hypocrite!" and the strong things about wars, earthquakes and death that He had taught yesterday.

Luke had gotten up early and was busy at his notes when Peter ambled over and collapsed against a pack saddle to talk. Luke had copied down the whole prophecy and was adding a point that he explained to Peter.

"What he said about Daniel is important, Peter," he said earnestly. "Remember Antiochus Epiphanes and how the temple was desecrated?"

"Sure. Everybody does," was Peter's tired response.

"Well, Jesus said something just like that was going to happen again—that apparently, instead of Him taking over right away, He may begin a revolution that results in the Romans coming here and destroying the temple all over again!"

"But why?" Peter said incredulously. What kind of a revolution is it that results in another sack of Jerusalem and the destruction of the temple?"

"He seems to believe all this will be replaced by an even greater, larger, more beautiful one. Remember how He said that we would see the powers of the heavens shaken, and the sign of the Son of Man coming with clouds and great glory?"

"I have added a warning here," he said, showing Peter his note scroll, "because if anyone reads what He said later I want them to really think about this reference to the 'abomination of desolation' He made. See? I said, 'Let him that reads understand.' "

"Yeah, I see," Peter said, "but I still don't quite get it. You mean we will have to *leave* Jerusalem, and that the temple will be completely destroyed?"

"Sure, we will. That's what He said! He said there would be a time of greater world trouble than ever before, and that some of us would even be killed!"

"But He also said 'not a hair of your head would perish'!" said Peter.

"Yes, but He only meant *some* of us, not all of us," countered Luke.

"Well, if we're going to bring about such a reaction from the Romans, then when do you think the war will be finally over?"

"I'm not sure exactly. But if I could figure out when the 'times of the gentiles' are to be over, I think I could tell you."

"Do you think that's what He meant about Jerusalem being trodden down of gentiles?" Peter asked, rubbing his aching eyes.

"I know it!" Luke responded, rolling up his notes and carefully placing them in his pack. "He said it would only be after some great destruction here that His Father in heaven would intervene, and then some great miracle —the greatest in all of history, like millions of people actually seeing Jesus up in the skies surrounded by billions of angels or something—would happen, and He said it could happen practically any time."

"Well, not just *any* time," Peter countered. "He also said there had to come a lot of preliminary things, like wars and famines.

"I didn't mean like right this minute, but He warned many of these things would happen before the end of this generation!"

"That's true. I think I may have missed part of that. Can I read over your notes later, Luke?" Peter asked, knowing that he might be asked questions by Jesus and not wanting to be caught short.

"Sure, you can. I'm having a special copy made by a scribe right here in Jerusalem. He's a friend of Joseph of Arimathaea and can be trusted. Besides, Joseph wants to have a copy, and that way he's willing to pay, since I couldn't have afforded the copy work."

"Who knows? I might even try writing a little of my own thoughts down sometime," Peter said. "But I don't know where I'll ever find the time."

"Peter," Luke said.

"Yes?"

"Something terrible is going to happen to Jesus this Passover; I know it in my bones. He is more detached, more remote, more serious than I have ever seen Him."

"I know. I've seen the same thing, and I was so upset by the long, powerful message last night, especially about the wars, all the suffering—I keep seeing my wife and family involved, I guess—but do you think He isn't capable of handling everything, or even performing some fantastic sign to set it right?"

"Probably," Luke said without conviction. "But He seems very preoccupied with something, and I've had to write about what He said, remember."

"That's right. So I suppose you have a way of remembering what the rest of us tend to forget."

"Not that I am worried much," Luke responded. "But when He said what He did about being 'lifted up,' do you know what He meant?"

"No. I supposed He meant exalted, or placed up on a high place where everybody could see Him, like up on the corner of the East Wall or someplace."

"He might have. But I keep thinking about the scroll of the Torah, and the brazen serpent of Moses. There is a tradition, you know, that a great man must die for the sins of the people."

"I've heard of such traditions, but would a man who has raised the dead—and, remember, I was *there* at Nain and right there at Lazarus' tomb—would such a man fear death, or ever submit to it?"

"I just don't know. But we'd better keep our eyes open because something's up. Even John feels it, and you know how close he is to Jesus."

"Well, I just can't believe He meant it when He said He would be delivered up within two days to be 'crucified.' I think He must be intending to perform some great miracle to turn all the people to Him, even all the chief priests and the Pharisees," Peter said.

"I know. That last statement about being crucified I was afraid to even include. Matt said he wrote it down, and he claims Jesus was definite, that He said in only two more days!"

# XIX

Two days later they held a special Passover.

During these past days Peter saw an increasing number of pilgrims flocking to Jerusalem for the Passover and Days of Unleavened Bread. Many sheep and goats could be heard blatting and bleating along the trails below them as the herdsmen drove their animals along. Ceremonial preparations were common in homes at this time of the season. A careful search would be made through every nook and cranny of each private home for any scraps of bread or leaven, cleaning all of it out for the approaching Days of Unleavened Bread.

The servants in the temple were busily scrubbing the pots, pans and utensils, and collecting bitter herbs in preparation for the baking of unleavened cakes and the roasting of the Passover lamb. Peter was mystified that Jesus had instructed him to go into the city to prepare to ''keep this Passover,'' and yet Jesus seemed to want to sit down to eat with them on the evening *before* the ceremonial sacrifice of the Passover.

Peter and John went to the large home that belonged to Joseph of Arimathaea, a wealthy and well known man in the area, and remained there for hours assisting the servants, overseeing the seating arrangements, helping to fill the large amphorae with water and being useful where they could.

Joseph's servants were quizzical and had questioned their master more than once, but he calmed them with an impatient gesture of the hand and simply told them, "The Lord knows what He's doing."

The household help couldn't seem to understand why all the frantic preparations for a big supper about eighteen hours early.

Following Jesus' lengthy teaching sessions of the temple that day, they wound their way through the streets, mingled with the crowds around the pool of Siloam, went out the water gate and traversed up to the main gate, seeking to lose themselves from any hangers-on who would identify them and report where Jesus was.

Winding their way through the narrow streets, sticking to the lengthening shadows of the taller buildings where they could, they came to the court below Joseph's house and, pulling the bell rope at the gate, were admitted by one of the maids.

Passing through the open courtyard and climbing the stairway to the large public room at the rear of the house, they entered the room where the servants had made ready.

There were more than one hundred and thirty of them in the room, counting the servants, and after they had all taken their seats and fallen quiet Jesus asked the blessing over the meal in a somber tone.

He looked around before bowing His head and said, "I have a deep desire to eat this Passover with you before I suffer. Because I'm telling you this is the last time I will eat it on this earth until it is fulfilled in the Kingdom of God!"

This saying disturbed Peter, but hope leapt within his breast, for he felt Jesus must mean that *tomorrow,* the day of the Passover, would be the day of the great final coup and the beginning of His kingdom. And, if He established Himself on the throne of Israel, then surely by next year He would be partaking of this same supper with His disciples *in His kingdom!*

After the sober blessing, the disciples were all talking excitedly among themselves, Peter discussing animatedly with Simon the Canaanite, Bartholomew and Cleopas, who was also there, how the Roman garrisons had been nearly doubled in size, and that very likely Jesus would seize the opportunity of the Passover on the very next night to rally the people by an overwhelming series of miracles!

The talk ebbed and flowed, servants replaced empty bowls with fresh ones, and the men ate with relish, for Joseph's household had prepared an exceptional Passover meal. There was roast lamb, kid and succulent dishes of cooked greens spiced with leeks. The mixture of bitter herbs and garlic gave a tangy taste to the lamb stew, and the hot, chewy loaves of unleavened bread had a little of the herb flavor too.

There were bowls of gruel made of barley and grape leaves, and there were cleverly arranged trays of nuts, dates, raisins and other delicacies to whet the appetite.

Peter reached for a specialty he liked, little rolled leaves of the grape stuffed with bits of chopped lamb, herbs, steamed barley kernels and wheat.

Peter noticed Judas was leaning over to speak in Bartholomew's ear now and then, and it seemed that Simon the Canaanite and the son of Alphaeus were nodding in agreement from time to time.

Peter listened as the conversation focused on who would be "the greatest" in the coming kingdom, and noticed both James and John animatedly arguing.

Peter had been disgusted more than once with the wife of Zebedee attempting to gain some special influence with Jesus, insisting that her two sons be given the chief seats, "seated on His right hand and His left" when He set up His kingdom. Not that Peter resented either one of them; he just felt Zebedee's wife and even the two men themselves were a little too eager to decide on just who was going to occupy what great high "office" in the kingdom.

As the meal wore on, Peter noticed four or five raising their voices in a full-fledged argument.

Jesus picked up a utensil and rapped sharply on the table with it, saying, "Now, wait just a minute! You all know that the kings of gentile nations exercise lordship over their subjects, and they that have authority over the people are usually called 'benefactors.' " Peter heard the distinct sarcasm in His voice, for the record of these so-called "benefactors" was bestiality and brutality of every sort, including the oft-repeated story of Herod's infamous assassination of all the children at about the time of Jesus' own birth.

"But among you it must not be that way! He that is greatest among you, let him become as if he were the youngest. And he that is the chief as if he were only a servant. Which is the greatest, he that sits at the table partaking of the meal or he that is doing the serving? Obviously it is he that is sitting at his table partaking of his own meat! Yet, here I am in the midst of you as one who *serves*. And you are those special few that have continued with Me in all My temptations and trials up to this time. I tell you I am appointing unto you a kingdom, even as My Father has appointed that kingdom to Me. You will eat and drink at My table in My kingdom, and you will all sit on thrones judging the twelve tribes of Israel!"

They were all struck by these words, and an excited babble again broke out around the table, Peter sitting back, locking his big hands around one knee to ease his aching shoulders, and musing over Jesus' words. Jesus was showing them that this bright new kingdom would expand into all four corners of the globe and that soon nations where the "Diaspora" and those Jews of the Dispersion that were rumored to be in the isles far beyond the Gates of Hercules would be brought into lesser kingdoms, actually underneath the authority of these twelve men!

Peter was stuffed. He had partaken liberally of the delicious roast lamb and had helped himself to another serving of the entire course. He settled back, knowing Jesus would use this pleasant time for a long talk.

Peter remembered other Passovers, but never one like this—never such a supper, with everyone present and taking it one day early! Of course Peter realized Jesus knew what He was doing, and there was no prohibition to eat roast kid and lamb, as they were doing this evening, at any meal. After all, they had not ceremonially sacrificed any animals.

Jesus had been explaining how deeply desirous He had been, wanting to eat this special supper with them.

All through the evening Peter was struck by the somber, heavy tones in Jesus' voice, the strange things He was saying, and a growing excitement was building in him. Probably there would be no time for any formal meals after Jesus pronounced Himself King tomorrow; the meal they were eating might be the last pleasant time together for a long time to come, Peter mused.

Jesus must know something really monumental, something that would happen tomorrow!

There was no surer way of spreading the news throughout the entire known world than accomplishing the coup while Jews and proselytes were here from nations a thousand miles and more distant.

They were usually the wealthy and the influential. The average family could afford no such pilgrimages, what with the high costs charged by the average ship captains or caravan masters. Some saved for years just to make one trip of a lifetime, so there were always elderly, poorer folk of modest means in the city for the Holy Days, but they were usually in the minority.

The Romans had strengthened their garrisons; arrivals from the seaports told of a squadron of three sails that had stopped first at Tyre and then at Joppa, debarking several hundred soldiers.

Roman history made much of Hannibal's occupation of most of Italy, only little more than one hundred and seventy years ago, Peter knew. Why, the Carthaginian general had won over most of Spain and Gaul, fought his way over the Pyrenees, eluded the Roman force along the Rhone River and then come down into northern Italy by crossing the soaring Alpenine Mountains with his strange African cavalry: elephants! Though losing half his force, he succeeded in occupying the northern plains and later conquered cities clear to Taranto, save Rome itself.

The Roman military made it a policy to keep a nervous eye on potential Hannibals, and there was no more potentially volatile part of their shaky empire than right here in Judea!

Theudas had gathered his little force, and it took a long time, many soldiers and not a few deaths to catch

him. Barabbas was no Hannibal, but there were plenty of
the poor folk who would shelter him and who listened to
his speeches about freedom.

The desperate desire for a promised Messiah was
rumored even in the courts of Rome, and, while the Caesar
himself may have scoffed at these simple peoples with
their notions of one God and devotion to their fathers and
prophets, he couldn't entirely ignore the fact that religious
fervor was usually the fuel to fire a major revolution.

When would Jesus speak out plainly? When would
He tell each man what his specific responsibilities were to
be?

He talked of each disciple seated on a separate throne,
judging over the tribes of Israel, and that meant some of
them would be headed toward Gaul and the Norman Islands, beyond Hercules. Some would be crossing the
mountains past Dacia, and others would be going east
toward Babylon.

Would they use groups of men recruited from their
earlier journeys? Would they need months, or years, to
raise up a force in the countries to which they would
journey?

Would they astound the local people with a series of
great miracles first, coming among them like lesser Mes-
siahs, of a sort, and gaining their respect?

They had the training for this, as Peter well knew.
That had been a brilliant decision on Jesus' part, twice
sending large groups out, two by two, and giving them the
amazing powers to cast out demons from the poor souls
who were paralytic, lunatic and sore troubled; healing
blindness, deafness and dumbness; and preaching powerfully about the coming new kingdom to the people!

Peter was content to wait.

Jesus cleared His throat and began speaking again.

"All of you will be offended, because it is written, 'I
will smite the shepherd, and the sheep shall be scattered
abroad.' However, after I am raised up I will go before you
into Galilee."

Peter sat up suddenly, his face reddening. Jesus was
going to be *smitten?* And what did He mean "raised up"?

Why would He be headed back up to Galilee, and why would all of them be going there again?

Peter was about to speak when Jesus looked over at him and said, "Simon, Simon, Satan has desired to have you so he can sift you like wheat, but I have prayed for you that your faith does not fail. And I want you to do something, after you have turned again: strengthen and establish your brethren."

Peter was aghast.

Was Jesus implying he, Peter, would *leave* Jesus?

Did He mean He was going somewhere Peter could not follow, or suggesting that Peter wouldn't be able to keep up or stand the pace?

"Lord," Peter said firmly, "though every one of the others here should be offended, I never would! Why, I am ready to follow You no matter where You lead. I'll go to prison, if that's what's needed—I'll die beside You!"

"Will you, Peter?" was the quiet reply.

No one else spoke. All eyes were on Jesus, and several glanced between Jesus and Peter. Judas was enjoying this, liking to see the big fisherman discomfited, and there were a few knowing smiles.

"Will you really die for Me, Peter?" Jesus asked. "I'm telling you truly, before the night is over—this very night—before the cock crows you will deny me thrice!"

"No! No, Lord, never!" was Peter's impassioned response. Several more chimed in and said, "No! We would never do anything like that!"

"Even if they kill me, I will *never deny you!*" Peter said, and John said likewise, being joined by all the others, nodding and speaking out their affirmation that they would remain loyally by His side.

Jesus seemed to want to change the subject.

He asked, "When I sent you out without a purse or wallet, and without shoes, did you lack anything?"

"No, Lord, nothing," they answered, puzzled.

"But now he that has a purse let him take it, and him that has a wallet had better carry it. Anyone that has none should buy a cloak and, if he has none, buy a sword. I'm telling you that this which was written must be fulfilled,

"And He was reckoned among the transgressors.' ''

At this, Peter and Andrew reached beneath the pallets and showed Him two swords. "Here are two, Lord," said Peter.

"That will be enough, Peter," He said—and then changed the subject again.

Peter decided not to press the issue, for he didn't want Jesus to say anything of a negative nature to him again this night.

Jesus got up from the table, laid away the outer layer of His garments until He was wearing only His loin cloth.

He then reached behind Him to a peg, took one of the large towels hanging there and wrapped it around Himself. Then He turned to one of the large stone amphorae, dipping into it with a basin, and began to fill a large bowl before Him.

He carried it carefully to the end of the table and, kneeling in front of Thaddeus and Simon, began to wash their feet!

Peter looked in amazement and watched Judas' face as he winked, rolled his eyes and grinned in hopelessness, shrugging his shoulders, as Jesus, head and shoulders bowed, began to wash his feet.

Peter became more and more concerned, realizing that Jesus was trying to drive home the lesson of being "among you as one that serves," but feeling He was overdoing it.

Finally, it was Peter's turn.

He said, "Lord, what in the world do You think You're doing? Are You going to wash my feet?"

Jesus looked at him steadily and said, "What I am doing now you don't understand, Peter, but you will understand afterward."

Peter blurted, "You're *never* going to wash my feet!"

Jesus retorted, "Peter, if I don't wash your feet you have nothing to do with Me whatever."

Peter was shamed—and his ears rang. Did Jesus really *mean that?*

Here it was again, one of those final turning points

where Jesus laid it out for him plainly. Either he was going to duck his head and show the humility that the others had shown, and allow himself to be subjected to the same ablutions, or Jesus was saying they could break off their relationship right then and there.

Peter shook his head, and a grin tugged at the corner of his mouth. Finally, smiling broadly, he said, "Lord, You go right ahead—and wash my hands and my head as well!"

Jesus was grinning back and said, "He that has had a bath does not need to wash anything but his feet, but is clean every bit—" then, looking at Judas, continued, "—and you are clean, but not all of you."

Jesus finished the washing of the feet of the twelve, replaced the basins, removed the water jars, swabbed up remaining water with a towel and, hanging it back on its peg behind the low table, got into His clothes again.

He sat down and the conversation stopped. "Do you know what I have done to you? You all refer to Me as Master and Lord, and you say well, for so I am.

"If I, then, your Lord and Master, have washed your feet, you also ought to wash one another's feet. Because I have given you an example that you should also do as I have done unto you!

"I'm telling you plainly that a servant is not greater than his lord, neither one who is sent greater than the one who sends him.

"If you know these things blessed are you if you do them. And I'm not talking to every one of you, because I know each of you that I have chosen, and the scriptures must be fulfilled that say, 'He that eats his bread with Me lifted up his heel against Me.'

"It's true that he who receives whomever I send is doing the same thing as receiving Me; he who receives Me will receive Him that sent Me!"

Only moments later Peter heard Jesus say loudly for several to hear, "I'm telling you the truth that one of you right here at this table is going to betray Me! His hand is partaking of the food right here at this table, and that very hand is going to betray Me! But I'll tell you this," Jesus continued in a sober but piercing tone: *"Woe* be unto that man through whom I am betrayed!"

Peter was shocked.

Who could it be? Peter looked narrowly at Thaddeus, Bartholomew, over at Cleopas, and especially at Judas. Peter had wondered about Judas' influence that had been growing over Simon the Canaanite and several of the others, knowing that Judas had freely criticized Jesus from time to time.

John, seated a little beyond Peter, leaned further back, laying his head on Jesus' chest, and appeared to be whispering into his ear.

Peter and James also heard what Jesus said to John when He answered with a low voice, "It's the one to whom I'm going to give the sop."

With that, Jesus picked up a piece of the loaf, dipped it in the common vessel, swabbing up slivers of roast lamb with its juice, and leaned well over the table and handed it to Judas Iscariot.

Judas whitened, becoming angry. He sneered, "I suppose You think it is I, don't You, Rabbi?" Jesus said, "Well, you have said it!"

Peter watched Judas become nearly apoplectic with anger, his trembling hand reaching up to stroke his black beard as he struggled for composure and self-control. As the conversation began to grow again at the other end of the table, Judas found a time to lurch to his feet, hurriedly gather his garments and go hastily down the stairs.

Peter noticed Jesus was talking to John quietly again, and that John was looking up at Jesus, hanging onto His every word.

Then, as they were eating, a platter of steaming fresh bread was brought and set before Jesus, and He stood up and beckoned for silence.

He bowed His head and gave God thanks for the bread, and then began to break it into individual pieces. The flat loaves broke easily, for they were unleavened, and He began handing it to the disciples, walking along the tables, saying, "Take this and eat of it, for this is My body which is given for you. This *do* in remembrance of Me!"

Peter realized Jesus was instituting some new custom in memory of this memorable night! He was showing that His whole being was totally dedicated as a sacrifice to His cause, to His great gospel message of the great good news about the coming kingdom. How often had He used the analogy of His own *body,* as if to encompass everything that He intended accomplishing? The recollection of how He had spoken of His body and blood that time, and how many were offended and quit as disciples, came to Peter.

Now He was taking a large vase of wine and asking God's blessing over it. With that, He passed it around, saying, "Drink of it, all of you, for this is My blood of the *new covenant,* which is shed for many! I will not drink any further of the fruit of the vine until that day when I drink it anew with you in My Father's kingdom, the Kingdom of God!"

Peter drank solemnly, wondering at the great meaning of these solemn words. Jesus' whole life was fully committed, he understood. He had spoken of the *new covenant,* a whole new approach to the laws of God and the dealings of men, a way of life that would so far transcend the narrow, bitter hardships of his people in this land that the mind could not imagine the difference.

He spoke of this being the last time He would partake of wine until they were all drinking it together in the kingdom!

Peter was sure that Jesus would never go back on His word.

All the anxieties and doubts seemed to melt away as Peter's satisfied stomach, laced with the fine wine they had taken and the soaring importance of Jesus' speech, had its effect. He was sure now. Tomorrow was it. While fleeting moments of curiosity about Jesus' statements concerning death, and "going somewhere" where others couldn't follow, puzzled Peter, he fully intended following Jesus' admonition. He would have faith.

He would strengthen the others when they doubted.

He most certainly would stand by Jesus, no matter what, and he would show them all, especially Jesus, that he would never deny Him, that he could loyally fulfill his self-appointed role of protector and bodyguard.

After they had been seated again, Jesus spoke non-stop for about an hour. He spoke of Himself as the vine, and said they were branches that could bear no fruit except as they remained in Him. He talked of how the whole world would turn against them and hate them, saying, "If they persecuted Me, they will persecute you. If they keep my sayings (and they haven't), then they will keep yours also . . . If I had not spoken unto them of their sin, they would have a cloak for it, but now they have no cloak for their sin, and no excuse."

He talked of beatings and scourgings and of persecution.

During a pause, Peter was asked, "What was that He said, about 'a little while and you will see Me no more, and then a little while and you will see Me'?"

"I don't know," Peter answered, puzzled himself. "Why don't you ask Him?"

Several others were musing over the saying, not understanding it, when Jesus overheard the conversations.

He said, "Why do you inquire among yourselves concerning this that I said, 'A little while and you will behold Me not, and again a little while and you shall see Me'? Truly, truly, I am telling you that you will weep and lament, but the world will rejoice. You will be sorrowful, but your sorrow will be turned into joy. A woman when she is in travail has sorrow because her hour is come, but when she is delivered of the child she doesn't remember the anguish for joy that a man child is born into the world. You have sorrow now, but I will see you again and your heart shall rejoice, and no one will ever take your joy away from you."

Peter was unable to follow the majestic things Jesus was saying, the way He slipped from analogy and simile back to reality. But soon, Jesus explained, "I have spoken to you in parables, but the hour comes when I will not speak to you any more in parables, but will speak plainly of My Father."

"Now we know you speak plainly and are not speaking any proverb," someone down the table said.

"I will pray the Father for you, because the Father loves you, and because you have loved Me and have believed that I came forth from the Father. I came from the Father, and I came here into this world. Now I leave this world and go to the Father."

"Now you're talking plainly and speaking in no parables," someone else said.

"Yes. We believe and we know You are come from God. You don't need to ask anyone anything, and we know and believe that You have come forth from God," said another.

"Do you believe now?" He responded. "Look, the hour is coming—yes, it is here—when you will be scattered, every man looking out for himself, and will leave Me alone. Yet, I am not alone because the Father is with Me."

Peter didn't know what to say to such a strong remark.

He certainly didn't want to get involved again in any rebukes, so, instead of repeating his strong statement that he would never leave Jesus alone, he said nothing.

Peter wished it were possible to turn to lighter subjects, to somehow talk Jesus out of this terribly heavy mood He was in, to ask questions about their schedule tomorrow, what they would be doing first, and what tasks Jesus would ask them to carry out.

Would they be going to the temple again? Would they go to Annas' house, or to Caiaphas'? Would Jesus enlist the aid of Nicodemus and the others of the Pharisees who had at least some sympathies toward Him? Would He try to see Pilate and tell him this revolution need not involve the Romans?

There was so much to be done, and if tomorrow was going to bring forth some action Peter wanted to be ready.

The sword under his pallet was making him uncomfortable, so he shifted it slightly.

Jesus seemed to have finished his lengthy statement, almost like the most important single teaching He had ever given them since that time long ago, up on a mountainside overlooking Galilee, Capernaum and Bethsaida, when He had spoken for so long a time.

Now He finished by saying, "These things I have spoken to you that in Me you may have peace. In the world you will have tribulation, but be of good cheer. I have overcome the world."

He used the Greek, and Peter knew Jesus had indeed completely kept Himself from any involvement in, or defilement by, the rottenness of this present society. The orgies of the Romans held no fascination for Him, and He had walked a perfect line, never deviating from His lofty principles once, never making a single misstep when it came to God's law, and was one of the most remarkable men when it came to controlling His own physical appetites that Peter had ever known.

He had seen Jesus drink wine but had never once seen Him take a drop too much, never seen Him join in any ribald remarks or make a pass at a servant girl, or pay any attention to money, preferring to let Judas handle their financial affairs.

He had certainly "overcome" the world. But Peter thought the remark went further. To him it meant Jesus had triumphed. He had prevailed. The current society was not fit to continue; it needed total change and a whole new way of things; that was why He had spoken about the "new covenant" that Jeremiah had described, and why He spoke of a government that exercised mercy and forgiveness.

Peter remembered the way Jesus had spoken to the woman taken in the very act of adultery, the way He had spoken mercifully and kindly to her, and yet had firmly said, "Go, and sin no more."

As Peter was thinking over the final statements of Jesus, he looked over at Him in time to see Him raise His eyes, and, looking up toward heaven, begin an eloquent, moving prayer.

Peter bowed his head and listened intently.

The prayer lasted for quite some time, and Peter was moved by the intensity of it, and especially how Jesus concluded by praying that the kind of love He felt for them would be in all of the disciples, and that the kind of love God had for Jesus would be inside them, and that He,

Himself, would be like a part of them.

At length the supper was over. The men were sobered and not a little disturbed. Jesus had spoken of so many things, and had seemed desirous to communicate deeply to them, and then finished with that moving prayer.

When He concluded there were moist eyes about the table, and even some of the servants were moved, Peter saw, as they busied about the table cleaning up.

But Jesus sat still, looking about upon them all as if to savor these moments, and suggested a song.

The others agreed, and Jesus singled out a special one He loved from the Psalms. Looking around with a smile, He gestured out a beat and began.

The room rang with sound, and the men put back their heads and sang the hymn together, each thinking his own thoughts. Peter sang with his gruff voice, being careful to avoid letting too many hear him, for he couldn't carry the tune like Jesus could and thought of the many other times they had all fallen silent, listening to Jesus sing the songs of this land and of the Psalms.

At length the song was over, and Jesus sat for a few moments as if still hearing the last tones. Then He stood, and, beckoning them to follow, said it was time to start out of the city, cross Kidron and go back up to the Mount of Olives.

So they would be sleeping out again, Peter thought.

Well, it would be a tired, sleepy walk, and Peter had hoped they would be safe enough right here, but if Jesus went to Olives, Peter would go where Jesus wanted to go.

The last good-byes were said at the door, quietly, and they began quietly trudging along the streets, now sparse with foot traffic and nearly deserted, the noise of their passing arousing little attention. The lowing of cattle and bleating of sheep and goats were heard outside the main gate where the flocks were being kept.

The sounds fell behind them, and finally the low murmur of Kidron's waters could be heard. Jesus turned to the right, traversed the slopes and headed toward the garden they called Gethsemane.

# XX

Peter, James and John were terribly sleepy. Twice they had fallen asleep despite the distant sounds that came to them now and then through the trees as a chance draft of wind carried Jesus' voice to them.

Twice He had come back and found them nodding with heavy heads, unable to stay alert. Each time He had seemed irritated with them and had said to Peter, "What? Are you sleeping? Couldn't you watch with Me for one hour? *Watch* and *pray* so you don't enter into temptation; the spirit is willing, but the body is weak."

He had turned on His heel then and disappeared into the night again.

Peter tried praying.

"Our Father, who art in heaven," he began. Soon he found his mind wandering as he fought sleep and, ashamedly, tried to force his tired mind back to the things he prayed for, especially that Jesus could somehow be strengthened and overcome this deeply heavy mood He was in. But again Peter found himself almost repeating the same things until, without realizing it, even in prayer, he had nodded off.

This time he jerked awake with a start.

Peter's buzzing head tried to sort out where he was. Oh, yes, he had been praying again, only a few minutes ago. But Jesus was saying He had been gone for another *hour*, at least. He looked at James, John, and then at Peter, and said with a tone of resignation, "Go ahead. Sleep now, and take your rest. The hour is at hand, and the Son of Man is betrayed into the hands of sinners.''

The saying startled Peter; he recognized the touch of sarcasm. Apparently Jesus knew something terrible was about to happen and was rebuking them again for being unable to hold their eyes open and not watching for Him.

But with that statement Peter knew it would be impossible to sleep again this night. How could he doze off and give sleep to his aching body when Jesus was wide awake and watching them so closely, obviously disgusted with them all?

Peter thought he heard a distant clinking of metal.

It was still night, punctuated only by the inquiry of a night bird off below them and the cry of a child from the valley. The crystal skies glittered brightly from these nippy heights, with the stars seeming to dance and wink from the distance. A rustling sound wafted to them, and Peter thought he heard the hooves of an animal striking stone. Winking torches shone now and then, moving in a jerky fashion as if a group of men were doubling back on a series of steep switchbacks along the trail.

Peter wondered what could possibly send a group of men out at this unearthly hour. Perhaps it was another coterie of soldiers chasing Barabbas again. Peter had heard he was only hours away from capture.

Standing, Jesus stared down the hill, seeing the winking torches and hearing the dull clatter and jingle of many animals and men laboring along the pathways. A muffled cry came to them as someone stumbled over an obstacle in the night.

''Get up!'' Jesus said urgently, and with a note of resignation He added, ''Let's be on our way now, because the one that betrayed Me is here at hand!''

*Betrayed* Him?

Who? Who could have done such a thing? Peter thought they were safe enough here. The Mount of Olives was up above all the normal trails; only goats and herdsmen ever came up here. It was a steep, laborious climb from the trail below that went to Bethany. He knew they could easily escape only by slipping down the other side.

Instead of turning to the east and climbing higher, toward the topmost ridge and so to escape, however, Jesus beckoned them to follow Him back along the route they had come.

When they came to the small clearing, it was to see obscure shapes rising here and there as several of the other disciples were piling out of their robes at the increasing noise of the arriving party.

Without warning, a group of officers lit lanterns above them, and another armed contingent trotted around below and began climbing to cut off escape from the route they had just traversed.

There must have been more than two hundred of them, Peter realized, and many of them had been creeping up in the dark while the main party was making plenty of noise coming up the trail. The torches burned sullenly, giving off black wisps of soot and casting yellowed light upon the motley looking crowd.

Here was Judas, standing right next to several of the high priests, and several of the leading scribes. Here were members of the Sanhedrin, Peter saw with a shock!

*What was happening?*

They were surrounded—and nothing they could do about it now! But *why?* Why hadn't they gotten away when they still had the chance?

There was no way they could have been trapped so effectively unless someone had known exactly where to look. That someone was Judas! Peter knew it now!

Spears and burnished helmets gave off flickers of torchlight as the armed men moved into a circle, drawing swords, while others were fixing arrows into their bows.

Jesus walked right up to the leaders and said, "Whom do you seek?"

There was some mumbling and Peter heard one say, "Jesus of Nazareth."

Jesus said, "I am He!"

At that, the front rank seemed to step involuntarily back. One little rotund fellow tripped over the hem of his long robe and fell into a soldier behind him with a long spear planted on the ground. He fell, and the spear swung a wicked arc, slashing another across the chest, who threw up his arms and shouted, falling back into another man behind him.

Peter's incredulous eyes saw the entire group falling away backward in a tangle of clothing, spears, torches and weapons! A muffled shout, and three men came flying apart, one of them stamping uselessly on a torch, beating at sparks glowing from his clothing. Another was yelling loudly, trying to extricate himself from two others who were standing on his robes.

The high priest, his dignity destroyed, came to his hands and knees and then slowly stood up, brushing at his clothing, speaking sharply to the little scribe at his side. The scribe tried to rearrange his clothing and, drawing a note scroll from his pack, took out writer's pen and held it poised over the sheet of papyrus, beckoning to one of the men who was retrieving a blazing torch to hold it nearer, and steady the thing so he could see.

Peter's hand was on his sword; they had missed a marvelous chance.

Somehow Jesus must have done that just by His word! He had said, ''I'm the One,'' or something like that, and suddenly they just began toppling over like so many cornstalks in a high wind. Peter had never seen anything quite like it. If it weren't for the deadly danger here, he was sure he would have laughed uproariously at the sight of these dignified religious fanatics all tangled up in a welter of arms, legs, spears, bows and torches.

Judas sidled forward, dark eyes glittering, and grasped Jesus on the shoulders, kissing Him lightly on the cheek, saying, ''Master!''

''Judas! Do you mean you would betray the Son of Man with a *kiss?*'' Jesus asked. Judas looked away, not answering. The priest's servant reached for Jesus to seize Him.

This was it!

Now they knew without a doubt exactly which one was Jesus Christ!

Now Peter *had* to do something!

Peter drew his sword and with a bellow of rage tried

to kill the closest man. He was the servant of the high priest, standing closest to the priest and next to Judas. Peter knew the others would be grabbing weapons from the men who were still trying to untangle themselves, and knew bows would be useless at this range, as would the longer spears. Swords would do it—daggers, and bare fists!

And Peter was ready! All the pent-up rage and frustration of three and a half years of waiting burst forth like a broken dam inside Peter, and he saw red.

He seized his Roman short sword and brought it down in a glistening arc atop the first man's head that stood in the way.

Malchus saw it coming and with a scream threw up an arm and dodged. Peter's sword missed the top of his head and severed his ear! The man fell to his knees, hand held to his head, blood welling from between his fingers.

Several of the other disciples made as if to grab at the men closest to them, and two of the soldiers tried to level their spears. Swords whistled out of scabbards, and one man leapt atop a rock and reached into his quiver for an arrow. Shouts echoed amongst them, but Jesus' voice quieted them all.

*"Put up your sword!"* he shouted to Peter. His voice was so commanding that Peter could only stand, sword at his side, looking at Malchus, who was staring at his ear lying in a pool of blood.

Everyone halted right where he was, the man on the rock with an arrow only half drawn from the quiver on his back, and Romans with spears poised.

"Put your sword back into its scabbard!" He ordered Peter and the others. "Don't you know that those who take up the sword shall die by the sword?" He said, powerful voice rising!

"Don't you understand that I could beseech My Father and He could send Me more than *twelve legions* of angels?"

Stooping, He picked up Malchus' ear and, wiping off the dirt clinging to it, gently took the sobbing Malchus' hand away and placed the ear back against his head.

Looking up to heaven, He spoke a brief word and took away His hand.

Peter's eyes about bulged from his head! Malchus' ear was whole! It stayed right there—no more blood—exactly as it had been! Jesus had healed it!

A mutter went through the crowd at this, but most had not seen what happened, their view being blotted out by the night and those in front of them.

One of the men seized Jesus' arms and began winding a rope about His wrists. "Are you come out here against Me like I was a robber, with swords and spears to arrest Me? I sat there daily in the temple teaching, right out in public, and you didn't take Me! But I'm telling you this is happening that the Scriptures might be fulfilled, and this is your hour, your terrible hour of darkness . . ."

Peter looked wildly about and faded back into the night at Jesus' rebuke. As Jesus was seized, Peter began mingling with the others. The rear guard was rushing toward them now, attracted by the shouts and the flicker of the torches that had been dropped.

In the confusion Peter found John and said, "I'm getting out of here before they kill us all!"

John dropped behind a large olive tree and, ducking his head, began sliding on his heels straight down the hill. Peter ran crabwise, scuttling along from boulder to boulder and tree to tree. He saw other running shapes here and there and once collided with another man, who let out a muffled yelp of fear, and continued on. They were all scattering like a covey of quail.

As he ran, a growing, unreasoning, blind rage seized him. He was trembling with shame and anger! *He* had been betrayed, he thought! What *was* Jesus? *Why* had He allowed this to happen? Why? He could have stopped it!

Should he have disobeyed Jesus' ringing command? Should he have killed a soldier or one of the priest's servants, or the priest himself?

But, if Jesus could raise Lazarus after four days, and had just stuck Malchus' ear back on his head, wouldn't He just have spoken the word and the sword wound would have been healed?

Peter felt hopelessly frustrated.

He had been *so sure* the other day when Jesus ascended the steep trail across the way on the old man's new foal, and when the thousands had shouted about Him being king! *So sure* when He had again overthrown the money changers' tables and confronted the Pharisees in the temple!

But now He had *willingly* let them take Him!

Peter's breath came in ragged gasps, his big legs churning, chest heaving, sweat running down his back as he moved as fast as he could along the steep slopes, dodging around the shadowy shapes of olive trees, stones, a small retainer wall now and then, and leaping over stumps and deadfall branches.

Probably by now He was dead, Peter thought. Like a magnificent castle in the sky, his hopes and dreams came crashing down into the blackness of this chaotic night. Now there was nothing left but his laboring breath and the distant torches back up there on the hill that were now beginning to form into a file and move along slowly.

Finally, exhausted, he stopped.

He had traveled perhaps three furlongs or more, completely around the lower shoulder of the mountain, until he was now about three hundred feet lower and within an easy walk of the main trail to Bethphage and Bethany.

His chest was heaving wildly, and his breath came in wheezing gasps, his heart pounding so noisily he could hear its beat against his ears. His back dripped with rivulets of sweat, and his hands were slick. He wiped them on his skirt and saw a lantern lit in a home below. Sweat dripped down inside his beard and tickled his chin.

He was alone here and safe for the moment, so slumped against the deadfall he had just jumped. He tried to rest momentarily. His thoughts raged on, a confused jumble of screams, torches, shouts, Jesus' commands and Judas' leering face as He kissed Jesus. Peter had never known a feeling of such utter, total defeat.

He wondered if he should have allowed himself to be arrested with Jesus, wondered if he should have disobeyed that command and struck out again and again until he had killed as many as he could before they ended his life.

He was suffering the shame and doubts of cowardice, and yet he excused himself, remembering how he was the only one who had possessed the courage to take action. Everyone else had stood meekly by, he rationalized, while he, Peter, had staked his life on that first blow.

How could he have imagined Jesus would stop him?

To Peter, the statement about selling your very clothing for a sword was the signal that Jesus meant business this time, that the beginning of the revolution was at hand!

He shouldn't feel cowardly, but his conscience tormented him for ducking and running like that. ''Better a living dog than a dead lion'' though, he quoted from Solomon, feeling little comforted.

He would have to work his way back to Joseph's town house, where he figured some of the others would be gathering. Among the whole ten dozen of Jesus' followers, there weren't more than three who actually owned property in Jerusalem, but Nicodemus and Joseph of Arimathaea had substantial houses there, and they would be safe, though he hated to compromise Nicodemus, knowing that he would be unwillingly dragged into the mess.

Was Jesus dead? Had they killed Him on the spot?

More likely they intended making some public display to offset all the furor His teachings had caused.

And to think *this was the Passover!*

Why, only *hours* ago they had sat there eating, never thinking anything like this could happen. Only hours ago they had sung that song together.

When daylight came they would be readying the Passover sacrifice down in the main courts of the temple, and people would be going about their business as usual. Probably the Romans were alerted to all this; nothing took place without them knowing, and Pilate tolerated no nonsense from the token government, even if he remained aloof from their weird religion, talking to his Roman gods and wondering at these voluble, excitable people.

Peter's breathing slowed and he stood, looking this way and that, listening.

The procession of torches came into distant view; it

appeared their number had grown now, and they were climbing the trail up the east slope below the city, intending to go into the main gate, no doubt.

Peter took out his sword again and, seeing a trace of blood on its blade, wiped it on the grass, hitched up his belt, wiped his beard and face again and set out. He crossed Kidron far below the others and started up the steep slopes.

Climbing rapidly, he paralleled the route of the mob, remaining above them and staying well back in the shadows, entering the city behind them.

Peter doubted he would be recognized, for it was past midnight and quite dark here in the narrow streets.

Peter hung well back as the boisterous crowd went to Annas' house, unable to hear anything that transpired. Soon they came to some decision, for they turned up another street that led to a large courtyard, flanked by the house of the high priest, Caiaphas. Annas was the father-in-law to Caiaphas. Peter knew, and Caiaphas was the priest of the yearly course, so they must have wanted counsel from Annas first.

As they shouted and shoved their way along, the curious lighted upper windows and called out to the crowd below, asking what was happening. Peter was surprised when he saw another furtive figure like himself drifting along from shadow to shadow behind the last of the hangers-on of the crowd.

The court of the high priest was just ahead, and the crowd had filed through the gate, which was being closed in the face of several of those who had followed. However, after noisy consultation it was reopened, and Peter saw the shapeless form of a servant girl clad in a bulky robe against the chill night tending the gate latch.

Peter paused opposite the other man when a sound came from that direction.

"Peter?" a voice asked.

"John, is that you?"

"Yes, it's me—where are all the others?"

"I don't know," Peter said ruefully. "I haven't seen any of them since everyone took off in all directions back up in the olive groves.''

"I guess everyone got scared and ran—I did," John said, crossing the narrow street and standing beside Peter in the shadow of the wall.

"So did I," Peter said quietly. "So did every single one of us, except that rotten Judas!"

"Yes, I caught a glimpse of him not long ago. It looked like he was arguing with one of the priests and not getting anywhere."

"I wonder what they paid that traitorous dog?" Peter rasped, thinking of Judas' thieving, secretive ways and the simpering way he had singled out Jesus with a kiss.

"Don't know, but I'll bet it was plenty, if they ever let him live to collect it. You know how tight some of those men are with money. They might have bribed him with an empty promise and Judas might find out his treachery comes back on his own head."

"I hope so, but I hope even more that I get to find him again someday. I'd like to take his precious money bag and cram it down his throat!"

"I know," John sighed. "No matter how much we have been taught against violence, when the violent resort to violence it sometimes triggers something inside us and we react."

"You think I shouldn't have struck out at Malchus?"

"I'm not judging you, Peter. I wanted to do something myself. But you know I'm not armed, and Jesus rebuked you pretty sternly, even though it meant His arrest."

"Well, I'm not going to abandon Him yet. He may need us soon, if He's going to attempt some great sign or perform some wonder, to escape!" Peter said.

"Let me go on into the courtyard. That servant girl doesn't know I'm one of the disciples."

"Can you get me inside too?" Peter asked.

"I'll try. Stay here until I talk to her."

It was chilly now, and the sweat coursing down Peter's back made his inner wrap stick tightly to his shivering body. Probably it was more than just the crisp night that made him shiver.

John had been inside for some minutes now, and the shouts and arguments from the large, lighted room across the courtyard came clearly to Peter. The dancing colors on the higher walls bespoke a large fire in the court, and Peter found himself dearly longing to turn his shivering back to its warmth.

He moved back in the shadows and crept closer to the gate, dodging out of sight when two more men came running up and were given entrance.

The gate was left slightly ajar this time, and yellow light came from within. The maid must have accompanied the two newcomers away from the gate, and Peter slid noiselessly closer, peering over the gate to see inside.

He was just in time to see John talking to the servant girl, who turned, looked at Peter's distant form by the open gate and ran over to him. Probably she thought she would be in trouble for leaving the gate untended, the latch open and the gate ajar.

She opened it wider, beckoning Peter inside the courtyard, and made as if to close the gate, when she stopped, peering closer at Peter, and asked, "Are you one of this man's disciples?"

Peter paled.

What would he do? If he turned and ran, she would scream to some of those Romans by the fire, and the courtyard was alive with men. The shouts and noise of the brightly lit room beyond came echoing clearly across the stones of the court, and two of the men by the fire had turned their way and were staring curiously at Peter and the maid.

Nothing to do but brazen it out now. Peter lied.

"I am not!" he said, haughtily, hoping his tone implied that a mere snip of a servant girl had no business questioning one of her betters.

He brushed by the girl and went to the fire in the center of the courtyard, drawn to the fire by the cold that seeped through his body. He hitched up his sword, smiled at two or three of them and sat down on the stones, turning his back to the flames and keeping his face in the shadows.

John was nowhere to be seen, and Peter wondered

where he was—wondered, too, if Matthew or Luke or anyone else had been able to conceal himself and join the crowd; whether they were even now inside, with Jesus and His tormentors. Peter knew it was worth his life to walk into that room, for Malchus would be in there, and his master, Caiaphas.

How could they do it? *How* could a man who had just experienced one of the most amazing miracles of his whole existence be in there calling for the death of the very One who had put his miserable little ear back on his head? Did he convince himself it hadn't really happened? Did he imagine it was some kind of black magic? Peter shook his head.

Surely they knew better!

The men around the fire were talking quietly. Obviously they were some who had surrounded Jesus and the disciples on the Mount of Olives. Peter kept his eyes averted from them except for a covert glance now and then, seeing that three of them wore their burnished breastplates, helmets, leather-plaited skirts, heavy leather and metal greaves, and were armed with swords. One man had a plumed helmet that marked him as an officer. Two of them had laid down their shields, and two short spears lay beside the shields on the other side of the fire. They were illiterate Carthaginians, Peter thought, mercenaries conscripted from the villages of North Africa and given the choice of the galleys or the army. No one given such a choice would choose anything except the Roman legions. Years in a strange land with little pay, harsh quarters and brutal toil were better than pain-wracked, sure, slow death laboring at a chained seat in a slave galley.

Peter knew he was no swordsman, and knew the other men were trained well in their military arts. His life was in jeopardy every moment here, especially dependent on the outcome of that kangaroo court taking place over there in that large, lighted room from which terrible sounds were coming.

Peter gathered up his skirt about his legs and clutched his hands around his knees, stretching his back out toward the fire.

The large inner room used for hearings opened directly onto the court, and Peter saw a considerable crowd inside. Now and then he saw arms raised, fists clenched, falling on someone within the crowd.

Epithets reached him.

"Prophesy!" someone shouted.

"Yes, Prophet," a sneering voice raged. "Since You can't see, tell us who is striking You!" The smacking sound of fists hitting flesh could be heard, and Peter heard several loudly spitting—and laughing.

The swirling crowd parted momentarily for the high priests to address Jesus again.

Peter moved around the fire, peering toward the opening, which had not been covered against the cold for the press of bodies within. Caiaphas demanded, "Are You the Christ, the Son of the Blessed?"

Peter heard part of Jesus' answer. Where was John? Had he actually gotten inside with the others?

". . . I am . . . see . . . Son of Man . . . clouds of heaven . . ." Peter heard, indistinctly.

The quick glimpse he got of Jesus showed they had tied His hands behind His back and had covered His eyes with a blindfold. There was spittle glistening on His brow, in His hair and on His short beard.

Peter saw the priest, Caiaphas, grasp his vestment and tear at it in frenzied rage. "What further need of witness have we?" he shrieked. "You have all heard this blasphemy!"

The crowd roared again and began pummeling Jesus anew.

Peter was sickened, and kept urging Jesus in his mind: "Do something! I can't fight them all!" He found his hands clammy with sweat, and he was trembling again.

The group had knocked Jesus down, and as the mob swarmed about Him He was lost to Peter's view. Though Peter could hear the sounds of a beating, he never heard Jesus cry out once.

Sickened, wondering what would happen, Peter could only turn back to the fire, the indecision in him complete. He could hardly charge in there and assault

more than a hundred men! These rough and burly fellows
outside with him, and the two beside the gate, were all
armed, and the light shone off the tips of spears inside.
They would surely kill him before he could even reach
Jesus' side. Failing that, they would arrest him for trying
to interfere with constituted authority or some other
charge, and then they would stone him to death.

One of the men at the fire rubbed his hands together,
glanced at the door and then studied Peter closely. The
maid left the outer gate, came to the fire, speaking quietly
to two of the men, and put out her hands to the flame.

"You were with that Nazarene, weren't you?" she
asked.

Peter pretended not to hear, glancing away inno-
cently and looking again at the crowd inside.

"You—the big man with the Roman sword—you
were with that Nazarene inside. You're one of His followers, aren't you?" she persisted, more loudly. The others
were looking narrowly at him now, and Peter tried to bluff
it out.

"Woman, I have no idea what you are talking about. I
don't know of whom you speak!"

"No, you were with Him," she said again.

"Blast it!" Peter said, loudly, as if trying to put this
mere servant in her place. "I don't know what you're
talking about!"

"But you're a Galilean, by your voice," said one of
the men.

At this, seeing several of them had quit talking and
were listening to the exchange, Peter began to curse and
swear vehemently! He *had* to get them to quit boring in on
him that way; he *had* to divert their attention, or he would
be captured and be of no use to Jesus in any way!

He swore like a Sidonian fish trader and said loudly,
"I don't know the Man!"

As the saying died on his lips, there was silence from
within, and the men came with no ready retort. Peter heard
the cock crow in the distance. The men shuffled their feet,
and one of them let his sword, half drawn, slide slowly
back into its scabbard.

"Truly, you must be one of them," the maid said again.

Peter lost his temper completely. He ranted and raged, cursed and swore, and shook his fist at the maid. "I don't know the Man! I have never met Him! I am not one of His followers!"

Just then the group inside stopped quickly. Peter glanced that way, seeing one of them retrieve the blindfold that had been ripped from Jesus' eyes during the buffeting they were dealing Him. In that split second, Peter heard a cock crow and found himself looking across the distance, straight into the puffy, bleeding, spittle-flecked face of Jesus! The eyes looked at him sadly, knowingly, dull with pain.

With a stifled sob, Peter tore himself away from the fire and, striding to the gate, opened it quickly and hurled himself into the street. The men let him go, thinking he was still angry with the maid and was leaving because of her.

Peter remembered, with a strangled sob, that only hours ago Jesus had said, "Before the cock crows twice, you shall deny Me thrice!"

Peter had claimed he would never deny Him!

But he had. Sickened, he knew he had.

He found a darkened doorway to one of the public buildings and, placing a brawny forearm against the stones, cried as if his great heart would break.

What followed was like a scene out of Gehenna.

# XXI

Peter trailed along with the hangers-on to the council quarters of the Sanhedrin, where they formally condemned Jesus. He heard most of what transpired and caught a glimpse of John, and even Matthew, in the crowd!

He dragged his weary feet through the streets when they took Jesus, bound and beaten, to Pilate. He followed when Pilate, after two lengthy talks with Jesus in private, had the captors half drag, half carry Jesus to Herod's palace.

When they came back out of Herod's quarters, Jesus was attired in one of the king's own cast-off purple robes, and they had untied Him.

They surged along through the streets, now lighter with the dawn of a new day, and led Him back to Pilate's residence again. The mob had grown with daylight; there were more than a thousand people milling about now, which in one way made Peter feel a little better, for it was easier to lose oneself in the crowd. He was staying away from the armed guard, for he didn't wish any of the men who had stared at him to see him again.

A great tumult was taking place in the courtyard below Pilate's balcony when Peter rounded the corner with the tail end of the crowd. A chant had been set up. They were screaming, *"Crucify Him! Crucify Him! Crucify Him!"*

At length, the doors opened onto the balcony and

Pilate appeared. The mob fell silent, and Pilate made as if to return, but instead gestured behind him.

What Peter saw then would remain emblazoned across his mind for the rest of his life. Two soldiers dragged a hideously deformed Man, one eye swollen completely shut, lips shredded, a piece of scalp hanging reddishly over one brow, out onto the balcony. It was Jesus!

A loud argument ensued between Pilate and the crowd.

Beckoning for silence, Pilate said to them, "I can find no fault in this Man, and I prefer to release Him!"

Peter's heart leapt!

If they would just let Him go, if He could have Pilate's protection, Peter and the others could take Him quickly to Mary's in Bethany and tend to His wounds. He would heal in time. Perhaps He could be miraculously healed, even heal Himself!

But the crowd was screaming out, "If you release this Man, you are no friend to Caesar! You would be disloyal to Caesar himself!" Pilate brought Jesus out and then, assisted by the big Roman guards, took Him to the raised area in the midst of the square called "The Pavement," or "Gabbatha." The crowd was silent for a time, as Jesus' faltering footsteps failed to carry His weight now and then.

Peter gasped at the sight of Him!

Why, they must have used a Roman *scourge* on Him! His robe was plastered to His back, soaked with blood! There were terrible, livid stripes on His neck, shoulders and arms. His legs were bloody and scarred. Spittle glistened from His hair and His beard, and blood slowly dripped from His nose and congealed in His ears and face.

It was now about six a.m., Peter judged. And he waited, shaking with fear and cold, his reddish eyes incredulous, his senses, though drugged with exhaustion, sharpened to some higher degree. Everything seemed in sharper focus: the colors brighter, the noise louder, the tiniest details standing out sharp and clear, especially Jesus' horrible wounds.

It was a miracle He yet lived!

The tumult began again, and the crowd, now more

than two thousand strong, chanted over and over, *"Crucify Him! Crucify Him!"*

An argument ensued between the leading Jews and Pilate. The high priest and members of the Sanhedrin were there, as were some of the temple scribes, civic leaders, temple officers and armed guards.

Finally, Pilate called out to a servant, and moments later two maids brought a large basin to Pilate. He beckoned for silence again, and the crowd fell silent, expecting some dramatic moment.

Pilate dipped both hands in the basin and, rubbing them together, began washing. He raised dripping hands several times, saying loudly, "I am entirely innocent of the blood of this righteous Man! It's your decision, not mine, so see you to it!"

At this, one of the leaders screamed out, "Let His blood be on us! And let His blood be on our children!"

"Let His blood be on us!" hundreds more took up the saying. "And let His blood be on our children," chanted more than a thousand!

Peter was shocked.

Was there no reprieve? Only moments before it had appeared Pilate might actually *let Him go*. Now he was plainly absolving himself of any responsibility, and claiming the Romans wouldn't interfere with Jewish justice! He had said Christ was "innocent" and "righteous," but it made no difference to the frenzied mob.

Peter stared in disbelief at the people. Many of them he recognized, for he had peered at their upturned faces often enough. Why, many of these same men and women had sat, enraptured, listening to Jesus teach in the temple! Many of them had said they *"believed"* on Him!"

Peter wanted to bellow with rage and take on the whole mob! He grasped his sword until his big hand ached, but did nothing, feeling completely helpless.

Pilate turned and made his way back into the palace, and the soldiers took a staff and began cruelly beating Jesus on the head, jamming a false crown of thorns into His scalp, pretending He was a king.

And here came some soldiers, bearing a large stake.

Behind them came several more soldiers, dragging along two prisoners, whose leg chains clanked as they were pulled over the rough stones. Both had been terribly beaten, and two more large stakes were brought up and laid over their backs.

The procession began then, headed for the main street. The whole city was alive with sound and violence. Throngs were lining each main intersection, and the whole of the main street to the main gate. Thousands of them were here, from all parts of the world. There were Jews from Crete, Arabia, Bithynia, Cappadocia, and from Dacia and beyond. There were proselytes from Persia, and Libya, and from Greece and Rome.

The soldiers kept shouting ahead, and a large armed guard cleared the way along the street. And here came a staggering figure, back bent under the weight of the large tree they had prepared, dragging it along the street behind Him.

As He walked, a guard would lash out and hit Him across the side, or around the legs with a whip. He would stumble, cry out with pain and fall flat under the stake, only to be jerked back to unsteady feet and pushed into motion again.

Behind Him, two men staggered under the weights of their stakes, progressing slowly through the screaming, jeering, laughing crowds.

Peter found tears coursing down his head, and saw others in the crowd crying.

As the procession drew nearer Peter's perch along a low wall, he saw a group of several women crying loudly. Jesus stumbled and fell near them, and, as the Romans pushed Him into motion again, He said, in a surprisingly strong voice, through split and torn lips, ''Daughters of Jerusalem! Don't weep for *Me* — weep for yourselves, and for your children! Behold, the days come in which they will say, 'Blessed are the barren, and the wombs that never bear, and the breasts that never give suck!''

''Then they will begin to mourn and say to the mountains, 'Fall on us and cover us,' for if they do things like this in the time of the green tree, what will be done in the dry?''

With a curse and a shove, one of the Romans pushed Jesus into motion again, and, staggering, He continued along, around the corner past Peter's view.

Peter climbed down and, managing to fight his way out of the throngs, headed down a side street, where he began to run to head off the grisly column again, nearer the main gate. *When would Jesus do something?* His mind raged.

He found a way to the road of the roofs alongside a large home and leapt up the outside stairway, gaining the parapet. Finally he detected by the noise where the column was and peered over.

He was in time to see Jesus lying on the street, the heavy beam having rolled off His back, pinioning one arm in the dust. Jesus was terribly bloody, the dirt sticking to His body. The soldiers lifted the big stake.

One of them turned and, seeing an obviously well-to-do man in the crowd, grabbed him and dragged him over to the prostrate figure in the dust.

Peter recognized the man, for he was well known. He was Simon of Cyrene, a sage and an elder in Israel. He was the father of Alexander and Rufus, who were both known as men of stature.

Two of the soldiers picked up Jesus and began half dragging Him along through the streets again. Simon followed, bearing the heavy stake across his old, stooped back, screaming out when a vicious Roman dealt him a blow with a whip.

It was the ultimate day for the Romans now. Their ''hour of darkness'' was indeed here. These illiterate beasts in army uniform were heaping their scorn and abuse on the Jews by taking an elder such as Simon right out of the crowd and forcing him to carry Jesus' stake!

Peter sobbed aloud, frantic with fear for Jesus, and flung himself back along the rooftops to the stairs he had mounted earlier, descending rapidly, and then ran to reach the main gate.

He arrived as the procession left the gate, turned to its left and began traversing a rocky, stony area that was used for animal auctions and where herdsmen gathered their flocks.

There was a garden beneath that bluff over there, Peter remembered, with several tombs in it, sheltered in the solid rock of the bluff, which leered at Peter with its hollowed caves, that made it look like a sad, forbidding skull.

It was known as "the place of the skull" to the people. "Golgotha," they called it.

The Romans knew where they were going, to the very top of this limestone outcropping, right up to the grassy knoll above the grinning face of the caves and the tombs, where the crosses would be seen for a great distance, and where no one could approach without climbing one of the steep paths.

Peter followed as close as he dared.

A low wail escaped the rear ranks of the crowd, toiling along behind the large procession that had gained the heights, and Peter's startled view saw first one, and then another, and then a third grisly shape being hoisted into the air by the soldiers. They had fastened the hands of the men, including Jesus, to the cross pieces, and were slowly hoisting them to the top of the stakes, which had been planted in their deep holes that had been dug.

There was an inscription atop Jesus' stake, Peter saw, and the people were all exclaiming about it. Several women were keening aloud, weeping and wailing, and a number of men were crying too.

It was growing darker now, with lowering clouds forming a darkening overcast, and the light of the sun barely filtering through.

Here came a loudly complaining delegation from the high priests, arguing among themselves over the inscription and saying they would take it directly to Pilate! Peter watched them pass, again averting his gaze lest he be singled out from among the crowd.

He edged nearer and saw they had printed on the plank: "This is Jesus of Nazareth, the King of the Jews."

Peter was weeping with the agony of the moment. Jesus was surely dead or dying. The form on the stake was naked now, for the soldiers had reached up and torn his garment from Him before hoisting Him aloft, and nailing His feet to the stake. Peter recognized the robe, for it was seamless and made of the finest wool and beautifully done. The soldiers were guarding the site, gesturing now and then at some in the crowd who came too close.

Peter kept working his way closer, through the crying, jeering, screaming, taunting crowd. Some were crying as if they would never stop, and others taunted them and hurled epithets at the form on the stake, saying, "Hey there! You! You 'Son of God' up there on the stake that claimed You could destroy our temple and build it again in just three days!"

"Yeah!" taunted another, turning with a big grin to his fellows! "If You're the 'Son of God,' then why don't You just climb back down from there right now?" The others guffawed at this, and Peter choked on the sobs of rage, pain, disbelief and sympathy for Jesus that wracked his big fisherman's body.

Peter noticed several women in the crowd, over there near the foot of the stake that pinioned Jesus. There was John! Peter edged closer. It was Mary, Jesus' mother, and there was her sister, Mary, who was Cleopas' wife, and Mary Magdalene.

They, like hundreds of others, were looking upward with terrible anxiety, tears coursing down their dust-streaked faces as they stared, transfixed, at the disfigured, purpled, bloody, swollen, beaten, almost unrecognizable figure up there above them hanging on a cross.

Peter didn't know how the women could stand it, how they managed to keep from swooning away in a dead faint!

Just then the figure stirred, and all in the crowd fell silent, some who had been tormenting Him with their jibes expecting He might have some weak retort. The one eye blinked and peered narrowly; the other was totally closed and swollen. The purpled, shredded, swollen lips parted a little, and muffled sounds came from the bloodied mouth. Blood dripped from the nostrils and from both ears. Reddish drops coursed down over His belly and legs, and livid weals showed where they had struck out, even at His manhood, now exposed.

Peter heard the sounds, but he doubted if Jesus saw him, standing in a crush of people nearby. Jesus was speaking to John and Mary. He said through broken lips, "Woman, behold your son!" indicating John with His glance, the one eye shifting to him.

"Behold, your mother!" He said to John, staring at him, hoping to convey as much meaning as He could, as if the effort of saying anything pained Him terribly.

Several muttered about the light; it was fading fast. Peter was in the depths of the greatest agony of his life, paying no attention to anything but that hideously tragic figure up there, almost feeling the cruel pains that must be torturing Jesus' body, as he stared at the wounds and at the way they had driven big spikes through His hands and through His feet.

"*Crucified!*" Peter said. His stomach turning in revulsion, unable to accept what his own eyes told him. "They actually *crucified* Him!"

Others were taking up chants against Him again, and Peter saw the soldiers sitting around the bases of the three crosses were gambling over Jesus' clothing! The filthy brutes were so heartless they were actually stopping to play with some colored stones one of them carried, thinking to decide by gambling who got the robe!

Several exclaimed about the clouds, for they were lowering, and it was growing very dark. Anxious faces peered upward, and Peter saw the soldiers get back to their feet and, fixing torch holders in the ground, light torches around the crosses to give off feeble light against the darkening day.

Peter didn't remember a much darker sky, not even in some of the very worst of the storms that had turned the Sea of Tiberius, as some called his Galilee, into a raging ocean of huge waves. Low and dark, yes, but not *this dark!* It was as if it was very late evening now, and yet it was only about one hour after noon on this fourteenth of Nisan.

Peter stayed back in the crowd as the soldiers were busy arranging the torches. Many of the people were beginning to drift away while dozens toiled out of the city and up the hill to see.

It was growing darker still. It wouldn't be long until the Passover ceremony, Peter thought with a start.

He had been awake now since those moments when he nodded off, back there in the Garden of Gethsamene. It seemed like a *month* ago, and the thoughts of those moments tortured Peter's conscience. If only he had *stayed awake*. If only they had been *watching*.

But was it really his fault?

His thoughts raged this way and that, as he stared, hopelessly, at the emaciated figure up there on that cross. Peter hung his big head and sobbed deep in his heart again, seeing everything he had lived for, worked for, prayed for, sacrificed for, everything in which he had believed, all the hopes and dreams of a new Israel, of a great kingdom stretching in the purple distance, across this land and far beyond to Persia, Egypt and Rome, the hopes and dreams of centuries and the promise of a great Messiah, a leader to restore their beloved Israel, their self-respect as a people, their commerce and their industry, their culture and their religion, to an end. Jesus had been that Man, Peter was positive. And yet, yet . . . there He was up there, apparently dead, or very near death. Apparently His mysterious powers were really broken!

Was He like Sampson? Had they discovered some flaw in His strength?

Where, now, were the powers that had healed the blind, calmed the waves and wind, changed water into wine and raised Lazarus? Peter wanted to scream out with the others, not in a jeer, but in a frantic, urgent cheer to Jesus, urging Him on to victory, to overcome this blackest of all moments! He wanted to say, "Lord, *come down from there! You can do it!*"

Peter couldn't stand it any more. He stumbled away through the crowd, thinking to find some of the other disciples if he could, and seek some solace, some understanding, in the company of his friends. He was afraid to go too near John and the three women just now, and he wondered at John's boldness.

It was as dark as if the sun had been down for an hour,

and Peter found the streets of the city alive with noisy, fearful, chattering people. Some were returning from Golgotha and exclaiming to others about what they had seen. Some were slowly working their way toward the temple, and here and there families carried or drove their unblemished lambs, intent on fulfilling the ancient sacrifice of the Passover, taking them to the court, for the high priest's first ceremonial slaughter. Others were hurrying out of the city, wanting to see the spectacle atop Golgotha for themselves.

He found Joseph's house and discovered several of the others hiding there. He related to them in hushed, broken, defeated tones what had happened. Several of the disciples had not known until now of Jesus' beating, and the terrible, tortuous trail through the city, or of the fact that He had been crucified.

They couldn't believe it! Some cried, and others shouted that it couldn't be true. Surely the Sanhedrin would never have turned Him over to the Romans.

"A couple of them said, without conviction, that they ought to go up there and rescue Him.

Peter took two of them with him and decided to go back out of the city and up the hill; he couldn't watch, and he couldn't stay away. People were quieter now, and speaking in awed tones, wondering at the unusual weather.

Distant lightning crackled, and minutes later an ominous, throaty rumble of thunder rippled mutteringly in the distance, like a great, powerful Being complaining to the earth below. The thin white pencil of light danced, flickered and knifed to the ground miles away, and the clouds reflected its whitish flash, while the second long, somnolent, complaining rumble came to them with its bass voice.

They gained the outer edges of the crowd just before the third hour after midday, and it was dark as midnight now! It was *some kind of sign,* Peter was convinced!

Hoping against hope, disbelieving and hurt, yet still clinging to that one chance in ten thousand, Peter wondered if Jesus was calling out to His Father, and if a great army of angels would appear, if Jesus would be released and healed instantly, and if all the detractors, persecutors, tormentors and murderers would be instantly seized!

It was only moments away from the ceremony of the Passover in the temple court, the same high priest that had condemned Jesus, Caiaphas, would be preparing the ceremonial knife, and the servants would be ready with their basins to catch the blood. Nothing, not even this history-breaking darkness and these black, black clouds and the thunder and flashing lightning could interrupt this ancient ceremony.

At their arrival, Peter and the others were shocked to see a Roman soldier hoisting the butt of his spear toward Jesus' mouth with a sponge on it. He pressed it to Jesus' lips, and Peter heard someone say, "They're giving Him vinegar. He probably asked for water!"

Some laughed at this, chuckling at the cruel joke.

Peter nearly collapsed then, when, with a derisive laugh, the soldier suddenly reversed his spear, shook off the sponge and, holding the lance tip poised in both hands, casting yellowish reflections from the many torches encircling the brutal scene, jammed the spear into Jesus' side!

*"Oh, no! no! no!"* Peter found himself screaming! *"Don't do that—don't do that—!"*

But it was too late!

Jesus screamed out in pain, and His head arched backward, hitting the stake with a solid thunk Peter could hear. The limbs strained upward momentarily, quivering and trembling, the muscles spasmodically jerking, and Peter heard the shredded lips say, "Father, I commend My Spirit into Your hands!"

The muscles relaxed then, and the head lolled forward on the beaten chest, blood dripping darkly from the beard. A great stream of bubbling stomach fluids and blood stained His side, and coursed down his leg to stain the stake and form a slowly spreading pool on the ground. The body became ashen gray, paling as if turning bluish in the flickering lamplight.

Little did Peter know that at this precise instant Caiaphas' hand descended in a swift arc as he slit the throat of the first sacrificial lamb of this Passover season!

At that moment, like the distant thunder was suddenly right beneath them, Peter felt a sickening, dizzying sensation! The three stakes trembled, swaying slightly, and many people fell to the ground or clutched each other.

A deep, subterranean noise, like a low, muttering, complaining rumble, roared through the ground, and Peter's startled eyes saw the buildings in the city swaying lightly, dust rising everywhere. Like steam or geysers, spurts of dust flew into the air.

The earth cracked, and the streets and pathways buckled!

Parapets sent showers of tiles into the streets, and frantic people screamed, dodging the deadly missiles hurtling down from above them.

The Roman soldiers grabbed up shields and swords, and knelt on the ground, facing outward, their shields before them in defense, and looked at one another, eyes wide with fear.

Then it began to rain.

The rain came in sheets—gusts whipping it onward, blinding, pelting, stinging rain.

Peter's awed gaze saw the reddish blood being washed from Jesus' hair, the pinkish hues running freely, and the rain lashing at the exposed bodies on the stakes.

One of the Romans said in his own tongue fearfully, "Surely this must have been the *Son of God!*"

Peter's scalp prickled. His heart was breaking, and he was dumbstruck!

Jesus was *dead*. They had done it! They had actually killed Him; the kindest, gentlest, wisest, best. He sobbed anew, big shoulders shaking with grief as he knelt there with the world insane around him. The earth shook, the rain hissed down in a roar, and lightning crashed, filling the air with a sulfuric, acrid odor and deafening Peter's ears.

Women were wailing, men were crying, children screamed, and even the soldiers were yelling at the top of their lungs.

But gradually the rain grew less, and the sickening motion of the earth stopped. The clouds began to take on a slightly grayish hue, and the terrible blackness began to abate.

The people nearest Peter and the other two were getting to their feet, and cries came from the city, where injured people were lying.

A frantic man came running to tell his friends that a tomb had been completely unearthed, and, as the rain cleansed it of the dust of years, the big stone lid of the sarcophagus had lifted and the man had seen a body. It had stood up and stepped out of the tomb!

"I saw a *dead* man—walking!" he screamed. His friends quieted him, telling him it couldn't have been true. Perhaps someone had just been sleeping in an unusual place, or maybe he had seen a vision.

"There are very strange things happening this day," said one, trying to calm him.

Peter, his clothes plastered to his body and water dripping in a steady stream from his hair and beard, grabbed Bartholomew's shoulder and growled at him that they had better get back to Joseph's house; there was nothing further they could do here.

The skies were lighter now as Peter and the others toiled back along the slippery pathway, whose center had turned into a muddy brook. He glanced backward now and then, unable to avoid it, Jesus' dead figure looking so totally alone and forlorn. It grew smaller and smaller until, as he turned into the gate, the bodies were only indistinct shapes up there among the blackened ring of torches that had been extinguished by the downpour.

When they got to Joseph's house, it was to find Nicodemus and several of his servants there talking with Joseph and others.

They were going to get permission to prepare the body for burial. Nicodemus thought he could do it, even though he knew the Romans had been instructed to keep a guard over the body and the tomb.

Later here came John, Mary, Jesus' mother, Mary

Magdalene, even Zebedee's wife was here, James and John's mother.

Peter listened to them talking of burial while they were hanging dripping garments up to dry, drying their hair and faces—and he couldn't take any more. He sent a servant to the wineskin, took it gratefully and mounted the stairs to a rear sleeping room. There he put back his big head and drank deeply, and then, getting out of his wet clothes and lying down, tried to sort out the stupefying thoughts that assailed his mind.

Like the reliving of a fight, Peter's thoughts kept singling out various parts of these past tumultuous hours until at last, in a torpor of confused thoughts and revolting stomach, the effects of the wine sent him into troubled, exhausted sleep.

# XXII

By the next day, the first day of Unleavened Bread and a Thursday, a sobered, silent group of forlorn disciples ate a quiet meal with Joseph and Nicodemus, breaking their unleavened bread and quietly talking of the events of that apocalyptic Passover.

Peter knew it was all over now, and toyed with the idea of leaving soon, getting out of Jerusalem and returning home, sorting out what was left of his fragmented life.

The next day was preparation for the weekly Sabbath, and the women worked at grinding up leaves and roots they had purchased, making spices they said they wanted to use on Jesus' body, hoping to gain entrance to the tomb before the fourth day, after which both common sense and Jewish law prohibited it.

Peter felt detached, uninvolved, almost like watching others from a vast distance.

Nicodemus was musing over what Jesus had said to him about "being born again," and remembering the tradition that a man had to "die for the sins of the nation."

This was a puzzle to Peter, though he accepted it as something that would happen to someone, someday—he couldn't connect it with Jesus.

Jesus was dead. It was over.

Peter expressed his dismay that they could sit there and talk about such distant, philosophical, otherworldly things when the reality of a crucifixion and their beloved leader lying lifeless up there in Joseph's new tomb was reality—the here and now!

Nicodemus said, "True, Peter, but remember one thing!"

"What's that?" Peter asked doubtfully.

"He said He would rise again!"

Joseph looked up sharply, and Peter half smiled.

"I'll believe that when I see it happen!" Peter said.

"I know you will, Peter. And I believe you'll see it happen!" Nicodemus said.

Peter could only smile at him and shake his head, wonderingly. He had been tormented by too many false hopes and had chased too many shattered dreams to ever get his hopes up about something so farfetched as that. Had he not been there and seen Jesus die with his own eyes, perhaps he could hope for some such ultimate, unthinkable miracle.

The others were equally skeptical. Nicodemus had made no headway whatever with his quiet expectation that Jesus would rise again; no one believed it possible.

The hours that followed were torture for Peter.

He was filled with shame and self-condemnation over what he had done, thinking what he could have done, what he should have done. He thought for the hundredth time how he could have prevented Jesus' arrest, how he could have been more effective with his sword, and he doubted that Jesus would have healed a split head!

He hoped, desperately, that the others didn't know how he had cursed and lied!

The shock and shame gnawed at Peter's vitals like a rusty fishhook, festered and poisonous. He flung himself about, raging to himself over the simplest things. He was beside himself with grief, rage, shock, hurt, humility, self-pity, guilt; it was impossible to sort out the feelings that swept through him like a burst torrent, like a raging sea, like a roaring wind.

He couldn't find a way out. His thoughts tormented him so: the specter, the ugly scene of those motley soldiers and priests with that little filthy squirt of a high priest's servant, the one Peter had tried to kill, and Judas, always Judas, the swarthy, handsome, glittering-eyed one with the deft fingers, smooth manner, ridiculous little mustache and constant talk about his impeccable "integrity" concerning money matters. Yet there he had been, with the filthy lucre weighting down his rotten pouch at his side, his clammy palms still sweating from the greed and jealousy that had consumed his soul. Yet, try as he could, Peter could not take the gnawing blame he felt and shift it onto the shoulders of some other person.

He sighed with a shuddering gasp.

*How could he have done it?*

Him! Peter, the so-called "pebble," the "rock"! Some *rock,* he thought ruefully—like a piece of camel dung that looked like a rock lying half rotted under a stone, more to the point! He had boasted, blustered and threatened!

His neck pulsed, and his palms sweated anew, as the red crawled up the back of his neck into his ears, remembering!

Stupid Peter! He had said, "If it is You, Lord, then bid me to walk out there on the water to You!" *He* was the one who had blurted out about making tabernacles to stay with Jesus on the heights of Hermon—why? Did he just want to appear "righteous" and impress the Lord? *He,* Peter, had gotten disgusted up there in Nazareth and left Jesus to return to his nets, and *he,* Peter, had tried to assume the role of self-appointed protector, guide and chief right-hand man!

Now He was dead. *Dead!* Peter couldn't believe it! It was absolutely *impossible!* He was so positive, so *sure* Jesus would never let them take Him! He was so sure he had staked his life, his family, his friends, his security, *everything,* on this glowing new kingdom Jesus had described. He was so wrapped up in it that for three and a half long years now it had been his life!

That dumb little chambermaid! *Why* had she felt it necessary to make idle chitchat with those stupid Roman mercenaries around that fire? So what was it to *her* that she had to blurt out, "Weren't you one of those Galileans I saw with Him?" He could have stuffed a pound of overripe figs into her dumb, turned-down, quizzical mouth! All he

needed then to add to his unbearable anxieties was some
stupid flip of a skinny chambermaid standing there sticking her reddish, runny nose into Peter's private affairs!

He raged on, kicking himself, excusing himself,
thinking "what if" at least a thousand times.

But it was too late now—it was all over.

How he had wanted to *believe* Jesus, to accept the fact
that He really *was* the very Son of God, the promised
Messiah, who would redeem His people and begin a grand
new kingdom. And he *had* believed, in a way. Oh, Jesus
had surprised him many times and disappointed him now
and then, but all in all He had been a remarkable Man,
strongly convinced of His own place in life, of His own
destiny.

Now that Peter thought back to those last few weeks,
and how concerned he and many others had become at
Jesus' dark sayings about being delivered up and about
being persecuted and whipped in the synagogues; how he
had been up before dawn and away by Himself to pray, and
how He had been losing weight and seemed to fast more
than usual; well, it all added up.

Did he somehow sense He might fail? Did Jesus
Himself have a sense of foreboding that things might go
wrong? Peter agonized like this for three days and nights.

On the morning of the first day of the week, Peter
didn't know whether to believe Mary, Jesus' mother, and
Mary Magdalene or not. They claimed to have been at the
tomb and to have seen two *angels* inside and to have been
actually *spoken* to by them! They said they had turned back
and seen this disfigured, stooped, terrible looking man
they thought was a graveskeeper and had asked him, "Sir,
if you are the one who has carried His body away, please
tell me where you have laid Him and I will come and claim
the body."

At that, they reported the man had said "Mary" to
Mary Magdalene.

The voice was the same, she said, with tears and
trembling hands, though He looked so *terribly different*.
She had blurted out "Rabboni," meaning "Master,"
quickly, and had tried to embrace Him, but He drew back

quickly and said, "Touch Me not, for I have not yet ascended unto the Father. But go unto My brethren and say to them, I ascend unto My Father, and your Father, and My God and your God."

Excited almost beyond containment, the two women related the story to Peter and John. Joanna and the other women kept affirming it was true!

Peter was still rubbing the sleep from his reddened eyes, having endured another tortured night of tumbled dreams and thoughts, when the two Marys had come pounding at the door and saying, "Peter! Peter! Is John with you?"

Hearing their story, Peter couldn't believe it. Why? Did they intend further parading of His dead body? But Jewish law wouldn't permit it, surely. Would even the rabid mobs that had screamed out their hatred, demanding *"Crucify Him! Crucify Him!"* stand still for the Romans parading His mutilated body through the streets?"

Without turning to see if he was following, Peter grabbed up a robe from the peg inside the sleeping room and said, "Come on, John, we're going to the tomb."

They hurried through the streets, increasing their pace once outside the main gate, and Peter was panting from his running when they came to the tomb site. It seemed temporarily unguarded, for some reason, but the huge, rounded stone they had wedged firmly against the door was rolled back!

The door of the sepulcher showed black, empty of any guard.

John stooped and peered inside, saying to Peter he could faintly see some linen clothes lying about! With a gasp of shock, Peter shouldered past John and entered the tomb. The feeble light from without revealed it was large; large enough for perhaps four or more bodies. Right there, before Peter's eyes, were the linen grave clothes that had been used to wrap Jesus' body, the bloodstains clearly visible. Lying further away, as if carefully folded, was the napkin they had used to wind about Jesus' head.

"John!" Peter said, voice choking with disbelief and fear. "Come . . . come here!"

John timidly entered then, and gasped.

"Peter—He is gone. He is risen!"

Turning, Peter stepped back outside, and his eyes were momentarily blinded by the harsh light. John joined him outside, where the two men looked around, wondering about the tale of the women concerning the two in white. There was no one else in sight, and Peter supposed the Roman guards had hurried off to report to their centurion.

"How do you suppose the stone was rolled back?" Peter asked.

"I don't know, unless angels did it—"

"Do you suppose the Romans took His body somewhere?"

"But *why?* What would they do this for? Pilate washed his hands of the whole thing, and he is over the whole Roman garrisons. Surely some centurion would not dare disobey him."

"The Sanhedrin, then?"

"If they did, they would be violating the traditions about touching dead bodies, and right in the middle of the Passover and Days of Unleavened Bread."

"But who, then?" Peter asked, puzzling.

"Perhaps He is risen—just as He said?"

"Do you really believe that, John?" Peter queried. "But how is this possible? *Alive,* I know Jesus could do great miracles—but dead?"

"All I know is, He said He would rise again the third day!" John said as they walked along the pathway toward the city. They continued puzzling over the empty tomb, racking their brains as to some logical explanation all the way back to the house. Their late breakfast was more of the same as they had the women relate their experience at the tomb to the whole group, and Peter and John added details about what they had seen.

So went the whole day, and on into the evening. No one dared to venture out during the day for fear of being recognized.

Peter was particularly wary. What if one of those Roman mercenaries with whom he had shared that fire saw him? What if that chambermaid pointed him out? For days he went out only by night.

They were all huddled together, talking almost non-stop in bewilderment over all the events of the past few days, and listening to Mary Magdalene tell this incredible story that same evening, when an apparition appeared!

Suddenly there was a person that appeared to be Jesus!

But He was so *different!*

His skin was deathly pale, almost white, and the terrible, livid scars gaped with brutal ugliness. The scalp had been ripped and torn; great gashes had disfigured the face; and the lips were shredded. Terrible, torn holes appeared in the feet and hands.

He said, "Why are you so frightened? Why are you reasoning and arguing inside yourselves? See My hands and My feet? It's *Me*. Come here and handle Me and see for yourselves. See? A spirit has not flesh and bones as you see I have."

They were exclaiming, saying, "But it's *impossible, it can't* be," and "Lord, is it really You?"

At this He had asked, "Have you anything here to eat?"

One of them turned back to the table and handed Him a piece of broiled fish, and He began to eat it before them. They stared, incredulous.

Peter was terribly frightened, afraid this was only a frightening vision, like up there on Hermon, and afraid that it could be true at the same time.

The vision of that same body, naked and bloody, hanging high above the heads of the tormentors and Roman soldiers, reawakened Peter's agony as he had watched, wanting to shout with rage and slay every Roman in sight, but afraid. He thought of that black, black day, with flashing lightning and the rumbling noise of an earthquake, the way the Roman soldier had reached up with his spear and jammed it cruelly into His side, the way His head smacked backward and then slumped on His chest. Peter gaped at the hands with their huge scars dexteriously pulling away a piece of fish, and watched Jesus eat, chewing carefully, looking at first one of them and then the other.

Suddenly He vanished! Several of them cried out, and John knelt to pray right then and there.

Thomas came in about an hour later with a report on the streets.

They began babbling to him about the appearance, and Thomas scoffed.

"You're crazy!" he said. "Except I could see in His hands the print of the nails and actually put my own finger into them, or put my hand into His side, I will not believe any of this!" That next eight days was one of the worst times in Peter's memory.

One day blended into the next, with most of them remaining indoors nearly all day, daring only to go out for a walk around the neighborhood at night, and even then with fear of being singled out.

Repairs were under way everywhere. Rumors were that the priests had gathered together for a special dedication of prayer at the installation of the new tapestry that had been made for the Holy Place, and many a parapet and rooftop had been repaired. Arrests were being made too, but the authorities weren't able to find many witnesses who claimed to know many of the disciples.

The frightened pilgrims from other countries had long since taken a hurried departure, some of them not even remaining for the Days of Unleavened Bread. Of course, even bigger crowds would likely be present for the Feast of Pentecost, especially now that the news of these strange occurrences was being spread throughout this part of the world.

Messengers on fast horses had spread out in all directions, some of them under pay of the chief priests, of course, and others to inform some of the Roman garrisons.

The people were shocked that Barabbas had been released, and that Jesus of Nazareth, a good and gentle Man who had healed many of them, or so they said, had been crucified! Two other criminals had died too, the news said, and the Romans were on alert and had requested reinforcements from Asia.

The next ships arriving at the ports from Tyre to

Rhodes and from Alexandria to Rome would bear the news.

Every day they sat endlessly discussing this or that latest rumor, waiting for something to happen, seemingly paralyzed into numbing inactivity by the furor in the city. It could have cost them their lives to have been recognized.

One of the strangest rumors came from Bethphage in the form of a servant of Joseph's who claimed the grandfather of his best friend had walked up and began exclaiming about all the changes that had been made in the house!

The family had screamed and run away, the story went, leaving the old man standing there scratching his head and calling to them. It wasn't until one of the very youngest got up his courage and approached the old man that the rest got over their fright and began questioning him.

The story was that he had been dead for more than a year!

Other rumors, equally strange, had it that several more of the best-known men of recent years, men of some note in the city, and two who were thought to be sages and prophets, had been seen *alive!*

With such rumors flying thick and fast, Peter thought, the people are in the mood to expect *any* relative who had been buried to come walking up and say hello. Maybe it all went back to the raising of Lazarus. Maybe people had talked themselves into some sort of mass hysteria, and were just seeing things.

And maybe the Romans, or the high priests themselves, were just spreading these rumors to keep the people upset and to make them think rumors about Jesus being seen alive were only some more empty tales, like the rest of them.

# XXIII

The days passed, with Peter becoming increasingly anxious to get out of the city.

Exactly eight days after Peter and the others had seen that apparition that appeared to be Jesus, suddenly *here it was again!*

A ripple of amazement went through the room, and Peter involuntarily stood up, feeling his skin prickle into gooseflesh. They had been casually chatting about latest rumors during dinner when, suddenly, Jesus stood in the exact center of their four low tables and said, "Shalom!"

With a gasp, everyone turned to see, and some stood.

Thomas was seated across from Peter, and he too got to his feet.

The Spirit said, "Thomas, come over here and reach out with your hand and put your finger into My hands and My feet."

Thomas, who had been the loudest of the skeptics, and who had just about convinced the staunchest of them that it was a hoax, or that they just dreamed it, went warily forward.

Reaching out, he took the right hand in his left, and, turning the hand palm upward, put his index finger into the gaping, livid wound. He gasped, eyes widening with fear, and stood looking closely into the scarred face, unable to move or speak.

"Now, Thomas, reach your hand out there and put it into My side."

The man drew back His garment, exposing a ragged incision several inches wide and very, very deep.

Thomas, moving zombielike, breath coming in quick, short gasps, a clammy film of perspiration covering his brow and upper lip, reached a trembling hand toward the wound.

Peter's stomach knotted up, and his heart beat so loudly he thought he could hear it. There wasn't a sound in the room. All were craning their necks to witness this unreal scene.

Thomas inserted his hand into the wound and thought he would faint!

The wound was huge—long and deep—and it was so *cold*. It felt exactly like placing his hand inside a cold cut of meat, except it was not moist, but dry. Thomas withdrew his shaking hand, and, standing with his whole body trembling visibly, drew back and exclaimed with a breaking voice, *"My Lord and my God!"*

As if unstopping all the mouths at once, several others said similar words, pronouncing His name, and several dropped to their knees and bowed their heads.

Jesus let the garment fall back into place and looked around on them all.

In a strong, clearly recognizable voice, He said, "Because you have seen Me, you have believed. *Blessed* are those that have *not seen, and yet have believed!"*

With that, He *disappeared!*

A noisy babble of voices broke out then.

Peter and John, together with Mary Magdalene, Cleopas, Luke and Matthew, talked far into the night about what would happen next.

Surely *Jesus was alive!* Somehow He had made good on His promise that He *would not remain* in that tomb for more than three days and three nights.

They began comparing.

"It was on the preparation day, right before the slaying of the Passover, remember," said Cleopas.

"Yes, and the day following was Thursday, the High Day, so we all rested, thinking Jesus was dead and buried," Mary added.

The women told how they had prepared spices and oils on that Friday, and then had rested on the weekly Sabbath as they habitually did, and had sought permission to gain access to the body before the fourth day, when it would be too late, for they felt He had not had a proper burial and there had been no preparation of the body, just a hasty wrapping in grave clothes, but no oils or spices.

"We wanted to get there before the morning and beat any curious people to the tomb, because the leaders were parading many people by every day, showing them the guards and the stone and saying Jesus was dead," said Mary Magdalene.

"Yes," added His mother. "And we wanted to get to the tomb before they changed the night guard, and when the men would be very tired and more likely to let us in without argument. It was still very black when we got there . . ." she said, and briefly repeated, for probably the twentieth time, their experiences of the next few hours.

But Jesus had not been there; the stone was rolled back, and the guards were passed out cold, and then they had seen the two angels.

Peter remembered how John had gained the mouth of the tomb just ahead of him but had stopped and tried to peer inside. Peter had rushed right on past him and entered the tomb, looking around. There were niches for several bodies, but not one in sight—just the linen clothes lying there with the napkin that had been around His head rolled up in a separate bundle by itself.

So He had been in the tomb *exactly* three days and three nights, then. Having been buried late that Wednesday, before the High Day Sabbath, which was the first day of the Days of Unleavened Bread, He had spent Wednesday night, Thursday night, Friday night and all day Sabbath until late in the afternoon, at precisely the same time of day that He had been buried, in the tomb.

Then, Peter thought, that stone was not rolled away to let Jesus *out;* it was rolled away to let John and him *in.*

He discussed this with the others, and they began talking about His ability to appear and disappear right through stone walls.

"Then He must have actually gone right through the stone walls of the tomb," because He was already risen—gone—by the time Mary got there, and that was still hours before daylight!" Peter said.

The others agreed, with much shaking of heads and talk about miracles.

Mary said Jesus had told her, "Fear not, and go and tell My brethren that they should leave now and go up to Galilee and there they will see Me."

When Peter heard that, he was relieved. He wanted quit of this city, and nothing could be better right now than going back up to Galilee. He had intended doing so as soon as it was safe to travel, and was about to leave on his own. But now Mary said the Lord wanted them to go up there.

Galilee. The sea.

It had all begun there. Peter remembered that sunswept morning when the Lord had walked by and said, "I know you! You're Simon, Jona's son, the fisherman. Come with Me and I'll make you a fisher of *men*."

Peter remembered the feelings he had experienced that day when Jesus had come striding along the quay followed by a large crowd and asked Peter if He could use his boat so He could escape the crowd and speak to them in safety. That was after the near disaster in Nazareth when he had tried to begin His public ministry there and had nearly died—*after* Peter had left Him once in disgust and in fear.

He remembered that time up on the heights of the Syrian mountains when Jesus had spoken so sharply to him about his doubts and about the time He had so gently thanked Beth and the children for their hospitality. It all came flooding back; Jesus asleep in the 'tween decks and Peter screaming, "Lord, we're about to drown! *Don't You care?*" and Jesus, telling Peter to go and catch a fish and that he would find a coin in its mouth.

Peter longed for the windswept vista of his whole life's experience, the Sea of Galilee, and the swoop and plunge of a solid boat under his feet. He longed for the time to sort out his thoughts aboard the boat, working, tugging, hauling, straining until he thought he would drop, with the shimmering, blinding reflection of a perfect noonday sun bathing his body with sweat. Galilee, the Galilee of his youth and of the times with Jesus that He treasured the most.

Suddenly he straightened, threw down the iron he had been using to toy with the coals of the fire and said to them all, "I don't know about the rest of you, but I'm going back to Galilee—right now."

That was the only cure for him—back to his boat, back to where it all began. And if he would glance over the thwarts on some moonlit night would he wonder if he saw an almost ghostly figure walking toward him? If he were to cast a hand line over the side, would he catch a fish with a coin lodged in its throat? If he were to work all day and then find a violent storm carrying him away, would the winds suddenly calm and the waves cease, and would he see Jesus coming to him across the water?

Peter was disgraced. He knew the others were murmuring about him, even though he had confessed only to John and Andrew his foolishness in his disclaimers (and had cried out to God for forgiveness for saying what he did), but he couldn't just stand around forever now—now that it was over.

Besides, there would no doubt be retaliations, and what about aged old Jona and his wife and the children?

"I'm going fishing," he said again, and walked away from the fire to begin arranging his pack.

"Surely you're not going to start *tonight?*" Andrew asked.

"Yes—now—tonight—I'll not wait another minute," Peter said.

"Then I'll come with you," said his brother.

Peter was flattered and grateful. Was it simple nostalgia? Why was it so important suddenly to go back to Galilee? He supposed it was because, like a wounded animal, he wanted to creep back into the arms of his own family, take up the tasks of his daily life the way it had been before this incredible three and a half years, see if the simple things of life—Beth and the children, his nets and the boats, the strain of working his muscles every day, rising well before sunup and working at his trade—didn't prove to be a healing to his bruised spirits.

Besides, hadn't Mary said Jesus told them to go to Galilee?

Peter's thoughts pulled and tugged at his conscience during the entire return to Galilee. He couldn't sleep well, tossing and turning and muttering in his sleep. He would wake up several times at night with a foul taste in his mouth, eyes like some wayward camel had kicked them full of the sand of the road, struggling to go back to sleep.

Even homecoming was a disaster.

Everyone was full of questions, Beth included. The rumors had reached Galilee about Jesus' death well ahead of them, and the villages were rife with stories about the mysterious black day and the earthquake, with some of the people claiming some of the saints had been resurrected and had appeared personally to relatives.

Leave it to some detractors to brace Peter and Andrew: "Well, whatever happened to that new government you were talking about?" and, "Hey, I thought you guys would be heading for Rome with an army by now."

Peter sought solace on the boat. Where had Jesus gone? Peter didn't know. He only knew he *thought* that was really Jesus they had seen following the strange events of that weekend when He had materialized right there in the room. He had even appeared to Thomas and told him to put his hand right into His side and to feel the wounds in His hands.

Why, He had even showed all of them the wounds and had said, "Why are you so alarmed? Why all the reasonings and arguments? See, these are My hands and My feet. It's *Me*. A spirit has not flesh and bones, as you see I have."

He had asked for something to eat, and they had given Him a piece of broiled fish and watched Him eat it right there before them.

It had been eight full days after that event, Peter remembered, when Jesus had again appeared to them inside closed doors, when Thomas had finally been convinced.

When Peter had said he was going up here to Galilee to go fishing, Thomas had said he was coming along, and so had James and John, Zebedee's sons (for their father was working with Peter and Andrew's father, Jona, in their fisheries business), and two of the other disciples. Even old Nathaniel had joined in.

With the men in place and the nets readied, they left the shore that late afternoon, intending to fish all night if need be, for the family needed the revenue from a good catch.

As the faint rays of early light painted the distant shore, they were working close to the north beach, casting and hauling again and again, tired from the night's work, and they hadn't caught a single fish.

With the growing light they saw a man standing on the beach.

The slightest sounds carried an incredible distance in this early dawn, with the sea as smooth as glass, no thermals yet disturbing its surface.

"Children, have you anything to eat?" the man called out to them.

"No," several of them called back, supposing it was an early-morning purchaser trying to buy fish, which was not uncommon.

"Then cast the net on the right side of the boat and you will find some," he said.

Puzzled, they wondered if the man had seen any fish rise, feeding. They were casting on the left side, away from the shore. Could he possibly have seen some fish feeding from that distance? They gathered in the net and cast it out the right side.

Peter ran aft, passing Andrew, who ducked under him to crisscross their lines and close the mouth of the net, and then four of them hauled away on the lines. They were using a cast net with its small floats and weights, and it took dexterity and skill to close it at the right time. As they began to haul the net, they saw the flash and dull, silvery sheen of many struggling fish! The net was sluggish and incredibly heavy, and it took all their strength to haul it close to the boat. And there, struggling in a flashing, shimmering mass, was a huge *school* of fish! The fish were large, larger than they were accustomed to catching, and the sodden weight of the mass of fish was too much for them to haul across the thwart and into the boat.

John was peering intently at the man on the shore, following their struggles, and Peter looked over at him, giving his line to Andrew.

"Peter, *it's the Lord!*" John said.

Peter gasped and, turning for his light, inner clothing (for he had been fishing naked, not wanting to ruin his clothes), he quickly put them on, cinched up the cord about his waist and, running along the boat, hit the water in a flat dive and began rapidly swimming toward shore.

The others grabbed the painter and hauled the little dinghy close to the larger boat and, snubbing the net lines around the cleats, piled into the dinghy and began to row ashore. The whole process took only minutes, but Peter was already only a distant splashing dot in the water, swimming with powerful strokes toward the land.

Peter felt weeds scrape his feet, and then sand. Gaining his feet, he hurled himself through the shallows, splashing out onto the beach, his brown beard dripping water and his feet becoming encrusted with the sand and small pebbles of the shore, running wetly toward the Man John had said was the Lord!

It *was* He!

There were livid marks there, on the face, and all about the scalp and cheeks, and the livid hues of deep wounds could still be seen on the hands. He was looking steadily at Peter with an enigmatic smile; Peter was trying to find words to say, choking with shock, wonder, surprise. His mind reeled with the miraculous fact that this really *was* Jesus—Jesus Christ of Nazareth! He had appeared before, several times, and here He was again, clear up here in Galilee! As Peter was about to speak, he heard the others scraping the keel of the dinghy onto the pebbly beach and the splashing and thump of their oars as they ran it ashore.

Peter followed the Lord's glance and saw that they had been unable to bring the net aboard the dinghy, pre-

ferring to tow it along behind them, for it was so heavy.
Jesus gestured toward them, and Peter ran to help. It took
all of them to drag the net ashore, where the fish were
slithering about, flopping and struggling, and making the
net move like some live thing.

Hauling the boat even further, they opened the net,
spilling out the fish and heaving them into the boat, counting as they did. Seventy-eight, seventy-nine, went the
count, until they had counted one hundred and fifty-three!
All of them large, the greatest catch Peter could ever
remember! Why, salted, smoked or sold fresh, this would
prove a real windfall to their families! Any one of those
fish would make a good meal for two people!

Strangely, Peter noticed that Jesus already had a fire
going, a grill laid out over coals resting on smooth rocks,
and there was a fish already broiling over the coals, and
bread! Where did it come from? Peter was afraid to ask,
moving as if in a dream, wondering, and with scalp tin-
gling, his pulse pounding.

Peter and Andrew deftly slit open and cleaned three
of the largest fish, and before long they were sizzling
pleasantly over the fire, the odor of hot, fresh bread mingling with the smoke, making Peter's mouth water. Their
conversation was strained, perfunctory. The weather, the
boat, the lake, the catch—many exclamations about the
size and the number of the fish—yet none of the disciples
dared ask directly, "Lord, is it really You?" even though
every one of them wanted to.

Jesus was tending the fire and turning the fish.

In due time He brought bread to the others, where
they were seated about on the beach near some large rocks
and logs, and said, "Come, and break your fast."

They ate in silence, casting furtive glances toward
Jesus now and again, watching Him eat and staring at the
livid wounds.

As they were gathering up the scraps and throwing
them into the fire, stirring it up to burn the leavings, Peter
was stunned when Jesus straightened, looked right at him
and asked, "Simon Peter, Simon, son of Jona, do you like
Me more than these others?"

"Yes, Lord. You know I like You," Peter said, hugely embarrassed.

"Simon, son of Jona, do you love Me?" Jesus asked the second time, using a stronger Greek word that meant more than "like," but which meant deep love.

Now Peter thought he knew what was coming. Here they were, standing about over a fire! The last time he had been standing over a fire and had seen Jesus was when they were buffeting Him, slapping Him around, spitting on Him and cursing Him, and while he, Peter, had cursed soundly, denied Him to that chambermaid.

*Three times* he had repeated the denial.

Now Jesus was asking whether he, Peter, "loved" Him.

Of course he loved Him. But it embarrassed him to think in such terms, though it seemed to come easy to John.

Now here he was, staring at Jesus over a fire, and Jesus had said, twice, "Then *feed My sheep.*"

Peter knew He meant those who were following along with them, the other disciples, and the mysterious "other sheep" of whom Jesus had spoken so long ago.

Peter's scalp prickled with apprehension, and he dug his toes in the sand, looking down, as the inexorable third question came.

"Simon Peter, do you deeply love Me?" Jesus asked.

"Lord, You know that I do love You," Peter answered again.

"Then *feed My sheep!* Peter, when you were young," Jesus continued in a sober tone, "you dressed yourself and went wherever you wished. But when you are old you will have to stretch forth your hands and another will dress you and take you where you wish they wouldn't. *Follow Me.*"

"And what shall this one do?" Peter asked, thinking about John, who had leaned on Jesus' breast at that last supper together.

"If I decide that he remain until I come, what is that to you? *You follow Me.*"

Peter raised his big head, feeling the morning breeze gently moving his beard and causing Jesus' robe to flap slightly against His legs, with their livid, purpled scars. He looked at the disfigured face, remembering. He saw the jagged wounds in the hands and feet, and looked at the deep scars across the nose and eyes that made Him look differently, almost like an older, wasted man who would be a gardener or a graveskeeper.

He seemed to hear the dull smacking sound of that cutting whip that lashed at Jesus as he had stayed outside, by that fire. He remembered bitterly his denials of Jesus and how he had wept afterward.

He gazed at this Jesus—this Christ, this Man who was God—who had been scourged, crucified and killed, and who had walked out of a tomb through solid stone!

He thought back to the time when he had seen Him fall under the weight of that big stake, and how Peter had raged within himself when he saw the Roman soldier reverse his spear and jam it up into this same Jesus' side.

And there was the very wound, visible now and then as the freshening breeze opened Jesus' garment a little.

He remembered Jesus' blunt, work-roughened hands touching a little child's sightless eyes, and the sound of His voice when He prayed. He remembered the tone of command at Lazarus' tomb, and the way He had wept at Mary's and Martha's disbelief. He thought back to the vision on Hermon, and the times up on the Sidonian seacoast, and at Sychem, and over in the Decapolis and down in Judea.

It all came flooding back now, the whole three and a half tumultuous, triumphant, disappointing, exciting, frustrating years. Jesus asleep, and arising out of His robes to go away and pray. The sound of His voice singing around their camps, and how the others would fall silent, enraptured to hear His strong baritone singing David's great psalms and the songs of the common folk; how Peter would see tears glistening in the eyes around the fire as He sang of their people, their families and their Galilee.

He thought of the times when He had turned stormy at the disciples for suggesting some mischief, like calling down fire on the Samaritans, or at Peter for grabbing Him and shaking Him for saying He would be arrested and taken; the way He had walked in and taken Peter's mother-in-law's hand when she was sick with a fever, and how the fever had left her immediately, and she got up to help Beth with the meal. How He had been so preoccupied and had tried so desperately to communicate what He must have been feeling on that last supper they had together just before His arrest, wanting them to understand, to share.

Peter looked at Jesus, remembering.

Jesus Christ of Nazareth, the very Son of the living God, was standing here before him, standing on the sands of the sea where it had all begun, where He had come walking up and told Peter, "Follow Me, and I'll make you a fisher of *men!*"

And to think I can't even catch a fish without Him! Peter thought ruefully, remembering the whole night's hard work and Jesus telling him where to throw the net.

He understood the big catch now, understood he couldn't do anything without Jesus standing right there to guide him, it seemed.

Jesus had said, *"You follow Me."*

Peter lifted his eyes to the shimmering sea, the pale shore lost in the distance, to the hills of Galilee. He smelled the morning breeze and looked at the little clouds forming, marching slowly across the sky. He knew now that the road would be long and tough.

He knew now that Jesus wanted him to go back down there to Jerusalem and wait for a great miracle from on high. He knew now, without the remotest shadow of a doubt, that he would catch those men, that he would feed those sheep.

He found his vision swimming. Jesus stood waiting, a faint smile, a knowing look of compassion on His cruelly marked face.

He stood like a proud warrior, wearing His scars of battle like medals, like honors. He was Jesus Christ. Jesus of Nazareth, the Jesus who was the very Son of the living God, and He was telling Peter to feed His sheep, to follow Him wherever He would go and whatever He would do.

Peter looked down, and the tears splashed over his beard.

He raised his big head, brushing a hand across his eyes and feeling the breeze in his hair and his clothing, looked at Jesus across the small fire. He would do it. He would go. He would feed those sheep.

"I'll follow You, Lord," he said, his voice breaking.

With that he turned, unfastened his belt and took his Roman sword from his waist. He took it by the haft and, striding to the water's edge, hurled it as far as he could. The sun sent winking lights from its sharply honed blade as it spun around and around and splashed into the water.

Peter tossed the horsehide scabbard onto the fire.

He walked to Jesus, gently put an arm around His shoulders and said, "I'll follow You, Lord, wherever You go."

The two of them turned and walked slowly down the beach together. The others stood silent and watched.

Suddenly, Peter was walking *alone!*

He turned, came back to the fire and said gruffly, "Let's go home and pack. We're going back to Jerusalem."